"Don't you want to kiss me, Eli?"

Kasey whispered the words to Eli's back, knowing that if he faced her, she wouldn't have the nerve to say them.

Eli stopped, half convinced that he'd imagined her saying words that he would have sold his soul to hear. Releasing the breath that had gotten caught in his throat, he turned around in slow motion until he stood facing her.

"More than anything in the world."

"Then what are you waiting for?"

He could have said that he couldn't kiss her because, technically, she was still Hollis's wife. Or that he couldn't because he didn't want to take advantage of her, or the situation. There were as many reasons to deny himself as there were leaves on the tree by his window. And only one reason to do it.

Because he ached for her.

COUNTRY
LEGACY

HER TEXAS
HERO

USA TODAY BESTSELLING AUTHOR

Marie Ferrarella

2 Heartfelt Stories

A Baby on the Ranch
and *The Cowboy and the Baby*

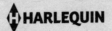

HARLEQUIN

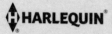

PLEASE RECYCLE

THIS PRODUCT IS RECYCLABLE

Recycling programs
for this product may
not exist in your area.

ISBN-13: 978-1-335-44886-6

Her Texas Hero

Copyright © 2022 by Harlequin Enterprises ULC

A Baby on the Ranch
First published in 2012. This edition published in 2022.
Copyright © 2012 by Marie Rydzynski-Ferrarella

The Cowboy and the Baby
First published in 2016. This edition published in 2022.
Copyright © 2016 by Marie Rydzynski-Ferrarella

This edition published by arrangement with Harlequin Books S.A.

For questions and comments about the quality of this book, please contact us at CustomerService@Harlequin.com.

Harlequin Enterprises ULC
22 Adelaide St. West, 41st Floor
Toronto, Ontario M5H 4E3, Canada
www.Harlequin.com

Printed in U.S.A.

CONTENTS

USA TODAY bestselling and RITA® Award–winning author **Marie Ferrarella** has written more than three hundred books for Harlequin, some under the name Marie Nicole. Her romances are beloved by fans worldwide. Visit her website, marieferrarella.com.

Books by Marie Ferrarella

Harlequin Special Edition

Matchmaking Mamas

Visit the Author Profile page at Harlequin.com for more titles.

A BABY ON
THE RANCH

To Kathleen Scheibling,
for wanting to see more.
Thank you.

Prologue

"Eli!"

The loud, insistent pounding worked its way into his brain and rudely yanked Eli Rodriguez out of a deep, sound sleep. Eyes still shut, he sat up in bed, utterly disoriented, listening without knowing what he was listening for, or even why.

He'd fallen into bed, exhausted, at eleven, too tired even to undress.

Was he dreaming?

"Eli, open up! Open the damn door, will you?"

No, he wasn't dreaming. This was real. Someone was yelling out his name. Who the hell was pounding on his door at this hour?

The question snaked its way through his fuzzy brain as Eli groped his way into the hallway and then made his way down the stairs, clutching on to the banister. His equilibrium still felt off.

Belatedly, he realized that it was still the middle of the night. Either that, or the sun had just dropped out of the sky, leaving his part of the world in complete darkness.

His mind turned toward his family. Had something happened to one of them? They were all well as of the last time they'd been together, but nothing was stationary.

Nothing was forever.

"Eli! C'mon, dammit, you can't be *that* asleep! Wake up!"

The voice started to sound familiar, although it was still hard to make it out clearly above the pounding.

Awake now, Eli paused for a second to pull himself together before opening the front door.

And to pick up a firearm—just in case.

The people who lived in Forever and the surrounding area were good people, but that didn't mean that unsavory types couldn't pass through. There'd been an incident or two in the past five years, enough to make a man act cautiously.

"Dammit all to hell, Eli!"

That wasn't an unsavory type—at least, not according to the general definition. That was his friend, Hollis Stonestreet. Except right now, he wasn't feeling very friendly.

With an annoyed sigh, Eli unlocked his front door and found himself face-to-face with Hollis.

A one-time revered high school quarterback, the blond-haired, blue-eyed former Adonis had become a little worn around the edges. Though he was still considered handsome, the past eight years hadn't been all that good to Hollis.

Eli rested the firearm he no longer needed against the wall. "You trying to wake the dead, Hollis?" he asked wearily.

"No, just you," Hollis retorted, walking into the front room, "which I was starting to think was the same thing."

"This couldn't wait until morning?" Eli asked, curbing his impatience.

Hollis was wearing his fancy boots, the ones with the spurs. They jingled as he walked.

Looking at the boots, Eli started getting a very bad feeling about this. What was Hollis doing here at this hour?

Last he'd heard, Hollis had been missing for almost a week now. At least according to his wife, Kasey. She'd said as much when she'd called him two days ago, apologizing for bothering him even though they'd been friends forever. Apologizing, and at the same time asking that if he wasn't too busy, would he mind driving her to the hospital in Pine Ridge because her water had just broken.

"The baby'll be coming and I don't think I can drive the fifty miles to the hospital by myself," she'd said.

He'd known by the tone in her voice that she was afraid, and doing her best not to sound like it.

His pulse had begun to race immediately as he'd told her to hang in there. Five seconds later, he'd torn out of his ranch house, dashing toward his Jeep.

That was the first—and the last—time he'd let the speedometer climb to ninety-five.

The following day, when he'd visited Kasey and her

baby—a beautiful, healthy baby boy—he knew boys weren't supposed to be beautiful, but in his opinion, this one was—Hollis still hadn't shown up.

Nor had he come the next morning when Eli had gone back to visit her again.

And now, here he was, pacing around in his living room at 2:00 a.m.

What was going on? Why wasn't he with Kasey, where he belonged? He knew that *he* would be if Kasey was his wife.

But she wasn't and there was no point in letting his thoughts go in that direction.

"No, it can't wait," Hollis snapped, then immediately tempered his mood. He flashed a wide, insincere grin at him. "I came by to ask you for a favor."

This had to be one hell of a favor, given the hour. "I'm listening."

"I want you to look after Kasey for me."

Eli stared at the other man. If he wasn't awake before, he was now. "Why, where are you going to be?" Eli asked. When Hollis didn't answer him, for the first time in their long relationship, Eli became visibly angry. "Did you even bother to go *see* Kasey in the hospital?"

Pacing, Hollis dragged a hand through his unruly blond hair. "Yeah. Yeah, I did. I saw her, I saw the kid." Swinging back around, Hollis watched him, suddenly appearing stricken. "I thought I could do it, Eli, but I can't. I can't do it," he insisted. "I can't be a father. My throat starts to close up when I even *think* about being a father."

Eli dug deep for patience. Hollis had never thought about anyone but himself. Because of his looks, everything had always been handed to him. Well, it was time to man up. He had a wife and a baby who were counting on him.

"Look, that's normal," Eli said soothingly. "You're just having a normal reaction. This is all new to you. Once you get the hang of it—"

He got no further.

"Don't you get it?" Hollis demanded. "I don't *want* to get the hang of it. Hell, I didn't even want to get married."

No one had held a gun to his head, Eli thought resentfully. If he'd backed off—if Hollis had left town five years ago—then maybe *he* would have had a chance with Kasey. And that baby she'd just had could've been his.

"Then why did you?" he asked, his voice low, barely contained.

Hollis threw up his hands. "I was drunk, okay? It seemed like a good idea at the time. Look, I've made up my mind. I'm leaving and nothing you say is going to stop me." He started to edge his way back to the front door. "I'd just feel better if I knew you were going to look after her. She's going to need somebody."

"Yeah, her husband," Eli insisted.

Hollis didn't even seem to hear as he pulled open the front door. "Oh, by the way, I think you should know that I lost the ranch earlier today."

Eli could only stare at him in disbelief. "You did *what?*"

Hollis shrugged, as if refusing to accept any guilt. "I had a straight—a straight, dammit—what're the odds that the other guy would have a straight flush?"

Furious now, Eli fisted his hands at his sides, doing his best to keep from hitting the other man. "Are you out of your mind?" Eli demanded. "Where is she supposed to live?"

The question—and Eli's anger—seemed to annoy Hollis. "I don't know. But I can't face her. You tell her for me. You're good like that. You *always* know what to say."

And then he was gone. Gone just as abruptly as he'd burst in less than ten minutes ago.

Eli ran his hand along the back of his neck, staring at the closed door.

"No," he said wearily to the darkness. "Not always."

Chapter 1

When she turned her head toward the doorway, the expression on Kasey Stonestreet's face faded from a hopeful smile to a look of barely suppressed disappointment and confusion.

Eli saw the instant change as he walked into her hospital room. Kasey hadn't been expecting him, she'd expected Hollis. *Hollis* was the one who was supposed to come and pick her and their brand-new son up and take them home, not him.

"Hi, Kasey, how are you?" Doing his best to pretend that everything was all right, Eli flashed her an easy smile.

He had a feeling that for once, she wasn't buying it or about to go along with any pretense for the sake of her pride.

Kasey pressed her lips together as a bitter disappointment rooted in the pit of her stomach and spread out. When he left her yesterday, Hollis had told her that he'd be here at the hospital long before noon. According to the hospital rules, she was supposed to check out at noon.

It was past noon now. Almost by a whole hour. When the nurse on duty had passed by to inform her—again—that checkout was at noon, she'd had no choice but to ask for a little more time. She hated the touch of pity in the woman's eyes as she agreed to allow her a few more minutes.

Excuses came automatically to her lips. Life with Hollis had taught her that. "He's stuck in traffic," she'd told the other woman. "But I know he'll be here any minute now."

That had been more than half an hour ago.

So when the door to her room finally opened, Kasey had looked toward it with no small amount of relief. Until she saw that the person walking in wasn't Hollis. It was Eli, her childhood friend. Eli, who always came when she needed him.

Wonderfully dependable Eli.

More than once she'd wondered why Hollis couldn't be more like the man he claimed was his best friend. It went without saying that if she had asked Eli to come pick her up before noon, he would have been there two hours early, looking to help her pack her suitcase.

Unlike Hollis.

Where *was* he?

The disappointment evolved into a feeling of complete dread, which in turn spilled out all over her as she looked up at the tall, muscular man she'd come, at times, to think of as her guardian angel.

When her eyes met his, the fear she harbored in her heart was confirmed.

"He's not coming, is he?" she asked, attempting to suppress a sigh.

Last night or, more correctly, Eli amended, this morning, when Hollis had left after delivering that bombshell, he'd suddenly snapped out of his fog and run after Hollis barefoot. He'd intended to either talk Hollis out of leaving or, that failing, hog-tie the fool until he came to his senses and realized that Kasey was the best thing that had ever happened to him.

But it was too late. Hollis was already in his car and if the heartless bastard saw him chasing after the vehicle in his rearview mirror, Hollis gave no indication. He certainly hadn't slowed down or attempted to stop. If anything, he'd sped up.

His actions just reinforced what Eli already knew. That there was no talking Hollis into acting like an adult instead of some errant, spoiled brat who did whatever he wanted to and didn't stick around to face any consequences.

Eli looked at the young woman he'd brought to the hospital a short three days ago. She'd been on the very brink of delivering her son and they had *just* made it to the hospital in time. Had she waited even five minutes before calling him, Wayne Eli Stonestreet would have been born in the backseat of his Jeep, with him acting as an impromptu midwife.

Not exactly a notion he would have relished. He had a hunch that Kasey wouldn't have been crazy about it, either.

The doctor who'd been on duty that night had mistaken him for the baby's father and started to pull him into the delivery room. He'd been very quick to demur, telling the doctor that he was just a friend who'd volunteered to drive Kasey here.

He'd almost made it to the waiting area, but then Kasey had grabbed his hand, bringing his escape to a grinding haul.

On the gurney, about to be wheeled into the delivery room, Kasey had looked at him with panic in her eyes. "Eli, please. I'll feel better if you're there. I need a friend," she'd pleaded. Her own doctor was out of town. With Hollis not there, she felt totally alone. "Please," she repeated, her fingers tightening around his hand.

The next moment he'd felt as if his hand had gotten caught in a vise. Kasey was squeezing it so hard, she'd practically caused tears to spring up in his eyes. Tears of pain.

Kasey might have appeared a fragile little thing, despite her pregnant stomach, but she had a grip like a man who wrestled steers for a living.

Despite that, it wasn't her grip that had kept him there. It was the look of fear he'd seen in her eyes.

And just like that, Eli had found himself recruited, a reluctant spectator at the greatest show in town: the miracle of birth.

He'd taken a position behind Kasey, gently propping her up by her shoulders and holding her steady each time she bore down and pushed.

The guttural screams that emerged from her sounded as if they were coming from the bottom of her toes and he freely admitted, if only to himself, that they were fraying his nerves.

And then, just as he was about to ask the doctor if there wasn't something that could be done for Kasey to separate her from all this pain, there he was. The miracle. Forever's newest little citizen. Born with a wide-eyed look on his face, as if he couldn't believe where he had wound up once he left his nice, safe, warm little haven.

Right now, the three-day-old infant lay all bundled up in a hospital bassinet on the other side of Kasey's bed. He was sound asleep, his small, pink little lips rooting. Which meant he'd be waking up soon. And hungry.

Eli took all this in as he cast around for the right way to tell Kasey what he had to say. But he hadn't been able to come up with anything during the entire fifty-mile trip here, despite all his best efforts. Consequently there was no reason to believe that something magical would pop up into his brain now as he stood in Kasey's presence.

Especially when she usually had such a numbing effect on him, causing all thought to float out of his head, unfettered. It had been like that since kindergarten.

So, with no fancily wrapped version of a lie, no plausible story or excuse to offer her, Eli had nothing to fall back on except for the truth.

And the truth was what he offered her, hating that it was going to hurt.

"No, he's not coming," he confirmed quietly. "Hollis asked me to pick you up because he said that the hospital was discharging you today." He offered her a smile. "Guess that means that you and the little guy passed the hospital's inspection."

His attempt at humor fell flat, as he knew it would. He hated that she had to go through this, that Hollis had never proven worthy of the love she bore him.

His attention was drawn to the sleeping infant in the

bassinet. He lowered his voice so as not to wake Wayne. "Hey, is it my imagination, or did he grow a little since I last saw him?"

"Maybe." Kasey struggled not to give in to despair, or bitterness. She shrugged. "I don't know."

It was clear that she was upset and struggling not to let her imagination take off.

But it did anyway.

Still, Kasey tried to beat it back, to deny what she felt in her soul was the truth. Her last sliver of optimism had her asking Eli, "Is he going to be waiting for us at the ranch?"

Dammit, Hollis, I should have taken a horsewhip to you instead of just let you walk out like that. You're hurting her. Hurting the only decent thing in your life. She deserves better than this. Better than you, he thought angrily.

It hurt him almost as much to say it as he knew it hurt her to hear it. "No, Hollis isn't going to be there."

Suspicion entered eyes as blue as the sky on a summer's day, momentarily blocking out her fear. "Why? Why are you so sure?" she asked, struggling to keep angry tears from falling.

When Hollis had come to see her, not on the first day, but on the second, he'd been full of apologies and even more full of promises about changing, about finally growing up and taking responsibility for his growing family. All right, he hadn't held Wayne, hadn't even picked him up when she'd tried to put the baby into his arms, but she told herself that was just because he was afraid he'd drop the baby. That was a normal reaction, she'd silently argued. First-time fathers had visions of their babies slipping right out of their arms and onto their heads.

But he'd come around, she'd promised herself. Hollis would come around. It would just take a little time, that was all.

Except now it seemed as if he wasn't going to come around. Ever.

She felt sick.

"Why?" she repeated more sharply. "Why are you so sure?"

He didn't want to say this, but she gave him no choice. He wasn't good at coming up with excuses—with lies—on the spur of the moment. Not like Hollis.

"Because he came by at two this morning and asked me to look after you and the baby."

"All right," she said slowly, picking her way through the words as if she were navigating a potential minefield that could blow her apart at any second. "Nothing he hasn't said before, right?" Her voice sped up with every word. "He's just probably got a job waiting for him in another town. But once that's over, he'll be back." A touch of desperation entered her voice. "He's got a son now, Eli. He can't walk out on both of us, right?" Her eyes searched his face for a confirmation. A confirmation she was silently begging for.

More than anything in the world, Eli wanted to tell her what she wanted to hear. That she was right. That Hollis had just gone away temporarily.

But he couldn't lie, not to her. Not anymore.

And he was tired of covering for Hollis. Tired of trying to protect Kasey from Hollis's lies and his infidelities. Tired most of all because he knew that he would be lumped in with Hollis when her anger finally unleashed.

He looked at her for a long moment, hoped that she would find it in her heart to someday forgive him, and said, "I don't think that he's coming back this time, Kasey."

She didn't want to cry, she didn't. But she could feel the moisture building in her eyes. "Not even for the baby?"

The baby's the reason he finally took off, Eli told her silently.

Rather than say that out loud and wound her even more deeply, Eli placed his hands very lightly on her slender shoulders, as if that would somehow help soften the blow, and said, "He said he was taking off. That he wasn't any good for you. That he didn't deserve to have someone like you and Wayne in his life."

Yes, those were lies, too. He knew that. But these were lies meant to comfort her, to give her a little solace and help her preserve the memory of the man Kasey *thought* she'd married instead of the man she actually *had* married.

"'Taking off,'" she repeated. Because of her resistance, it took a moment for the words to sink in. "Where's he going?"

Eli shook his head. Here, at least, he didn't have to get creative. He told her the truth. "He didn't tell me."

She didn't understand. It didn't make any sense to her. "But the ranch—with Hollis gone, who's going to run the ranch?" She was still trying to recover from the delivery. "I'm not sure if I can manage that yet." She looked back at the bassinet. "Not if I have to take care of—"

This felt like cruelty above and beyond the norm, Eli couldn't help thinking, damning Hollis to hell again.

"You're not going to have to run the ranch," he told her quietly.

Because this was Eli, she misunderstood what he was saying and jumped to the wrong conclusion. "Eli, I can't ask you to run the ranch for me. You've got your own spread to run. And when you're not there, I know that you and your brothers and Alma help your dad to run his. Taking on mine, as well, until I get stronger, would be too much for you."

He stopped her before this got out of hand. "You're *not* asking," he pointed out. "And I'd do it in a heartbeat—if there was a ranch to run."

"If there was…" Her voice trailed off, quaking, as she stared up at him. "I don't understand."

He might as well tell her all of it, this way he would pull the Band-Aid off all at once, hopefully minimizing the overall pain involved. As it was, he had a feeling that this would hurt like hell.

Eli measured out the words slowly. "Hollis lost the ranch in a card game."

"He…lost the ranch?" she repeated in absolute disbelief.

Eli nodded. "In a card game."

It wasn't a joke. She could see it in Eli's face. He was telling her the truth. She was stunned.

"But that was our home," she protested, looking at Eli with utter confusion in her eyes. "How could he? How *could* he?" she repeated, a note of mounting anger in her voice.

Good, she was angry, he thought. Anger would keep her from slipping into a depression.

"Gambling is an addiction," Eli told her gently. "Hollis can't help himself. If he could, he would have never put the ranch up as collateral." Hollis had had a problem with all forms of gambling ever since he'd placed his first bet when he was seventeen and lied about his age.

Stricken, her knees unsteady, Kasey sank back down on the bed again.

"Where am I going to go?" she asked, her voice small and hollow.

The baby made a noise, as if he was about to wake up. Her head turned sharply in his direction. For a moment, embalmed in grief, she'd forgotten about him. Now, having aged a great deal in the past ten minutes, she struggled to pull herself together.

"Where are *we* going to go?" she amended.

It wasn't just her anymore. She was now part of a duo. Everything that came her way, she had to consider in the light that she was now a mother. Things didn't just affect her anymore, they affected Wayne as well. Taking care of her son was now the most important thing in her life.

And she couldn't do it.

She had a little bit put aside, but it wasn't much. She had next to no money, no job and nowhere to live.

Her very heart hurt.

How could you, Hollis? How could you just walk out on us like this? The question echoed over and over in her head. There was no answer.

She wanted to scream it out loud, scream it so loud that wherever Hollis was, he'd hear her. And tell her what she was supposed to do.

Taking a shaky breath, Kasey tried to center herself so that she could think.

Her efforts all but blocked everything else out. So much so that she didn't hear Eli the first time he said something to her. The sound of his voice registered, but not his words.

She looked at him quizzically, confusion and despair playing tug-of-war for her soul. "I'm sorry, what did you say?"

He had a feeling she hadn't heard when she didn't answer or comment on what he'd just said.

This time, he repeated it more slowly. "I said, you and the baby can stay with me until we figure things out."

Eli wasn't making an offer or a generous gesture. He said it like it was a given. Already decided, Kasey thought. But despite his very generous soul, she wasn't his problem. She would have to figure this out and deal with it on her own.

As if reading her mind, Eli said, "Right now, you're still a little weak from giving birth," he reminded her. "Give yourself a few days to recover, to rest. You don't have to make any decisions right away if you don't want to. And I meant what I said. You're coming home with me. You and Wayne are going to have a roof over your heads for as long as you need. For as long as this takes for you to come to terms with—and that's the end of it," he concluded.

Or thought he did.

"We can't stay with you indefinitely, Eli," Kasey argued.

"We're not talking about indefinitely," he pointed out. "We're talking about one day at a time. I'm just asking you to give yourself a little time to think things through," he stressed. "So you don't make decisions you'd rather not because the wolf's at the door."

"But he is," she said quietly. That was the state of affairs she faced.

"No, he's not. I shot the wolf," he told her whim-sically. "Now, are you all packed?" It was a needless question, he knew she was. He'd found her sitting on her bed, the closed suitcase resting on the floor beside her foot. Rather than answer, she nodded. "Good. I'll go find the nurse. They said hospital policy is to escort you out in a wheelchair."

"I don't need a wheelchair," she protested. "I can walk."

"Make them happy, Kasey. Let them push the wheel-chair to the front entrance," he coaxed.

Giving in, she beckoned him over to her before he went off in search of the nurse. When he leaned in to her, she lightly caressed his cheek. "You're a good man, Eli. What would I do without you?"

He, for one, was glad that she didn't have to find out. And that he didn't have to find out, either, for that matter.

"You'd manage, Kasey. You'd manage." She was re-silient and she'd find a way to forge on. He had no doubts about that.

He might not have any doubts, but she did.

"Not very well," she said in a whisper meant more for her than for him. Eli had already gone out to notify a nurse that she was ready.

Even though she really wasn't ready, Kasey thought, fighting a wave of panic. She did what she could to tamp it down. She wasn't ready to face being a mother all by herself. This wasn't how she'd pictured her life at this very crucial point.

A tear slid down her cheek.

Frustrated, Kasey brushed it aside. But another one

only came to take its place, silently bearing testimony to the sadness within her.

The sadness that threatened to swallow her up whole, without leaving a trace.

Chapter 2

Kasey thought she was seeing things when Eli brought his vehicle to the front of the hospital and she caught a glimpse of what was in the backseat. She could feel the corners of her eyes stinging.

Leave it to Eli.

"You bought him an infant seat." Her voice hitched and she pressed her lips together, afraid that a sob might suddenly break free and betray just how fragile her emotions were right now.

Eli nodded as he got out of the Jeep and hurried around the hood of his vehicle to her side. The nurse who had brought the wheelchair had pushed Kasey and the baby right up to the curb and stood behind them, waiting for Kasey and her son to get into the vehicle.

Was Kasey upset, or were those happy tears shimmering in her eyes? Eli couldn't tell. Even though he'd grown up with Alma, he'd come to the conclusion that all women should come with some kind of a manual or at least a road map to give a guy a clue so he could properly navigate a course.

"I got the last one at the Emporium," he told her. "I know that Rick would cut me some slack if I took the baby home without a car seat, given the circumstances," he said, referring to the sheriff. "It's not like there's a whole lot of traffic around here. But I thought you'd feel safer if Wayne was strapped into his own infant seat when he's traveling."

"I do," she said with feeling, her voice just barely above a whisper as she struggled to keep the tears back. What might have seemed like a small act of kindness to a casual observer threatened to completely undo her. "Thank you."

Never comfortable with being on the receiving end of gratitude, Eli merely shrugged away her thanks.

He looked down at the sleeping infant in her arms. It almost seemed a shame to disturb him, he seemed so peaceful. But they did have to get going.

While he was fairly adept at holding an infant, strapping one into an infant seat was something else. Eli looked from Wayne to the infant seat in the rear of the Jeep and then slanted a glance toward the nurse. He didn't like admitting to being helpless, but there was a time to put pride aside and own up to a situation.

"Um…" Eli dragged the single sound out, as if, if he continued debating long enough, a solution would occur to him.

The nurse, however, was in a hurry.

"If you open the door—" the young woman pointed

to the side closest to the infant seat "—I'll strap your little guy into his seat for you," she offered.

Relieved, Eli immediately swung the rear door open for the nurse. "I'd really appreciate that. Thanks," he told her heartily.

"Nothing to it." With a nod in his direction, the nurse turned her attention to the baby in her patient's arms. "If you're lucky," she said to Kasey as she eased the infant from her arms, "he'll just sleep right through this."

Cooing softly to the baby that Kasey had just released, the nurse leaned into the Jeep's backseat and very deftly strapped Wayne Eli Stonestreet in for his very first car ride. Eli moved closer, watching her every move intently and memorizing them.

"You're all set," the young woman announced, stepping back onto the curb and behind the wheelchair. She took hold of the two handlebars in the back. "Time to get you into your seat, too," she told Kasey.

Eli offered Kasey his hand as she began to stand. Feeling slightly wobbly on her feet, Kasey flushed. "I didn't think I was going to feel this weak," she protested, annoyed. "After all, it's been three days. I should be stronger by now."

"You will be," Eli assured her. Getting her into the front passenger seat, he paused to thank the nurse again. The latter, holding on to the back of the wheelchair, was all set to leave. Eli flashed her a grateful smile. "Thanks for your help with the baby. I figure it's going to take me a while before I get good at all this."

The nurse released the brakes on either side of the wheelchair. "It won't take as long as you might think," she told him. "It'll all become second nature to you in a blink of an eye. Before you know it, you'll be doing all that and more in your sleep." She smiled as she nodded toward the back of the Jeep. "These little guys have a habit of bringing out the very best in their parents."

He was about to correct the woman, telling her that he wasn't Wayne's father, but the nurse had already turned on her heel and was quickly propelling the wheelchair in front of her, intent on going back and returning the wheelchair to its proper place. Calling after her wasn't worth the effort.

And besides, he had to admit that, deep down, he really liked the idea of being mistaken for Wayne's father, liked the way someone thinking that he and Kasey were actually a family made him feel.

You're too old to be playing make-believe like this, he upbraided himself. Still, the thought of their being an actual family lingered a while longer.

As did his smile.

With his passengers both in the Jeep and safely secured, Eli hurried around the front of his vehicle and slid in behind the steering wheel. A minute later the engine revved and he was pulling away from the curb, beginning the fifty-mile trip to Forever. More specifically, to the small ranch that was just on the outskirts of that town.

His ranch, he thought, savoring the burst of pride he felt each time he thought of the place. He was full of all sorts of big plans for it. Plans that were within his control to implement.

Unlike other things.

Because he didn't want to disturb the baby, Eli had left the radio off. Consequently, they drove in silence for a while. There was a time that Kasey had been exceedingly talkative and exuberant, but right now she was quiet. Almost eerily so. He wondered if it was best just to leave her to her thoughts, or should he get her talking, just in case the thoughts she was having centered around Hollis and her present chaotic state of affairs.

If it *was* the latter, he decided that he needed to raise up her spirits a little, although what method to use eluded him at the moment.

It hadn't always been this way. There was a time when he'd known just what to do, what to say to make her laugh and forget about whatever it was that was bothering her. Back then, it usually had something to do with her verbally abusive father, who only grew more so when he drank.

Eli was about to say something about the baby—he figured that it was best to break the ice with a nice, safe topic—when Kasey suddenly spoke up.

It wasn't exactly what he wanted to hear.

"I can't let you do this," she told him abruptly, feeling woven about each word.

"Do what?" he asked. The blanket statement was rather vague, although, in his gut, he had a feeling he knew what she was referring to. Still, he decided to play dumb as he stalled. "Drive you?" he guessed.

"No, have me stay at your ranch with the baby." She turned in her seat to face him. "I can't put you out like that."

"Put me out?" he repeated with a dismissive laugh. "You're not putting me out, Kasey, you're doing me a favor."

She looked at him, unconvinced and just a little confused. "How is my staying at your place with a crying newborn doing you a favor?"

"Well, you might remember that I grew up with four

brothers and a sister," he began, stating a fact tongue-in-cheek since he knew damn well that *she* knew. Growing up, she'd all but adopted his family, preferring them to her own. "That made for pretty much a full house, and there was always noise. An awful *lot* of noise," he emphasized. "When I got a chance to get my own place, I figured that all that peace and quiet would be like finally reaching heaven."

He paused for a second, looking for the right words, then decided just to trust his instincts. Kasey would understand. "Well, it wasn't. After living with all that noise going on all the time, the quiet got on my nerves. I found that I kind of missed all that noise. Missed the sound of someone else living in the place besides me," he emphasized. "Having you and Wayne staying with me will help fill up the quiet. So you see," he concluded, "you're really doing me a favor.

"Besides," he continued. "What kind of a friend would I be, turning my back on you at a time like this when you really need someone?"

"A friend with a life of his own," she answered matter-of-factly.

"You're right," he replied with a nod of his head. "It is my life. And that means I get to choose who I want to have in it." He looked into his rearview mirror, angling it so that he could catch a glimpse of the sleeping infant in the backseat. "And I choose Wayne. Since he's too little to come to stay with me by himself, I guess that means that I have to choose you, too, to carry him around until he can walk on his own power," he concluded with a straight face.

Repositioning the mirror back to its original position, he glanced toward Kasey. She hadn't said anything in response. And then he saw why. Was he to blame for that? "Hey, are you crying?"

Caught, she had no choice but to nod. Avoiding his eyes, she said evasively, "My hormones are all over the map right now. The doctor who delivered Wayne said it's because I gave birth, but it's supposed to pass eventually."

She was lying about the cause behind the tears and he knew it. He could always tell when she was evading the truth. But for the time being, he said nothing, allowing her to have her excuse so that she could have something to hide behind. It was enough that he knew the tears she was crying were tears of relief.

Shifting and taking one hand off the steering wheel, he reached into his side pocket and pulled out a handkerchief. Switching hands on the steering wheel, he silently held out the handkerchief to Kasey.

Sniffing, she took it and wiped away the telltale damp streaks from her cheeks. Eli's offer of a place to stay had touched her. It meant a great deal. Especially in light of the fact that the man she'd loved, the man she'd placed all her faith and trust in, not to mention given access to the meager collection of jewelry her late mother had left her, had thought nothing of just taking off. Abandoning her at a point in time when she very possibly needed him the most.

And, on top of that, he'd left her and their newborn son virtually homeless.

If Eli wasn't here…

But he was. And she knew he was someone she could always count on.

"I'll pay you back for this," she vowed to Eli. "I'm

not sure just how right now, but once I'm a little stronger and back on my feet, I'll get a job and—"

"You don't owe me anything," he said, cutting her off. "And if you want to pay me back, you can do it by getting healthy and taking care of that boy of yours. Besides," he pointed out, "I'm not doing anything that extraordinary. If the tables were turned and I had no home to go to, you'd help me." It wasn't a question.

"In case you haven't noticed," he continued, "that's what friends are for. To be there for each other, not just when the going is good, but when it's bad. *Especially* when it's bad," he emphasized. "I'll always be here for you, Kasey." It was a promise he meant from the bottom of his heart. "So do us both a favor and save your breath. You're staying at my place for as long as you want to. End of discussion," he informed her with finality.

She smiled then, focusing on his friendship rather than on Hollis's betrayal.

"I had no idea you could be this stubborn," she told him with a glimmer of an amused smile. "Learn something every day, I guess."

He caught the glimmer of humor. She was coming around, Eli thought, more than a little pleased. With any luck, Hollis taking off like some selfish bat out of hell wouldn't scar her. But then, above all else, he'd always figured that, first and foremost, Kasey was a survivor.

"There's probably a lot about me that you don't know," he told her as he continued to drive along the open, desolate road that was between Pine Ridge and Forever.

"A lot?" Kasey repeated, then laughed softly as she turned the notion over in her mind. After all, they'd known each other in what felt like close to forever. "I really doubt that."

He loved the sound of her laughter. Loved, he freely admitted, if only to himself, everything about Kasey—except for her husband. But then, he didn't have to love Hollis. Only she did.

It was because he'd accidentally found out that she loved Hollis that he'd kept his feelings for her to himself even though he'd finally worked up the nerve to tell her exactly how he felt about her.

But that was back in high school. Back when Hollis, the school's football hero, had attracted a ring of girls around him, all completely enamored with his charm, each and every one of them ready to do whatever it took to have him notice them.

Hollis, being Hollis, took all the adulation in stride as being his due. He took his share of worshipful girls to bed, too.

Even so, he always had his eye on Kasey because, unlike the others, while very friendly, she didn't fawn all over him. So, naturally, she was the one he'd had to have. The one he'd wanted to conquer. She'd surprised him by holding out for commitment and a ring. And he'd surprised himself by letting her.

One night, not long after graduation, drunk on far more than just her proximity, Hollis had given her both a commitment and a ring, as well as a whirlwind wedding ceremony in a run-down, out-of-the-way chapel that specialized in them, with no questions asked other than if the hundred-dollar bill—paid up-front—was real.

And just like that, Eli recalled, the bottom had dropped out of his world. Not that he felt he had a prayer of winning her heart while Hollis was busy sniffing around her. But Eli had honestly thought that if he bided his time and waited Hollis out, he'd be there when Kasey needed someone.

And he was.

It had taken eight years, far longer than he'd thought Hollis would actually last in the role of husband. More than anything, Eli wanted to be there for her. He'd take her gratitude—if that was all she had to offer—in place of her love.

At least it was something, and besides, he knew that unless he was dead, there was no way he wouldn't be there for Kasey.

He heard her sigh. This was all weighing heavily on her, not that he could blame her. In her place, he'd feel the same way.

"I want you to know that I really appreciate this and that I promise Wayne and I won't put you out for long."

"Oh, good," he quipped drily, "because I'll need the room back by the end of the week."

His words stopped her dead. Eli spared her a look, one that was a little long in length since he was fairly confident that there was nothing to accidentally hit on this stretch of lonely highway.

"I'm only going to say this one more time, Kasey. You're not putting me out. I want to do this. I'm your friend and I always have been and this is what friends do, they have each other's backs. Now, unless you really want to make me strangle you, please stop apologizing, please stop telling me that you're going to leave as soon as possible. And *please* stop telling me that you feel you're putting me out. Because you're not. It makes me feel good to help you.

"Now, I don't want to hear anything more about this. My home is your home for as long as you need a place to stay—and maybe for a little bit longer than that." He paused to let his words sink in. "Understood?"

"Understood," she murmured. Then, a bit more loudly and with feeling, she promised, "But I *will* make it up to you."

"Good, I'm looking forward to it," he told her crisply. "Now, moving on," he said deliberately. "You have a choice of bedrooms. There are two to choose from, pretty much the same size," he told her, then stopped when a thought occurred to him. "Maybe I should let you have the master bedroom. We can put the crib in that room, so you can have Wayne right there—unless you'd rather have him stay in his own room, at which point you can take one of the bedrooms and place him in the other."

Kasey felt as if she was still stuck in first gear, her brain fixated on something he'd said to start with. "The crib?"

Why did she look so surprised? he wondered. "Well, Wayne's got to sleep in something, and I thought a crib was better than that portable whatchamacallit that you had at your place. Or a dresser drawer," he added, recalling stories his father told him about his being so small to begin with, they had tucked him into the bottom drawer of a dresser, lined with blankets and converted into a minicrib. He'd slept there for a month.

Kasey pounced on something he'd only mentioned in passing. "You were there?" she asked eagerly. "At our ranch?" The *our* in this case referred to her and Hollis. When he nodded, her mind took off, fully armed to the teeth. "So that means that I can still go over there and get—"

He shook his head. The man who had won the ranch from Hollis had made it very clear that he considered everything on the premises his. Still, if she had something of sentimental value that she wanted retrieved, he would be there in less than a heartbeat to get it for her. The new owner would just have to understand—or be made to understand.

"The guy who won the ranch from Hollis is living there," he told her. "I had to talk him into letting me come in and get some of your things. Actually—" never one to take any undue credit, he felt he needed to tell her "—having Rick and Alma with me kind of gave me the leverage I needed to convince the guy to release your things so I could bring them to you."

"Rick and Alma," she repeated as that piece of information sank in with less than stellar results. "So they know? About Hollis leaving me?" she asked in a small, troubled voice.

He knew that she would have rather kept the fact that Hollis had walked out on her a secret, but secrets had a way of spreading in a small town the size of Forever. And besides, the sympathy would all be on her side for reasons beyond the fact that she was a new mother with an infant to care for. Everyone in and around the town liked her.

That couldn't be said of Hollis.

"They know," Eli told her quietly. "I figured they— especially Rick, since he's the sheriff—should hear it from me so that they'd know fact from fiction, rumors being what they are in this town," he added.

Kasey felt as if there was a lead weight lying across her chest. There was a very private, shy woman beneath the bravado. A woman who wanted her secrets to remain secrets.

"How many other people know?" she asked him.

"For now, just Rick and the deputies."

For now.

"Now," she knew, had an exceptionally short life expectancy. As Eli had said, rumors being what they were, she had a feeling that everyone in town would know that Hollis had taken off before the week was out—if not sooner.

It was a very bitter pill for her to swallow.

But she had no other choice.

Chapter 3

"I guess you're right. No point in pretending I can hide this," Kasey finally said with a sigh. "People'll talk."

"They always do," he agreed. "It's just a fact of life."

Fact of life or not, the idea just didn't sit well with her. She wasn't a person who craved attention or wanted her fifteen minutes of fame in the spotlight. She was perfectly content just to quietly go about the business of living.

"I don't want to be the newest topic people talk about over breakfast," she said, upset.

"If they *do* talk about you, it'll be because they're on your side. Fact of the matter is, Hollis more or less wore out that crown of his. People don't think of him as that golden boy he once was," Eli assured her. Over the years, he'd become acutely aware of Hollis's flaws, flaws that the man seemed to cultivate rather than try to conquer. "Not to mention that he owes more than one person around here money."

Kasey looked at him, startled. Her mouth dropped open.

Maybe he'd said too much, Eli thought. "You didn't know that," he guessed.

Kasey's throat felt horribly dry, as if she'd been eating sand for the past half hour.

"No," she answered, her voice barely above a shaken whisper. "I didn't know that."

If she didn't know about that, it was a pretty safe bet that she certainly didn't know about her husband's dalliances with other women during the years that they were married, Eli thought.

Hollis, you were and are a damn fool. A damn, stupid, self-centered fool.

He could feel his anger growing, but there was no point in letting it fester like this. It wasn't going to help Kasey and her baby, and they were the only two who really mattered in this sordid mess.

"Are you sure?" Kasey asked. She'd turned her face toward him and placed a supplicating hand on his upper arm, silently begging him to say he was mistaken.

It was as if someone had jabbed his heart with a hot poker. He hated that this was happening to her. She didn't deserve this on top of what she'd already gone through. All of his life, he'd wanted nothing more than to make life better for her, to protect her. But right now, he was doing everything he could. Like taking her to his ranch.

Dammit, Hollis, how could you do this to her? She thought you were going to be her savior, her hero.

The house that Kasey had grown up in had been

completely devoid of love. Her father worked hard, but never got anywhere and it made him bitter. Especially when he drank to ease the pain of what he viewed as his dead-end life. Carter Hale had been an abusive drunk not the least bit shy about lashing out with his tongue or the back of his hand.

He'd seen the marks left on Kasey's mother and had worried that Kasey might get in the way of her father's wrath next. But Kasey had strong survival instincts and had known enough to keep well out of her father's way when he went on one of his benders, which was often.

Looking back, Eli realized that was the reason why she'd run off with Hollis right after high school graduation. Hollis was exciting, charming, and fairly reeked of sensuality. More than that, he had a feeling that to Kasey, Hollis represented, in an odd twist, freedom and at the same time, security. Marrying Hollis meant that she never had to go home again. Never had to worry about staying out of her father's long reach again.

But in Hollis's case, "freedom" was just another way of saying no plans for the future. And if "security" meant the security of not having to worry about money, then Hollis failed to deliver on that promise, as well.

Eli had strong suspicions that Kasey was beginning to admit to herself that marrying Hollis had been a huge mistake. That he wasn't going to save her but take her to hell via another route.

Most likely, knowing Kasey, when she'd discovered that she was pregnant, she had clung to the hope that this would finally make Hollis buckle down, work hard and grow up.

Eli blew out a short breath. He could have told her that Hollis wasn't about to change his way of thinking, and saved her a great deal of grief. But lessons, he supposed, couldn't be spoon-fed. The student could only learn if he or she *wanted* to, and he had a feeling that Kasey would have resisted any attempts to show her that Hollis wasn't what she so desperately wanted him to be.

Eli tried to appear as sympathetic as possible. As sympathetic as he felt toward her. This couldn't be easy for her. None of it.

"I'm sure," he finally told her, taking no joy in the fact that he was cutting Hollis down.

Kasey shook her head. She felt stricken. "I didn't have a clue," she finally admitted, wondering how she could have been so blind. Wondering how Hollis could have duped her like this. "What's wrong with me, Eli? Am I that stupid?"

"No, you're not stupid at all," he said with feeling. "What you are is loyal, and there's nothing wrong with you." To him, she'd always been perfect. Even when she'd fallen in love with Hollis, he hadn't been able to find it in his heart to take her to task for loving, in his opinion, the wrong man. He'd just accepted it. "Hollis is the one who's got something wrong with him. You've got to believe that," he told her firmly.

Kasey lifted her slender shoulders in a helpless shrug and then sighed again. It was obvious that she really didn't want to find fault with the man who'd fathered her child. The man whom she'd loved for almost a decade. "He was just trying to get some money together to make a better life for us," she said defensively.

The only one whose lot Hollis had *ever* wanted to improve was his own, Eli thought grudgingly, but he knew that to say so out loud would only hurt Kasey, so he kept the words to himself.

After pulling up in front of his ranch house, he turned off the engine and looked at her. "Until you're ready, until you have a place to go to and *want* to go there," he added, "this is your home, Kasey. Yours and Wayne's. What's mine is yours," he told her. "You know that."

He saw her biting her lower lip and knew she was waging an internal war with herself. Kasey hated the idea of being in anyone's debt, but he wasn't just anyone, he silently argued. They were friends. Best friends. And he had been part of her life almost from the time they began forming memories. There was no way he was about to abandon her now. And no way was he going to place her in a position where she felt she "owed" him anything other than seeing her smile again.

"Don't make me have to hog-tie you to make you stay put," he warned.

The so-called threat finally brought a smile to her lips. "All right, I won't."

Feeling rather pleased with himself, at least for the moment, Eli unfolded his lanky frame out of the Jeep and then hurried over to Kasey's side of the vehicle to help her out. Under normal circumstances, he wouldn't have even thought of it. She'd always been exceedingly independent around him, which made her being with Hollis doubly difficult for him to take. Kasey couldn't be independent around Hollis.

Hollis enjoyed being in control and letting Kasey *know* that he was in control. That in turn meant that he expected her submission. Because she loved him, she'd lived down to his expectations.

Unlike Hollis, he was proud of the fact that Kasey could take care of herself. And also unlike Hollis, he liked her independent streak. But at the moment, that had to take a backseat to reality. It was obvious that her body was having a bit of difficulty getting back in sync after giving birth only a few days ago. Eli just wanted to let her know that he was there for her. Whether it meant giving her a hand up or a shoulder to cry on, she could always rely on him.

She knew he meant well, but it didn't help her frame of mind. "I don't like feeling like this," she murmured, tamping down her frustration.

Eli took her hand and eased her to her feet. "It'll pass soon and you can go back to being Super Kasey," he quipped affectionately.

Just as she emerged from the passenger side, the tiny passenger in the backseat began to cry.

"Sounds like someone's warming up to start wailing," Eli commented, opening the rear door. "You okay?" he asked Kasey before he started freeing Wayne from all his tethers.

She nodded. "I'm fine." A sliver of guilt shot through her as she watched Eli at work. "I should be doing that," she said, clearly annoyed with herself. "He's my responsibility."

"Hey, you can't have all the fun," he told her good-naturedly, noting that she sounded almost testy. He took no offense, sensing that she was frustrated with herself—and Hollis—not him.

The baby was looking at him, wide-eyed, and for a moment he had stopped crying. Eli took that to be a good sign.

"Hi, fella. Let's get you out of all those belts and buckles and into the daylight," he said in a low, gentle voice meant to further soothe the little passenger.

In response, the baby just stared at him as if he was

completely fascinated by the sound of his voice. Eli smiled to himself, undoing one belt after another as quickly as possible.

Behind him, he heard Kasey say, "I'm sorry, Eli."

He looked at her over his shoulder, puzzled. "About what?"

"About being so short with you." He was being nothing but good to her. He didn't deserve to have her snapping at him.

"Can't help being the height you are," he answered wryly.

"I meant—"

He didn't want her beating herself up about this. God knew she had reason to be upset and short-tempered.

"I know what you meant," he told her, stepping back from the Jeep and then straightening. Holding Wayne securely in his arms, he changed the subject. "I can't get over how little he is. It's like holding a box of sugar. A wiggling box of sugar," he amended as the baby twisted slightly.

He saw that the infant's lips were moving. "Rooting," he thought the nurse had called it on one of his visits to hospital. It was what babies did when they were hungry and searching for their mother's breast.

"I think your son is trying to order an early dinner," he told her. Wayne had latched on to his shirt and was sucking on it. Very gently, he extracted the material from the infant's mouth.

Wayne whimpered.

Eli was right, Kasey realized. The nurse had brought her son to her for a feeding approximately four hours ago. She needed to feed him.

Kasey took the baby from Eli and Wayne turned his

little head so that his face was now against her breast. As before, he began questing and a frustrated little noise emerged from his small, rosebud mouth.

"I think you're right," she said to Eli, never taking her eyes off her son.

She still wasn't used to Wayne or the concept that she was actually a mother. Right now, she was in awe of this small, perfect little human being who had come into her life. Holding him was like holding a small piece of heaven, she thought.

That her best friend seemed so attuned to her son made her feel both happy and sad. Happy because she had someone to share this wondrous experience with and sad because as good and kind as Eli was, she was supposed to be sharing this with Hollis. Her husband was supposed to be standing beside her. He should be the one holding their son and marveling about how perfect he was.

Instead, Eli was saying all those things while Hollis was out there somewhere, heading for the hills. Or possibly for a good time. And it was Hollis who had gambled their home right out from under them and then hadn't been man enough to face her with the news. He'd sent in Eli to take his place.

What kind of man did that to the woman he loved—unless he didn't love her anymore, she suddenly thought. Was that it? Had he just woken up one morning to find that he'd fallen out of love with her? The thought stung her heart, but she had a feeling that she was right.

Meanwhile, Wayne was growing progressively insistent and more frustrated that there was nothing to be suckled from his mother's blouse. All that was happening was that he was leaving a circular wet spot.

Glancing toward the protesting infant, Eli abandoned the suitcase he was about to take out.

"I'd better get you inside and settled in before Wayne decides to make a meal out of your blouse," he said. Nodding at the suitcase, he told her, "This other stuff can wait."

With that, he hurried over to the front door and unlocked it. Like most of the people in and around Forever, he usually left the front door unlocked during the daytime. But knowing he was going to be gone for a while, he'd thought it was more prudent to lock up before he'd left this morning.

Not that he actually had anything worth stealing, but he figured that coming into a house that had just been ransacked would have been an unsettling experience for Kasey, and he'd wanted everything to be as perfect as possible for her.

Despite their friendship, coming here wasn't going to be easy for her. Kasey had her pride—at times, that was *all* she had and she'd clung to it—and her pride would have been compromised twice over if she'd had to stay in a recently robbed house. If nothing else, it would have made her exceedingly uneasy about the baby's safety, not to mention her own.

She had more than enough to worry about as it was. He wanted to make this transition to his house as painless, hell, as *easy* as possible for her. That meant no surprises when he opened the front door to his house.

"Don't expect much," he told her as he pushed the front door open. "I'm still just settling in and getting the hang of this place. It'll look a lot better once I get a chance to get some new things in here and spruce the place up a bit."

Walking in ahead of him, Kasey looked around slowly, taking everything in. She knew that Eli had bought the ranch in the past couple of months. Though she'd wanted to, she hadn't had the opportunity to come by to visit. It wasn't so much that she'd been too busy to spare the time, but that she'd had a feeling, deep down, Hollis hadn't wanted her to come over. That was why, she surmised, he'd kept coming up with excuses about why he wasn't able to bring her over and he'd been completely adamant about her not going anywhere alone in "her condition," as if her pregnancy had drained all of her intelligence from her, rendering her incapacitated.

Not wanting to be drawn into yet another futile, pointless argument, she'd figured it was easier just to go along with what Hollis was saying. In her heart, she knew that Eli would understand.

Eli always understood, she thought now, wondering why she'd been such a blind fool when it came to Hollis. There were times, she had to reluctantly admit, when Hollis could be as shallow as a wading pool.

At other times…

There *were* no other times. If he'd had a moment of kindness, of understanding, those points were all wiped out by what he'd done now. A man who'd walked out on his family *had* no redeeming qualities.

She forced herself to push all thoughts of Hollis from her mind. She couldn't deal with that right now. Instead she focused on Eli's house.

"It's cozy," she finally commented with a nod, and hoped that she sounded convincing.

He went around, turning on lights even though it was still afternoon. The sun, he'd noticed shortly after buying the ranch, danced through the house early in the morning. By the time midafternoon came, the tour was finished and the sun had moved on to another part of the ranch, leaving the house bathed in shadows. It didn't bother him, but he didn't want to take the chance that it might add to Kasey's justifiably dark mood.

"By 'cozy' you mean 'little,'" he corrected with a laugh. He took no offense. By local standards, his ranch was considered small. But everything had to start somewhere. "I figure I can always build on to it once I get a little bit of time set aside," he told her.

She nodded. "I'm sure your brothers would be willing to help you build."

"And Alma," he reminded her. "Don't forget about Alma."

His sister, the youngest in their family and currently one of the sheriff's three deputies, was always the first to have her hand up, the first to volunteer for anything. She was, and always had been, highly competitive. At times he had the feeling that the very act of breathing was some sort of a competition for Alma, if it meant that she could do it faster than the rest of them.

His sister had slowed down some, he thought—and they were all grateful for that—now that Cash was in the picture. The one-time resident of Forever had gone on to become a highly sought-after criminal lawyer, but he was giving it all up to marry Alma and settle down in Forever again. He knew they all had Cash to thank for this calmer, gentler version of Alma. Eli could only hope that Alma was going to continue on this less frantic route indefinitely.

"Nobody ever forgets Alma," Kasey said fondly. Wayne, his cries getting louder, was now mewling like a neglected, hungry kitten. She began to rock him against her chest, trying to soothe him for a minute longer. "Um, could you show me where we'll be staying?"

Because Hollis had caught him by surprise, he hadn't had time to do much of anything by way of getting her room ready for her—or, for that matter, make up his mind about which room might be better suited to her and the baby. He was pretty much winging it. Stopping to buy the infant seat, as well as bringing over the baby's crib, was just about all he'd had time for before driving to the hospital.

"For now, why don't you just go into the back bedroom and use that?" he suggested. When she continued looking at him quizzically, he realized that she didn't know what room he was talking about. "C'mon—" he beckoned "—I'll show you."

Turning, Eli led the way to the only bedroom located on the first floor. Luckily for him—and Kasey—the room did have a bed in it. It, along with the rest of the furnishings, had come with the house. The previous owner had sold him the house on the one condition that he wasn't going to have to move out his furniture. That, the old widower had told him, would be one big hassle for him, especially since he was flying to Los Angeles to live with his daughter and her family.

Eli, who hadn't had a stick of furniture to his name, had readily agreed. For both it had been a win-win situation.

Opening the bedroom door, he turned on the overhead light and then gestured toward the full-size bed against the wall. It faced a bureau made of dark wood. The pieces matched and both were oppressively massive-looking.

"Make yourself comfortable," Eli urged. Stepping

to the side, he added, "I'm going to go out and get your suitcase. Holler if you need anything."

And with that, he turned and left the room.

Kasey watched him walk away. With each step that took him farther away from her, she could feel her uneasiness growing.

I'm hollering, Eli. I'm hollering, she silently told him.

You're not the only one in the room, she reminded herself.

Smiling down at Wayne, she turned her attention toward quelling her son's mounting, ever-louder cries of distress.

Chapter 4

Eli kept looking at the door to the downstairs bedroom, waiting for it to open. It seemed to him as if Kasey had been in there with the baby for a long time.

Was that normal?

He debated knocking on the door to ask if everything was all right. But on the other hand, he didn't want Kasey to feel as if he was crowding her, either.

He didn't know what to do with himself, so he just kept watching the door for movement. He had no idea how long it took to actually feed an infant. Alma was the last one born in their family and since he was only eleven months older, he never had the opportunity to be around an infant.

Dragging a hand through his unruly, thick black hair, he blew out an impatient breath. No doubt about it, he'd never felt so out of his depth before.

When he glanced down at his watch, he noted that twenty minutes had passed. Again he wondered if he should be worried that something was wrong. Though she'd tried to hide it, Kasey had been pretty upset when she'd gone into the bedroom with the infant. Not that he could blame her. The man she'd wanted to count on had abandoned her without so much as a shred of consideration for how she would feel about the situation. Hollis certainly hadn't had the courage to face her before he'd pulled his disappearing act.

She really was better off without him, but, if he said anything like that now, it might strike her as cold.

Frustrated, concerned, Eli ran his hand through his hair again, trying to think of a possible way to make things better for Kasey.

Maybe Hollis should have at least left her a letter or some sort of a note, apologizing for his actions and telling her that he just needed to get his head straight. That once that happened, maybe he could come back and do right by her. The more he thought about it, the more certain he became that Kasey would have taken comfort in that.

But there was no point in reflecting on that, since Hollis hadn't even been thoughtful enough of her feelings to do something as simple as that—

Eli stopped thinking of what was and began thinking of what should have been.

If it helped, why not?

He looked at the door again, and then at the old-fashioned writing desk butted up against the far wall in the living room. Weighing the pros and cons, he wavered for less than a moment, then quickly crossed over to the desk, took out a piece of paper, a pen and an envelope.

With one eye on the entrance to the living room, watching for Kasey, he quickly dashed off a note of apology to her, doing his best to approximate Hollis's handwriting, then signed it *Hollis*.

He'd just finished sealing the envelope when he heard the bedroom door opening. The very next moment, he heard Kasey calling to him.

"Eli? Eli, are you down here?" Her voice sounded as if she was coming closer.

Stuffing the envelope into his back pocket, Eli raised his own voice slightly. "Out here. I'm in the living room."

The next moment Kasey walked into the room. Both she and the baby looked somewhat calmer.

"Well, he's all fed and changed, thanks to the disposable diapers in that little care packet the hospital gave me." Even as she said it, Kasey caught her lower lip between her teeth.

He was so tuned in to her, he could almost read her mind. She was already thinking ahead to all the things she was going to need, including a veritable mountain of disposable diapers.

"Well, unless we can get Wayne potty-trained by tonight, you're going to need more of those," he commented, taking the burden of having to mention it from her. "Tell you what, why don't you make up a list of what you'll need and I'll take a quick trip into town?" Eli suggested.

Kasey smiled, grateful for his thoughtfulness. How did one man turn out like this while another—

Don't go there, she warned herself. There weren't any answers for her there and she would drive herself crazy with the questions.

"Sounds like a good idea," she agreed. Then her eyes narrowed as she saw the long envelope sticking out of his back pocket. "What's that?" she asked.

Appearing properly confused, Eli reached behind himself. He pulled out the envelope, looked at it and slowly allowed recognition to enter his expression.

"Oh, in all the excitement of bringing you and Wayne home, I totally forgot about this."

Kasey cocked her head, curious as she studied him. "Forgot about what?"

"When Hollis came over in the middle of the night to ask me to look after you, he wanted me to give this to you." And with that, he handed her the envelope.

She stared at it, then looked up at Eli. "Hollis left me a letter?" That really didn't sound like the Hollis she knew. He would have made fun of anyone who actually put anything in writing.

"I don't know if it's a letter or not, but he left something," Eli told her vaguely. "Here, why don't you let me hold on to the little guy so you can open the envelope and see what's inside." Even as he made the offer, Eli was already taking Wayne away from her and into his arms.

Really puzzled now, Kasey nodded absently in Eli's direction and opened the envelope. The letter inside was short and to the point. It was also thoughtfully worded. She read it twice, and then one last time, before raising her eyes to Eli's face. She looked at him for a long moment.

Swaying slightly to lull the baby in his arms, he looked at her innocently. "So? What did Hollis have to say?"

She glanced down at the single sheet before answer-

ing. "That he was sorry. That it's not me, it's him. He
doesn't want to hurt me, but he just needs some time
away to get his head together. Until he does, he can't be
the husband and father that we deserve. In the meantime, he'll send money for the baby and me when he
can," she concluded. Very deliberately, she folded the
letter and placed it back in its envelope.

Eli nodded. "That sounds about right. That's more
or less what he said to me before he left," he explained
when she looked at him quizzically. "At least he apologized to you."

"Yes, at least he apologized," she echoed quietly,
raising her eyes to his. Still looking at him, she tucked
the letter into her own pocket. There was an odd expression on her face.

Did she suspect? He couldn't tell. There were times,
such as now, when her expression was completely unreadable.

The next moment Kasey took her son back from Eli
and sat with the infant on the sofa. A very loud sigh
escaped her lips.

Eli perched on the arm of the sofa and looked into
her face. Hollis was clearly out of his mind, walking
away from this.

"Are you all right, Kasey?" he asked solicitously.

She nodded her head slowly in response. When she
spoke, her voice seemed as if it was coming from a
very far distance. And, in a way, she supposed it was.
With each word he uttered, she closed the door a little
further to her past.

He was about to ask her again when Kasey abruptly
began to talk.

"I guess, deep down, I knew that Hollis wasn't the

father type. As long as it was just him and me, he could put up with some domesticity, provided it didn't smother him."

Her eyes stung and she paused for a moment before continuing. She didn't tell Eli about the times she suspected that Hollis was stepping out on her, that he was seeing other women. There was no point in talking about that now.

"But then I got pregnant, and once the baby was here, it really hit Hollis that he might have to..." Her voice trailed off for a moment as she struggled with herself, vacillating between being angry at Hollis and feeling disloyal to him for talking about him this way. For once, anger won out. "That he might have to grow up," she finally said.

"First of all, you didn't just 'get pregnant,'" Eli corrected. "Last time I checked, it took two to make that happen. Hollis was just as responsible for this as you were," he pointed out.

Kasey smiled affectionately at him then. Smiled as she leaned forward and lightly touched his face. Both the look and the touch spoke volumes. But Eli had no interpreter and he wasn't sure just what was hidden behind her smile or even *if* there was something hidden behind her smile.

All he knew was that, as usual, her smile drew him in. There were times, when he allowed his guard to slip, that he loved her so much that it hurt.

It would be hard having her here under his roof, sleeping here under his roof, and keeping a respectful distance from her at all times.

Not that he would ever disrespect her, he vowed, but God, he wanted to hold her in his arms right now. And more than anything in the world, he wanted to lean over and kiss her. Kiss her just once like a lover and not like a friend.

But that was impossible, and it would ruin everything between them.

So he rose off the arm of the sofa and got down to the business of making this arrangement work. "If you could just give me that list of things—"

"Sure. I'm going to need a pen and some paper," Kasey prompted when he just remained standing there.

"Right."

Coming to life, Eli was about to fetch both items from the same desk he had just used to write that "note from Hollis" to her when there was a knock on the front door.

The first thing Eli thought of was that Hollis had had a change of heart and, making an assumption that Kasey would be here, had returned for his wife and son.

A glance at Kasey's face told him she was thinking the same thing.

As he strode toward the door, Eli struggled to ignore the deep-seated feeling of disappointment flooding him.

Kasey followed in his wake.

But when he threw open his door, it wasn't Hollis that either one of them saw standing there. It was Miss Joan and one of her waitresses from the diner, a tall, big-boned young woman named Carla. Miss Joan was holding a single bag in her exceptionally slender arms. Carla was holding several more with incredible ease, as if all combined they weighed next to nothing.

"Figured you two had probably gotten back from the hospital by now," Miss Joan declared. Her eyes were naturally drawn to the baby and she all but cooed at him. "My, but he's a cutie, he is."

And then she looked up from the baby and directly at Eli. "Well, aren't you going to invite us in, or are you looking to keep Kasey and her son all to yourself?"

Eli snapped to attention. "Sorry, you just surprised me, that's all, Miss Joan," he confessed. "C'mon in," he invited, stepping back so that she and the waitress had room to walk in.

He watched the older woman with some amusement as she looked slowly around. Miss Joan made no secret that she was scrutinizing everything in the house.

As was her custom, Miss Joan took possession of all she surveyed.

"I don't recall hearing about a tornado passing through Forever lately." She raised an eyebrow as she glanced in his direction.

Eli knew she was referring to the fact that as far as housekeeping went, he got a failing grade. With a shrug, he told her, "Makes it easier to find things if they're all out in the open."

Miss Joan shook her head. "If you say so." She snorted. "Looks like this could be a nice little place you've got here, Eli." Her eyes swept over the general chaos. "Once you get around to digging yourself out of this mess, of course." She waved her hand around the room, dismissing the subject now that she'd touched on it.

"Anyway, I got tired of waiting for an invite, so I just decided to invite myself over." Pausing, the older woman looked at Eli meaningfully. "Thought you might need a few things for the new guy," she told him, nodding at the baby in Kasey's arms.

"Oh, I can't—" Kasey began to protest. The last thing she wanted was for people to think of her as a charity case.

"Sure you can," Miss Joan said, cutting Kasey off with a wave of her hand. Then she directed her attention to the young woman who had come with her. "Just set everything down on the coffee table, Carla," she instructed. She shifted her eyes toward Kasey. "I'll let you sort things out when you get a chance," she told her. "Brought you some diapers and a bunch of other items. These new little guys need a lot to get them spruced up and shining." She said it as if it was a prophesy.

Miss Joan was right. She couldn't afford to let her pride get in the way, or, more accurately, Wayne couldn't afford to have her pride get in his way.

"I don't know what to say," Kasey said to Miss Joan, emotion welling up in her throat and threatening to choke off her words.

"Didn't ask you to say anything, now, did I?" Miss Joan pointed out. And then the woman smiled. "It's what we do around here, remember? We look out for each other." She nodded at the largest paper bag that Carla set down. Because she had run out of room on the coffee table, Carla had deposited the bag on the floor beside one of the table legs. "Thought the baby might not be the only one who was hungry, so I brought you two some dinner. My advice is to wait until you put him down before you start eating."

"What do I owe you?" Eli asked, taking his wallet out.

Miss Joan put her hand over his before he could take any bills out. "We'll settle up some other time," she informed him.

Kasey wasn't about to bother asking Miss Joan how the woman knew that she was here, at Eli's ranch, rather than at her own ranch. Even when things were actually kept a secret, Miss Joan had a way of knowing about them. Miss Joan *always* knew. She ran the town's only diner and dispensed advice and much-needed understanding along with the best coffee in Texas.

Joan Randall had been a fixture in Forever for as long as anyone could remember and had just recently given in to the entreaties of her very persistent suitor. She and Harry Monroe had gotten married recently in an outdoor wedding with the whole town in attendance. Even so, everyone still continued to refer to her as Miss Joan. Calling her anything else just didn't feel right.

Having done everything she'd set out to do, Miss Joan indicated that it was time to leave.

"Okay, Carla and I'll be heading out now," she announced, then paused a moment longer to look at Kasey. "You need anything, you just give me a call, understand, baby girl?" And then she lowered her voice only slightly as she walked by Eli. "You take care of her, hear?"

He didn't need any prompting to do that. He'd been watching over Kasey for as long as he could remember.

"I fully intend to, Miss Joan," he told her with feeling.

Miss Joan nodded as she crossed the threshold. She knew he meant it. Knew what was in his heart better than he did.

"Good. Because she's been through enough." Then, lowering her voice even further so that only Eli could hear her, she told him, "I ever see that Hollis again, I'm going to take a lot of pleasure in turning that rooster into a hen."

Eli had absolutely no doubts that the older woman was very capable of doing just that. He grinned. "Better not let the sheriff hear you say that."

Miss Joan smiled serenely at him. "Rick won't say anything. Not with Alma helping me and being his deputy and all. Your sister doesn't like that bastard any better than any of us do," she confided. Then, raising her voice so that Kasey could hear her, she urged, "Don't wait too long to have your dinner." With a nod of her head, she informed them that "It tastes better warm."

One final glance at Kasey and the baby, and the woman was gone. Carla was right behind her, moving with surprising speed given her rather large size.

"I didn't tell her about Hollis" was the first thing Eli said as he closed the door again and turned around to face Kasey. He didn't want her thinking that he had been spreading her story around.

Kasey knew he hadn't. This was Miss Joan they were talking about. Everyone was aware of her ability to ferret out information.

"Nobody ever has to tell that woman anything. She just *knows*. It's almost spooky," Kasey confessed. "When I was a little girl, I used to think she was a witch—a good witch," she was quick to add with a smile. "Like in *The Wizard of Oz*, but still a witch." At times, she wasn't completely convinced that the woman *wasn't* at least part witch.

He grinned. "Out of the mouths of babes," he quipped. "Speaking of babes, I think your little guy just fell asleep again. Probably in self-defense so that he didn't have to put up with being handled." He grinned. "Carla looked like she was dying to get her hands on him." He had noticed that the waitress had struggled to hold herself in check. "But then, I guess that everyone loves a new baby."

The second the words were out, he realized what he'd said and he could have bitten off his tongue.

Especially when Kasey answered quietly, "No, not everyone."

He could almost *see* the wound in her heart opening up again.

Dammit, he would have to be more careful about what he said around Kasey. At least for a while. "Let me rephrase that. Any *normal* person loves a new baby."

Kasey knew he meant well. She offered Eli a weak smile in response, then looked down at her son.

"I'll try putting him to bed so that we can have our dinner. But I can't make any promises. He's liable to wake up just as I start tiptoeing out. Feel perfectly free to start without me," she urged as she walked back to the rear bedroom with Wayne.

As if he could, Eli thought, watching her as she left the room.

The truth of it was, he couldn't start anything anywhere, not as long as she continued to hold his heart hostage the way she did.

Shaking free of his thoughts, Eli went to set the table in the kitchen. With any luck, he mused, he'd find two clean dishes still in the cupboard. Otherwise, he would actually have to wash a couple stacked in the sink.

It wasn't a prospect he looked forward to.

Chapter 5

Eli wasn't sure just when he finally fell asleep. The fact that he actually *did* fall asleep surprised him. Mentally, he'd just assumed that he would be up all night. After all, this was Kasey's first night in his house, not to mention her first night with the baby without the safety net of having a nurse close by to take Wayne back to the nursery if he started crying.

Granted, he wasn't a nurse, but at least he could be supportive and make sure that she didn't feel as if she was in this alone. He could certainly relieve her when she got tired.

Last night, when it was time to turn in, Kasey had thanked him for his hospitality and assured him that she had everything under control. She'd slipped into the same bedroom she'd used earlier. The crib he'd retrieved from her former home was set up there.

Her last words to him were to tell him that he should get some sleep.

Well *that* was easier said than done, he'd thought at the time, staring off into the starless darkness outside his window. He'd felt much too wired. Besides, he was listening for any sound that struck him as being out of the ordinary. A sound that would tell him that Kasey needed help. Which in turn would mean that she needed him, at least for this.

He almost strained himself, trying to hear if the baby was crying.

It was probably around that time that, exhausted, he'd fallen asleep.

When he opened his eyes again, he was positive that only a few minutes had gone by. Until he realized that daylight, not moonlight, was streaming into his room. Startled, he bolted upright. Around the same moment of rude awakening, the aroma of tantalizingly strong coffee wound its intoxicating way up to his room and into his senses.

Kicking off a tangled sheet, Eli hit the ground running, stumbling over his discarded boots on his way to his door. It hurt more because he was barefoot.

Even so, he didn't bother putting anything on his feet as he followed the aroma to its point of origin, making his way down the stairs.

Ultimately, the scent brought him to the kitchen.

Kasey was there, with her back toward him. Wayne wasn't too far away—and was strapped into his infant seat. Sometime between last night and this morning, she'd gotten the baby's infant seat out of the car and converted it so that it could hold him securely in place while she had him on the kitchen table.

Turning from the stove, Kasey almost jumped a foot off the ground. Her hand immediately went to her chest, as if she was trying to keep her heart from physically leaping out.

"Oh, Eli, you scared me," she said, struggling to regain her composure.

"Sorry," he apologized when he saw that he'd really startled her. "I don't exactly look my best first thing in the morning." He ran his hand through his hair, remembering that it hadn't seen a hint of a comb since yesterday.

"You look fine," she stressed. No matter what, Eli *always* looked fine, she thought fondly. She could count on the fact that nothing changed about him, especially not his temperament. He was her rock and she thanked God for him. "I just wasn't expecting anyone to come up behind me, that's all." She took in a deep breath in an attempt to regulate her erratic pulse.

"What are you doing up?" he asked.

"Well, I never got into the habit of cooking while I was lying in bed," she stated, deadpan. "So I had to come over to where the appliances were hiding," she told him, tongue-in-cheek.

But Eli shook his head, dismissing the literal answer to his question. "No, I mean *why* are you up, cooking? You're supposed to be taking it easy, remember?" he reminded her.

She acted mystified. "I guess I missed that memo. Besides, this *is* how I take it easy," she informed him. "Cooking relaxes me. It makes me feel like I'm in control," she stressed. Her eyes held his. "And right now, I need that."

He knew how overwhelming a need that could be.

Eli raised his hands in surrender. "Okay, cook your heart out. I won't stand in your way," he promised, then confessed, "And that *does* smell pretty amazing." He looked from her to the pan and then back again. He didn't remember buying bacon. Maybe Alma had dropped it off the last time she'd been by. She had a tendency to mother him. "And that was all stuff you found in my pantry?"

"And your refrigerator," Kasey added, amused that the contents of his kitchen seemed to be a mystery to him. "By the way, if you're interested, I made coffee."

"Interested?" he repeated. "I'm downright mesmerized. That's what brought me down in the first place," he told her as he made a beeline for the battered coffeepot that stood on the back burner. Not standing on ceremony, he poured himself a cup, then paused to deeply inhale the aroma before sampling it. *Perfect,* he thought. It was a word he used a lot in reference to Kasey.

He looked at her now in unabashed surprise. "And you did this with *my* coffee?"

She merely smiled at him, as if he were a slightly thought-challenged second cousin she had grown very fond of. "Yours was the only coffee I had to work with," she pointed out. "Why? You don't like it?"

He took another extralong sip of the black liquid, waiting as it all but burned a path for itself into his belly.

"Like it?" He laughed incredulously at her question. "I'm thinking of marrying it."

Outwardly he seemed to be teasing her, but it was his way of defusing some of the tension ricocheting through him. He was using humor as a defense mechanism so that she didn't focus on the fact that he struggled not to melt whenever he was within several feet of her. Though he had brought her here with the very best of intentions, he had to admit that just having her here was all but undoing him.

"Really, though," he forced himself to say, putting his hand over hers to stop her movements for a second, "you shouldn't be doing all this. I didn't bring you here to be my cook—good as you are at it."

She smiled up at him, a thousand childhood memories crowding her head. Memories in which Eli was prominently featured. He was the one she had turned to when her father had been particularly nasty the night before. Eli always knew how to make her feel better.

"I know that," she told him. "You brought me here because you're good and kind and because Wayne and I didn't have a place to stay. This is just my small way of paying you back a little."

He shook his head. "This isn't a system of checks and balances, Kasey. You don't have to 'pay me back,'" he insisted. "You don't owe me anything."

Oh, yes, I do. More than you can ever guess. You kept me sane, Eli. I hate to think where I'd be right now without you.

Her eyes met his, then she looked down at his hand, which was still over hers. Belatedly, he removed it. She felt a small pang and told herself she was just being silly.

"I know," she told him. And that was because Eli always put others, in this case her, first. "But I want to." Taking a plate—one of two she'd just washed so that she could press them into service—she slid two eggs and half the bacon onto it. "Overeasy, right?" she asked, nodding at the plate she put down on the table.

They'd had breakfast together just once—at Miss Joan's diner years ago, before she'd ever run off with

Hollis. At the time, he envisioned a lifetime of breakfasts to be shared between them.

But that was aeons ago.

Stunned, he asked, "How did you remember?" as he took his seat at the table.

She lifted her slender shoulders in a quick, dismissive shrug. "Some things just stay with me, I guess." She took her own portion and sat across from him at the small table. "Is it all right?" she asked. For the most part, it was a rhetorical question, since he appeared to be eating with enthusiasm.

Had she served him burned tire treads, he would have said the same thing—because she'd gone out of her way for him and the very act meant a great deal to him. More than he could possibly ever tell her, because he didn't want to risk scaring her off.

"It's fantastic," he assured her.

The baby picked that moment to begin fussing. Within a few moments, fussing turned to crying. Kasey looked toward the noise coming from the converted infant seat. "I just fed him half an hour ago," she said wearily.

"Then he's not hungry," Eli concluded.

He remembered overhearing the sheriff's sister-in-law, Tina, saying that infants cried for three reasons: if they were hungry, if they needed to be changed and if they were hurting. Wayne had been fed and he didn't look as if he was in pain. That left only one last reason.

"He's probably finished processing his meal," he guessed. "Like puppies, there's a really short distance between taking food in and eliminating what isn't being used for nutrition," he told her.

With a small, almost suppressed sigh, Kasey nodded.

She started to get up but he put his hand on her arm, stopping her. She looked at him quizzically.

"Stay put, I'll handle this." Eli nodded at his empty plate. "I'm finished eating, anyway." He picked Wayne up and took him into the next room.

She watched him a little uncertainly. This was really going above and beyond the call of duty, she couldn't help thinking.

"Have you ever changed a diaper before?" she asked him.

He didn't answer her directly, because the answer to her question was no. So he said evasively, "It's not exactly up there with the mysteries of life."

Changing a diaper might not be up there with the mysteries of life, but in his opinion, how something so cute and tiny could produce so much waste *was* one of the mysteries of life.

"This has got to weigh at least as much as you do," he stated, marveling as he stripped the diaper away from the baby and saw what was inside.

Making the best of it, Eli went through several damp washcloths, trying to clean Wayne's tiny bottom. It took a bit of work.

Eli began to doubt the wisdom of his volunteering for this form of latrine duty, but he'd done it with the best of intentions. He wanted Kasey to be able to at least finish her meal in peace. She didn't exactly seem worn-out, but she certainly did look tired. He wondered just how much sleep she'd gotten last night.

After throwing the disposable diaper into the wastebasket, he deposited the dirty washcloths on top of it. The latter would need to be put into the washing machine—as soon as he fixed it.

Dammit, anyway, he thought in frustration, recalling that the last load of wash had flooded the utility room.

Served him right for not getting to something the second it needed doing. But then, life on a ranch—especially since he was the only one working it—left very little spare time to do anything else, whether it was a chore or just kicking back for pleasure.

And now that Kasey and her son were here—

And now that they were here, Eli amended, determined to throw this into a positive experience, there was an abundance of sunshine in his life, not to mention a damn good reason to get up in the morning.

There! he thought with a triumphant smile as he concluded the Great Diaper Change. He felt particularly pleased with himself.

The next moment he told himself not to get used to this feeling or the situation that created it. After all, it could, and most likely *would,* change in a heartbeat.

Hadn't his life come to a skidding halt and changed just with Hollis banging on his door, abandoning his responsibilities on the doorstep? Well, just like that, Kasey could go off and find her own place.

Or Hollis might come back and want to pick up where he'd left off. And Kasey, being the softhearted woman she was, would wind up forgiving him and take Hollis back. After all, the man *was* her husband.

But that was later, Eli silently insisted. For now, Kasey was here, in his house with her baby, and he would enjoy every second of it.

Every second that he wasn't working, he amended.

Picking Wayne up, he surveyed his handiwork. "Not a bad job, even if I do say so myself," he pronounced.

Ready to go back out, he turned around toward the

door with the baby in his arms. He was surprised to find that Kasey was standing in the doorway, an amused expression on her face.

What was she thinking? he couldn't help wondering. "Have you been standing there long?" he asked.

She smiled broadly at him. "Just long enough to hear you evaluating your job," she said. Kasey crossed to him and her son. "And you're wrong, you know," she told him as she took Wayne into her arms with an unconscious, growing confidence. "You're being way too modest. You did an absolutely *great* job." There was admiration in her voice. "The nurse had to walk me through the diapering process three times before I got the hang of it," she told him with a wide smile. "You never told me you had hidden talents."

"Didn't know, myself," he freely confessed. "I guess that some people just rise to the occasion more than others."

She thought about him opening his home to her. They were friends, good friends, but that didn't automatically mean she could just move in with him. He had been under no obligation to take her in. She certainly hadn't expected him to do that.

Looking at him pointedly, she nodded. "Yes, they do," she agreed softly.

For one shimmering second, as he stood there, gazing into her eyes, he felt an incredibly overwhelming desire to kiss her. Kiss her and make a full confession about all the years he'd loved her in silence.

But he sensed he might scare her off. That was the last thing that either one of them wanted, especially him. He needed to put some space between them. He thought about his ever-growing list of things that needed his attention. Just thinking about them was daunting, but he needed to get started.

Eli abruptly turned toward the door.

"Well, I'd better get to work," he told Kasey. "Or the horses will think I ran off and left them." But instead of heading outside, the smell of a diaper that was past its expiration date caught his attention. "But the horses are just going to have to wait until I take care of this," he told Kasey, nodding at the wastebasket and its less-than-precious pungent cargo.

"Don't bother," Kasey said. "I'll take care of that." To make her point, she placed herself between Eli and the wastebasket. "Go, tend to your horses before they stampede off in protest."

Instead of getting out of his way, she leaned forward and impulsively kissed his cheek. "Thank you for everything," she whispered just before her lips touched his cheek. "Now *go*," she repeated with feeling.

His cheek pulsated where her lips had met his skin.

Eli didn't quite remember going upstairs to put on his boots or walking out of the house and across the front yard, but he figured he must have because when he finally took stock of his surroundings, he was on his way to the stable.

It wasn't as if she'd never kissed him before. She had. She'd kissed him exactly like that a long time ago, before she'd become Hollis's wife and broken his heart into a million pieces. But back then, she'd brushed her lips against his cheek, leaving her mark by way of a friendly demonstration of affection.

And the results were always the same. His body temperature would rise right along with his jumping pulse rate.

Just being around her could set him off, but that went doubly so whenever she brushed by him, whether it was her hand, her lips or the accidental contact of different body parts.

It made him feel alive.

It also reminded him that he loved her. Loved her and knew that he couldn't have her because it was all one-sided.

His side.

But he'd made his peace with that a long time ago, Eli reminded himself as he continued walking. It was enough for him to know that he was looking out for her, that he was ready to defend her at a moment's notice, Hollis or no Hollis. And because of that, she would be all right. If on occasion he yearned for something more, well, that was his problem, not hers.

During the day, he could keep it all under control, enjoying just the little moments, the tiny interactions between them as well as the longer conversations that were exchanged on occasion.

It was only in his sleep that all these emotions became a good deal more. In his dreams he experienced what he couldn't allow himself to feel—or want—during his waking hours.

But that was something he could never let her even remotely suspect, because in disclosing that, he'd risk losing everything, especially her precious friendship.

He wanted, above all else, to have her feel at ease with him. He wanted to protect her and to do what he could to make her happy. That couldn't happen if she thought he might be trying to compromise not just her but her honor, as well.

His own happiness, he reasoned, would come from

her feeling secure. *That* he could do for her. For them, he amended, thinking of the baby.

Reaching the stable, he pulled open the doors. The smell from the stalls assaulted him the moment he walked in. Babies weren't all that different from horses in some ways. They ate, digested and then eliminated.

Mucking out the stalls would allow him to put changing a small diaper into perspective.

"Hi, guys," he said, addressing the horses that, for now, made up his entire herd. "Miss me?" One of the horses whinnied, as if in response. Shaking his head, Eli laughed.

Approaching the stallion closest to him, he slipped a bridle over the horse's head, then led Golden Boy out of his stall. He hitched the horse to a side railing so that the animal would be out of the way and he could clean the stall without interference.

"Well, I've got a good excuse for being late," he told the horses as he got to work. "Wait till I tell you what's been going on...."

Chapter 6

Eli worked as quickly as he could, but even so, it took him a great deal of time to clean out the stalls, groom the horses, exercise and train them, then finally feed them.

There were five horses in all.

Five horses might not seem like a lot to the average outsider who was uninformed about raising and training quarter horses, but it was a lengthy procedure, especially when multiplied by five and no one else was around to help with the work.

The latter, he had to admit, was partially his own fault. He didn't have the money to take on hired help, but that still didn't mean that he had to go it alone if he didn't want to.

It was understood that if he needed them, he could easily put out a call to one or more of his brothers and they'd be there to help him for the day or the week. He had four older brothers, ranchers all, and they could readily rotate the work between them until Eli was finally on his feet and on his way to making a profit.

But for Eli it boiled down to a matter of pride—stubborn pride—and this kept him from calling any of his brothers and asking for help. He was determined that, as the youngest male in the Rodriguez family, he would turn the ranch into a success without having to depend on any help from his relatives.

Ordinarily he found a certain satisfaction in working with the horses and doing all the chores that were involved in caring for the animals. But today was a different story. Impatience fairly hummed through his veins.

He wanted to be done with the chores, done with the training, so that he could go back to the house and be with Kasey. He really didn't like leaving her alone like this for the better part of the day.

He sought to ease his conscience by telling himself that she could do with a little time to herself. What woman couldn't? His being out here gave her the opportunity to get herself together after this enormous emotional roller-coaster ride she'd just been on—gaining a child and losing a husband.

Not that losing Hollis was really much of a loss.

In addition Eli was fairly certain that Kasey wouldn't want him around to witness any first-time mistakes that she was bound to make with the baby. In her place, *he* certainly wouldn't want someone looking over his shoulder, noting the mistakes he was making.

Even if he wanted to chuck everything and go back up to the house to be with her, he couldn't just up and leave the horses. Not again. Not twice in two days.

He'd already neglected their training segment yesterday when he'd gone to bring Kasey and the baby home from the hospital in Pine Ridge.

Not that he actually neglected the horses themselves. He'd made sure that he'd left food for the stallions and God knew they had no trouble finding the feed, or the water, for that matter. But the stalls, well, they were decidedly more ripe-smelling than they should have been. Breathing had been a real problem for him this morning as he mucked out the stalls.

Raising horses was a tricky business. He knew that if they were left on their own for too long, the horses could revert back to their original behavior and then all the hours that he'd put into training them would be lost.

Now they wouldn't be lost, he thought with a wisp of satisfaction. But he was really, really beginning to feel beat.

He was also aware of the fact that his stomach had been growling off and on now for the past couple of hours. Maybe even longer. The growling served to remind him that he hadn't brought any lunch with him.

Usually, when that happened, he'd think nothing of just taking a break and going back to the house to get something to eat. But he really didn't want to risk just walking in on Kasey. What if she was in the middle of breast-feeding Wayne?

The thought generated an image in his head that had him pausing practically in midstep as his usually tame imagination took flight.

He had no business thinking of her that way and he knew it, but that still didn't help him erase the scene from his brain.

Taking a deep breath, Eli forced himself to shake free

of the vivid daydream. He had work to do and standing there like some oversexed adolescent, allowing his mind to wander like that, wouldn't accomplish anything—except possibly to frustrate him even further.

Silver Streak, the horse he was currently grooming, suddenly began nudging him, as if clearly making a bid for his attention. The horse didn't stop until he slowly ran his hand over the silken muzzle.

"Sorry, Silver," Eli said, stroking the animal affectionately. "I was daydreaming. I won't let it happen again."

As if in response, the stallion whinnied. Eli grinned. "Always said you were smarter than the average rancher, which in this case would be me," he added with a self-deprecating laugh.

Since it was summer, the sun was still up when Eli fed the last horse and officially called it a day. He had returned all five of the quarter horses to their stalls and then locked the stable doors before finally returning to his house.

Reaching the ranch house, Eli made as much noise as he could on the front porch so that Kasey was alerted to his arrival and would know that he was coming in. He didn't want to catch her off guard.

Satisfied that he'd made enough of a racket to raise the dead, Eli finally opened the front door and called out a hearty greeting. "Hi, Kasey, I'm coming in."

"Of course you're coming in," Kasey said, meeting him at the door as he walked in. "You live here."

Eli cleared his throat, feeling uncomfortable with the topic he was about to broach. "I thought that maybe you were, you know, *busy*," he emphasized, settling for a euphemism.

"Well, I guess I have been that," she admitted, shifting her newly awakened son to her other hip. "But that still doesn't explain why you feel you have to shout a warning before walking into your own home."

He didn't hear the last part of her sentence. By then he was too completely stunned to absorb any words at all. Momentarily speechless, Eli retraced his steps and ducked outside to double check that he hadn't somehow stumbled into the wrong house—not that there were any others on the property.

The outside of the house looked like his, he ascertained. The inside, however, definitely did not. It bore no resemblance to the house he had left just this morning.

What was going on here?

"What did you do?" he finally asked.

"You don't like it," Kasey guessed, doing her best to hide her disappointment. She'd really wanted to surprise him—but in a good way. Belatedly she recalled that some men didn't like having their things touched and rearranged.

"I don't *recognize* it," Eli corrected, looking around again in sheer amazement. This was his place? Really?

The house he had left this morning had looked, according to Miss Joan's gentle description of it, as if it had gone dancing with a tornado. There were no rotting carcasses of stray creatures who had accidentally wandered into the house in search of shelter, but that was the most positive thing that could have been said about the disorder thriving within his four walls.

He'd lived in this house for the past five months and in that amount of time, he'd managed to distribute a great deal of useless material throughout the place. Each room had its own share of acquired clutter, whether it was dirty clothing, used dishes, scattered reading material or some other, less identifiable thing. The upshot was that, in general, the sum total of the various rooms made for a really chaotic-looking home.

Or at least it had when he'd left for the stables that morning. This evening, he felt as though someone had transported him to a different universe. Everything appeared to be in its place. The whole area looked so *neat* it almost hurt his eyes to look around.

This would take some getting used to, he couldn't help thinking.

The hopeful expression had returned to Kasey's face. She'd just wanted to surprise and please him. She knew she'd succeeded with the former, but she was hoping to score the latter.

"I just thought that I should clean up a little," she told him, watching his face for some sign that he actually *liked* what she had done.

"A little?" he repeated, half stunned, half amused. "There was probably less effort involved in building this house in the first place." This cleanup, he knew, had to have been a major undertaking. Barring magical help from singing mice and enchanted elves, she'd accomplished this all herself.

He regarded her with new admiration.

She in turn looked at him, trying to understand why he didn't seem to have wanted her to do this. Had she trespassed on some basic male ritual? Was he saving this mess, not to mention the rumpled clothes and dirty dishes, for some reason?

"You want me to mess things up again?" she offered uncertainly.

"No." He took hold of her by her shoulders, enunciating each word slowly so that they would sink in. "I don't want you to *do* anything. I just wanted you to relax in between feedings. To maybe try to rest up a little, saving your strength. Taking care of a newborn is damn hard enough to get used to without single-handedly trying to restore order to a place that could easily have been mistaken for the town dump—"

She smiled and he could feel her smile going straight to his gut, stirring things up that had no business being stirred up—not without an outlet.

Eli struggled to keep a tight rein on his feelings and on his reaction to her. He succeeded only moderately.

"It wasn't *that* bad," she stressed.

She was being deliberately kind. "But close," he pointed out.

Her mouth curved as she inclined her head. "Close," Kasey allowed. "I like restoring order, making things neat," she explained. "And when he wasn't fussing because he was hungry or needed changing, Wayne cooperated by sleeping. So far, he's pretty low maintenance," she said, glancing at her sleeping son. "I had to do *something* with myself."

"Well, in case you didn't make the connection, that's the time that you're supposed to be sleeping, too," Eli pointed out. "I think that's a law or something. It's written down somewhere in the *New Mother's Basic Manual*."

"I guess I must have skipped that part," Kasey said, her eyes smiling at him. His stomach picked that moment to rumble rather loudly. Kasey eyed him knowingly. "Are you all finished working for the day?" Eli nodded, trying to silence the noises his stomach was producing by holding his breath. It didn't work. "Good," she pronounced, "because I have dinner waiting."

"Of course you do," he murmured, following her.

He stopped at the bedroom threshold and waited as Kasey gently put her sleeping son down. Wayne continued breathing evenly, indicating a successful transfer. She was taking to this mothering thing like a duck to water, Eli couldn't help thinking. He realized that he was proud of her—and more than a little awed, as well.

He looked around as he walked with her to the kitchen. Everything there was spotless, as well. All in all, Kasey was rather incredible.

"You know, if word of this gets out," he said, gesturing around the general area, "there're going to be a whole bunch of new mothers standing on our porch with pitchforks and torches, looking to string you up."

She gazed at him for a long moment and at first he thought it was because of his vivid description of frontier justice—but then it hit him. She'd picked up on his terminology. He'd said *our* instead of *my*. Without stopping to think, he'd turned his home into *their* home and just like that, he'd officially included her in the scheme of things.

In his life.

Was she angry? Or maybe even upset that he'd just sounded as if he was taking her being here for granted? He really couldn't tell and he didn't want to come right out and ask her on the outside chance that he'd guessed wrong.

His back against the wall, Eli guided the conversation in a slightly different direction. "I just don't want you to think that I invited you to stay here because I really wanted to get a free housekeeper."

Kasey did her best to tamp down her amusement. "So, what you're actually saying is that I could be as sloppy as you if I wanted to?"

He sincerely doubted if the woman had ever experienced a sloppy day in her life, but that was the general gist of what he was trying to get across to her. She could leave things messy. He had no expectations of her, nor did he want her to feel obligated to do anything except just *be.*

"Yes," he answered.

Kasey shook her head. The grin she'd been attempting to subdue for at least five seconds refused to be kept under wraps.

"That's not possible," she told him. "I think you have achieved a level of chaos that few could do justice to."

Somewhere into the second hour of her cleaning, she'd begun to despair that she was never going to dig herself out of the hole she'd gotten herself into. But she'd refused to be defeated and had just kept on going. In her opinion, the expression on Eli's face when he'd first walked in just now made it *all* worth it.

"How long did you say you've lived here?" she asked innocently.

He didn't even have to pause to think about it. "Five months."

Kasey closed her eyes for a moment, as if absorbing the information required complete concentration on her part. And then she grinned. "Think what you could have done to the house in a year's time."

He'd rather not. Even so, Eli felt obligated to defend himself at least a little. "I would have cleaned up eventually," he protested.

The look on her face told him that she really doubted

that, even though, out loud, she humored him. "I'm sure you would have. If only because you ran out of dishes and clothes." Now that she thought of it, she had a feeling that he'd already hit that wall several times over without making any lifestyle changes.

At the mention of the word *clothes,* Eli looked at her sharply, then looked around the room, hoping he was wrong. But he had a sinking feeling that he wasn't.

"Where did you put the clothes?" he asked her, holding his breath, hoping she'd just found something to use as a laundry hamper.

"Right now, they're in the washing machine." Where else would dirty clothes be? Kasey glanced at her watch. "I set the timer for forty-five minutes. The wash should be finished any minute now."

She'd wound up saying the last sentence to Eli's back. He hurried passed her, making a beeline for the utility room.

"What's wrong?" she called after him, doubling her speed to keep up with Eli's long legs.

Eli mentally crossed his fingers before he opened the door leading into the utility room.

He could have spared himself the effort.

Even though he opened the door slowly, a little water still managed to seep out of the other room. Built lower than the rest of the house, the utility room still had its own very minor flood going on.

Right behind him, Kasey looked down at the accumulated water in dismay. Guilt instantly sprang up. She'd repaid his kindness to her by flooding his utility room.

Way to go, Kase.

Thoroughly upset, she asked, "Did I do that?"

"No, the washing machine did that," Eli assured her, his words accompanied by a deep-seated sigh. "I should have told you the washing machine wasn't working right—but in my defense," he felt bound to tell her, "I wasn't anticipating that you'd be such a whirlwind of energy and cleanliness. Noah could have really used someone like you."

"It wouldn't have worked out," she said with a shake of her head. "I have no idea what a cubit is," she told him, referring to the form of measurement that had been popular around Noah's time.

Although she was trying very hard to focus on only the upbeat, there was no denying that she felt awful for compounding his work. She'd only wanted to do something nice for Eli and this definitely didn't qualify.

"I'm really very sorry about the flooding. I'll pay for the washing machine repairs," she offered.

Kasey wasn't sure just how she would pay for it because she had a rather sick feeling that Hollis had helped himself to their joint account before leaving town. But even if everything was gone and she *had* no money, she was determined to find a way to make proper restitution. Eli deserved nothing less.

Eli shook his head. "The washing machine was broken before you ever got here," he told her. "There's absolutely no reason for you to pay for anything. Don't give it another thought."

There had to be at least two inches of standing water in the utility room, Kasey judged. The only reason it hadn't all come pouring into the house when he'd opened that door was because the utility room had been deliberately built to be just a little lower than the rest of the house—more likely in anticipation of just these kinds of scenarios.

"But I caused this." She gestured toward the water. None of this would have happened if she hadn't filled up the washing machine, poured in the laundry detergent and hit Start.

"I want to make it up to you," Kasey told him earnestly.

He had a feeling that he just wasn't destined to win this argument with her. Besides, she probably needed to make some sort of amends to assuage her conscience.

Who was he to stand in the way of that?

But right now, he really had a more pressing subject to pursue.

"You said something about having to make dinner?" he asked on behalf of his exceptionally animated stomach, which currently felt as if it was playing the final death scene from *Hamlet*.

"It's right back here," she prompted, indicating the plates presently warming on the stove. "And I don't have to make it, it's already made," she told him.

"That's perfect, because the washing machine was already broken. Looks like one thing cancels out the other." Satisfied that he'd temporarily put the subject to bed, he said, "Let's go eat," with the kind of urgency that only a starving man could manage. "And then I'll fix the washing machine," he concluded. "That way you get to keep Wayne in clean clothes," he added.

And you, too, she thought as she nodded and led the way back to the kitchen. *I get to keep you in clean clothes, too.*

She had no idea why that thought seemed to hearten

her the way it did, but there was no denying the fact that it did.

A lot.

She smiled to herself as she placed his plate in front of him. If the smile was a little brighter, a little wider than normal, she really wasn't aware of it.

But Eli was.

Chapter 7

"So how's it going?"

Busy taking a quick inventory of the groceries he'd placed in his cart, Eli glanced up. He was surprised to discover his sister standing at his side. She hadn't been there a moment ago.

Or had she?

He'd been completely focused on picking up the supplies Kasey said they needed and getting back to the ranch as quickly as possible. That described the way he'd been doing everything these past three weeks: quickly. He'd do what had to be done and then get back to being with Kasey and the baby. He was eager to get back to his own private tiny piece of paradise before it suddenly vanished on him.

Eli had no illusions. He *knew* that it wasn't going to be like this forever. Life wasn't meant to be cozy, soul-satisfying and made up of tiny triumphs and small echoes of laughter. But while it was, he intended to make the very most of it, to enjoy every single second that he could and count himself extremely lucky. These moments would have to last him once she was gone.

Alma had been taking her turn at patrolling the streets of Forever when she'd passed Eli's familiar Jeep. She'd immediately parked and gone into the Emporium looking for him. They hadn't talked since the day he'd brought Kasey back from the hospital when she and the sheriff had gotten some of Kasey's things, as well as the baby crib, out of the house that her no-account husband had lost in a poker game.

Her brother looked tired, Alma thought. Tired, but definitely happy.

Happiness didn't come cheap. She knew all about that. She also knew that when happiness showed up on your doorstep, you grabbed it with both hands and held on as tightly as possible.

"Alma Rodriguez, remember?" she prompted, pretending to introduce herself to him. "Your sister," she added when he just stared at her. "I know it's been a while, but I haven't changed *that* much. I recognize you," she told him brightly.

Not wanting to come back to the store for at least a week, Eli began to move up and down the aisles again, filling his cart. Alma matched him step for step.

"Very funny, Alma."

"No," she said honestly. "Very sweet, actually. All this domesticity seems to be agreeing with you, big brother." She examined him more closely for a moment, her head cocked as if that helped her process the information better. Eli continued moving. "Are you gaining weight, Eli?"

That stopped him for a second. "No," he retorted defensively although he really had no way of knowing that for certain. He didn't own a scale, at least not one for weighing people. Usually his clothes let him know if he was gaining or losing weight. For as long as he could remember, he'd worn jeans that proclaimed his waist to be a trim thirty-two inches, and they fit just fine these days, so he took that to be an indication that his weight was stable.

Although he wouldn't have really been surprised if he *had* gained weight. Kasey insisted on cooking every night, and that woman could make hot water taste like some sort of exotic fare fit for a king.

Seeing that her brother wasn't in the mood to be teased, Alma decided to back off. She knew firsthand what it felt like to be in a situation that defied proper description even though her heart had been completely invested.

She'd always had her suspicions about the way Eli had felt about Kasey and now, judging by what was going on, she was more than a little convinced that she was right. But saying so would have probably put her on the receiving end of some rather choice words.

Or, at the very least, on the receiving end of some very caustic looks.

Still, her curiosity was getting the better of her.

Watching his expression, she felt her way slowly through a potential minefield. "I'm sorry I haven't been able to get out to visit you and Kasey—"

"Nobody was holding their breath for that," he told her quickly, dismissing her apology along with the need

for her to make an appearance at his house. For the time
being, he rather liked the fact that it was just the three
of them: Kasey, the baby and him.

"Duly noted," she replied, then reminded him, "You
didn't answer me." When he appeared confused, she
repeated, "How's it going?"

He shrugged, as if he had no idea what she was waiting for him to say. He gave her a thumbnail summary.
"I'm helping Kasey pull herself together. Hollis walking
out on her like that really did a number on her self-es-
teem and her confidence. I'm trying to make her understand that she doesn't have to face any of this alone."

"How about the part that she's so much better off
without him?" Alma asked.

"That'll come later. Right now, we're still gluing the
pieces together."

And he felt as if he was making some serious head-
way. Kasey seemed more cheerful these days than when
she'd first arrived.

"You're doing more than that," Alma pointed out.
"You took her in."

He waited to answer his sister until Alice Meriwether
passed them. Anything that went into the woman's ear
instantly came out of her mouth. He nodded at Alice
and then moved on.

"Yeah, well," he finally said, lowering his voice, "she
didn't have any place to go and even though it's summer right now, she can't exactly sleep on the street."

"She wouldn't have," Alma assured him. "I'm sure
Miss Joan would have happily put her and the baby up
in her old house. She still hasn't gotten rid of it even
though she moved in with Cash's grandfather."

Just saying Cash's name brought a wide smile to her

lips. He'd come back for his grandfather's wedding and wound up staying in Forever for her. They were getting married in a little more than a month. And even though there was now a growing squadron of butterflies in the pit of her stomach, the fact that she and Cash were finally getting married was enough to make a person believe that happy endings did exist.

Which was, ultimately, what she was hoping that Eli would come to discover. His own personal happy ending with a young woman he obviously loved.

Alma crossed her fingers.

Her brother shrugged, doubting that moving into Miss Joan's house would have been a viable solution for Kasey. "Kasey would have felt like she was on the receiving end of charity. She really wouldn't have been comfortable accepting Miss Joan's offer," he told her.

Miss Joan was like everyone's slightly sharp-tongued fairy godmother—just as quick to help as she was to offer "constructive criticism."

"But she's comfortable accepting yours?" Alma asked so that her brother didn't suspect that she knew how he felt about Kasey.

"We've been friends since elementary school," Eli said. "That makes my letting her stay with me an act of friendship, not charity."

Alma congratulated herself on keeping a straight face as she asked, "So this is just like one great big sleepover, huh?"

Eli stopped short of coming up to the checkout counter. He pinned his sister with a deliberate look. "Something on your mind, Alma?"

"A lot of things," she answered blithely. "I'm the

sheriff's deputy, remember? I'm supposed to have a lot on my mind."

His patience begun to fray a little around the edges. "Alma—"

"I saw you through the store window," she told him. "And I wanted to make sure that you were still going to be at the wedding." He'd gotten so wrapped up around Kasey, she was afraid that he'd forget that she and Cash were getting married. But before Eli could say anything in response, she deliberately sweetened the pot for him by adding, "You know that Kasey and the baby are invited, too, right?"

His instincts had prevented him from bringing up the subject of Alma's upcoming wedding and Kasey hadn't asked him about it. "She didn't say anything to me."

"That's because when the invitations went out, she was still Hollis's wife and he kept her on a very tight leash. Most likely, he got rid of the invitation before she ever saw it," Alma ventured.

"She still *is* Hollis's wife," he pointed out, even though just saying it seemed to burn a hole in his gut.

"Which reminds me, Kasey can go see either Rick's wife, Olivia, or Cash to have them start to file divorce papers for her."

Both Olivia and Cash had had careers as high-powered lawyers in the cities that they'd lived in before coming here to Forever. In effect, they'd traded their six-figure incomes for the feeling of satisfaction in knowing that they were doing something worthwhile for the community.

"She's got the perfect grounds for it," Alma said when her brother made no comment. Didn't he want Kasey free of that deadbeat? He'd inherited the ranch

they'd lived on from his late parents and had all but ruined it. He certainly had let it get run-down. "Abandon-
ment," Alma said in case her brother wasn't aware of it.

But he was.

"I know that," Eli responded curtly.

Well, that certainly wasn't the reaction she'd expected from him. Alma tried to figure out why her
brother seemed so short-tempered. Could it be that
Kasey was still in love with that worthless excuse for
a human being and had said as much to Eli?

Alma rather doubted that, not after Kasey had lived
with Eli these past few weeks. Living with Eli gave the
new mother something positive to measure against the
poor excuse for a human being she'd been shackled to.
For her part, she might tease her brother mercilessly,
but she knew that the difference between Eli and Hollis
was the proverbial difference between night and day.

"I never said you didn't," Alma assured him gently,
then explained, "I was just trying to make myself clear,
that's all. It's a habit I picked up from Cash." Her tone
changed to an assertive one. "By the way, you're coming to the wedding." It was no longer a question but a
command. "I've decided that I'm not accepting any excuses," she added. "Now, is there anything I can do for
you or Kasey?" she asked. "I mean, other than shooting
Hollis if he tries to creep back into town?"

Having reached the checkout counter, Eli had un-
loaded most of the items he'd picked up. He'd gotten
everything on Kasey's list, plus a candy bar he recalled
she'd been particularly fond of when they went to high
school. Finished, he fished out his wallet to pay the
clerk. That was when Alma had said what she had about
Hollis.

The thought hit him right between the eyes. He'd all but convinced himself that Hollis was gone for good. "Do you think that he actually might...?"

There was really no telling *what* someone with Hollis's mentality and temperament would do. "I've found that it's really hard to second-guess a lowlife," she told her brother. "No matter how low your expectations, they can still surprise you and go lower. But in general, I'd say no, probably not." She knew that was what he wanted to hear and for once, she decided to accommodate him. Besides, there was a fifty-fifty chance she was right. If she was wrong, worrying about it ahead of time wouldn't help, and if she was right, then hours would have been wasted in anticipation of a nonevent.

Alma moved closer to him so that none of the customers nearby could overhear. She knew how much Eli's privacy meant to him.

"So then it's going well?" she asked for a third time.

He wasn't sure what she meant by *well* and he wasn't about to answer her in case Alma was too curious about whether something had blossomed between Kasey and him in these past few weeks. He knew how Alma's mind worked, especially now that Cash had come back and they were getting married soon.

Instead he gave her something safe. "She's learning how to survive motherhood and I'm getting the hang of changing diapers," he told her, then pointedly asked, "Is that what you wanted to hear?"

"I just wanted to know how you and she were getting along," she told him innocently. "And you getting the hang of diapering is bound to come in handy."

"Why?" He wasn't following her drift. Glancing at the total the supplies had come to, he peeled out a number of bills and handed them to the clerk. "Horses don't need to have diapers changed."

"No, but babies do." Her eyes met his, which were hooded and all but unreadable. She hated when he did that, shut her out like that. "And you never know when that might come in handy."

His expression cleared somewhat as a light dawned on him. "You wouldn't be angling for a babysitter, now, would you?"

Actually she was referring to the possibility that he could become a father in the future—especially if he and Kasey finally got together the right way—but for now, she let his take on her words stand. It was a great deal simpler that way—for both of them.

"Not a bad idea," she told him. "I'll keep you in mind should the need ever arise down the line. Well, I've got to get back to patrolling the town—not that anything *ever* happens here," she said, rolling her eyes. *Boredom* happened here. Excitement? Hardly ever. "Give Kasey my love," she said as they parted company right beyond the front door. "Unless, of course, you've already given her yours." She winked at him and then turned on her heel to walk to her vehicle.

"You almost made it, Alma," he noted, calling after her. Alma turned around to hear him out. "Almost left without making that kind of a comment. I must say I'm impressed."

Alma laughed. "Didn't want you thinking that I'd changed *that* radically," she quipped just before she headed to the official vehicle she was driving. She had a town to patrol—and boredom to fight.

Eli watched his sister walk away. Shaking his head,

he was grinning as he deposited the various bags of supplies he'd just paid for into the Jeep.

He was still grinning when he arrived home half an hour later.

He caught himself doing that a lot lately, he thought, just grinning like some sort of happy idiot.

Eli had never been one of those brooding men that supposedly held such attraction for all women, but there hadn't been all that much to be happy about, either: hard life, hard times, and then his mother had died. That took its toll on a man.

He wasn't like Alma. She was upbeat and optimistic to a fault. But he was, he'd always thought, a realist. Although, for the time being, ever since he'd brought Kasey here, the realist in him had taken a vacation and he was enjoying this new state of affairs just as it was.

Dividing the grocery bags, he slung five plastic bags over each wrist. He tested their strength to make sure they'd hold and moved slowly from the vehicle to the house. He brought in all the groceries in one trip.

Setting the bags down on the first flat surface he came to, Eli shed the plastic loops from his wrists as quickly as he could. But not quickly enough. The plastic loops bit into his skin and still left their mark on his wrists.

Rubbing them without thinking, Eli looked around for Kasey and found her sitting in an easy chair, the baby pressed against her breast.

It took him a second to realize that he'd done exactly what he'd always worried about doing: he'd walked in on Kasey feeding Wayne.

Breast-feeding Wayne.

His breath caught in his throat. He had never seen anything so beautiful in his life.

At the same moment it occurred to him that he had absolutely no business seeing her like this.

Even so, it took him another few seconds to tear his eyes away.

Then, hoping to ease out of the room without having Kasey see him, Eli started to slowly back out—only to have her suddenly look up from what she was doing. Her eyes instantly met his.

He'd never actually felt embarrassed before. He did now.

"I'm sorry, I didn't realize you'd be doing that out here. I mean—I'm sorry," he said again, his tongue growing thicker and less pliable with each word that he stumbled over.

"There's no reason for you to be sorry," she told him softly. "If anything, it's my fault for not going into my room with Wayne." She raised one shoulder in a careless shrug and then let it drop again. "But you were gone and he was fussing—this just seemed easier."

Belatedly, he realized that he was still facing her and that he still didn't know just where to put his eyes. He immediately turned on his heel, so that he was facing the front door and had his back to her.

He couldn't let her blame herself. He'd walked in on her, not the other way around.

"It's my fault," he insisted. "I should have called out when I walked in," he told her.

"Why?" she asked, just as she had that first evening when he *had* called out before walking in. "After all, it's your house, you have every right to walk into it whenever you want to. If anything, I should be the one apologizing to you for embarrassing you like this. I'm the intruder, not you."

"You're not an intruder," he told her firmly. How could she even *think* that he thought that about her? "You're a welcomed guest. I didn't mean to— I shouldn't have—"

Eli sighed, frustrated. If anything, this was getting harder, not easier for him. He couldn't seem to negotiate a simple statement.

He heard her laughing softly and the sound went right through him. Right *into* him.

"It's all right, Eli. You can turn around now," she told him. "I'm not feeding Wayne anymore."

He sighed, relieved. "Thank God," he murmured, then realized that he'd said the sentiment louder than he'd intended. Swinging around to face her, he damned himself for his display of incredible awkwardness. He couldn't remember *ever* being this tongue-tied. "I'm sorry, that didn't come out right."

On her feet, still cradling the baby against her, Kasey crossed to him and then caressed his cheek as she laughed at his obvious dilemma.

"It's all right," she told him. "Really," she emphasized. "I know it was an accident and, like I said, it's my fault, not yours."

He was behaving like a jackass, Eli upbraided himself. Worse, he was behaving like an *adolescent* jackass. And Kasey was being wonderfully understanding. They were friends and friends sometimes had to cut each other some much needed slack.

"It's nobody's fault," he said with finality, absolving both of them.

Kasey smiled up at him. For the most part Eli had

always known just what to say to make her feel better. She was happy to be able to return the favor, in whatever minor capacity that she could.

"I like the sound of that," she told him with approval.

He looked down at the baby in her arms. Wayne seemed to be growing up a storm. In the few short weeks he'd been here, the baby looked as if he'd all but doubled in size. If Wayne wasn't careful, he would be the first giant in kindergarten.

Ever so gingerly, he touched the downy head of blond hair. "Sorry, little guy, I didn't mean to interrupt your mealtime."

The infant made a gurgling noise as he stared up at Eli.

Kasey was delighted. "I think he recognizes your voice, Eli." Her smile broadened as she looked from the baby to him. "He's responding to you," she declared, both amazed and happy.

And he's not the only one, she added silently.

The very thought of *that* made her smile even wider.

Chapter 8

"Godfather? Me?" Eli asked, staring incredulously at Kasey. "Are you sure that you want *me* to be Wayne's godfather?"

Morning was still in the formation stage, since the sun wasn't close to coming up yet. Eli had thought that he might start his day even earlier than usual so that, if everything went right, he could get to spend a little more time with Kasey and Wayne before the baby was put down for the night.

His plan was to just quietly slip out, easing the front door closed so that he wouldn't disturb or wake Kasey. But he should have known better.

She'd sensed the intended change in his schedule and she'd gotten up ahead of him. He'd come down the stairs to the smell of strong coffee and something delicious being created on the grill. Kasey was making him breakfast as well as packing him a lunch.

She'd been doing the latter ever since the second day she was here. She told him she did it so that he didn't have to go hungry or take the time to come back to the house to eat if he didn't want to.

Kasey always seemed to be at least one step ahead of him, or, at the very least, intuiting his every move, his every need.

Without making it official, they had slipped into a routine and become a family. The kind of family he used to daydream about having someday.

With her.

He used to envision what it would be like if Kasey agreed to marry him, to have his children—to have *their* children, he amended with feeling. And now, here he was, working the ranch, coming home to Kasey and the baby. It was all too good to be true—and he was more than a little aware of that.

He knew he was on borrowed time and he was trying to make the most of it without somehow scaring Kasey away.

Sometimes he'd quietly slip into the baby's room— which was upstairs now, right next to hers. They'd decided to move Wayne's crib into an adjoining bedroom so that Kasey could sleep a little more soundly. Slipping in, he'd just watch the infant sleep. Nothing was more peaceful and soothing than watching Wayne sleep.

As for their forming a family unit, he never said anything about it out loud because he was afraid of spoiling it, afraid that once he gave a name to it, the situation would change. He didn't want to take a chance on jinx-

ing it. All he wanted to do was to savor every moment
of it, knowing full well that it wouldn't last. That eventually, Kasey would become stronger, more confident,
and want to move on.

But now this request of hers would forever bind them
together. Being Wayne's godfather firmly placed him
in Wayne's life and, by association, in hers.

Did she understand the full implication of what she
was suggesting? He looked at her and repeated, "You're
sure?"

She smiled at him, the kind of smile that always went
straight to his gut. "I was never more sure of anything
in my life," she told him. "Unless you don't want to,"
she qualified suddenly.

Until this moment it had never occurred to her that
he might not be willing to do this. Though he kept insisting that he wasn't, maybe Eli *did* already feel bur-
dened by having her and her son stay here with him.
That meant that asking him to be Wayne's godfather
was just asking too much.

"Because if you don't," she continued quickly, "it's
all right. I understand. I mean, you've already done so
very much for—"

She was talking so fast there was no space, no pause
where he could stick in a single word. Eli didn't know
any other way to stop her except to place his fingertips
to her lips, halting their movement. She raised her eyes
to his quizzically.

"Of course I *want* to. I was just surprised—and
touched," he confessed, "that you asked. To be honest,
I never saw myself as the type to be someone's godfather. That's a very big—"

Kasey was nodding her head. "I know. Responsibility," she said, thinking she was ending his sentence for him. She didn't want him to feel that she was putting any sort of demands on him, not after he had been so wonderful to them.

"I was going to say 'honor,'" he told her patiently. "Being a godfather is a very big honor and I just didn't think I was worthy."

Eli watched, fascinated, as her eyes widened. How many times had he felt as if he could literally go wading in those eyes of hers? Lose himself completely in those fathomless blue eyes?

It took a great deal of effort on his part to keep himself in check and just go on talking as if nothing was happening inside of him. As if he didn't want to just sweep her into his arms and tell her that he loved her, that he would always be there for her and for Wayne and that there was really no need for any formal declarations.

"Not worthy?" Kasey echoed. "I've never known a better man than you in my whole life and if you do agree to become Wayne's godfather, then we're the ones who will be honored, not you," she told him.

Eli shoved his hands into his pockets to keep from touching her face. He laughed in response to her statement, shaking his head.

"All right. Then consider yourself honored," he quipped. "I would *love* to be Wayne's godfather. Just tell me where and when."

"This coming Saturday," she told him. "We can go to the church together. I'll just let the pastor know." She paused for a second, letting the first part sink in before she told him of her other decision. "I was thinking of asking Miss Joan to be his godmother." She watched his face for a reaction. "What do you think?"

Eli nodded, approving. He had a feeling that it would mean a great deal to the woman. "I think she'd like that very much."

Pleased, Kasey picked up the full pot of coffee. It had just finished brewing when Eli walked by the kitchen. She'd called to him, but she had a feeling that it was the coffee aroma that had lured him in.

"Well, that's settled," she said, pouring him a cup. "Now come and have your breakfast. I've already packed your lunch for you."

He doubted that she had any idea how good that sounded to him. He would never take this for granted.

"I keep telling you that you don't have to do this," he said, taking a seat at the table.

Admittedly his voice was carrying less and less conviction each time he told her that there was no need to get up and serve him like this. But that was because, beneath his protests, he was thoroughly enjoying sharing his meals with her. It would have taken nothing on his part to get used to a life like this.

Simple, without demands.

Just the three of them...

He knew he was dreaming, but dreams cost nothing, so for now, he indulged himself.

"And I keep telling you that it's the least I can do," she reminded him.

He stared at the plate that Kasey had just put on the table in front of him. There was French toast, sausage and orange juice, as well as the cup of black coffee. And over on the counter was his lunch all packed and standing at the ready, waiting to be picked up on his way out. Life just didn't get any better than this.

"If this is the least," he told her in appreciation, between bites, "then I don't think I'm ready to see the most."

She laughed, delighted. It occurred to her that she'd laughed more in these past five weeks than she had in all the years that she'd spent with Hollis. That could have been because with Hollis, there'd always been one problem after another, always something to worry about. All the bills—and finding the funds to pay them—had always fallen on her shoulders.

It wasn't like that with Eli. *He* was the one bent on taking care of her, not on being waited on, hand and foot, by her.

It was a completely different world. She had to admit that she rather liked it and could, so easily, get used to it....

"I'm working on it," she told him with a wink.

The wink set off its own chain reaction. Eli could feel his toes curling, could feel anticipation racing through him to the point that he could barely sit still long enough to finish his breakfast.

He couldn't recall *ever* being happier.

The following Saturday, Eli carefully dug out the suit that he'd worn to Miss Joan's wedding. Brushing off a few stray hairs that had found their way to the dark, navy blue material, he put the suit on.

As Wayne's godfather, he wanted to look his best, he thought, carefully surveying himself from every angle in the mirror. He scrutinized his appearance with a very critical eye. The last thing he wanted to do was to embarrass Kasey by looking like some weather-beaten cowboy.

He was going for a dignified look. For that, he

needed to wear a tie, but the thing insisted on giving him trouble, refusing to tie correctly.

Ties were nothing but colorful nooses, but a necessary accessory to complete the picture, and as such, he had to wear one.

Easier said than done.

When his third attempt at forming a knot turned out even worse than the first two, Eli bit off a curse as he yanked off the offending garment. He was never going to get this right. Alma had tied his last tie for him, but Alma wasn't here.

He had a hunch that all women were born knowing how to tie ties.

Impulsively, clutching the uncooperative tie in his hand, he went to Kasey's room and knocked on her door.

"Be there in a minute," he heard her call out.

He hadn't meant to rush her. "No hurry," he assured her. "I just wanted to ask if you knew anything about tying ties."

He should have just slipped his tie off over his head the last time he'd worn it. Then he'd be ready to go by now instead of walking around with his tie crumpled in his hand.

Just as he finished chewing himself out, Kasey's door opened. She wore a light blue-gray dress that stopped several inches above her knees.

The word *vision* throbbed in his brain.

"You look beautiful," he told her, his voice only slightly above a whisper.

She smiled at the compliment, finding his tone exceptionally sexy.

Her eyes lit up the way they had a tendency to do

when she was happy. And as they did, he could feel his very soul lighting up, as well.

He ached for her.

"You're very sweet, Eli," she told him.

"And very inept," he concluded, feeling it best to change the subject and not dwell on anything that could get him into a whole lot of trouble. "You'd think a grown man could finally get the hang of tying a tie," he complained.

She didn't want him to get down on himself. "That grown man is too busy doing good deeds and trying to make a go of his new ranch while lending moral support to a friend. I'd say that tying a tie doesn't even make the top one hundred list of things that need to be learned." She stood in front of him for a moment, studying his tie, then said, "I'm going to have to stand behind you to do this—if you don't mind having my arms around you for a couple of minutes," she interjected.

Mind? Did she think he was mentally deficient? What man in his right mind would balk at having a beautiful woman put her arms around him under *any* pretext?

"No, I don't mind," he assured her, doing his best not to grin like a reject from a Cheshire cat competition as he said it. "Do whatever you have to do to get this thing finally on straight."

"I'll do my best," she promised.

The next moment she was behind him, reaching around his body to take hold of the two ends of his tie. Even though he was wearing a jacket, he was aware of her soft breasts pressing up against his back. Aware of the gentle fragrance of her shampoo as it filled his head. Aware of the hunger that coursed through his veins.

He took in slow, measured breaths, trying to reduce the erratic pounding of his pulse.

"I'm not making this too tight for you, am I?" she asked, her breath lightly tickling the skin that was just above his collar.

"No." He didn't trust himself to say any more words than that.

Within another minute and a half, Kasey was finished. With a tinge of reluctance, she stepped back, away from his hard, firm body, although not away from the sensations that contact with that body had created and left behind.

Eli was her friend. She wasn't supposed to think this way about him, wasn't supposed to react this way to him. More than anything else, she didn't want to risk losing his friendship. At times, knowing that Eli was there for her was all that kept her going.

Kasey came around to stand in front of him and examine her work.

She'd tied a perfect knot, a Windsor knot, it was called. "Not bad," she pronounced. And then, raising her eyes to his, she told him, "I think we're good to go. I'll go get Wayne."

He placed his hand on her arm, stopping her. "Let me," he offered. "After all, he's my godson—or my 'almost' godson. And once Miss Joan arrives at the church, I won't be able to get within shouting distance of him, much less hold him."

Kasey laughed at the exaggeration. "Right. Like you don't already hold him every chance you get," she teased, following behind Eli as he went to her son's bedroom.

Walking into Wayne's room, Eli went straight to the boy's crib.

Wayne was on his back, watching in fascination as his fingers wiggled above his head. Everything at his age was magical. Eli envied him that.

As he stood above the boy, Wayne focused on him and not his fingers. Recognition set in and Wayne began to get excited. This time when he waved his arms, it wasn't to watch his fingers. It was a form of supplication. He wanted to be picked up by this man.

Wayne didn't have to wait long.

Holding the infant to him, Eli picked up the thread of the conversation between them. He feigned ignorance regarding her last statement. "I don't know what you mean."

Oh, yes, he did, Kasey thought. He knew *exactly* what she meant.

"I hear you, you know. In the middle of the night, I hear you. I hear you going into Wayne's room when he starts to whimper. I hear you picking him up, rocking him, walking the floor with him sometimes. You're spoiling him, you know," she told Eli. Then she added with a wide grin, "And me."

Some people didn't get spoiled. Ever. She was one of them. "Never happen," he assured her.

Oh, but it's already happened, she couldn't help thinking. She'd gotten used to relying on him, used to experiencing the feeling of well-being that he generated for her.

Shaking herself free of her thoughts, she declared, "All right, enough fraternizing." She took the baby from him, tucking Wayne against her shoulder. "It's time to take your godson to church."

His godson.

He liked the sound of that. But then, he liked the

sound of anything that came from her lips, he thought. He always had.

"Yes, ma'am," he said, pretending to salute her.

Squaring his shoulders like a soldier, Eli led the way out of the house and to his Jeep. The vehicle had been washed and polished in honor of the occasion.

Now if he could just keep it clean until the day was over....

The baptism itself was a very simple ceremony, but touching nonetheless.

The solemnity of the occasion was interrupted when Wayne attempted to drink the drops of water that lightly cascaded from his forehead, his little tongue working overtime to catch as many drops as he could.

"The boy's got a sense of humor about him," Miss Joan declared with no small approval, nodding her head as she watched his failed efforts to make contact with the water. Because she wanted to hold the boy for a few more minutes, she allowed the moment to linger. Then, with a barely suppressed sigh, Miss Joan handed the boy back to his mother.

In her heart, she was reliving moments of her life when she'd held her own son this way, thinking how much promise was contained within the small boy.

She fervently hoped that the boy whose godmother she'd become today had a better, longer future ahead of him than her own son had had.

"All right," Miss Joan suddenly said, clearing her throat and raising her voice so that everyone in the church could hear her. "We've dunked him and promised to stand by him and stand up for him. Now let's all go and celebrate over at my place."

Her place, as everyone in town knew, referred to Miss Joan's diner. Forever's only restaurant had been suitably decorated to celebrate Wayne's christening. As with the Christmas holidays and the Fourth of July, all the women in town who'd been blessed with the knack had banded together and cooked up a storm, making everything from baby-back ribs to pies and cakes, some of which were so light Miss Joan's husband, Harry, claimed they had to be tied down to keep them from floating away.

The diner was soon filled to capacity. And then some.

Because it was warm, the establishment doors were left open and the party soon spilled out of the diner and onto the grounds surrounding it.

The celebration, fueled by good food, good company and boisterous laughter, continued until darkness overtook the sun, sending it away, and the stars came out to keep the moon company.

"I think we might have finally tired him out," Eli commented, looking at his brand-new godson. At close to six weeks old, the boy had miraculously taken to sleeping through the night—most nights, at any rate.

Kasey smiled her approval of this latest development. "I can take him home," she volunteered. "But you don't have to leave right away. You can stay here longer if you like."

He looked at her as if she wasn't making any sense. "My mother always taught me to go home with the girl I brought to the dance."

"This wasn't a dance," Kasey pointed out, amused.

"Same concept," he told her. "Besides, why would I

want to stay here without you—and Wayne?" he purposely added.

The smile she offered him stirred his heart—again. "I just wanted you to know you had options. I don't want you to feel I'm taking advantage of your kindness or that I'm monopolizing you."

He wondered what she would say if he told her that he *wanted* her to take advantage of him, *wanted* her to monopolize him to her heart's content.

Probably look at him as if he'd gone off the deep end, and he supposed he had. He couldn't think of a better way to go than loving Kasey until his last minute on earth was up.

But if he even so much as hinted at that, Kasey would probably be packing by morning. Not about to experiment and find out, he decided that it was for the best to just keep his feelings to himself.

"C'mon," he said, "I'll take the two of you home."

Tired, Kasey was more than willing to leave. She held the baby against her as Eli guided her out of the diner and toward his car. Without even realizing it, she was leaning into his arm as she walked.

Eli slipped his arm around her shoulders to help guide her, savoring the warm glow he felt.

Chapter 9

Kasey supposed that she'd been feeling a little sad and vulnerable all day. She didn't know if it was because of all the couples at the christening, which in contrast made her feel isolated and alone, or because her hormones were still slightly off.

It could have also been due to her finally accepting that she would be facing life as a single mom.

Or maybe it was a combination of all three.

Whatever it was, her emotions were all very close to the surface. She did her level best to rein them in. The last thing she wanted, after he'd been so nice to her, was to burst into tears in front of Eli. He'd think that it was his fault, but it wasn't. After her son, Eli was the best thing in her life right now.

As they drove back to Eli's ranch, she felt an intense loneliness creeping in despite the fact that Eli was in the Jeep with her, as close as a prayer. Certainly close enough for her to touch.

Maybe she just needed to make contact with another human being, she thought. The sadness made her feel extremely vulnerable.

For whatever reason, she found herself reaching her hand out to touch Eli's arm just as he pulled the vehicle up in front of the house.

Turning off the ignition, Eli looked at her, assuming that she'd touched him to get his attention because she wanted to say something. Kasey had been exceptionally quiet all the way home. He'd just thought she was too tired to talk, but since she'd touched his arm, he figured that it was to get him to center his attention on her.

As if *all* his attention *wasn't* centered on her all the time.

Because she wasn't saying anything, he prodded her a little.

"What?" he asked her softly, deliberately keeping his voice low so as not to wake the little sleeping passenger in the backseat.

Embarrassed, she could feel color rising in her cheeks. He would probably think she was crazy. "Nothing, just proving to myself that you're close enough to touch. That you're real."

He looked at her, somewhat puzzled. "Of course I'm real. Why wouldn't I be?" he asked good-naturedly.

She shrugged, avoiding his eyes. After all he'd done for her, she owed him the truth, but she was really afraid that he'd laugh at her.

"Because sometimes I think you're just too good to be true."

Eli did laugh, but it wasn't at her. It was at what she'd

just said. Turning off the Jeep's headlights, he removed his key from the ignition. "Obviously it's been a long time since you've talked to Alma."

This time, she did raise her eyes to his. "I don't need to talk to Alma to know how good you've been to me. How kind. Trust me, Eli, you're like the answer to a prayer."

And you are all I ever prayed for, he told her silently, knowing better than to say something like that out loud.

"I think you might have had a little too much to drink," he guessed, coming around to her side of the vehicle. Opening the door, he took her hand to help her out.

Shifting forward, she rose to her feet and found herself standing extremely close to Eli. So close that when she inhaled, her chest brushed ever so lightly against his.

Electricity zigzagged through her and she didn't immediately step back. When Eli did instead, the sadness within her became larger, coming close to unmanageable.

"I didn't have anything to drink," she protested. "At least, nothing with alcohol in it." She was still nursing Wayne, although he was beginning to favor the bottle. She had a feeling that her days of nursing her son were numbered. "My mind isn't clouded, if that's what you're thinking," she told him. "I see everything very clearly."

And just like that, Eli was waging an internal struggle, wanting more than anything else to lose the battle and just go with his instincts. Go with his desires.

He came within an inch of kissing her. In his mind's eye, he'd already crossed that bridge. But that was fan-

tasy and the reality was that he didn't want to do anything to jeopardize what he had at this moment.

He pulled back at the last moment and turned toward
the rear of the vehicle.

"I'd better get Wayne out of the Jeep and into his
crib," he said. "He's had a pretty long day."

She said the words to his back, knowing that if Eli
was facing her, she wouldn't have been able to get
them out. And she desperately needed to. Her voice
was hardly above a whisper. "Don't you want to kiss
me, Eli?"

Eli grew very rigid, half-convinced that he'd imagined hearing her voice. Imagined her saying words that
he would have sold his soul to hear.

Releasing the breath that had gotten caught in his
throat, he turned around in slow motion until he stood
facing her.

Looking at her face in complete wonder.

In complete surrender. "More than anything in the
world," he told her.

It had to be the moonlight, playing tricks on his vision, but he could have sworn he saw tears shimmering in Kasey's eyes.

"Then what are you waiting for?"

He could have said that he couldn't kiss her because, technically, she was still Hollis's wife. Or that
he couldn't because he didn't want to take advantage of
her, or the situation, or the fact that she was probably
overtired and not thinking straight.

There were as many reasons to deny himself as there
were leaves on the tree by his window. And only one
reason to do it.

Because he ached for her.

Before he could stop himself, he took hold of Kasey's shoulders—whether to hold her in place or to convince himself that she was real and that he wasn't just dreaming this, he wasn't sure.

The next moment there was no more debate, no more speculation. Because he was lowering his mouth to hers and waking up his soul.

His body temperature rose just as his head began to spin, completely disorienting him from time and space and hurling him toward a world of heat, flashing lights and demanding desires.

She tasted of all things wonderful. Unwilling to back away the way he was convinced he should, Eli deepened the kiss, thus temporarily suspending all rational thoughts and riding a crest of billowing emotions.

Tears slid free from the corners of her eyes. Eyes she'd shut tight as she focused on the wild, wonderful sensations shooting all through her like brightly lit Roman candles.

Kasey threw her arms around his neck, holding on for dear life as she followed him into a world filled with the promise of wondrous, fierce passions.

Words like *chemistry, soul mates* and *joy* flashed through her mind at the speed of light, so fast that it took her a few moments to realize that she was experiencing everything the words suggested. Experiencing it and wanting more.

Craving more.

So this was what it was like, to truly *want* to be with someone. To *ache* to be one with someone. She realized that she'd never known it before.

In all the time she'd been with Hollis, in all the years she thought she was in love with him, she'd never felt anything even remotely like this. Never had this huge, overwhelming desire to make love with him—or die.

Never felt this physical ache that something was missing.

Even though it had been.

When the kiss ended, when Eli stepped back so that their bodies were no longer pressed against one another, they looked at each other for what seemed like an isolated eternity. Each was surprised that the longing insisted on continuing.

He shouldn't have allowed this to happen. Shouldn't have given in to his weakness. It was up to him to be the one in control.

"Kasey, I'm sorry," Eli began, searching for words that would give him a way out, that would allow her to absolve him. Words that would convince her to continue staying at his ranch.

And then she said something that completely took his breath away.

"I'm not," she whispered, her eyes never leaving his. His lips might lie to her, but his eyes never would. She could tell what he was really feeling by looking at them. "I'm only sorry that it didn't happen sooner."

Did she know?

Did she realize the power she had over him? He'd walk through fire for her and gladly so. He'd been in love with her since the world began.

He wanted to take her there. To make love with Kasey with wild, abandoned ardor right here on the ground, in front of the house. But that sort of behavior was for animals in heat, not a man who had waited in silence for more than a decade.

"We'd better get him to his crib," Eli murmured, turning to unbuckle Wayne from his infant seat.

The little guy was so tired that he didn't wake as he was being lifted from the seat, nor did he wake when he was being carried into the house and then up the stairs to his room.

Kasey followed in Eli's wake, just in case Wayne woke up and needed her. But he continued sleeping.

Gratitude swelled in Eli's chest. As he gently lay the infant in his crib, he whispered to him, "Thanks, little guy, I owe you one."

He could have sworn that the baby smiled in his sleep just then. He knew that experts would claim that it was only gas, but he knew better.

Taking Kasey's hand in his, Eli moved quietly out of the infant's room and slowly eased the door closed behind him.

The second he was out in the hallway, he could see by the look in Kasey's eyes that this was no time to tender any apologies or lay the blame for his previous actions on lack of sleep.

There was no blame to be laid.

Instead, though every fiber of his body begged him to just sweep her into his arms and carry her off to his room, Eli held himself in check long enough to ask Kasey one crucial, basic question.

"Are you sure?"

Kasey didn't answer him. At least, she didn't answer him verbally. Instead she threw her arms around Eli's neck, went up on her toes as far as she could go and kissed him even more soundly than she had just in front of the house.

She made him feel positively intoxicated.

"I guess that's a yes," Eli breathed out heavily when they finally paused because they had to come up for air.

He was rewarded with the sound of her light laughter. It rippled along his lips, making hers taste that much sweeter.

Like the first ripe strawberries of the summer.

It was all he needed. The next moment he was acting out his fantasy and this time he *did* sweep her into his arms and carry her into her room.

Anchoring herself to him with her arms around his neck, she leaned her head against his shoulder, content to remain just where she was for all eternity—or at least for the next few hours.

As he came into her room, he didn't bother pushing the door closed with his elbow. There was no one here except for them. And the baby was months away from taking his first step, so they were safe from any prying eyes.

When Eli set her down, the raw desire he saw in Kasey's eyes melted away the last shred of resistance-for-her-own-good he had to offer.

Besides, as he'd carried her into her room, she'd pressed her lips against his neck, setting off all sorts of alarms and signals throughout his body. Making him want her more than he thought humanly possible.

Eli kissed her over and over again, savoring the feel of her, the exquisite, wildly erotic taste of her and the sound of surrender echoing in his head.

Unlike the sensations she'd evoked within him, the details of what transpired were somewhat sketchy. Under oath he couldn't have recounted how Kasey and he went from being two rational, fully dressed people to two naked adults who had thrown all caution, all reason, to the winds.

Eli had always thought that if he'd *ever* be lucky enough to have an evening of lovemaking with Kasey, he would proceed slowly, affording every single part of her the time, the worship and the reverence it so richly deserved.

But somehow, even with the game plan still lodged somewhere in his brain, it had turned into a race. The eagerness he felt only intensified, growing stronger as his hands passed over her body, exploring, claiming.

Loving.

She was just as exquisite as he'd always dreamed she'd be.

And she was, at least for the night, his.

His.

If this wasn't the perfect example of dying and going to heaven, then nothing was.

With each passing moment, as each sensation fed on itself and grew, Kasey found she was having a hard time believing that this was happening. That this was actually true.

Lovemaking with Hollis had always been about what Hollis wanted, about what turned Hollis on. Her needs, when she'd still had a glimmer of them, were just collateral. The way he saw it, he'd once told her with more than a few shots of whiskey in his system, was that if she should happen to climax, that was great. If she didn't, well, women didn't really need that the way men did.

Or, at least that was the philosophy that Hollis lived by.

And she had believed him. Or, more accurately, believed that he believed.

Until Eli.

Everything she'd previously believed—that she didn't need to feel the kind of sensations, the kind of surges and peaks that a man did—they had been and continued to be all lies.

Lies.

Because what she was feeling, what Eli *made* her feel, was supremely, incredibly wonderful.

Moreover, it seemed as though the more she got, the more Eli aroused her, the more she wanted. Eli had opened up a brand-new, wonderful world for her.

A world she wasn't willing to leave that quickly.

And when he kissed her all over, leaving the imprint of his warm lips along all the sensitive parts of her body, waking them up and making them come alive, she felt eruption after eruption. They were happening all along her body, not just within her very core.

What *was* this delicious sensation, this throbbing need that he'd brought out of her? And how did she get it to go on indefinitely?

But the itch for the final peak got to be too great, too demanding.

She was primed and eager when Eli finally stopped paying homage to the various parts of her whole and finally positioned himself over her.

Even this was a far cry from the way lovemaking had gone with Hollis—especially toward the end. With Hollis, she could never shake the feeling that she could have been anyone. That in the end, his partner didn't matter to Hollis. He just wanted to reach his climax.

And, as for her, all she'd wanted at that point was just to get it over with. There was no romance, no excitement left between them. That had ended a long time ago.

Had it not been for Eli, she would have never known that her body was capable of feeling like this. That making love could be like this, all generosity, thoughtfulness—and fire.

And when they finally became one, Kasey was as eager to be with him as she sensed he was to be with her.

After the first moment, there was no time for thought at all. Because they were both hell-bent for the final climb. They took it together and shared the light show when they attained the top of the covert peak.

He made her breathless.

Chapter 10

All too soon, the bright, shooting stars dimmed and the all-encompassing euphoria faded away.

Bracing herself, Kasey waited for the sadness to return, for the cold feeling to wrap itself around her like a giant snake.

Neither happened.

The sadness and the cool feeling were both kept in abeyance because Eli didn't turn away from her, didn't, after having her, withdraw and just fall asleep, the way Hollis, her only other lover, had. Instead, when Eli shifted his weight off her, he turned so that he was lying next to her. Tucking his arm around her, he pulled her closer to him.

A wave of tenderness made its way all through her. And it intensified when Eli pressed a kiss to her forehead with such gentleness, it brought fresh tears to her eyes. They slid out before she could stop them.

With his cheek against hers, he felt the dampness, and remorse instantly raised its hoary head, rebuking him. Taunting him that he *had* taken advantage.

Raising up on his elbow, Eli traced the path of the tear that had slipped out with the tip of his finger.

"Oh, Kasey, I'm so sorry." The words sounded so ineffectual, but he didn't know how else to apologize. "I shouldn't have pressed—"

For a moment his apology threatened to slash apart all the wondrous sensations that had just come before, as well as the happy feeling she was holding on to now. But then she realized just *why* Eli was saying what he was saying.

In her rush to set him straight as to *why* she appeared to be crying, her words got all jumbled on her tongue, making little coherent sense as they emerged.

"Oh, no, no. I'm not— You didn't— Do you think that I'm actually *regretting* what just happened here between us?" Hadn't he *been* there? How could he possibly believe that making love with him could have upset her? It was the most fabulous experience in her life.

The way he saw it, what other conclusion could he have come to? That was a tearstain on her cheek, not a stray raindrop.

He looked at her, confused. "Aren't you?"

"No!" she cried emphatically. How did she go about phrasing this? How did she make him understand what he'd stirred up within her without incurring his pity? She decided if there *was* pity, she'd deal with that later, but right now, she needed to make him understand what he had done for her.

"Oh, my God, Eli, all these years, I never knew."

"Never knew?" he echoed, not following her. "Never knew what?"

The corners of her mouth curved. The smile slipped into her eyes as it spread. "I never knew it could be like that."

She debated a moment, wondering if she should continue. She didn't want him thinking she was just an inexperienced housewife, but it was important that he understood exactly what this meant to her. To do that, she would have to tell him about what had come before.

"Hollis was never interested in...in holding me afterward. And, to be honest, he didn't exactly take all that much of an interest in my pleasure, only in his."

She paused, knowing that putting herself out there—naked—wasn't wise, but she couldn't help that. It was part of explaining what he'd made her feel and why. She didn't expect anything in return for this baring of her soul, not his commitment or even the promise that this would happen again. But she did want him to know that he had made her earth move and she was grateful for what they'd just shared.

"I think I saw fireworks going off. I definitely saw stars," she confessed with a soft laugh.

Eli threaded his fingers through her hair, framing her face, memorizing every contour, although there was no need. Every nuance that comprised her features was permanently imprinted on his brain.

Part of him still couldn't believe that they had actually made love. That his most cherished fantasy had really come true.

"Me, too," he told her.

God help her, she would have loved to believe that. Even so, she could feel herself melting again. Being stirred up again. There was something incredibly sexy about being on the receiving end of kindness.

She'd always felt that way. And never more than after she'd gotten married and learned to do without it. Hollis wasn't knowingly cruel to her and he hadn't abused her, but thoughtfulness, kindness, all that seemed to be beyond his comprehension.

"You're making fun of me," she protested.

"No, I'm not," Eli was quick to assure her. "What I *am* doing is still wondering how I managed to get so damn lucky."

She looked up at him, wondering why she'd never realized before what a knight in shining armor Eli was. Or how really handsome he was. Hollis had been a golden boy, all flash and fire. But Eli had substance. More important than his good looks, he made a woman feel safe.

"Why waste time wondering when you could be doing something about it?" she asked in a husky whisper that rippled all through him. Exciting him.

He wasn't sure if he lowered his mouth to hers, or if she pulled him down to her, but the logistics didn't really matter. What mattered was that the fireworks were going off again, in full force, accompanied by anticipation and heat.

In the end, they made love a total of three times before they lay, completely exhausted and utterly satisfied, huddled into one another in her bed.

And Wayne had come through like a trouper. The little guy had been complicit in his mother's sensual awakening by doing his part. He'd slept all through the night without so much as one whimper.

As for Eli, while Kasey might have been stunned and surprised by what she'd experienced, he hadn't been. In his heart, he'd always known it would be like this. Making love with Kasey had been every bit as incredible as his fantasies. She'd filled his soul with light, with music.

Again he wondered how Hollis could have willingly walked away from this, how he could have sacrificed exquisite nights like this because he didn't have the will-power to man up—to *grow* up. He would have crawled over glass on his knees for this, and Hollis had just thrown it all away.

One man's adversity was another man's good fortune, he couldn't help thinking, secretly grateful that Hollis had been so selfish.

Kasey finally broke the silence. "You're awfully quiet," she observed.

"That's because I'm too exhausted to talk," he told her with a self-mocking laugh. "You're a hard woman to keep up with."

Kasey pressed her lips together, knowing she shouldn't comment, shouldn't push this. But she *had* to know.

"Is that a good thing or a bad thing? You being tired," she added, just in case she'd rambled a little too much again.

He turned to her and she could actually *feel* his smile. It undulated all through her.

"A good thing," he told her. "A very good thing." He paused, savoring her closeness, content just to fall asleep holding her like this. But there was still something he needed to get out of the way, a question that he needed to ask, because he'd gotten so carried away so quickly. "I didn't hurt you, did I?" he asked. "It was just that—"

He stopped himself, wondering if his admission

would push her away. Telling her that he'd loved her all this time, that he'd yearned for her even before she'd run off with Hollis, well, that could very well spook her. That was the very last thing he wanted. After finally having *found* her, after having her willingly become a part of his life, he couldn't just lose her again. He didn't think that he could bear that.

"Just that what?" she queried when he didn't finish his sentence.

"Just that I got so carried away, so caught up in the act, I was afraid that I might have hurt you. I'd completely forgotten that you had just given birth and all," he reminded her.

"Five weeks ago," she pointed out. Had he forgotten about taking her, as well as Wayne, to the doctor the other day for a dual checkup? The doctor had been pleased to proclaim that they were both the very picture of health. "And according to Dr. Davenport, I've bounced back incredibly well."

"You won't get an argument from me about the 'incredible' part," Eli told her. If his grin had been any broader, it would have come close to cracking his face.

"Good," she murmured. "Because I'm much too exhausted to argue," she told him with what felt like her very last bit of available energy. The very next moment, she drifted off to sleep.

The sound of her even breathing was like music to his ears. Lulling music. Eli drifted off to sleep, himself, within minutes of Kasey.

With the sharp rays of daylight came even sharper rays of guilt. After having just had the greatest night of his life, Eli woke to the feeling of oppressive guilt.

As wondrous as making love with Kasey had been, it didn't negate the fact that he had taken advantage of her at an extremely vulnerable time.

He should have been strong enough to resist his urges, strong enough to hold her at arm's length rather than closer than a breath.

But he hadn't been.

Even now, he wasn't.

Looking at her now, he wanted nothing more than to pull her into his arms and make love with her all over again. And keep making love with her until he completely expired.

But that would be indulging himself again and not being mindful of her.

Dammit, he wasn't some stallion in heat. He was supposed to have willpower. That was what separated him from the horses he was training.

Or at least it was supposed to.

Holding his breath, Eli slowly got out of bed, then silently made his way across the floor and out of the room. He first eased the door open, then eased it closed again, moving so painfully slow he was certain she'd wake before he made good his escape.

Once out of the room, he hurried quickly to his own room. Throwing on the first clothes he laid his hands on, he was gone in less than fifteen minutes after he'd opened his eyes.

Working, he put in a full day and more, all on an empty stomach. After a bit, it ceased complaining, resigning itself to the fact that a meal wasn't in its future anytime soon. Eventually, after he'd done every single conceivable chore he could think of and had brought his horses back to their stalls, putting them away for the night, he ran out of excuses to stay away from the house. And her.

It was time to go home and face the music. Or, in this case, the recriminations.

Bracing himself, he opened the front door, hoping against hope that he wouldn't see the look of betrayal in Kasey's eyes when he walked in.

The first thing he saw when he shut the door behind him was not the look of betrayal—or worse—in Kasey's eyes. What he saw was a suitcase. Her suitcase. Kasey had left it standing right by the door and he'd accidentally knocked it over as he came in.

Righting it, Eli felt its weight. It wasn't there by accident. She'd packed it.

She was leaving him.

The moment he realized that, he could feel his stomach curling into itself so hard it pinched him. Badly. And it definitely wasn't caused by a lack of food.

A feeling of panic and desperation instantly sprang up within him.

He knew he should just let her leave, that he shouldn't stand in the way of her choice. But another part of him wasn't nearly that reasonable or selfless. That part urged him to fight this. To fight to keep Kasey in his life now that he had finally discovered what loving her was like.

Kasey instantly tensed as she heard him come in. She'd been listening for him all day, literally straining to hear so much that her nerves were all stretched to their limit, ready to snap in two at the slightest provocation.

"You're leaving." It wasn't really a question at this point. Why else would a packed suitcase be left right by the door?

She needed to get through this as fast as possible. She should have actually been gone by now. Why she'd waited for him to come home, she really didn't know. Ordinarily, she avoided confrontations and scenes, and this could be both.

Maybe she'd waited because she'd wanted Eli to talk her out of leaving. She'd wanted him to explain why he'd bolted the way he had this morning. And, more than anything, she wanted him to tell her that he didn't regret what had happened between them.

"Don't worry, you won't have to drive me." If her mouth had been any drier, there would have been sand spilling out when she spoke. "I'll call Miss Joan." It was the first name she could think of.

"Why?" he asked, his voice barely above a whisper.

She wanted to cry, to double up her hands into fists and beat on him in sheer frustration. She did neither. Instead, in a voice deliberately stripped of any emotions, she said, "Because I thought she might let me stay with the baby at her place."

"No." His eyes all but bore into her. "Why are you leaving?"

Why was he torturing her this way? What was it he wanted from her? "Because you want me to," she cried, her voice breaking.

He stared at her incredulously. Had she lost her mind? "Why the hell would you think that?" he demanded, stunned.

"The bed was empty when I woke up," she told him. "The house was empty when I woke up."

She was shouting now, unable to harness her emotions. She felt completely betrayed by him. She'd thought that last night had meant something to him, other than a way of easing his tension, or whatever it was that men told themselves when they slept with a woman and then completely erased her existence from their minds the next morning.

"You didn't even want to talk to me. What else am I supposed to think?" she cried heatedly, then struggled to get hold of herself. She couldn't have a complete meltdown like this, if for no other reason than because Wayne needed a functioning mother. "Look, I get it. You don't owe me anything. You've been more than kind, giving me somewhere to stay, being my friend. Last night was incredible, but I don't want to lose your friendship, so I thought that it might be best if I got out of your sight for a while." She went to pick up the suitcase.

He pushed it out of the way with his foot. "You thought wrong."

He'd said it so low, she wasn't sure if she heard him correctly. "What?"

"You thought wrong," he repeated, this time with more conviction. "I left before you woke up because I needed some time to try to figure out a way to save our friendship."

"Save it?" she repeated, completely confused. Why would he possibly think that their friendship would be in jeopardy because they had made lyrical love to-gether?

"I didn't want you worrying every time you turned around that I would suddenly pounce on you without warning."

"'Pounce,'" she repeated. As she said the word, an image of Eli "pouncing" materialized in her head. This time there was no confusion evident in her voice. But there was a hint of a smile.

"Pounce," he said again.

All things considered, "pouncing" had definite merits, she thought, relieved. Maybe she'd been worried for no reason.

"Did it ever occur to you that maybe I'd actually *want* you to pounce on me?" she asked Eli.

"What are you saying?"

She tried again, aware that she'd been more coherent in her time. "I'm saying that while I don't expect any promises—we're both in brand-new territory here—I would like to have something to look forward to once in a while." Was that really her, actually *asking* him to say that making love with her wasn't totally out of the picture? *Wow* was all she could think to say. "Or at least think it was a possibility."

"Then, just to be perfectly clear," he qualified, more for himself than for her, "what happened last night, that didn't offend you? Didn't make you feel uneasy about having me hanging around?"

"Eli, you're my best friend. How could I be uneasy about having you around? And, for the record, when have you *ever* just been 'hanging around'? You're running an entire ranch by yourself, helping me with Wayne and I *know* that you get up to tend to him when he starts to cry in the middle of the night."

She'd caught his attention with the first line. He was having trouble getting past that. "A best friend who slept with you," he pointed out.

Her smile expanded. "I don't recall much sleeping going on until a lot later," she reminded him. "Eli, if you think that you took advantage of me, let me put your mind at ease. You didn't. What you did do was make me feel alive again.

"You made me feel like a desirable woman instead of an unattractive, discarded one whose husband didn't even think enough of her to tell her face-to-face he was leaving. If anything," she said quietly, "I took advantage of you."

That was an out-and-out lie and it wasn't just his male pride that said so. But he didn't want to argue about it. Or about anything else. "Then I guess we could call it a draw."

Her eyes crinkled as she nodded. "Works for me."

Relief settled in.

"Me, too." And then, because his stomach decided to speak up again, voicing a very loud complaint, he asked, "What are my chances of getting some dinner tonight? Actually, it doesn't have to qualify as dinner. At this point, anything'll do. If you have some boiled cardboard lying around, I can make do with that."

"'Boiled cardboard,'" she repeated.

He raised his shoulders in a careless shrug, then let them drop again. "What can I say? I'm easy."

"There's easy, and then there's just selling yourself too cheap. Cheap isn't good," she said, pretending that they were having an actual sensible conversation.

"I'll have to keep that in mind," he said.

"You do that." She hooked her arm in his as she led him to the kitchen. "In the meantime, why don't I see what I can come up with to satisfy that stomach of yours so it can stop whimpering like that."

"My stomach doesn't whimper, it rumbles."

"Whatever you say."

"It does," he protested. As if on cue, his stomach made a noise. "See, there it goes again."

She managed to keep a straight face. "All I hear is whimpering," Kasey said as she opened the refrigerator door.

Eli knew better than to argue. Besides, he was too busy making love to her with his eyes even to consider arguing with this woman who made his world spin off its axis.

Chapter 11

In the evenings, if Eli wasn't with her, Kasey always knew just where to find him. With Wayne. He'd either be playing peekaboo with the baby, reveling in the gleeful, infectious laughter that emerged from her son, or he'd be attending to the boy's needs. Eli had gotten better at changing Wayne than she was.

If Wayne was already in his room for the night, Eli could be found in the rocking chair, holding Wayne and reading a bedtime story to the boy. Once the boy was asleep, Eli would often just stand over the crib and watch him breathe rhythmically.

It was a scene to wrap her heart around.

That was the way she found him tonight. Staring down at Wayne as if mesmerized by the very sight of the boy sleeping.

"There you are," she whispered, coming up behind Eli. "Dinner's ready."

"I'll be right there," he promised, but he made no effort to move away from the crib.

She couldn't help herself—she had to ask. "You're looking at him so intently, Eli. What is it that you think you see?"

Eli's smile deepened at her question—she noticed that he *always* smiled around Wayne. "That he has a world of endless possibilities in front of him. Right now, he could be anything, do anything, dream anything. He could even grow up to have the most beautiful girl in town fall in love with him." A whole beat passed before he realized what he'd just said and the kind of interpretation she was liable to put to it: that he thought she was in love with him. He knew better than to assume that. "That is, I didn't mean to imply that I thought—"

His tongue just kept getting thicker and more unmanageable as he tried to quickly dig his way out of his mistake.

But if he was afraid what he'd said would push her away again, he could have saved himself the grief. She had focused on something entirely different in his sentence.

"You think I'm beautiful?"

He slowly—and quietly—released a sigh of relief, even as he wondered why she looked so surprised. The woman had to own a mirror. "Of course you are."

"The most beautiful girl in town?" she questioned in wonder, repeating the words he'd used. She looked at him as if she hadn't seen him before. And maybe she hadn't. Not in this light. It put everything in a brand-new perspective.

"Absolutely," he affirmed, then added, "And you always have been to me."

Gently touching his face, she leaned into him and lightly brushed her lips against his. Not like a vain woman rewarding someone for giving her praise, but like a woman whose heart had been deeply moved by what she'd just heard him say.

"Dinner," she reminded him.

He nodded, remembering. "Dinner," he repeated, following her out of the room and into the hall.

Turning, he eased the door closed behind him. His sister, in keeping with her practice of always being one step ahead, had bought them a baby monitor. One of the four receivers was set up in the kitchen so that there was no need to be concerned that something might happen to the infant while they were busy elsewhere. They were able to hear every sound the baby made. Having the monitor definitely eased the fear that they wouldn't know if Wayne suddenly became distressed for some reason. It allowed them to have some time with one another without guilt and without involving diapers and spit-up.

Eli had had one of those days that seemed as if it was going to go on indefinitely. He felt completely wiped out and bone-tired as he sank into his chair in the kitchen.

"Need help?" he asked automatically.

"Sit there," she instructed. "You look like you just might fall over on your face if I have you doing anything."

Was there something she needed him to do? He tried his best to look like he was rallying.

"No, I'm good, really," he protested, going through the motions of getting up, even though somehow, he remained sitting where he was, his torso all but glued to the chair.

She turned to glance at him for a second, a smile playing on her lips that went a long way toward banishing the exhaustion from his body—at least temporarily.

"Yes," she agreed, punctuating the single word with a wink. "You are."

"Kasey?" he asked, not sure exactly what she was saying to him, only knowing that he was completely fascinated by what could only be described as a sensual expression on her face.

Ignoring the question in his voice, Kasey set a tureen on the table right between their two place mats. The contents were hot enough to emit a plume of steam.

"I made your favorite," she told Eli. "Beef stew."

She was rewarded with a look of pleasure that rose in his brown eyes.

It occurred to her—not for the first time—that they'd settled into a comfortable, familiar pattern, Eli, the baby and she. Mornings she'd get up—no matter how exquisitely exhausting the night before with Wayne might have been—and make Eli breakfast. After he ate, she'd send him off with a packed lunch and a kiss—and secretly begin counting the minutes until he walked through the front door again.

There was no point in pretending otherwise. She knew she was in love, although she refused to actually put a name to the exhilarating sensation coasting through her body. She was afraid if she neatly labeled it, love would arbitrarily disappear.

After all, she'd been in love before and it had turned out very badly. She didn't want to risk having what she had with Eli turn to ashes on her just because she'd called it by its rightful name. So, for now, she was just living each day, *enjoying* each day, and refusing to think beyond the moment or, at the very most, if she *had* to make plans, beyond the week she was in.

And each evening, Eli would walk through the door, and just like that, her heart would begin to sing. Everything seemed a little brighter, a little warmer. She didn't even have to be in the same room with him to know that he'd come home. She could just *feel* it. Even Wayne seemed to light up when he saw him. God knew, she certainly did.

And then, while she put the finishing touches on dinner, Eli would play with the baby. Or, like tonight, if Wayne was already in his crib, he'd tiptoe in just to check on him.

Wouldn't he be surprised to know how much that single thoughtful act on his part turned her on?

Once he came to the table, they'd eat and talk—sometimes for hours—then he'd help her tidy up and eventually they would go to bed. Together.

In the beginning, after that first night when they'd made love, there'd been just the slightest bit of hesitation—on his part rather than on hers.

That was due to his incredible chivalry again. He was always thinking of her, of Wayne. He never put himself first, which still astounded her because of all the years she'd spent with Hollis. Hollis had always thought of himself first. He believed that in the marriage, he was the one who really counted.

Hollis had told her once that his needs had to come first because he had to be in the right frame of mind to be able to take care of her. Looking back, she realized just how slow-witted she must have seemed, silently accepting his opinion without questioning him or challenging him.

She'd done a lot of growing in these past two-plus months, she thought. And it was all thanks to Eli.

"How is it?" she asked, watching Eli as he took his first forkful of dinner.

"Fantastic. As always," he added. "I don't think you could put together a bad meal even if you actually tried to."

She laughed at the compliment and the simple faith that was behind it. "You'd be surprised" was all she allowed herself to say.

There was no reason for her to go into detail about the first few disasters she'd had preparing meals, or how small Hollis had made her feel when he looked at her with belittling annoyance, saying that he thought she knew how to cook.

"Yeah, I would be," Eli agreed, continuing to eat with complete and obvious gusto. He seemed amazingly content. "You really outdid yourself this time," he told her with enthusiasm.

Kasey sat opposite him, taking a much smaller portion for herself. "You know what I think?" She didn't wait for his answer. "I think I probably could serve you boiled cardboard and you'd find something nice to say about it."

He was just that kind of person, she thought. Handsome, sexy *and* kind. It just didn't get any better than this.

Eli grinned in between forkfuls. "This is definitely *not* boiled cardboard," he told her with feeling. "If I'm not careful, I'm going to 'outgrow' my clothes and not in a good way. I'll wind up having to wear pants made out of burlap and tying them with a rope to keep them from falling down."

Kasey tried very hard not to laugh at the image that created in her mind. She didn't want to risk hurting his feelings.

"I don't think you have anything to worry about. You certainly don't appear as if you've gained any weight to me—and, if you remember, I *have* seen you up close— and personal," she added, her eyes dancing.

Funny, she and Hollis never had these sorts of sweet, intimate conversations. Most of the time, they really hadn't talked all that much at all. She'd been on edge around Hollis, waiting for him either to point out some failing of hers or to complain that there never seemed to be enough money around for him to do what he really wanted to do. Heaven knew she was often aware that there wasn't enough money available in their account to pay all the bills that kept cropping up.

But even she hadn't realized just how bad his gambling problem had gotten, she thought now. Not until he'd lost his family's ranch and her along with it.

"How could I forget?" Eli patted what was essentially a very flat middle. "Well, I guess if I've passed your inspection, it's okay for me to have a second helping tonight," he said, once again moving his now empty bowl up against the tureen. He ladled out another generous serving of beef stew. Tiny splashes were made by the tumbling vegetables.

This serving was even bigger than the first had been. Kasey shook her head in wonder. *Where* did he put it all? "Sure you don't have a tapeworm?"

Eli shrugged away the thought. "If I did, he'd be out of luck because I'm not about to share this food with any outsider."

What made it even better in his opinion was that she'd made the meal knowing that it was his favorite. She'd paid attention to learn what his favorite meal was. He found this to be very pleasing—and humbling, in a way. That he knew what her favorite things were went without saying, but then, he knew absolutely everything about her. To him, that was just a normal part of loving someone.

"But you really don't have to make an extra effort like this," he told her. "I'd be satisfied with anything you made—like a sandwich," he suggested off the top of his head.

"Sandwiches are for emergency trips, they're meant to keep you going. They're definitely *not* supposed to take the place of a real meal. Besides, I *like* cooking for you." They'd had this conversation before. She was determined to get her answer to register in Eli's brain this time. "Eli—" leaning forward, she covered his hand with her own "—I'm only going to say this once and I want you to listen to me. I never do *anything* because I have to, or feel obligated to. I'm doing it, whether it's cooking, or keeping house, or something else—" she paused for half a beat, allowing the last part to sink in

"—because I *want* to. Because you *make* me want to. I just wish I could do more."

"That's not possible," he assured her with feeling.

He could feel his emotions surging within him. Once again it was on the tip of his tongue to tell her that he loved her. That she'd made him happier in these past two months than he ever thought possible.

And once again, he was afraid that putting his feelings into words would spell the beginning of the end. Most likely, he'd spook her, making her back away from him, possibly even *run* away from him.

Who knew? Kasey might even be considering moving out on her own right now. He just didn't know. But the one thing he did know was that if he said anything that remotely *resembled* a declaration of love, he'd find her packing her things within the hour.

He wanted to avoid, or at least to forestall, the end for as long as possible. And that meant keeping his feelings to himself even though he was all but dying for them to finally come out.

"You are so very good for my ego," Kasey was telling him, savoring what he had just said. Rising, she took her empty bowl to the sink to rinse it out before she placed it in the dishwasher. The dishwasher was a recent purchase. She knew he'd bought it for her, even though he'd told her it was one of those things that he'd been meaning to get around to buying for himself.

Eli didn't lie very convincingly, which was another point in his favor. Hollis could lie like a pro. He did it so smoothly that after a while even he was convinced he was telling the truth. The upshot of it was, she never knew what to believe.

Whereas with Eli, she knew that if he said the moon had suddenly turned to pink cheese, she would race outside to see the phenomenon for herself. She trusted him beyond any words, any vows, any promises made between a man and a woman.

Kasey turned around to say something to him, but the words never came out. The serious expression on his face drove any and all coherent thought out of her head.

Why did he look like that? "What's the matter?" she asked in a hushed voice.

He raised his hand, silently asking for *her* silence. He cocked his head, listening intently. Then, rather than explain or answer her question, he was up on his feet, leaving the room. Hurrying to the second floor and Wayne's room.

Since he'd been listening to the baby's monitor, it had to be something concerning Wayne. The moment that occurred to her, concern and worry flooded her.

Hurrying after Eli, she ran up the stairs in his wake, trying to catch up.

"Eli, what's the matter?" she asked. "Why are you running?"

"He's wheezing" was all he had time to say, tossing the words over his shoulder. The next moment he burst into Wayne's room. Crossing to the crib, he saw the problem instantly. The baby was on his stomach, his face all but buried against the stuffed rabbit that had been propped up next to the inside of his crib.

Reaching the infant first, Eli turned the boy onto his back. Then he checked to see if perhaps the baby had gotten something stuck up his nose or in his throat.

But the passages were all clear and once he was on his back, the baby began to breathe more easily.

Eli removed the rabbit, tossing him onto the rocking chair he'd bought for Kasey to celebrate her first week on his ranch.

And then it hit him.

"Kasey, I left Wayne on his back, the way I always do." His eyes met hers. "Do you know what this means?" he asked as he picked the fussing infant up and began to gently sway with him.

"He turned over by himself." She said the words out loud, partially in amazement. She paused, thinking of what she'd found in the *Parenting During the First Year* book—also a present from Eli. He had a way of spoiling her, she thought fondly, then forced herself to get her mind back on track. "Isn't he a little young to be doing that?"

"Not for an exceptional baby," Eli assured her, then looked at the infant in his arms. "And you are exceptional, aren't you, Wayne?"

For his part, Wayne looked up at him with wide, serious eyes, as if he was hanging on Eli's every word.

"Well, since I'm here…." Eli said, pretending to resign himself to the chore. "I guess we might as well finish that story I was reading to you last night," Eli said as if the little boy understood every word.

Picking up the large, rectangular book from the top of the bookcase, he settled in to read. "Let's see what that little mouse has been up to since we left him," he said, taking a seat in the rocking chair. He arranged the baby so that he could turn the pages more easily while still holding Wayne against his chest.

Kasey lingered in the doorway for a couple of minutes, listening and wondering whether, if she prayed very hard and was the best person she could possibly be, she could keep living inside this dream for a little longer. She knew all good things came to an end, but that didn't mean it had to be right now, did it?

The sound of Eli's voice, reading to Wayne, followed her all the way down the hall until she reached the stairs. Her smile lasted a great deal longer.

Chapter 12

Something was bothering her.

Eli could see it in her eyes. Kasey hadn't really said anything yet and she was moving around the kitchen, getting breakfast, acting as if nothing out of the ordinary was going on.

That was the problem. She was *acting*. He could tell the difference when it came to Kasey. For instance, he'd noticed that she had paused in midmotion several times, as if wrestling with a thought or searching for the right words to use before she said anything to him.

A sliver of uneasiness pricked him.

He knew he should give Kasey space and let her say something—or not say something—when she was ready. But he would be going out to the stable soon and wondering what was on her mind would bedevil him the whole time he was gone. Not to mention that if she decided she *did* want to talk to him, she would have to trek out to the corral with Wayne since that was where he would be for most the day, training the horses.

No, asking her outright was by far the easier route all the way around, despite the fact that he really didn't like invading Kasey's territory, or making her feel pressured.

"Something on your mind, Kasey?" he asked, trying to sound casual.

What she said in response threw him off a little. At the very least, it wasn't what he'd expected her to say. Or, in this case, ask.

"How are your training sessions with the horses going?"

"They're going well," he answered slowly, never taking his eyes off her expression, waiting for something to tip him off. She'd never asked him about his training sessions before. "As a matter of fact, I'm ahead of schedule." He paused, waiting. She said nothing. "Why?" he finally asked.

She answered his last question in a roundabout fashion, like someone feeling their away around a brand-new situation.

"Then would you mind not training them? Just for today, I mean," she added quickly. There was no missing the hope in her voice.

He noticed that she'd wrapped her hands around the mug of coffee she'd poured for herself. Her hands were shaking a little.

Something was *definitely* wrong.

"No, I wouldn't mind," he told her, watching her more intently than ever. He curbed a sudden surge of impatience, knowing that would only make her more reticent to explain whatever had prompted her request. "Why?" he asked gently. "What do you have in mind, Kasey?"

She pressed her lips together, half-annoyed with herself for not being stronger. She'd done so much by herself in these past few years, taking care of the ranch, trying to make a go of her marriage. She should have been able to do this alone, as well.

But this was a huge step she was about to take. Heaven help her, but she wanted someone to lean on, someone to turn to for emotional support. She was afraid that if she didn't, if she went alone, she might change her mind at the last moment.

She blew out a shaky breath. "I'm thinking of going into town today."

He waited for her to continue. When she didn't, he picked up the fallen thread of conversation. "All right. I can certainly put some things off for a day. Any particular destination in town you have in mind?" he asked mildly.

She was pressing her hands so hard against the mug, he was surprised it didn't just shatter. "I thought I'd go see Olivia. The sheriff's wife."

He smiled at the addendum. "I know who Olivia is, Kasey." And then the pieces started coming together for him. "This isn't going to be a social call, is it?"

She shook her head slowly from side to side. "No, it's not."

If she was going to do what he thought she was going to do, she needed to at least be able to put it into words, to say it out loud so that she could begin getting used to the idea.

"Why are you going to see Olivia?" he persisted.

She didn't answer him right away, trying to get comfortable with the idea. What she knew she *had* to do.

Kasey took in a deep breath. This would be her reality now. She had already forced herself to face the fact that her marriage was over.

Technically, it had been over for longer than just these past two and a half months. It had been over the moment she'd become pregnant. She'd only fooled herself during those nine months before Wayne was born, telling herself that Hollis would change once the baby was here. Telling herself that he'd want to finally grow up because he was responsible for a brand-new little human being and behaving recklessly was no longer the answer.

But despite her ongoing optimism, in her heart, she'd always known better. Always known that Hollis was *not* the man she'd hoped he was beneath all the bad-boy trappings.

The roof of her mouth felt like sandpaper as she told Eli, "I want to file for a divorce. Hollis isn't coming back and I need to move forward."

Although this was *exactly* what he'd hoped for, Eli didn't want her feeling pressured to take this step. Not that he had pressured her, even remotely, but maybe just the very fact that he had taken her into his home somehow made her feel obligated to take this step. Especially since they were now sleeping together.

"Are you sure you want to do this, Kasey?"

The question, coming from him, surprised her. Was he afraid that once she was a free woman again, she'd try to get him to marry her? Well, he could rest easy. She was not about to repay his kindness with any undue expectations.

She'd been blind before, blind to all the wonderful qualities Eli possessed, but that was on her. She'd missed out on a great deal—on the life she would have ideally wanted. But again, there were no "do-overs" in life and she was just grateful to have Eli in *her* life. More importantly, with any luck, the bond he was forming with her son would continue. She knew that Wayne would be the richer for it. As would she.

"Very sure," she answered.

He wanted to reach out to her, to hold her and assure her that he'd always be there for her. But, considering this step she was taking, he didn't want her to feel crowded or stalked in even the vaguest sort of way.

"All right, then," he told her. "Let me just take care of a few basic things with the horses and then I'm all yours." Finished with breakfast, he was already on his feet and heading for the back door.

As she turned away to clear the table, Kasey smiled sadly to herself.

If only.

But she knew that she had no one to blame but herself for that. And wishing for a do-over was more than useless. It was a waste of time.

A few hours later, Olivia Santiago, Forever's legal Jill of all trades, ushered in her first client of the morning. Eli, Kasey and Kasey's son were welcomed into the office before the lawyer asked them just what it was that had brought them to her.

"How can I help you?" Olivia asked, looking from Kasey to Eli. And then her gaze came to rest on the cooing baby.

"My daughter used to drool something awful at about

his age," Olivia confided. "I couldn't wait until she out-
grew it. Now I wish those days were back." And then
she laughed. "It's true what they say, you know," she
told Kasey. "They *do* grow up much too fast. Cherish
every moment you get."

Kasey nodded her agreement, but when she spoke, it
wasn't in reference to Olivia's last observation. It was
to answer her initial question.

"I need to know if I can file for divorce if my—"
Unable to refer to Hollis either by his name, or by what
he was supposed to have been to her, she fell back on a
euphemism. "If the other party isn't around."

She paused for half a second to pull herself together,
searching for inner strength. The encouraging smile Eli
flashed at her seemed to do the trick.

"He walked out on me. On us," Kasey amended,
looking at Wayne.

The infant was obligingly drifting off to sleep, but
fighting it as best he could. His eyes had popped open
twice, as if he was aware that once they really closed,
he'd be sound asleep and missing out on whatever was
going on here. But within moments he'd given up the
fight and the sound of soft, regular breathing noises
could be heard coming from his small mouth.

Olivia appeared extremely sympathetic to what
Kasey had just told her.

"You have grounds for a divorce," she assured the
other woman. Then she put it into a single word. "Aban-
donment. I can also get the paperwork going to sue him
for child support and make sure that he never gets joint
custody—"

The laugh that emerged from Kasey's lips echoed of
sadness. "You don't have to go through the trouble of

that," she told Olivia. "The last thing in the world Hollis wants is to be responsible for Wayne. That was why he left to begin with."

Olivia raised an eyebrow. "Oh?" She looked to Eli for confirmation and he gave her a very discrete nod.

Steeling herself as best she could, Kasey went over the events of the past. "He said he couldn't take the idea of being a father. And I don't want to sue him for child support." She didn't want a single thing from Hollis, other than to be left alone. "I'll take care of Wayne myself. I just don't want Hollis coming back into our lives, thinking that he could just pick up where he left off."

"I understand how you feel," Olivia assured her new client. "You do know, however, that he is responsible for at least half of your son's care and feeding. More if he can afford it."

But Kasey was already shaking her head. It was a lovely scenario that Olivia painted, but it just wasn't about to happen.

"I know Hollis. He won't pay it."

"In that case, he can be a guest of my husband's jail," Olivia told her in a no-nonsense voice.

Even so, Kasey remained adamant. She wanted to have nothing further to do with Hollis. Dealing with him was just a reminder of the kind of fool she'd been.

"If it's all the same to you," she said to Olivia, "just file the divorce papers, please."

Olivia seemed eager to talk her out of this pacifistic stance, but Kasey remained firm on this issue.

With a sigh, Olivia said, "You're in the driver's seat. I'll draw up the necessary papers and bring them on over when they're ready. That should be in a few days."

She raised her eyes to Eli, who had been quiet throughout the conversation.

Kasey nodded, relieved that it would finally be over. And yet, at the same time, there was a bit of residual sadness, as well.

"I'll have to pay you in installments."

It killed her to admit, but there was no getting around the fact that she had very little in the way of money right now. She might as well let the attorney know that up front. Paying her in installments would be the case no matter what the charge. And, no matter what the cost, she was determined to pay her own way.

It occurred to Kasey at that point that she was still missing one crucial piece of information. "You haven't told me your fee."

Olivia waved a hand at the question as she accompanied the young couple and the infant to the door of her office.

"Don't worry about it, we'll work something out," she promised. And then, curious, she asked Eli, "Will I see you at the wedding?" A second later, she laughed at her own question. The answer was perforce a no-brainer. "Of course I will. I forgot for a minute that Alma is your sister, isn't she?"

Eli smiled as he nodded. "That she is." A dozen memories came crowding back to him. He wondered if he should send Cash a condolence card. Poor guy didn't know what he was getting himself into.

"Rick thinks the world of her," Olivia confided. "And my closedmouthed husband doesn't often speak highly of people. I can't say I know much about your sister's future husband, though."

"Actually, Cash is originally from around here," Eli

told Kasey's new lawyer. "He and I and Gabriel were best friends back in elementary and high school. We lost touch when he went off to college to become a lawyer." That had been Cash's doing, but it was all in the past now. Cash would be part of the family. Eli pretended to lower his voice as he said, "You know what they say about lawyers."

"That they're the salt of the earth?" Olivia interjected, tongue-in-cheek.

Eli smiled, going with her description. "I don't know about any other place, but they are around here."

Olivia smiled her appreciation at the kind words.

Extending her hand, she first shook Kasey's, then his. "I think we're going to get along fine. And don't worry," she told Kasey. "I'll be sure to handle everything. All you'll have to do is sign on the dotted line."

"Just like that," Kasey murmured a few minutes later as they were walking back to Eli's Jeep. Eli looked at her quizzically, not really following her train of thought. "Just like that," she repeated. "I sign on the dotted line and the marriage is dissolved, almost like it never happened."

Was that regret he heard in her voice? What kind of regret was it? Was it regret over the end of her marriage, or that she had married Hollis in the first place? And if it was the first, what did he do? Did he try to change her mind, or did he let her sort it out by herself, without any interference—praying that he would come out the victor?

"Having second thoughts?" he asked, watching her expression in case she chose to lie to him.

She didn't. "No, just amazed at how quickly something can be erased, that's all."

"Not everything," he assured her, slipping his arm through hers and lending her a hand.

She smiled at that, taking enormous comfort in just the sound of his voice as well as in what he was subtly telling her. That his presence in her life was steadfast.

"Nice to know," she murmured.

Chapter 13

Miguel Rodriguez was not a man who gave in to sentiment easily.

Except for the time when he held his dying wife in his arms, feeling the weak flicker of life slowly ebbing away from her, he kept his emotions tightly under wraps. It was important to him to remain on an even keel no matter whether it was an occasion for anger or for joy. The father of six always met both in the same manner. With thoughtful reserve.

But today was different.

Today his youngest born, his baby, his Alma, was getting married. The first of his children to do so. And, he realized as emotions vied for space within him, all but choking him, she looked absolutely beautiful in her mother's wedding gown.

He'd known Alma was going to be wearing it. He

was the one who had offered to take it down for her from the attic.

But he hadn't seen her in it.

Until now.

He hadn't expected her to look so much like his young bride had all those many years ago.

Long-ago yesterday, he thought now, because that was what it felt like. As if he and Dolores had just exchanged their vows yesterday.

It was hard to believe that a lifetime had passed since then.

He hadn't been prepared for the kick to his gut that he'd received when he first saw Alma in the wedding dress. Popping his head into the room where Alma and some of her bridesmaids were getting ready—after first knocking to make sure he wouldn't be surprising anyone—Miguel was the one who found himself on the receiving end of a big surprise.

It took him a second to remember to breathe and far longer to tear his eyes away.

He felt moisture forming along his eyelashes.

Miguel cleared his throat, trying to sound as if nothing was out of the ordinary, but it so obviously was. "For just a moment, I thought your mother was back. That I was looking at her, not you, on our wedding day. She was a beautiful, beautiful bride," he told her. "As are you," he added reverently, patting her hand.

Moved, Alma had to take a moment before she could say anything to her father. And that was when she saw it, the glisten of unshed tears in his eyes.

"Dad, you're not going to cry, are you?" she asked in a disbelieving whisper. She didn't know whether to be horrified—or touched. What she was without thinking, was stunned.

Miguel shook his head, tilting it backward a bit, as if relying on gravity to hold his tears in abeyance.

"Of course not. A man does not cry," he told her. "I just wanted to see if you were ready yet, that is all."

She nodded, letting him have his white lie. "It must be the lighting in here," she said after a moment's speculation.

Still, as she gave his hamlike hand a squeeze, Kasey tucked a handkerchief into it—just in case.

Miguel glanced down at his hand and then back at her, a glimmer of surprise in his eyes. She merely winked at him, as if to tell him that this would be their little secret.

"I will be waiting for you outside the church doors," he told her. Then, after a sweeping glance that took in all of the other bridesmaids, all women who had grown up in Forever—except for Olivia Santiago, the sheriff's wife—he put his hand on the doorknob, ready to leave. "Ladies," he said politely, bowing his head as a sign of respect, "I will see you all inside."

"Your father looks very happy about you marrying Cash," Kasey commented.

Although not a bridesmaid, Kasey had offered to be a last-minute gofer for Eli's sister. Not encumbered by the flowing gray-blue bridesmaid's dress, she pointed out that she could move around far more easily than the members of the bridal party.

Having witnessed the exchange between Alma and Miguel, Kasey couldn't help wondering what that felt like, having a father, much less one who so visibly approved of her and what she was doing. One who was so completely invested in her happiness.

Her own father had been nothing like that. If anything, he'd seemed resentful of her, of the attention she'd received from her mother when she was very young. Attention that he felt had been taken away from him. Some men were just not cut out to be fathers and he was one of them.

Like Hollis, she thought, although at the time, when she'd happily accepted his proposal that night and fled her father's house, she hadn't even been thinking about that possibility.

Her father was dead now, but she found herself wondering if, like the sheriff's mother, he would have attempted to make amends for his obvious shortcomings. Would he have professed to regret his actions the way she had?

The sheriff and his sister, Ramona, the town veterinarian now that her mentor had retired, had both gone through a very rocky period when their mother suddenly returned to Forever asking for their forgiveness. It had been harder on Mona than on Rick, but in the end, they had come around and softened, forgiving the repentant woman. Their mother had since become a very important person in their lives, watching their children grow the way she hadn't when they had been that age.

It was the sheriff's mother who had volunteered to watch over all the children today so that their parents could have a few hours of enjoyment at the wedding.

Some stories did have happy endings, Kasey thought. Would hers?

"Your father looked really very moved to see you in that wedding dress," she commented to Alma as she helped her with the full-length veil, spreading it out so that it didn't get tangled underfoot.

Alma was silent for a moment, solemnly scrutinizing her reflection in the mirror. The young woman looking back was her—and it wasn't.

"I hadn't realized how much I looked like my mother," Alma said in a quiet voice. It had taken her father's shaken observation to make her see that. "Funny, growing up, I didn't think I looked a thing like her."

"That's because, growing up, you were always covered with dirt, running after all of us and trying so hard to compete," Eli said.

After running into his father just now and hearing what he'd said about Alma, Eli wanted to see the resemblance to his mother for himself. Standing in the doorway now, he could see both sides of his sister, thanks to the position of the full length, wood-framed mirror in the room.

Although he had obviously only seen photographs from that day, he could see an eerie similarity between his one-time tomboy sister and the genteel, dark-eyed woman who had been their mother.

Alma turned from the mirror. "What do you mean, 'trying' to compete?" she challenged, pretending to rise to the bait. "I usually *beat* all of you boys—especially you."

"You didn't *beat* me," he corrected. "I just felt sorry for you and didn't want to be the one who delivered a final death blow to that 'fragile' ego of yours," he informed her with a laugh. Walking into the room, Eli paused for a second, taking in the full effect of the vision his sister cast. "Dad's right. You do look beautiful,

Alma," he acknowledged, becoming serious for just a moment. "Cash is a lucky guy."

Alma could feel herself growing emotional, just as her father had earlier. She'd promised herself to keep a tight rein on her more sensitive feelings. Tears just ruined makeup.

"Don't be nice to me, Eli," she chided. "You know I don't know what to do when you're nice to me." Alma blinked several times, warding away the tears that threatened to betray her.

He took her words in stride and nodded. "Okay, I'll go get a switch and beat you with it. Be right back," he promised, backing away.

Watching the exchange between Eli and his sister, Kasey realized all over again what a very special man he really was. And how very lucky she was to have him in her life, however briefly that turned out to be.

Don't go there now, she chastised herself. *Nothing good'll come of it. Just enjoy the moment and pray it continues.*

On his way out, Eli paused by her. Raising his voice, he said to his sister, "If you're through with Kasey, I'd like to steal her back for a while."

"I'm all set," Alma announced. "She's free to do whatever she wants." Glancing in her direction, Alma said, "Thanks for your help, Kasey."

"I did next to nothing," Kasey protested.

"Nothing's good," Eli quipped, only to have his shoulder hit. "Hey, careful," he chided. "I bruise easily."

But curiosity kept Kasey from verbally sparring with him. Turning toward Eli so that she blocked anyone's visual access to him, she asked in a lowered voice,

"What's wrong?" There was uneasy anticipation in her eyes as she waited for him to say something.

"Nothing," he whispered in her ear. "I just want you to myself, that's all."

A warm glow, initiated by the feel of his breath against her ear and neck and fed by his words, spread rapidly through her.

Her heart swelling despite all her logical reasoning, Kasey grinned. "Careful what you wish for," she whispered back.

That might be true, at times, in other cases, Eli thought, but not in this one. Because right at this precious moment, he was happier than he could ever remember. The girl he'd been in love with since forever was right next to him when he woke up each morning and when he went to bed each night.

And he was absolutely crazy about her son. When things settled down a little after Alma's wedding and after Kasey's divorce was finalized, he was going to ask her to marry him. And if she said yes—he didn't want to think about how he would feel if she turned him down—he would ask her if she had any objections to his adopting Wayne and making the boy his son in the eyes of the law.

He couldn't think of anything he wanted more, the perfect woman and the perfect family. That would be all he'd need.

Ever.

But for now, Eli kept his thoughts to himself, not wanting to make Kasey feel as if he was rushing her. Even without words, he was fairly certain that she knew how he felt about her. He knew it was certainly there, in his eyes, every time they made love, or laughed together, or just shared a quiet moment together. He couldn't hide his love for her, not even if his very life depended on it.

She had become very important to his world.

Hell, she *was* his world.

And he had never felt luckier.

The actual wedding ceremony was simple and all the more beautiful for it.

Simple or not, Kasey was struck by the contrast between Alma and Cash's ceremony and the one that she'd had when she'd married Hollis. The whole thing had lasted five minutes—if that much—from start to finish.

And afterward, when they'd checked into a motel that had looked better cloaked by the night than it did in the light of day, the lovemaking that followed had been conspicuously short on tenderness and—for her—long on disillusion.

But for that she had only herself to blame. After all, no one had forced her to build up fantasies that, Hollis quickly made her aware of, belonged to a child, not a woman. Certainly not one who knew what the real world was like.

It was only after she'd experienced making love with Eli that Kasey realized her fantasies *could* become a reality. To her unmitigated joy, she'd found everything she'd ever been looking for—and so much more—in Eli's arms.

There was a collective sigh, followed by applause and cheers, when the ceremony concluded and the priest pronounced Cash and Alma to be husband and wife in the eyes of God and the law.

Kasey, Eli noted, had been awfully quiet throughout

the whole thing. Even at the very end when Cash had kissed Alma so long that their relatives and friends had all begun to rhythmically clap as if they were keeping time with the beat, Eli noticed that Kasey was just going through the motions as she watched the couple intently.

Her palms hardly touched as she clapped.

Was she thinking about her own wedding? Was she thinking about Hollis? Or worse, was she missing him?

He had no right to be jealous, especially since Hollis was no longer around, but he was. Hollis didn't deserve to have one minute wasted on him with thoughts of regret. Definitely not after what he'd done to Kasey. She should erect a piñata with his face on it so that she could take a stick to it, not pine for his return.

Still, he didn't want her being uncomfortable, and the wedding might be bringing up past hurts and longings for her. It wasn't like her to be this quiet this long. "Do you want to leave?" he asked.

The question startled her. Without thinking, she wrapped her hand along her neck, as if pressing the warmth of his breath into her skin permanently.

"No, why?" Was *he* the one who wanted to leave for some reason? "Do you?"

This was his sister's wedding, why would he want to leave? He shook his head in response. "No, but I just thought—" He stopped and tried again, determined to sound coherent. "You just looked like you were a million miles away."

Or however far away Hollis was these days, he added silently.

"Did I?" she questioned. "I wasn't, really. I was just thinking how happy they looked. And how happy I am for them," she added with feeling. Just because her own

172 A Baby on the Ranch

circumstances hadn't worked out didn't mean she wanted other people not to have a shot at happiness and attaining their own happily ever after. "Especially Alma."

She looked at Eli as they filed out of the rows of chairs, following behind the bride and groom.

"Did you know that she was once in love with Cash?" She suspected that Alma had never really stopped loving the man, but she hadn't pressed the issue when Alma had confided in her.

For the most part, Kasey was not the type to be eaten up by curiosity. She could wait for something to be told to her, no matter how long it took to own up to. But that didn't mean she didn't have her suspicions.

"It's nice to know that sometimes happy endings do happen," she said wistfully, more to herself, actually, than to Eli.

"It's not a happy ending," Eli pointed out. When she looked at him, confused, he explained. "It's a happy beginning."

"I do like the way you think, Eli," Kasey confessed. He had such a positive outlook on things, and yet it wasn't without some sort of a basis, a solid foundation. There was *logic* behind his positive thinking. Whereas Hollis always had a tendency to build castles in the sky, shooting for improbable things that hadn't a prayer of coming true. He had no solid base, no foundation.

How different the two men were, she thought now. One was charming and attractive and about as deep as a thimbleful of water. The other was a rock, someone she could trust, someone she could lean on.

Someone, she now realized, who put her first, before himself. The bottom line was that Eli was a man, while Hollis was an attractive bad boy.

But as sexy as it might initially be, the latter attraction wore thin in the real world, she mused, realizing how lucky she was and how grateful she was to have been given a second chance to do it right.

A second chance to discover that Eli had feelings for her, at least for now. Of the two, it was Eli who was the better man. She just hadn't realized it before, at least not consciously. She'd been too blind, too dazzled by a man with no substance.

Eli had substance.

Thanks to the efforts of some very skilled amateur musicians, music filled the air.

"Dance with me, Eli?" Kasey proposed suddenly, putting out her hand to him.

Reluctantly he took her hand but didn't move. "I don't dance, Kasey," Eli told her.

"Yes, you do," she insisted. "You danced with me. At the prom, remember?"

At the time Hollis had temporarily disappeared on her and when she'd come to him, asking if he knew where Hollis had gotten to, he had feigned ignorance, then asked her to dance to distract her.

He'd known that Hollis had ducked out with another girl who was very willing to gratify his more basic needs. Hollis had gone missing for approximately half an hour, then returned to claim "his date." Hollis had also accused him with a laugh of "stealing his girl."

For his part, Eli had come extremely close to confronting Hollis about cheating on Kasey that night, but he hadn't wanted to humiliate her in front of the whole senior class, so he'd kept his mouth shut and said nothing.

And Kasey went on believing Hollis's stories.

"I remember," Eli said. Then, with a shrug, still holding her hand, he led her to the small area that had been cleared for dancing. "I'm really rusty. I can't remember dancing since then, so you're doing this at your own risk. Don't say I didn't warn you."

"Consider me warned," she told him, a smile playing on her generous mouth. "I've decided to chance it," she said bravely. "Besides, you would never hurt me."

And knowing that was an immense comfort to her.

And almost a burden for him.

Chapter 14

The reception, held outdoors on Miguel Rodriguez's ranch, was deliberately an informal affair. In the spirit of camaraderie, attendance was open to anyone who wanted to stop by to add their good wishes for the happy couple.

Which was how the man who wound up casting a shadow over the event had come to be there.

One moment Eli was holding Kasey in his arms, swaying to a slow dance and allowing himself to make plans for their future. The next moment a chill went down his back as he heard a familiar voice uttering a phrase out of the past.

"Thanks for taking care of my girl, but I can take over now."

It was like being on the receiving end of an upended bucket of ice water. Both he and Kasey immediately froze in place, then, ever so slowly, they turned around to look at the man who had just spoken.

Her mouth went dry at the same time that her heart rate sped up.

This can't be happening. It has to be a nightmare.

The thought pulsed in Kasey's brain over and over again, repeating itself like an old-fashioned record playing on a Victrola with its needle stuck in a groove.

"Hollis," she finally whispered hoarsely in sheer disbelief. What was he doing here? *Why* was he here?

Hollis smiled at her then, that wide, golden smile that had once captured her heart and so firmly captivated her soul. A smile that now left her utterly cold.

"In the flesh," he told her, spreading his hands in front of himself like a showman. He completely ignored Eli, looking only at her. "May I have this dance?" he asked, acting as if it were a sheer formality, that he didn't expect any resistance.

"The music stopped," Eli said, still holding Kasey to him. His voice was cool enough to freeze an ice-cube tray filled with hot water.

Hollis didn't even bother sparing his one-time friend so much as an extra glance.

"So it did." He had eyes only for Kasey. "I guess I'll just have to wait for the next song."

Eli squared his shoulders, shifting slightly so that he was between Hollis and Kasey. "I don't think so." He ground the words out between clenched teeth.

Hollis finally glanced in his direction. There was more than a little mocking contempt in his tone. "Don't get carried away, Eli. When I asked you to look out for her, I didn't mean when I was around. Your job's done here."

For two cents—less—he would have decked the pompous jerk he'd once thought his friend. But this was Kasey's call. So Eli turned to her, waiting for Kasey to say something, to tell him whether she wanted Hollis to go—or to stay.

Kasey remained where she was, making no effort to move around Eli. "Don't cause a scene, Hollis" was all she said.

"Hey, I'm not the one acting like some big superhero," Hollis protested, dismissing Eli's presence with a sneer. He eyed Kasey, his demeanor growing serious. "I'm back and I want to make amends. I've missed you, Kasey," he told her, sounding more sincere than she'd ever heard him. "We need to talk."

She was not about to allow him to draw the focus away from Alma and Cash. This was *their* day and she didn't want it marred by a potential ugly scene. It gave her the courage to tell him, "Not here."

Kasey was willing to talk to Hollis, Eli thought, even after he'd walked out on her. Willing to hear the man out despite all the things he'd done to her. But then, Kasey was usually willing to hear a person out, willing to be more than fair no matter how poorly they'd treated her. He remembered how she used to make excuses for her father's behavior.

He had a bad feeling about this.

Hollis had a golden tongue when he set his mind to it. The gift of gab, some people called it. Gift or not, all Eli knew was that Hollis could talk a wolf into buying a fur coat in the middle of July.

While he, well, he had a habit of getting tongue-tied and not being able to say just the right thing when the time came for persuasive arguments. The right words would come to him *after* the fact, when it no longer mattered.

Eli could feel his stomach tying itself into a hard knot, but there was nothing he could say. Nothing he *would* say. He didn't want Kasey looking at him someday and accusing him of having talked her out of reuniting with her husband.

Husband, Eli thought bitterly. Whether he liked it or not, until the papers were final, Hollis was Kasey's husband.

As for him, he was just the man who'd loved her forever. In silence.

The bad feeling he had grew.

"Where and when?" Hollis asked, his grin widening. "You just name the time and place, Kase, and I'll be there, waiting with baited breath." He watched her for a long moment, his grin fading, his voice growing serious. He lowered it as he said, "I didn't mean to hurt you."

Kasey gave no indication that she'd even heard the last words he'd said. Instead she addressed the question he'd put to her. "I'll let you know."

"I'll be waiting," he promised, then added for good measure, "My fate is entirely in your hands." No doubt feeling himself to be on solid ground, he glanced at Eli and said magnanimously, "You did a good job looking out for her. Thanks."

Eli knew he should just ignore Hollis altogether. He shouldn't let the man get under his skin like this, but he couldn't make himself just stay silent, either. "I didn't do it for you."

Hollis surprised him by quietly acknowledging, "I know."

"Problem?"

The question, mildly put, came from Rick. His manner was nonthreatening as he asked the simple question, but there was no doubt in anyone's mind that Rick could become all business at a moment's notice if necessary.

Finally, Eli spoke up, taking the opportunity to defuse the possibly explosive situation. "No, no problem, Sheriff. Hollis here was just leaving." He looked at his former friend expectantly. "Weren't you, Hollis?"

Hollis had no choice but to nod, confirming Eli's statement. "I just wanted to pay my respects to the happy couple," he said pointedly.

"Then you've got your 'happy couples' confused," Rick informed him in a pseudo-expansive voice. "Alma and Cash are the ones sitting at the head table." Rick nodded over in their direction. "Just follow me, I'll take you to them." It wasn't an invitation but a thinly veiled order. "I'm walking right by them." He eyed the man expectantly, waiting for Hollis to fall into step beside him.

Reluctantly, Hollis finally did.

But just as he left, Hollis looked over his shoulder at Kasey. "I'll see you soon," he promised.

And she knew he intended to. Until they had that conversation that Hollis had alluded to when he'd said they needed to talk, she was certain that he would continue popping up when she least expected it.

Or wanted it.

If she was to have any peace of mind, she had no other choice but to get this over with sooner than later. She'd hear him out and then—

"You're really going to see him?" Eli asked, snapping her back into the immediate present. Eli didn't seem exactly happy about the turn of events.

That made two of them.

"I don't think that I have much of a choice," she told Eli. He probably had no idea how much that bothered her, not to have any options, but instead to have her path cut out for her by someone whose motives were highly suspect.

Eli frowned. He took her response to mean that she *wanted* to see Hollis. *And why shouldn't she?* a voice in his head taunted. Hollis had been her husband, was *still* her husband. And during their marriage, he had managed to throw her equilibrium off so much that logic had no place in her life.

A person just had to reflect on her past. She'd gone against her parents because of Hollis, run off and married Hollis against her parents' expressed wishes.

Had he really expected her to choose him over someone as dynamic, as mesmerizingly compelling as Hollis? That kind of thing only happened in his dreams. He had a sinking feeling that reality had a completely different kind of outcome in store for him.

Kasey turned her brilliant blue eyes on him and said something unexpected. "Unless you don't want me to talk to him."

No, don't talk to him! Don't ever *talk to him. Not one single word, because he'll twist everything around, make himself out to be the victim here. And you'll take him back, warts and all.*

But out loud, all Eli said was, "I have no right to tell you what to do or not to do."

If he had to tell her not to talk to Hollis, well, then it didn't really count, did it? He wanted her to come to that conclusion on her own. He wanted her to cut Hollis off without so much as a prayer. It wouldn't count if he asked her to do it.

The corners of Kasey's mouth curved just a little. The fact that Eli didn't tell her what to do was part of the reason why she loved him the way she did. But even so, a small voice within her questioned what he'd just said.

Didn't he care that Hollis was obviously trying to get her back? Had she been just a pleasant interlude for Eli? Someone to warm his sheets for a while? Didn't he *want* something permanent with her? Was she wrong about him after all?

All these questions and more crowded her mind, making her uncertain about what to expect next when it came to Eli and herself—if there actually *was* such a duo.

Expect nothing. That way, you can't be disappointed.

Kasey could feel the frustration building up inside of her.

For now, she forced herself to push all that aside and go on pretending that they were the same two people who had arrived at the ceremony just a few short hours ago.

As the music started up again, she looked up at Eli pointedly as she held out her arms to him. "We have a dance to finish."

And this might be the last time he got to hold her in his arms, Eli thought.

"So we do," he acknowledged, pulling Kasey to him again. And they danced, each determined to block out everything that threatened to rend their fragile world apart.

The reception ended by degrees rather than by any sort of agreement. Eventually there were only a few people left. The bride and groom, accompanied by a wealth of good wishes, cheers and applause, had driven off in their car some forty minutes ago, in a hurry to begin their honeymoon. The people attending the reception had begun dispersing around then.

Tired, Kasey murmured, "I think it's time to leave."

Eli reluctantly agreed, although he couldn't shake the feeling that once they left here, they would also be leaving something precious behind.

The possibility of a life together.

As if on cue, he saw Hollis approaching them.

Had Kasey's delinquent almost-ex-husband been lying in wait all this time?

Eli glanced at Kasey. If the same thought had occurred to her, she didn't show it. Instead she turned to him just as Hollis came up to her and said, "Would you mind giving us a few minutes, Eli?"

Yes, he minded, minded a hell of a lot. But again, if he voiced his objections, if he had to deliberately place himself in the way, stopping her from talking to Hollis, then what they had—what he *thought* they had— wasn't really there at all.

"I'll go get Wayne," he told her, his voice devoid of any emotion. As he walked away, he told her, "Take as much time as you need."

Kasey stared after him. *To do what? To say no? To say yes?*

More than anything, she wished Eli had said something definitive so she knew how he felt about Hollis's unexpected appearance here. Did Eli *want* her to go with Hollis, or was he hoping she'd tell her ex to get lost?

Well, either way, she would have words with the man. She resigned herself to the confrontation.

The old Kasey would have run from this confrontation, avoiding it like the plague. But the new Kasey had too much respect for herself to behave like some limp dishrag, allowing herself to be used, then discarded, only to be picked up again at will.

"Hi, this too soon to have that talk?" Hollis asked with a grin.

She had visions of wiping that smile off his face. How could she have ever been naive enough to have fallen for this shallow, shallow man? Especially when there had been a man of substance just around the corner for the better part of her life.

"No, it's as good a time as any," she told Hollis. There was no inviting smile on her lips and when he went to kiss them, she turned her head, giving him a mouthful of hair instead. "I said we'd talk. That's not code for kiss, or grope, or anything else, is that understood?"

"Okay." He put up his hands, as if pushing away any further dialogue about his aborted attempt to kiss her. "I get that."

Her eyes narrowed. "Get what?"

"That you're angry. You have every right to be angry," he acknowledged. "I made a huge mistake. I should have never left you," he told her, and he sounded so sincere, she found herself believing him. And then he *really* surprised her by saying, "I should have taken you with me."

She stared at him, stunned. Taking hold of her hand, Hollis continued, making his plea. "Come with me, Kasey. I don't belong in this two-bit, flea-bitten town. I have to be where the action is," he stressed. "I was dying here, but out there, out there is a whole big world, just waiting for us." His eyes fairly glowed as he added, "Just ripe for the picking."

She didn't ask him what that meant, although she had a sneaking suspicion she knew. But there was a far more pressing question to ask him as he spun his grand plans about escaping Forever with her.

"What about Wayne?"

His words coming to a skidding halt, Hollis looked at her blankly. "Who?"

"Wayne," she repeated a bit more firmly. When there appeared to be no further enlightenment on his part, she added, "Your son."

"Oh." It was obvious that not only had he forgotten about the child, he really hadn't even given him any thought. He shrugged. "Well, he can come, too." His mind appeared to race, searching for a way to make this all work out. "We'll get a sitter for him." Problem solved, he continued in a far more enthusiastic voice. "I want to show you things, Kasey. I want to put Las Vegas at your feet."

"Las Vegas," she repeated incredulously. What in heaven's name would she want to do there? She had absolutely no desire to spend any time in a place that revolved around pitting yourself against luck for a monetary outcome.

Hollis took her tone to mean that she needed more input on the subject to be won over. And he was more than prepared.

"Yes. You wouldn't believe the luck I had out there. I won enough money to buy back the ranch if I wanted it," he confided, then smirked. "But then I thought, why? It would only tie me down to this place, and like I said, there's a whole big world out there." He took her hand in his, coaxing her. "What d'you say, Kase? Come with me." It wasn't a request so much as a statement. He expected her to eagerly agree.

She looked at this man who thought he was tempting her. He didn't even know her well enough to understand that what he said held absolutely no allure for her.

Again she couldn't help wondering, what had she ever seen in him? Especially since Eli had always been around, there whenever she needed him. Comparing the two was like comparing fool's gold to the real thing. One's shine didn't go beyond the surface, the other had to be mined before he showed his full worth. His *significant* worth.

"You're right," Kasey acknowledged quietly. "You don't belong here—"

Hollis took her agreement to mean that he'd won. He all but beamed, triumphant. "Oh, Kasey, wait'll you see—"

Kasey cut him off. "I didn't finish," she pointed out sternly. "*You* don't belong here," she stressed. "But I do. For me, this *is* where the action is and I don't have any intentions of ever leaving it."

"Not leave?" Hollis asked, confused and unable to process the very idea that she would turn him down. That she would pick living here over living with him. Hollis looked at the woman he'd come back for as if she had just turned slow-witted on him. "How could you not want to go?"

"Because my life's here," she stated. Didn't he get it? "My son is here. My friends are here—"

"And Eli?" His tone was accusing, contemptuous. "Is he the reason you want to stay?"

If Hollis meant to make her feel guilty, he was out

of luck. It wasn't going to happen. She smiled as she said, "He is a good reason for wanting to stay in Forever, yes," she agreed.

As she watched, Hollis's complexion turned red and his anger erupted. "And that's what you're settling for?" he demanded. "Being with Eli?"

"Being with Eli wouldn't be settling," she informed him coldly. "But for the record, he hasn't asked me to be with him. I just don't want to be with you—here or in Las Vegas. I don't want to be with you in any kind of setting."

Hollis seemed unable to believe her. He had never been turned down before, not by any woman. "You're just saying that because I hurt you when I left."

She had come to view that segment of her life in a completely different light.

"Your leaving me just might have been the kindest thing you ever did for me," Kasey told him. "You forced me to open my eyes, to finally see you the way you were, not the way I wanted you to be. Don't misunderstand," she said quickly, "I don't begrudge you that life you want, Hollis. I just don't want to share it with you."

As Kasey turned to walk away, incensed, Hollis grabbed her roughly by the arm, jerking her around. "You're my wife, Kasey, and you'll do as I say."

Okay, he'd seen enough. Put up with enough. This was the final straw, Eli thought, stepping forward. He'd returned with Wayne in time to see Hollis grabbing Kasey to force her to stay.

Braced for a confrontation, he shifted Wayne to the crook of his left arm, turning his body so that he half shielded the infant.

"Let her go, Hollis," Eli ordered angrily. "You gave

up the right to call her your wife when you abandoned her."

The expression on Hollis's face was absolutely malevolent. "This is none of your business," he shouted angrily at Eli.

"This has *always* been my business," Eli contradicted. "Now I'm not going to tell you again. Let her go, Hollis."

There was pure fury in Hollis's eyes. "Or what?" he challenged, then jeered, "You're a big man, aren't you? Growling out orders. Meanwhile, just look at you! You're hiding behind a damn baby. Think that'll keep you safe?" he demanded, taunting him. "Well, think again, hotshot. You holding a kid in your arms isn't going to stop me from whipping you good," Hollis promised.

Eli didn't bother answering him. At least not verbally.

In less time than it took to think about it, his fisted right hand flew out, making solid contact with what had always been referred to as Hollis's glass jaw.

Hollis never knew what hit him. He dropped to the ground like a stone.

Chapter 15

Stunned, Kasey stared at Hollis, lying in an unconscious, crumpled heap on the ground, then raised her eyes to the man who had delivered the punch.

"Eli?"

She said his name as if she wasn't certain she'd seen what she'd just witnessed. As if she suddenly realized that there were even more hidden facets to this man than she'd already discovered in these past few months.

Kasey forced herself to glance one final time at Hollis, just to make sure he was still breathing. She put her fingers against his neck and found a pulse. It was then that she felt a sense of relief as well as a smattering of triumph. Hollis had finally gotten what was coming to him.

Eli found the expression on Kasey's face completely unfathomable.

Oh, damn, now he'd gone and done it, he thought, frustrated. She would probably feel sorry for Hollis. Kasey had a huge heart and she'd always had a soft spot in it for the underdog.

Eli saw no way to salvage or reverse the situation.

"Sorry," he told her, "but there's just so much I could take."

Eli watched her face intently, watched Kasey slowly nod as she appraised the crumpled figure on the ground again.

A feather would have done it. Or even the slightest summer breeze. Either would have easily knocked him over right after he heard her say, "About time."

Had she really said what he thought he'd heard her say?

"Excuse me?"

She raised her eyes to his. "I said 'about time.'" And then she elaborated, in case he still wasn't getting her meaning. "It's about time you stop letting that walking ego order you around like you were some sort of unpaid lackey of his. Hollis never appreciated you." She came closer to him, a soft smile blooming on her lips. "And I'm ashamed to say, neither did I." She thought of the past couple of months and what he had done for her, how he had made her feel whole. "At least, not completely. Not until you gave me that letter and said it was from Hollis."

He looked at her uncertainly. "I don't—"

"Don't you think I knew that you had written it? That you were just trying to save my feelings?"

"What gave me away?" he asked, then took a guess. "The handwriting?"

"The thoughtfulness. Hollis wouldn't have said that he was at fault. Hollis always found a way to blame everyone else except himself. You were trying to spare my feelings by giving me the words I needed to read. I think that was when I started to fall in love with you," she told him honestly.

Eli said nothing for a minute. And then, still holding a very cooperative Wayne in the crook of his left arm, Eli cupped the back of Kasey's head and kissed her with all the fervor that had suddenly seized every single fiber of his being. He kissed her with all the love he was feeling and instantly sent her heart, not to mention her head, reeling.

And it was exactly *that* moment when everyone still at the reception appeared, drawn by the initial noise. They gathered around them as well as the fallen Hollis.

Sensing their presence, Eli reluctantly pulled his head back, released his hold on Kasey and looked around. His brothers and father had surrounded them, as did Rick, Joe and several other people, including Miss Joan and her husband.

"What are you all staring at?" Eli asked, doing his best not to appear as self-conscious as he felt.

"A late bloomer, apparently," his brother Gabe answered for all of them. He was looking down at Hollis's prone body when he said it.

To underscore his opinion, Gabe began to clap, applauding Eli not just for seizing the moment with Kasey, but predominantly for decking Hollis. Within less than a minute, the sound of his palms meeting one another was echoed by the rest of the remaining guests.

Eli looked at Kasey. "I guess Hollis doesn't have a whole lot of friends around here anymore."

"None that I can see," Miss Joan agreed, raising her voice above the noise. "By the way, Stonestreet's car's parked out front," she told them. "Why don't some of you boys take the man to his vehicle and just put him inside? Maybe he'll take the hint when he wakes up, and drive away from Forever. The town doesn't need some mouthy gambler stirring things up and causing trouble." She turned toward Rick. "Do they, Sheriff?" she asked pointedly.

"No, they surely don't," he agreed heartily. "You heard the lady," he said, addressing Joe and several of the other men around him. "Let's go take the trash out. No reason to leave it lying around and have it ruin a fine wedding," he emphasized.

Within a couple of minutes, Gabe, Rafe, Rick and Joe, the sheriff's brother-in-law, deputy and friend, had each taken an extremity and were just short of dragging the unconscious Hollis out to the front of the house. His flaming red sports car sat just where Miss Joan had said it would be.

The man had no sense of subtlety, Eli thought, looking at the car as he followed behind the men carrying Kasey's ex. Moving around the men, he opened the driver's side door for them, then stepped back. The other men deposited Hollis into his car, draping the unconscious man's arms over his steering wheel and anchoring him there as best they could.

The message was clear: go away.

"That's some haymaker you've got, Eli," Rick commented, dusting off his hands. "Remind me never to be on the receiving end of it."

"No chance of that." Kasey spoke up. She'd followed the others, holding her son in her arms. "It takes a lot to get Eli angry."

"You want to press charges?" Rick asked Eli. He nodded toward the slumped figure in the car. "I could hold him for a few days for disturbing the peace," he offered. "Give you two a chance to get away if you wanted to."

But Eli shook his head. "Nobody's going anywhere, Sheriff."

"You're wrong there," Kasey told him. When he looked at her, obviously waiting for an explanation, she said, "Hollis can't wait to leave this two-bit, flea-bitten town behind. His words, not mine," she clarified when Rick raised a quizzical eyebrow.

"Well, then, by all means, let's oblige him," Rick proposed. "One of you boys do me a favor and drive our former citizen to the edge of town. I'll have Larry follow and he'll drive you back," he promised, referring to his other deputy.

"Sounds good to me," Gabe declared. "I'll do it," he volunteered.

"Guess then the rest of us will be going home," Rick declared, stating the obvious. Stepping back toward Miguel Rodriguez, he shook the man's hand. "Great reception, Mr. Rodriguez. Everyone had a great time."

"Some more than others," Miguel agreed, looking at his youngest son and the woman beside him. "You two are welcome to stay the night if you're too tired to drive back to your place," he offered.

Your place.

It had a nice sound to it, Kasey thought. A nice feel to it, as well. She knew in her heart that she belonged with Eli on his ranch. But it would take words to that effect from Eli before she could even think of settling in.

And, as of yet, he hadn't actually *said* anything about their future together. She'd noticed that he deliberately kept the scope of any conversation they had in the present, never mentioning anything even remotely far ahead.

Was that on purpose or just an oversight? She wished she knew.

"Thanks, Dad, but I think we'll just be going back to the ranch," Eli told his father.

There was no reference to the term his father had used, she noticed. Was that deliberate?

Or...?

You're going to drive yourself crazy. The man stepped up to defend you. He punched Hollis out when he tried to manhandle you. What more do you want?

What she wanted was commitment. The very concept that had frightened her just a few short months ago was now something she coveted.

But hinting at it wasn't her style—and even if it was, pushing the situation might make Eli balk. Men were unpredictable at bottom and maybe his throat would start to close up at the mere thought of settling down. Of committing to one woman. To her. It wasn't exactly unheard of.

One day at a time, Kasey.

"I wasn't going to go with him, you know," she said very quietly some fifteen minutes later as they were driving back to the ranch.

Kasey said the words so softly, for a second he thought he was just imagining her voice and it was just the breeze whistling through the trees.

"What?"

"Hollis." She turned to look at him. "Just before you decked him, he wanted me to leave town with him. I wouldn't have gone." When he made no comment in response to her declaration, she nervously went on talking, not knowing what else to do. "Would you believe that he didn't know who Wayne was?"

Eli looked at her, confused. "He didn't know Wayne was his son?"

This wasn't coming out right. Since when did she have trouble being coherent? Since she had so much riding on it, she thought, answering her own question.

"No, the name," Kasey corrected. "Hollis didn't remember that we named him—that I named him Wayne," she amended. "When he said he wanted me to go away with him and when I asked him what about Wayne, he looked at me as if he didn't know who I was talking about. He never once asked about him or wanted to hold him." She looked at Eli. "You holding Wayne certainly didn't stop him from threatening to hit you." The very thought made her furious.

Kasey's hands were fisted in her lap, just as his had been earlier.

"It all turned out well," Eli said, soothing her. "Hollis is pretty clear now how you feel about leaving and I've got a feeling he won't be bothering you anymore. His ego doesn't like rejection." He wasn't saying anything they both didn't know. "You'll be erased from his memory because you don't fit his cookie-cutter mentality of what a fawning woman should be like around him."

They were home. Eli pulled up in front of the ranch house. Turning the ignition off, he left the key where it was for a moment as he shifted toward her. "Does that bother you, being erased from his mind?"

"Why should it bother me?"

"Well, you love him," Eli answered quietly, treading lightly in this obvious minefield of emotions.

"Lov*ed*," Kasey stressed. "I *loved* him, dumb as that now seems to me. But I guess everyone's allowed one really bad mistake in their lives." And he was hers. "And when you look at the total picture, it wasn't a complete disaster."

As he listened, Eli expected to hear her say something about the nice moments that she and Hollis had had together. Instead, Kasey surprised him. "If I hadn't married Hollis, then I would have never had Wayne." Looking over her shoulder to the backseat, she smiled at the sleeping little boy secured in his infant seat. He'd be outgrowing it soon, she thought fondly. "The best baby in the whole world. Funny how that is, given Hollis's temperament," she commented.

"Well, it's obvious. Wayne takes after his mother," Eli told her.

She could always count on Eli to say something sweet and reaffirming. "Thank you for coming to my rescue back there," she said. She couldn't help smiling at the way that sounded, like bad dialogue from a damsel-in-distress movie.

Eli was never one to take credit if he could help it. "I had no choice," he told her simply.

"Why not?"

"Because" was all he said out loud. *Because I love you,* Eli told her silently. *I've loved you for as long as I can remember.* "He was threatening to take you away," he continued. "And, from the looks of it, you didn't want to go with him."

"What if I had? What if I was willing to just pack up and leave Forever with him? Would you still have punched him out like that?"

He wasn't a man who liked to bare his feelings. But he'd come this far, he might as well go all the way—and besides, he felt he owed it to her. "I would have wanted to, but no, I wouldn't have."

"Why not?" she returned, curious. "Why would you hold back?" If anyone had the right to tap-dance on Hollis's body, it was Eli. Eli who had put up with so much from the self-centered Hollis in the name of friendship.

"Don't you get it yet?" he asked, surprised that she hadn't caught on by now. "I want you to be happy. That's always been my bottom line. I would have wanted you to be happy with me, but if you would rather be with someone else—"

He didn't get a chance to finish. It was extremely difficult to talk when his lips were pressed up against another set. Especially if that other set was also wreaking havoc on his ability to think. He had no choice to do anything except to respond—physically and emotionally—to this passionate outside catalyst that completely stirred him as it effectively stripped his mind.

All he could think of was her.

Of having her, of loving her, of losing himself in her.

"Then you don't want to be with anyone else?" he asked hoarsely when she finally pulled away.

How could he even ask that question after a kiss like that? It had all but singed his eyelashes. "You're an idiot, you know that, don't you?"

"But a lucky one," he pointed out with a wide grin. "A damn lucky one."

He was riding on a crest. It was now or never. He threw down a challenge to himself. Either he asked her now, or he held his peace indefinitely. Maybe even forever.

He decided that indefinitely was more than he could bear.

"Just one thing would make me luckier," he told her.

A ripple of desire danced through her, heating her down to her very core.

She wasn't going to jump to conclusions, Kasey told herself. That would be greedy and she'd already been on the receiving end of so much. He wasn't necessarily talking about what she so passionately wanted him to be talking about.

So, very carefully and treading lightly, she asked, "And that would be...?"

He realized that she was an old-fashioned girl, after all, wanting to hear the words, go through the proper steps. She was an old soul inside of one incredibly well-rounded body.

"If you married me."

There were bells and whistles and banjos, all making wonderful music within her.

"You want me to marry you," she repeated.

"Yes, I do."

She pushed a little further—because she had to know

the truth. "Because it's the right thing to do and people are talking about the 'living arrangement' we have?" Was he just trying to make an honest woman of her, or was there more involved here?

She crossed her fingers.

Eli looked at her, stunned. Since when had other people's opinions ever meant a hill of beans to him? "When do I see people?" he asked. "When do I care about what they say?"

He sounded so defensive, she decided that he meant what he was saying. But that still left her with an unanswered question. "Then why are you asking me to marry you?"

"Best reason in the world," he said, lightly stroking her hair. "Because I love you."

There it was, she thought. The magic. The starbursts, all going off inside of her like a super Fourth of July celebration.

"You love me."

He laughed, shaking his head. "And I'd love you even more if you stopped parroting everything I say," he told her, deadpan. "But yes, I love you," he confirmed. "And when you're ready, I want you to marry me. No pressure," he assured her.

"Maybe I'd like some pressure," she told him, and then she grinned. "And I'd like to get married right away, before you realize what a catch you really are and start to have second thoughts about marrying me."

"That," he told her very seriously, "would never happen."

"How can you be that sure?" she challenged.

"Because those 'first thoughts' I'm having are just too damn sexy to give up."

Her eyes smiled at him. "Stop talking, Eli."

Had he said too much? Made her begin to have doubts? Looking at her more closely, he decided that wasn't the case. Looked as if he was home free. "Why?" he asked, tongue-in-cheek.

"Because I want you to kiss me."

His smile went straight to her heart. "I can do that."

"Then do it."

And he did.

Expertly.

* * * * *

THE COWBOY AND THE BABY

To
Dr. Steve Kang
For Giving Me Hope
That I Could
Wear High Heels Again

Prologue

Cody McCullough didn't like being late.

Ever.

It was a work ethic his big brother Connor had instilled in all of them. Connor had insisted on it that first time he had gathered them all together to tell them that, despite the recent death of their father, they were still going to be a family, still go on living under one roof. Connor had just turned eighteen at the time. That ultimately meant that, as the oldest, Connor was willing to give up his dreams of going away to college in order to become their guardian.

There was no one else to turn to and, besides, Connor had never been one to believe in buck-passing.

Taking care of three younger siblings and a modest cattle ranch was a hell of a responsibility to take on for an eighteen-year-old, so the rest of them—Cody, Cole and Cassidy—figured that the least they could do was not give Connor a hard time about anything, including the rules he saw fit to set down and enforce.

Connor's Code, they had all come to agree, was there for their own good. If they were to survive in a world that could—all too easily—be rough and cruel, they had to pull together.

And in exchange for not giving Connor any grief, their older brother returned the favor. He backed them whenever he could and never made them feel as if they were victims of a cold fate. He taught them that they were the masters of their own destinies. They just had to fight a little harder to forge them.

Even so, when Cody had decided to do something different with his life—change his career path to become a deputy—he was certain that Connor would voice his objections, or at least display a degree of displeasure with his choice.

Instead, Connor had heard him out when he made his case. At the end, he had nodded, saying, "If that's what you want to do, do it. You change your mind, the ranch is always going to be here for you. But if you're going to be a deputy, I want you to be the best damn deputy you can be. I don't want to hear anyone telling me that the sheriff regrets the day he took you on as Alma's replacement."

And Cody had promised to give the job nothing less than his best—which had turned out to be a challenge.

Alma Rodriguez Tyler might have been a small woman, as well as the first female deputy that Forever, Texas, had ever had, but Cody would have been the first one to say that she had left some pretty big boots to fill.

Even so, he had taken to the job like the proverbial

duck to water. Cody discovered that he really loved it. Loved putting on the uniform, the badge. Loved being a deputy the way he hadn't ever really loved being a rancher.

The only part of ranching that *was* near and dear to his heart was the horses. He loved riding, loved becoming one with the animal beneath him. While his other siblings gradually shifted over to getting around in the family truck or the second-hand Jeep they had all chipped in to buy, Cody loved riding. He had ever since he'd been a toddler and his late father, Josh, had picked him up and put him on the back of his first horse, a sleepy-eyed old mare named Libby.

Still, like any young man of twenty-five, Cody had given in to conformity and saved up to buy his own Jeep in the interest of the image he knew he had to project as one of Sheriff Rick Santiago's deputies.

Not that there was all that much for the sheriff's department to do. It wasn't as if Forever, population of a little over five hundred people these days, was exactly a hotbed of either criminal activity or underhanded dealings. There was the occasional argument that escalated to trading blows, and of course there was Miss Elizabeth, an eighty-nine-year-old widow who, from time to time, would be found wandering the streets of Forever, sleepwalking in her nightgown.

For the most part, theirs was a quiet little town. He and the two deputies, Joe Lone Wolf and Gabe Rodriguez, were seen more as friends than as lawmen.

But a man's word was his bond and Cody believed in being at his desk at the beginning of each workday because he was supposed to, not because he was waiting for some minor crime wave to break out so he could jump into action.

As fate would have it, his spirit might have been more than willing to arrive on time, but his Jeep's was not. For some reason, the vehicle had simply refused to turn over when he put his key in the ignition, despite the fact that the town's sole mechanic—thought to be a veritable wizard when it came to machinery—had overhauled it and pronounced it good as new.

Cody knew everything there was to know about horses and absolutely nothing when it came to car engines. After one more futile attempt to rouse the engine, he'd pocketed his key and thrown a saddle on Flint, a golden palomino he had raised from a colt.

A couple of minutes later, he was headed toward Forever at a quick gallop.

Entirely focused on not being late, Cody had almost missed seeing the beat-up pickup truck. The truck, which had definitely seen better days, was pulled over to the far side of the road. And even if he had seen it, it was in such poor condition, he would have just assumed it was abandoned.

Cody had already ridden past it when he thought he heard a scream.

Pulling up Flint's reins, he paused, cocked his head and listened again.

Nothing.

He was just about to chalk it up to either his imagination or the summer wind, which could, at times, make a mournful sound. Cody was on the verge of lightly kicking the palomino's flanks and resuming his journey when he heard it again.

This time there was no doubt in his mind. What he'd

heard was definitely a scream. It was loud, full-bodied and strong enough to not just make his blond hair stand on end, but to send a hard shiver down his spine, as well.

Automatically putting his hand over his holster to assure himself that he had remembered to strap on his weapon before heading out, Cody turned his horse around and galloped right back toward the clearly *not* abandoned pickup truck. Excitement coursed through his body.

Someone was in trouble.

Chapter 1

Oh God, this was such a bad idea. She shouldn't have driven out looking for him in her condition.

"Yeah, like you really had a choice," Devon Bennett mocked herself, sarcasm saturating each word.

Independent to a fault, accustomed to handling everything that came her way, Devon could never have resisted looking for Jack when she woke up to find him gone from the motel room.

At first, she'd thought he'd just gone out to get them breakfast—but he wouldn't have needed to take their suitcase for that. And it was missing, along with her credit cards and all the money out of her purse.

He did leave her the truck. But that wasn't because he'd had an attack of conscience, or even because she was carrying his baby and was due to deliver in about a week or so. Being coldly honest with herself, Devon knew that Jack hadn't taken the truck for one reason and one reason only. The truck was still there, parked right outside of the rundown motel, because Jack couldn't find the keys to it.

He wasn't able to find them because she'd had this uneasy feeling that Jack was having second thoughts about the plans they had laid out for their future. Not knowing what Jack might impulsively decide to do, she had tucked the keys to the truck under her pillow— smack in the center so that even if he did suspect they were there, he would have had to move her in such a way that she was certain to wake up.

Looking back now as she scanned the desolate area—weren't there supposed to be some *people* around this forsaken wilderness?—Devon couldn't have said exactly what had possessed her to hide the keys, but maybe, somewhere deep down, she didn't really trust Jack anymore. Oh, he'd smiled a lot and talked about these grand plans he had for the two of them, promising that everything would be wonderful once they got to Houston.

They'd left Taos, New Mexico, because Jack had come into their small apartment one morning telling her that he'd lined up another job—a much better job— and it was waiting for him in Houston. They'd been together for almost three years and they'd gotten engaged after four pregnancy tests had yielded the same answer: positive.

At the time, she'd thought that finding out she was pregnant would send Jack packing, but Jack surprised her. He stayed.

He'd even looked as if he was happy about it. The baby, the engagement, the promise of a new job—he

made it sound as if all they needed was a new beginning to make everything work out.

She'd had no reason to doubt him.

No reason except perhaps the nagging, sinking feeling in the pit of her stomach—something apart from
morning sickness for a change—warning her that
maybe, just maybe it was too good to be true.

And she had learned a long time ago that if something seemed too good to be true, then it usually wasn't.

"*Usually?* Always. It's always too good to be true,"
Devon retorted, the realization all but tearing her up.

Tears began to gather in her eyes, threatening to
fall, to make her come apart. Devon struggled to hold
herself together. She didn't even know where she was
going, other than just heading somewhere "due east"
because that was the direction they'd been driving in
when they'd pulled up to that sad little motel.

It hadn't been her first choice. She had located an
actually decent hotel that was about ten miles up the
road, but Jack had vetoed it, saying that hotel would eat
into "their" capital.

The only capital Jack was acquainted with was the
first letter to his name. The money was hers—or it had
been before he'd taken it, along with the gold cross her
mother, Amy, had left her and the earrings that might
or might not have been worth something. Whatever actual dollar amount the jewelry was worth, both pieces
had meant the world to her because they were all she
had left from her mother.

But to Jack the jewelry was just something to be converted into cash at his first opportunity.

So he'd left her with her truck and taken everything
else. Because she'd had no money to pay the desk clerk,

she'd been forced to sneak out while dawn was still creeping in. She'd assuaged her conscience by promising herself that she'd find him, that no good, sweet-talking thief—not because she wanted him back, but because she wanted to pay the motel clerk and, more than that, recover her mother's cross and earrings.

But where the hell could he have gotten to?

And where on earth was she?

When she'd tried to pinpoint her location on her smartphone's GPS, Devon could have sworn that if her phone had had actual hands, it would have been scratching its head.

She was in the middle of nowhere—and getting more deeply entrenched.

More tears stung her eyes.

"Serves me right for thinking that just once in my life, things were going to go WELLL! OMIGOD!"

The pain, sudden and sharp and completely unexpected, had come leaping out at her from nowhere.

Devon had been upset and overwrought and paying attention to the road, not to the signals her body was sending her. In her defense, she'd been experiencing strange sensations and odd little pains off and on for a while now.

Scanning her memory bank now, she realized that her lower half had been feeling very, very strange, but then, that could have easily described the way her bottom had been feeling ever since she'd found that she was pregnant.

Focused on hunting Jack down, she'd had no reason to believe that this "strange" feeling was any different than all the other strange feelings she'd been experiencing all along.

Except that it *was* different.

She'd never quite had this pain before. Never felt like two giant hands had each taken hold of one of her legs and were now about to make a wish just before they pulled them apart in two opposite directions.

"Can't you wait, Michael?" she begged, addressing her very swollen abdomen by the name she had selected. Not that she knew the baby's gender. She'd just assumed that it was male because it had been giving her such a hard time from the moment she'd conceived him. "You're not supposed to be here yet and, in case you haven't noticed, we're in the middle of nowhere. I can't do this alone. Sorry to disappoint you, little boy, but I am *not* the pioneer type.

"There, you have had the worst of it," she told her unborn son as the pain settled down a little. "Except that your father's a rat, but we'll talk about that later. Like in a week and a half," she stressed. "*Please* wait a week and a half."

She went on reasoning with the baby that seemed intent on kicking its way out now. "Please, please, PLEEEASE!" she shrieked, unable to contain the pain.

Sweat was pouring down from her brow and her tears were mingling with it, pooling along the hollow of her throat.

Devon couldn't believe that this was actually happening, that she was going to die in the middle of nowhere, giving birth.

"This is *not* happening now," she yelled at her stomach. "Do you hear me? I'm your mother and I forbid you to come out!"

Another scream tore from her lips, taking a tremendous toll on her body. She was beginning to feel as if she was hallucinating.

"You're not going to listen, are you?" she asked weakly. A deep, frustrated sigh emerged from the center of her very core. "Not even born and you're already a typical male."

The next wave of pain completely stole her breath away, making her pant.

Making her panic.

"No, no panicking. Panicking is bad," she admonished herself, trying desperately to exercise some measure of control, putting mind over matter.

But it wasn't helping.

Nothing was helping. She was coming apart at the seams, literally, and nobody would ever know what had happened to her.

The word throbbed in her brain.

Nobody.

The few friends she had all thought that she'd run off with Jack to Texas. They'd never know that she died before she got to her destination.

And she had no family. An only child, she'd lost her father when she was seven and her mother when she was a senior in high school.

So there was no one to worry about her.

No one cared.

That was probably why she'd been such an easy target for Jack. She'd always thought of herself as an independent soul, but the truth of it was she was lonely. She'd wanted to matter to someone, just *one* someone. And Jack had pretended that she mattered to him.

Tall, dark and handsome with an easy grin, Jack had drifted into her life and then taken her along for the ride.

She'd been a total fool, Devon thought disparagingly. Perspiration was beginning to soak through her clothing. She didn't know if the sun was hot, or if only she was. The end result was the same. Her clothes were damp.

"I thought your daddy loved me. Turns out he loved my meager little savings account. But we'll find him, you and I. We'll catch up to him and force him to give back all that money because you're going to need diapers—and food.

"Who am I kidding?" she said despondently. "We're not getting out of here alive. I'm sorry, Michael. Sorry to have done this to you. Sorry to have saddled you with a daddy who's a deadbeat. SORRYYYY!"

The pain was so bad that she'd almost bitten right through her bottom lip this time around.

She was clutching and clawing at anything she could find within reach. The pain was growing stronger, threatening to swallow her up completely. As it was, she was on the verge of passing out.

This was more than she could endure.

This was—

"Ma'am?"

Devon screamed again, this time in fear. A moment ago, there'd been no one here, not even a prairie dog. Now someone—or more accurately, some*thing*—was leaning in through her rolled-down truck window, peering in and apparently talking to her.

"Oh God, now I'm seeing things," she cried, doing her best to disappear into the cracked seat cushion. "Talking horses. Maybe I've already died."

Belatedly, Cody realized that the woman in the cab of the truck was looking at Flint. She sounded as if she was delirious.

Dismounting, he tied the horse's reins to the back

of the vehicle and returned to the open window. He looked in.

The woman was drenched and looked almost wild-eyed. "Are you alone?" Cody asked her.

"Not a horse, an angel," Devon realized out loud. The next moment, she closed her eyes tight as she felt yet another huge contraction coming. This one had all the signs of being even bigger than the last. "A hunky angel," she said to herself. "This is Texas, what did I EXPECCTTT?"

For a second, Cody could only stare at her in complete awe. Even wracked with pain, the dark-haired woman was beautiful. But he'd never seen a woman *this* pregnant before. She looked as if she was just about to pop at any moment.

"No disrespect, lady," he began politely, really wishing someone else was with him right now—Cassidy, for instance.

Women related to each other at a time like this. Or maybe Connor. Nothing rattled Connor. He could handle anything. Still, wishing didn't change anything. Cody was the only other human being out here and he was going to handle this.

He put a sympathetic expression on his face. "But what are you doing out here by yourself in your condition?"

She had no idea what possessed her. She didn't even remember doing it, but, suddenly, Devon found herself grabbing the front of the inquisitive angel's shirt and yanking on it with all the strength she had. She yanked on it so hard that she almost dragged him right in through the window.

"DYING!" she yelled back.

"So you *are* having contractions?" the cowboy asked.

Great, a Rhodes scholar. "What…gave it…away?" she panted, desperately trying to get away from the pain or at least ahead of it. She failed. It insisted on following her.

Cody ignored the woman's sarcastic comeback. "How far apart are your contractions?" he asked.

Devon was arching in her seat. No one had ever said it was going to hurt this badly. "Not…far… ENOUGH!"

Cody looked out into the horizon, in the direction he'd been riding when he'd heard her screams. Forever was about five, maybe seven, miles away.

"There's a clinic in town," he told her. "I can get you there fast."

But all she could do was shake her head—violently— from side to side. He'd never get her there in time. Besides, the idea of movement made everything worse.

"No…time," she panted. "Baby…coming… NOOOW-WWW!"

That was what he was afraid of.

Mentally, Cody rolled up his sleeves. Connor always insisted that they face all their challenges head-on, not hide behind excuses or shirk their responsibilities. This woman obviously needed him.

Whether he liked it or not, it was just as simple as that. He took a deep, fortifying breath.

"Okay, then," Cody told her. "Let's do this."

Maybe he *was* better than an angel, Devon thought. "You're…a…doctor?" she asked, digging her nails in the cab's seat again, bracing herself for what she now knew was coming.

"No," Cody answered honestly, "but I helped birth

a few calves on the ranch before I became a sheriff's deputy."

Terrific, he was a cowboy. Just her luck. "I'm... having...a... BABYYY," she cried, arching again, "not...a... CAAALF!"

Cody did his best to give her a confident smile. "Same difference," he assured her.

No, it wasn't, she thought. Not by a long shot. "I... am...in...so...much... TROUBLE!" Devon screamed, all but biting a hole in her lip.

"I know this is scary," he told her.

"You...don't...know...the... HALF... OF... IT!" she retorted, trying her best not to give way to hysteria as she dug her nails into his forearm.

He did what he could to comfort her. "I think I can guess," he told her, then began to introduce himself. "My name is Cody, and I'll be delivering your baby today," he ended with a warm smile.

At this point, Devon was no longer worrying about whether or not she was hallucinating. If this hallucination could help her get rid of this incredible piercing pain she was experiencing through her lower half, then she was all for it.

"PLEEEEASE!" she all but begged.

"What's your name?" Cody asked as he carefully climbed into the truck's cab, coming in from the passenger side. He gently shifted her so that she wasn't behind the steering wheel anymore.

What difference did her name make? "Are...you... filling...out...a...form?" Devon cried in disbelief.

"Just thought it'd be easier for both of us if I knew your name before I got personal," he replied.

She'd thought that she was way past embarrassment.

This was another low. Devon closed her eyes. "Oh… Lord…"

But the pain ramped up, becoming so intense that she was quickly at the point where she would do anything to get beyond it. "DEVON! MY NAME'S DEVON!"

"Nice to meet you, Devon." He braced himself for what he was about to say and do. "I'm going to have to have to lift up your skirt."

She knew that. He didn't have to narrate his actions, she thought in mounting agitation. She just wanted this to be over. If this baby wasn't coming out soon, Devon was certain that she was going to die out here in the middle of nowhere.

"Say…that…to…all…the…girls?" she managed to get out without screaming at him.

"Just the pregnant ones I find in abandoned trucks on the side of the road," he said dryly.

Feeling somewhat awkward about it, Cody slipped the woman's underwear off, all the while telling himself that this was nothing personal, that he had to do it in order to help her bring this baby into the world.

As he drew the material off her legs, he glanced at the hand that was clutching at him. It was the woman's left hand and he saw that there was a ring on it. Not a wedding ring, but a rather tiny engagement ring. At least, he assumed that's what it was. The stone at the center was missing.

He couldn't help wondering if the baby's father was just temporarily missing from this scene—or if there was more to the story than that.

It was a story that was going to have to wait for another day, Cody told himself. From what he saw, Devon appeared to be completely dilated and ready to become a mother.

"You're going to have to bear down and start pushing now," he told her.

She didn't answer him. And then he realized why. As he saw the perspiration popping out all along her brow, she ground out a bloodcurdling noise.

Cody saw that she was already complying with his instructions.

Chapter 2

Devon's face had turned a bright shade of red. In Cody's estimation, she was pushing too hard and too long. She had to take a break. Otherwise he had a feeling that she was going to rupture something.

"Okay, now rest," he told her. She didn't seem to hear him. Her eyes were screwed shut and her face was growing even redder. "Stop pushing!" Cody ordered more loudly.

Worn-out, Devon fell back against the seat, her hair damp and plastered against her brow. She was panting really hard.

"You...tell...the...cow...that...too?" she gasped.

Devon couldn't remember *ever* feeling this exhausted. She'd pushed so hard, she was seeing spots dancing before her eyes.

"No. I saw this on a medical drama on TV," he confessed. It was the summer he'd broken his leg and was laid up with nothing else to do. He'd picked up a lot of miscellaneous information that came in handy at the oddest times. Like now.

"Better…and…better," Devon retorted. This would have been funny if she wasn't so scared and in so much pain.

The next second, she went rigid again as another scream pierced the air. Without waiting for him to say anything, she began to bear down again.

Cody knew better than to interfere unless it was absolutely necessary, so he counted the seconds off out loud.

When she'd gone past the limit, he ordered, "Stop!"

This creature inside her—she'd ceased thinking of it as a baby—had taken charge of her body and she couldn't control the urge to push it out.

"I… CAN'T!"

"Breathe through your mouth." When she didn't seem to hear him, Cody put his hands on either side of her face and made her look at him. "Listen to me, unless you want to start possibly hemorrhaging, *breathe through your mouth*!" he ordered. "Like this."

And he proceeded to show her, recalling what he'd seen on that program he'd watched during his summer of forced confinement.

He could only pray he got it right.

Cody saw anger in the woman's eyes. Anger mingled with fear, but then she began to do what he'd told her. Blowing air out of her mouth, she stopped pushing for a moment.

And then he felt her growing rigid again. Her whole body looked as if it was in the throes of another contraction.

"Another one?" he asked.

It was a rhetorical question, but she answered anyway. "YES!" she hissed as she dug deep into her core to find the energy to expel this child out of her body once and for all.

"I see the head!" Cody declared in wonder as he tried his best to encourage her.

"Isn't…there…any…more?" she cried sharply.

She was going to die like this, she was certain of it. She could feel herself growing weaker and weaker as she seemed to float in and out of her head.

"There's more," he assured her. "There's more!" This time he said it because she was pushing again. Pushing and screaming. "You're almost there," he encouraged.

"AAAARRRGGGHHH!"

The word shattered the atmosphere as it accompanied the emergence of the infant who was sliding out of her body.

Euphoric, exhausted and close to delirious, Devon panted hard, trying to regain her breath. Trying to hear something beyond the sound of her heart, which was pounding like mad.

"He's not…crying," Devon said, panicking. "Why isn't…my…baby…crying?"

Cody didn't answer her. He was too busy trying to get the tiny human being he was holding in his arms to do just that.

Turning the infant over so that it was facing the ground, Cody patted the baby's back, then turned it over again to check its airway.

Quickly clearing it with his forefinger, he held the baby in one arm while unbuttoning his shirt with the other.

Devon attempted to use her elbows to prop herself up so she could see what was going on. She didn't have enough strength left to manage it.

"What—what are you doing?" Devon demanded weakly. Why was this man getting undressed? Fresh fear vibrated through her.

Parting the tan deputy shirt, Cody pressed the baby against his bare skin, all the while still massaging the tiny back.

A tiny whimper just barely creased the air. And then there was a cry. An indignant, lusty cry, followed by another one.

Cody breathed a sigh of relief. His own heart was racing in triumph and elation.

"She's going to be all right!" he declared.

Confusion slipped over Devon's face. "She?" Devon questioned, unable to process the deputy's words for a moment.

Shrugging out of his shirt one sleeve at a time, he passed the infant from one arm to the other as he did it. Once he had the shirt off, he wrapped the material around the newborn.

"Your baby's a girl," he told Devon. She was also the first infant he'd delivered and he was filled with a warm glow he couldn't begin to describe.

"Michael's a girl?" Devon asked, confused and happy at the same time. It was over. The baby was out and it was over! She realized that she was crying again.

"You might want to think about changing that name," Cody advised. Looking down at the infant, he smiled. "This is your mama," he told the baby as he transferred her into Devon's arms.

Her head spinning, feeling like someone in a dream,

Devon carefully accepted the swaddled infant into her arms. She felt completely drained as she held the infant against her.

She did her best to smile at her daughter. "Hi, baby."

Out of the corner of her eye, Devon thought she saw the man who had come to her rescue pull a knife out of the sheath within his boot. A wave of new fear shimmied through her.

"What are you going to do?" she asked in a horrified whisper, unable to gather the strength for anything louder.

Having struck a match—he always kept a book of matches in his pocket, although he rarely used them—Cody was passing the blade of his knife back and forth over the flame.

"The umbilical cord is still attached," he told her with an easy smile. "I figure it might get in the way after a bit."

Even though it was hard for her to focus, Devon was watching his every move. Her arms weakly tightened around the baby. "Will it hurt?"

"Can't really say for sure," Cody told her honestly, "but I don't think so." He looked up at her. "Got any alcohol in the glove compartment?"

Was he looking to toast the successful birth? Now? Had she not felt so exhausted, she might have seriously considered trying to get out of the truck with her baby.

"No," she cried.

"Too bad." He carefully lifted the umbilical cord at the baby's end. "It might have been good to disinfect the area, but this should be okay for now."

And then, just like that, before she could ask Cody when he was going to do it—he'd separated the infant from the cord. She felt the remainder, no longer of any use, being expelled out of her own body.

Sweating profusely, Devon didn't realize that she had taken in a sharp breath until she released it.

"That's it?" she asked.

Cody nodded. "As far as I know."

The reality of the situation and what he had just miraculously been a part of finally hit him. It took Cody a moment to get his breath back. The tiny infant nestled in the crook of Devon's arm looked at peace, as if she had always been a part of the scene rather than just newly arrived.

"How are you feeling?" Cody asked Devon, concerned. The color seemed to be draining out of her.

"Woozy," she answered. "Wonderful, but really, really light-headed."

"Well, you did good," he told her. Very carefully, he reached out and, ever so lightly, stroked the baby's downy head. "Feels like peach fuzz," he commented quietly with a warm smile.

"It'll grow," Devon told him, struggling not to slur. "My mom said… I was bald until I…was one, now it grows like…crazy."

She sounded exhausted. He didn't blame her. He was feeling a little depleted himself. He just had one more question for her. "What are you going to call her?" he asked.

She barely heard him at first, and then his words replayed themselves in his head.

"I don't know," Devon answered honestly. "I was… really sure I was having…a boy, so all I have…are… boys' names."

A thought hit him. It seemed almost like fate, he

thought. "My mom's name was Layla. I always thought that was a pretty name."

"Layla," Devon repeated weakly. "You're…right… It…is…pretty." She looked down at the baby in her arms. Her daughter was looking up at her with wide, wide blue eyes. A peacefulness was descending over Devon. Her mind began to drift, but she did her best to focus. "Layla," she repeated again to see if the name fit. It seemed to.

"You like that?" The infant made a tiny noise. It wasn't in response, but Devon took it that way. She glanced up at the man who had been there for her when he could have just kept going. "Looks…like it's…unanimous."

"What were you doing out here by yourself?" he asked. If he'd been in her place, he wouldn't have been driving around in the middle of nowhere. Where was the man who belonged to that ring? To that baby?

"Looking…for a cowboy…to deliver…my baby," she told him weakly.

She wasn't going to tell him, he thought. Well, that was her business, he supposed. He could respect that. Cody was just glad that he had been running late this morning. If his Jeep hadn't decided to die, who knew what might have happened to the pregnant woman?

He glanced at her face. She appeared frighteningly pale. "You need to be checked out by a doctor," he told her. He would have suggested it even if she looked fine, but, at the moment, she didn't.

"You have…one of those…with you, too? In… your…pocket?" He was so resourceful, she thought, she wouldn't have put it past him. But he'd have to have big pockets…

"Not with me," he said wryly. "But in town, we do.

We've got two of them, actually. They're both at the clinic," he told her. "Along with a couple of nurses. All really top-notch. They're certainly not in it for the money." He glanced over to the backseat. "Why don't I make you and Layla more comfortable in the backseat? There's more room to lie down there. And then I'll drive your truck into town."

Even if she'd wanted to protest, she didn't have the strength to do so. Devon felt way too tired.

"Whatever…you…say."

It was the last thing she recalled saying to the man who had come to her aid. In the next moment, everything suddenly and dramatically turned pitch-black.

She lost her hold on the world.

"Ma'am?" Cody asked uncertainly when he saw that she had shut her eyes. He got no response. "Devon?" he questioned more urgently, seeing her head nod to one side.

The next second, he quickly took the baby from her. Devon's hold had gone lax. The baby would have fallen if he hadn't moved fast.

"Damn," he mumbled. "New plan, Layla. We buckle your mom in where she is in the front seat and I drive into town, holding you in one arm. That okay with you?" He added under his breath, "Good thing Connor was always on us to multitask."

Getting out of the cab with the baby in his arms, Cody came around to the other side of the passenger seat to secure the seat belt as best he could around the unconscious woman.

He continued to talk to the baby, keeping his voice at a soothing level, the way he did when he worked with spooked horses or cattle.

"Connor's my big brother. You'd like him. He's kind of bossy, but he had to be. He stuck around to raise my brother and sister and me when our dad died. Our mom died some years before that. Old Connor, he always came through." As he talked, he found that the sound of his voice was not just keeping the baby calm, but it was helping to do the same for him.

This wasn't exactly something that was covered in his deputy's manual. He was fairly certain that as far as his duties went, this was all brand-new ground he was crossing.

Slipping the metal tongue into the seat belt receptacle, he secured it. When he looked to make sure it would hold, that was when he became aware of the blood. There was a great deal more of it than there had been just a few minutes ago when Devon was struggling to push out her daughter.

Adrenaline spiked all through his veins. This was serious. *Really* serious.

He had to get this woman a doctor and fast or the baby in his arms was going to be an orphan before the sun set.

It took him a split second to make another decision. Running around to the rear of the truck, still holding the baby, Cody untied his horse. If he drove into town at a normal pace, the horse could easily keep up. But this was now a race for time. He intended to go as fast as he could. If still attached, the horse would be dragged in the truck's wake.

He spared the stallion one look and shouted a command. "Follow the truck, Flint. Follow the truck! Town, Flint. Town."

Telling his stallion the destination—a command he'd

given often enough, except then it had been from the vantage point of a saddle astride the horse's back—he raced around to the driver's side and got in.

He didn't expect Flint to keep up, but, with luck, the horse would follow and reach town sometime after he did. If the horse didn't reach town by the time Cody would be able to look around for him, at least he knew that Flint wouldn't just run off aimlessly. Cody had spent long hours training the stallion. He was completely confident that, since the terrain was familiar to both of them, the horse would eventually find its way to Forever.

Climbing into the cab, still holding on to the baby who was now whimpering, Cody awkwardly buckled himself in. A quick check told him that, mercifully, Devon had left the keys in the ignition.

He started the truck, stepped on the gas and they were off.

Driving with one hand while holding the baby against him with his free arm proved to be tricky and definitely not something Cody had ever even *remotely* prepared for. But he didn't have the luxury of doubting that he was up to it or of looking around for an alternative method. There was no time for any of that. A woman's life—Layla's mother's life—depended on him being able to handle both the emergency and the baby.

Cody felt like he was running out of time.

He spared Devon an apprehensive glance. She was still unconscious, but he did see her chest rising and falling. At least she was still breathing.

"You hang in there, you hear me?" he ordered Devon. How could he have missed that she was still bleeding? How could he not have seen all that blood soaking through her dress? he upbraided himself. "I've never lost a mother after she gave birth to her calf and I sure as hell don't intend to start with you."

Cody stepped down harder on the gas. He could see Flint trying to keep up in the rearview mirror, but the stallion was falling behind.

"I've got a feeling that you're all this little girl has, so don't even think of checking out. You're going to live, you understand? You're going to live! We're almost there," he told her, saying anything and everything that came into his head.

If he stopped talking, he was sure he was going to lose Devon.

"The town's just over that hill. It's not all that much to look at, but Forever's got really good people. People who take you in and look out for you. They don't care what your story is—although Miss Joan'll ask. Miss Joan, that's the woman who runs the diner. She's like a mother to all of us. Acts all grumpy, but she's got a heart as big as the state. She'll make sure you're warm and fed—she did with the four of us after our dad died. Did it so that it didn't seem like charity because Connor, he wouldn't have accepted any charity. *Ever*," Cody said. "He's way too proud. But Miss Joan, she always found a way to get around that. She'll just melt when she sees this baby of yours, even if she tries not to show it. And she'll give you advice you'll think you don't need—but you will."

The road ahead was wide open and empty. One hand clutching the steering wheel, he allowed himself to look in Devon's direction.

She was still unconscious. Her head was moving ever so slightly because of the vibrations caused by the increased speed.

Fear clawed at him. Fear that he wasn't going to make it to the clinic in time.

"You're not going to die, you hear me?" he told her. "I've never filled out a death report because of someone dying on my watch and I'm not going to start now. They're too long. They've got to be at least nine, ten pages long. You can't put me through that after I helped to deliver your baby, you hear me?"

Pushing down on the accelerator as hard as he could, he saw the outskirts of Forever rushing closer to him. It was just up ahead, within reach.

And then he breeched the city limits.

Keeping an eye out for any pedestrians and other cars, both of which were scarce, Cody tore straight through the center of Forever. The next moment, he was passing the town square, where the annual Christmas tree was always displayed.

Veering to the right and then to left, he didn't slow down until he reached his destination.

He practically put his foot through the floor as he pushed down on the brake as hard as he could.

The tires screeched in high-pitched protest as they came to a halt inches away from the front of the clinic.

Chapter 3

As usual, the waiting room of Forever's lone medical clinic was very close to filled. It was the only available medical facility for fifty miles and the people of Forever were grateful for that. It wasn't all that long ago that the clinic had stood empty, its last physician having moved away thirty years ago. There was something comforting about having someone to turn to because they felt ill, or just because a husband or wife had nagged them into availing themselves of an annual—or bi-annual—exam.

Startled by the combined, unnerving sound of screeching tires and squealing brakes, everyone in the clinic's waiting room turned in unison toward the noise. As a rule, Forever was thought of by its residents as a sleepy little town that no one outside of the area ever really noticed and where nothing of consequence ever happened.

That meant that no one, either out of boredom or a sense of competitiveness, engaged in car races or harrowing displays of one-upmanship.

So when the teeth-jarring noise pierced the morning air, every patient within the waiting room, as well as the one nurse manning the desk, Debi White Eagle, instantly glanced in the direction of the bay window. The window looked out toward the front of the clinic.

"What the hell was that?"

Rancher Steven Hollis jumped to his feet, verbalizing what everyone else in the room was thinking.

The question didn't go unanswered for more than a couple of quick beats. Almost immediately thereafter, the roomful of patients witnessed what all would have readily agreed was a very unlikely sight: a bare-chested Deputy Cody McCullough bursting into the clinic with what appeared to be a newborn baby in his arms. The baby was wrapped in his uniform shirt.

Debi, a surgical nurse by vocation as well as one of the most recent additions to Forever's population, vacated her desk and rushed over to Cody.

"What happened?" she asked.

Cody quickly transferred Layla into her arms. "The baby's mother is in the truck. She's lost a lot of blood and I need help."

"Holly!" Debi yelled over her shoulder toward the rear of the clinic. "We need a doctor out here, STAT!"

It was an order she was accustomed to issuing when she worked at the hospital in Chicago. Here, however, the word left more than one of the patients looking at the others in bewilderment.

Grabbing the fresh lab coat she'd brought in for one of the doctors, Debi quickly removed Cody's shirt from around the tiny body and rewrapped the newborn in the lab coat. Acting in the interest of practicality, not to mention cleanliness, she figured the doctor would forgive her.

"Here," she said, giving Cody back his shirt. "You don't want to be out of uniform, Deputy."

With that, Debi immediately turned toward the most maternal patient available to her, Anita Moretti, who had five children and a brood of grandchildren of her own. "Anita, hold the baby," she requested, then looked at Cody. "Where's the mother?"

"Out here." He threw the words over his shoulder as, shrugging back into his shirt, he ran outside, secretly almost afraid of what he would see once he opened the truck's passenger door.

"Where is she?"

The question came from Dan Davenport, the doctor who had initially reopened the clinic and who was currently in charge of it as well as the care of the citizens of Forever.

Cody was already at the truck. He threw open the passenger door and unbuckled the seat belt that was the only thing holding Devon in place and semiupright.

As carefully as he could, he lifted Devon out of the vehicle. The lower half of her dress was soaked with her blood.

Dan attempted to take the unconscious woman from him, but Cody shook his head. He wasn't about to let her go. "No, I've got her."

"This way," Dan said needlessly as he and Debi went back into the clinic ahead of Cody. "What happened?" Dan asked. "Did you find her this way?"

More than a dozen set of eyes looked in their direction as Cody carried the woman in.

"No, she was conscious and screaming when I found her," Cody answered, giving no indication that he even saw the other people in the room.

"Was she still in labor or had she given birth already?" Dan asked, leading the way to the room where he and his partner, Dr. Alisha Cordell-Murphy, performed both the simple surgeries and the ones that were classified as emergencies.

"As far as I could see, she had just started," Cody told him, aware that every word was being greedily absorbed by all the people in the waiting room. "I tried to help her. When she gave birth, I thought she'd be okay," Cody went on. "I didn't realize…" His voice drifted off helplessly.

It was clear to Dan by Cody's tone that he felt guilty that the situation had somehow devolved to this point.

"Not your fault," Dan told him, indicating the freshly prepared gurney in the room. "People don't realize that there are a lot of unforeseeable elements that can go wrong as a baby's being born."

"What have we got here?" Alisha Cordell-Murphy asked, peering into the room in response to Holly's summons. Her eyes widened when she saw the unconscious woman. "Omigod, who is she?" she asked, looking from Dan to the man who was covered in the woman's blood. She had only been in Forever a little over a year now, but she was acquainted—at least by sight—with everyone who lived within the area. This one was definitely not anyone she knew.

"Cody found her and brought her in," Dan answered.

Cody gave her the highlights. "Her truck was pulled over on the side of the road. I wouldn't have even seen it if she hadn't screamed," he confessed.

"I need plasma," Dan declared. "It looks like she's lost more blood than she can afford to."

Debi, who had come into the room with them, was cutting away the woman's clothing, preparing to put a sterile gown on her. Holly, who had already brought in the plasma, was now wordlessly preparing what she assumed the doctors were going to need to stop the hemorrhaging as well as to get a transfusion going.

Cody took a step back, and then another, giving everyone else there room to work. He felt as if he was just in the way.

"I'll just wait outside," he said to no one in particular as he took another step back.

Dan looked up, sparing him a fraction of a moment. "Don't go too far away. I've got a few more questions you might be able to answer."

"I don't know more than I just told you, but sure, I'll just be in the waiting room," Cody told the doctor, but he knew he was talking to himself. Everyone else in the room was busy, doing their best to try to save the woman's life.

Concerned and more than a little agitated, Cody slipped out.

The minute he was back in the waiting room, a barrage of questions rose all around him, coming from all different directions.

"You know her?"

"Where'd you find her?"

"Is this her baby?"

"Where's the father?"

There were more, all mingling with one another until it was just a huge wall of sound.

"Everyone, hush," Anita Moretti scolded, raising

her voice to be heard above the rest. She was still holding the baby and rocking her as she patted the baby's bottom, doing her best to soothe the infant the way she had with each one of her children and grandchildren in turn. "Can't you people see that he's been through a lot, too?" Turning toward Cody, Mrs. Moretti smiled at him, the perennial, protective mother. "Don't pay them any mind, Cody. They're just looking for something exciting to talk about over dinner tonight. You don't have to say anything if you don't want to."

"There's not much to talk about," Cody told her, taking a seat and glancing around at the others. He was grateful for the woman's concern, but he was also very familiar with and understood a small-town mentality, especially since he'd become one of Sheriff Rick Santiago's deputies. "I was running late and only noticed the truck on the side of the road when I heard screams coming from it."

"She was on the side of the road?" Wade Hollister, one of the patients, asked.

Cody humored the man, despite the fact that he felt the answer was self-evident. "Well, she was in labor so I don't think she really felt like she was able to do any driving."

Rusty Saunders scratched his head. "Hell, what was she doing out there in her condition, anyway?"

Cody laughed quietly as he eased Layla out of Mrs. Moretti's arms. The woman looked at him skeptically, and then smiled and surrendered her precious package.

"I didn't get a chance to ask her," he told Rusty. "I was kind of busy at the time. We both were."

To underscore his point, he smiled at the baby in his arms.

"You delivered that?" Nathan McLane asked Cody. He was as close as possible to a permanent occupant at the Murphy brothers' saloon. His weathered expression was creased with awe.

Cody had never been one to embellish on a story or give himself credit if he could avoid it. He shrugged now. "I was just there to catch her. She more or less delivered herself," he told Nathan and the rest of the waiting-room occupants.

Travis Wakefield, ever the practical man, was obviously trying to work out the logistics to Cody's story. He'd gone to the window to look again at the truck Cody had driven over.

"You leave your truck back there?" he asked. "'Cause the one out there sure isn't yours."

That was when Cody suddenly remembered. He looked up. "My horse."

"What about Flint?" Red Yakima asked, getting up and moving closer to Cody.

Cody had risen to his feet as well and now walked over to the bay window, scanning as much of the area as he could make out from his present vantage point. Flint was nowhere in sight.

"I couldn't tie him to the back of the truck because I had to drive fast," he told Red. "I told him to follow me."

"You 'told' him to follow," Rosie Ortiz, one of the occupants in the waiting room, repeated skeptically. "And what, he said, 'Sure'?"

"Horses are smarter than most people," Red tonelessly informed the woman. He turned his attention back to Cody. "You want me to go out and see if I can find him for you?" the man offered.

Cody turned the matter over in his head. He could

either take the man up on his offer or turn the infant back over to Mrs. Moretti—and he did want to hang around to make sure Devon pulled through. There was a chance that she might not, although he really didn't want to entertain that idea for the baby's sake.

He had no idea why, but he felt that if he remained here, she wouldn't die. He knew he was being superstitious, but everyone around here had some superstition they clung to. His was that if he walked out, the door would be left open for bad things to transpire.

Cody looked at the weathered ranch hand he had known for most of his life. "I'd appreciate that, Red."

"Don't mention it," the man told him, waving a dismissive hand. "I'll stop at the sheriff's office and tell them you didn't fall into a ditch or off the side of the cliff, put Rick's mind at ease," Red added matter-of-factly.

"I owe you."

Red smiled for the first time. "Hey, buy me a beer next time we're at the saloon together and we'll call it even."

"You got it," Cody agreed, although in his opinion it didn't really even begin to repay the man for taking the trouble to track Flint down.

Red walked out of the clinic.

Less than a minute later, Holly came out, an apologetic expression on her face. She looked around the waiting room at the patients.

"It's going to be a while, I'm afraid," she told them. Braced for complaints, she was surprised when none were voiced. "The doctors have got their hands full. Your names are all on the sign-in sheet. If you'd like to come back tomorrow, you'll be seen in the order that you arrived today," she said, once again looking around the room, waiting for some sort of descent or grumbling.

"How long is 'a while'?" Oral Hanson wanted to know, obviously weighing his options.

Holly answered honestly. "At least a couple of hours." Honesty forced her to add, "Maybe more."

The man shrugged his wide shoulder. "Got nothin' I'm doing anyway, not since my boys took over the ranch. Seems they're always telling me to 'go take a load off' anyway, so I might as well do that and stay put." Smiling at the baby in Cody's arms, he added, "I'd like to find out if the little one's mama pulls through."

Most of the other patients were not of the same mind as Oral. They had busy lives to get back to, so they decided to leave the clinic and return the next day as suggested.

But a few, including Mrs. Moretti, remained. When Cody looked at the older woman quizzically, Mrs. Moretti said, "I thought maybe I'd stick around, give you a little help if you need it. You'll want to have your hands free if they call you back in there." Lowering her voice, she added, "You know, just in case."

It was obvious to Cody that Mrs. Moretti had already convinced herself that there was more going on between him and the woman he'd found today.

Anita Moretti wasn't a gossip by any stretch of the imagination, but the woman did enjoy a good story, both hearing one and, occasionally, passing one along. He couldn't fault her for being human, even though what he knew she was thinking was entirely a fabrication.

And Cody knew better than to protest or try to set the woman straight. Saying anything to the contrary would only get him more deeply entrenched. Mrs. Moretti would go on believing what she chose to believe.

Connor had always maintained that when you lost control of the situation, the best thing to do was to politely say "thank you" and then back away as quickly as possible.

"I appreciate that, Mrs. Moretti," Cody told the woman.

Because he was agitated and didn't know what to do with himself, Cody began to walk the floor. Layla seemed to enjoy the rhythmic movements and before long obligingly dozed off.

Making no secret of the fact that she was watching him, Mrs. Moretti smiled and gave him the thumbs-up. "You're a natural," she told Cody, beaming.

"I'm not doing anything but walking," Cody pointed out.

He heard the door behind him opening. Turning, he was about to tell whomever had come in that service was temporarily on hold until further notice.

But he didn't have to say anything. It wasn't a new patient. Red had returned to the clinic.

"Couldn't find Flint?" Cody asked the older man. Red hadn't been gone very long, but, then, Cody had no right to expect him to scour the area. After all, Flint belonged to him, not Red.

"Didn't really have to look," Red replied. "That is one loyal stallion you've got yourself there, McCullough. Saw him coming right into the outskirts of town, as pretty as you please, minding his own business like he didn't have a care in the world and was just out for a morning stroll. Had to gentle him a little before I tied him to the hitching post down the street, but that's to be expected. He's waiting for you there," the ranch hand informed him.

Well, that was a relief, Cody thought. He hadn't realized he was so concerned until just this moment. He supposed this morning's events had stretched his nerves taut to the very limit.

"I appreciate it," Cody told the man.

"Yeah, yeah," Red dismissed the words of gratitude. "I said a beer would square us, remember? Now I'll go tell the sheriff you're safe and sound. See you around, McCullough," he told Cody.

Inclining his head in a show of respect, Red nodded at Mrs. Moretti just before he left the clinic.

Chapter 4

As Cody tried to decide his next move, the infant he was holding against him began to make a noise he couldn't quite make out. It didn't exactly sound like a whimper or a cry, but the baby was definitely voicing some sort of discontent.

In a few seconds, he had his answer. The infant had turned her head into his chest and appeared to be rooting around, her tiny lips making noises as she attempted to suck on his shirt.

"Looks like she's hungry," Mrs. Moretti told him helpfully. "She's trying to get her sustenance out of your shirt."

"Sorry, Layla, I'm afraid you're out of luck there," Cody told the baby, very gently separating the tiny mouth from his shirt.

At a temporary loss as to what to do, he looked at Mrs. Moretti for help.

The older woman shook her head. "I'm afraid I don't have anything for her. I stopped carrying formula with me several years ago. All my grandchildren are older than she is. But let me see if I can get one of the nurses to find something for her."

Rising heavily to her feet, the woman approached the registration desk and looked over it in hopes of seeing someone coming out of the impromptu operating room. She didn't, but that didn't stop her.

Making her way around the desk, Mrs. Moretti continued to the rear of the clinic. The doors to four of the exam rooms were wide open. Mrs. Moretti zeroed in on the one that was closed. When Melissa, one of her granddaughters, had needed stitches for the gash she'd gotten on her forehead thanks to a game of hide-and-seek that had gone wrong, she'd been taken into that room.

Knocking on the door, Mrs. Moretti raised her voice. "Sorry to bother you, but the baby out here seems to be hungry. Is there any formula in the clinic?" she asked politely.

After a moment the door opened in response to Mrs. Moretti's question. Holly was in the doorway.

"You didn't have to come out, dear. You could have just told me where the formula's kept and I would have gotten it," the woman said to Holly.

If given a choice, Mrs. Moretti always preferred being self-sufficient instead of dependent on the help of others.

"It's just easier this way," Holly told the woman. Besides, the doctors really didn't want to have civilians rooting through their supplies. However, there was no polite way to say that to Mrs. Moretti, so she let that pass. "How's everyone out here?" she asked as she took the woman to the supply cabinet in the last exam room.

There were several bottles of formula on the bottom shelf. Taking one, Holly decided to look in on the baby before heating the formula up.

"Mostly gone," Mrs. Moretti told her matter-of-factly, still following behind her. "Except for a couple of us. And, of course, Cody and the baby. Poor little thing's *hungry*." She smiled sympathetically. "I guess being born was hard work for her."

"I guess so," Holly agreed. She walked out into the waiting room. "How's our girl?" she asked Cody.

He was rocking the baby back and forth in an attempt to soothe her. "Okay, I think." And then he flushed. "I've got more experience with newborn calves than humans."

It amazed Holly how someone who looked the way Cody McCullough did—broad-shouldered, athletic with a soft, sexy smile and soul-melting blue eyes—could be so humble.

"You're doing fine, Cody," she assured him. "I'll just go and warm up this formula for you." Holly paused for a moment, needing to ask him a question just to be sure. "You all right with feeding it to her?"

Cody nodded, adding, "Not much different than with a calf, right?"

She'd never heard it put quite that way before. She supposed that there were similarities. "As long as you make sure you don't try to get her to stand up while she's doing it."

Cody laughed. "I think I've already figured that part out."

Holly returned within minutes, the small bottle of formula warmed and ready to be given to the hungry infant. "There you go," she said, handing Cody the bottle.

She was about to coach him through it, but saw that she needn't have worried. Cody was doing just fine with feeding the baby.

Instead, she gave him an encouraging smile. Still, she had to admit to herself that there was a little concern on her part.

"You're sure you'll be all right out here?" she asked him.

"He'll be fine," Mrs. Moretti told the nurse, answering for Cody. "I'll stay on just in case," she volunteered.

Cody looked at the older woman as he fed Layla. "You sure? It might be a long wait to see one of the doctors, when they're finally free."

It was becoming obvious that the delay would be even longer than anticipated. "I can come back for that tomorrow, but I'll stay here with you as long as you feel I might be of some help."

"I don't want to keep you, Mrs. Moretti," Cody told her.

Mrs. Moretti laughed. "It's been a long time since I was a kept woman," she told him with a wink that both surprised and amused him. There was still a little bit of the young flirt within the older matron. And then she waved her hand, dismissing his protest. "Don't give it another thought."

Feeling that everything was under control, Holly told them, "I'd better be getting back in there."

A flash of anxiety came out of nowhere, surprising Cody. "How is she doing?" he asked.

"Better than when you first brought her in." That was all Holly felt comfortable saying at this point. She'd learned that it was better to say too little than too much.

With that, the young nurse left the waiting room and hurried back to the operating room.

Mrs. Moretti sensed Cody's concern.

"She'll be fine," she assured Cody, patting his hand in the same soothing fashion she'd employed with all of her own children. "They don't come any better than Dr. Dan and Dr. Alisha," the grandmother of six told him. "Those two are the best thing that ever happened to this little town," she said with conviction.

Half an hour passed. Layla finished the formula that Holly had brought out for her.

Though he strained his ears, Cody couldn't discern anything coming from the rear of the clinic. He didn't hear any voices, nor did he hear a door being opened.

This "operation" was going on much too long, he thought. Something was very wrong.

As if reading his mind, Mrs. Moretti leaned forward. Her eyes meeting his, she told him, "Remember, no news is good news."

"Yeah," he murmured without conviction.

Cody knew that the woman meant well, but the old saying didn't really comfort him at this point. He'd always been the kind of person who met everything head-on. He didn't have that option here. All he could do was wait and the inactivity was making him fidget inwardly.

"Well, I guess I'll come back tomorrow," Oral Hanson suddenly announced to the room, even though Cody and Mrs. Moretti were the only two occupants left.

After getting up, the man crossed over and paused in front of Cody. He looked down at the baby and allowed a nostalgic expression to pass over his face.

"Brings back memories," he explained, referring to

when his children had been that small. "You hang in there, Cody, you hear?"

Cody merely nodded. There wasn't anything else that he could do, really.

"You're doing a good thing," Oral said as he left the clinic.

"He's right, you know," Mrs. Moretti told Cody, adding her voice to the sentiment.

He was *really* beginning to feel guilty having the woman remain here with him.

"Mrs. Moretti, you don't have to stay any longer," he told her. "You've got a family to get back to."

He knew that because of extenuating circumstances, Mrs. Moretti was helping to raise two of her younger grandchildren. It wasn't fair to the woman to make her stay on his account. After all, it wasn't as if he was helpless.

But Mrs. Moretti shook her head. "I don't feel right about leaving you alone."

"Two doctors and two nurses is not 'alone,' Mrs. Moretti," he reminded her. "All I have to do is raise my voice and one of them is bound to come out. Really, go home to your family," he urged, then added, "Layla and I will be fine. Really."

Mrs. Moretti's dark eyes crinkled as she smiled at the sleeping infant in his arms. "Such a lovely name," she told him. "That was your mama's name, wasn't it?" she asked. Cody nodded in response. "All right," the older woman said with a resigned sigh as she rose to her feet. "I guess they'll be wondering what happened to me if I don't get home soon." Mrs. Moretti spared him one last encouraging pat on the shoulder. "Don't give up hope, Cody."

"No, ma'am, I won't," he promised her.

Nodding her head, Mrs. Moretti picked up her over-size purse and finally made her way out of the clinic.

"Looks like it's just you and me now," Cody whispered to the baby once the door had closed behind Mrs. Moretti.

"And then," he amended as he heard the door to the clinic opening again, "maybe not." Raising his voice so that the woman would turn around, Cody said, "Mrs. Moretti, really, it's okay. Go home."

"I'm not Mrs. Moretti and I'm not going home, at least not until I find out just what the hell is going on here."

Surprised, holding the baby pressed against his chest, Cody shifted around in his seat to see Connor walking into the clinic.

Anyone looking at them would have instantly known that Cody and Connor were brothers, but Connor, three years older and two inches taller, was leaner and more weathered-looking than Cody. And while they both had the same blue eyes, Connor's hair was a darker shade of blond than Cody's.

"Where did you get that?" Connor asked, nodding at the baby as he took a seat next to his brother.

"Mrs. Abernathy was having a yard sale," Cody cracked. "I couldn't help myself."

"I'll let that go," Connor told him. He studied his brother for a moment. "I hear that you've had a hard morning."

"Exactly what did you hear?" Cody asked. Because the infant was reacting to the sound of Connor's deep voice, Cody began to rock her gently.

The reaction did not do unnoticed by Connor, though

he made no comment. "Well, your truck's still where you parked it last night and your horse is missing, so I figured out that the damn thing wouldn't start—the truck, not the horse. And then there's your little midwife adventure."

"Who told you?" Cody asked. Connor had been out mending fences early this morning. How had his brother heard about any of this? he wondered.

Connor grinned. "You know that Rusty Saunders never could keep anything to himself for more than five minutes. He rode out to the ranch to tell me. I gather the thought of you as a midwife tickled him pink."

Cody blew out a breath as he shook his head. "Man always was easily entertained."

"Yeah, well, it doesn't take much for some," Connor agreed. "I brought you a change of clothes," he said to Cody. "I figured after the way he described you, you'd need it." Giving his brother the once over—Cody was still wearing the bloodied shirt he'd had on when he carried Devon into the clinic—Connor nodded. "Looks like he wasn't wrong."

He put the brown paper sack containing a clean shirt and jeans down on the floor next to his brother's feet. "So, that's the little one, huh?" he asked, softening marginally as he gazed at the infant. The next moment, he looked up at his brother, the expression on his face that of a man who felt vindication. "See, I always said helping out during calving season would come in handy for you someday."

Cody nodded. He knew better than to question his brother's memory. Besides, Connor probably had said something like that at one time or another. "That's what you told me."

"How's her mother?" Connor asked.

"I don't know," Cody told him honestly. "Nobody's really told me anything since the two docs got to work on her."

The words were simple, but Connor heard his brother's concern. Not that he expected Cody to be aloof, but there was a tad more feeling in Cody's tone than Connor was accustomed to hearing.

"They're good people" was all Connor said of the doctors by way of encouragement. Still, the implied endorsement spoke volumes. "You need anything?" Connor asked, getting ready to leave.

"Not me. But she might do with a miracle," he told Connor, nodding back toward the rear of the clinic, where the door to the fifth exam room was still closed.

"I figure that part was already covered when you showed up." Connor started to rise, then abruptly stopped. "I can stick around if you want," he offered.

Cody laughed. "You don't do 'sticking around' well and you know it. Leave you in one place for too long and you'll be climbing right out of your skin. Thanks for coming."

Connor merely shrugged off his brother's thanks. "Flint's at the hitching post down the street a ways," he told Cody.

"I know. He's a good horse. He followed me to town behind the truck." Proud of the animal, Cody felt he had to share that with Connor. "Red found him for me."

"Good man, Red. Well, I'll see you when I see you," Connor said on his way to the door. One hand on the doorknob, he paused just before leaving. "Want Cassidy to come by?" he asked.

"And have my ear talked off?" Cody laughed. "No, I've got this covered."

Connor nodded. "I figured you did." And, with that, he walked out, closing the door behind him.

The baby had dozed off again and slept in his arms. For a while, there was nothing but the sound of her breathing to keep him company. Cody kept glancing toward the rear of the clinic, but the door didn't open. It felt as if he was doomed to wait in vain forever.

And then, just as he had given up all hope, Cody heard the door finally open.

For a moment, he thought he'd imagined it. Even so, he anxiously rose to his feet. And then he heard voices. Happy voices, not agitated ones.

Within a minute, Dan walked out to the front of the clinic. He looked somewhat tired, but he definitely had the air of a man who had won the battle he'd fought.

"Is she all right?"

The words burst from Cody's lips before he even realized he was asking the question out loud.

Rather than answer one way or the other, Dan asked, "Why don't you go see for yourself?"

Cody didn't remember crossing the waiting room, didn't really remember Holly coming up to him to take the baby from his arms. And he was only marginally aware of the fact that his arms ached from having held the baby in that position for so long.

All he knew was that Dan was leading him into the room where a battle to save a woman's life had been fought—and won.

When he walked in, Devon's eyes were closed. No longer on the surgical gurney, she had been transferred onto the lone hospital bed the clinic had.

An uneasiness began to take hold of Cody as he drew closer to her.

She still looked so pale, he thought.

Apprehension came out of some dark, hidden place, drenching Cody as he asked Dan, "Is she—is she—she's not—is she?"

He had lived through a lot in his time—the death of first one parent, then the other, the possibility of having the family split up and winding up in foster care. But even with all that, Cody couldn't make himself say the words.

Dan, who had lost his only brother just before he came to Forever, empathized. He put a wide, comforting hand on the younger man's shoulder as he told him, "She's alive, Cody. She's just sleeping."

The wave of relief surprised Cody as it all but knocked him off his feet.

Chapter 5

Cody trusted the doctor and knew that Dr. Davenport wasn't about to mislead him or sugarcoat the situation. He just wanted to hear the doctor assure him again.

"She's just sleeping, Dr. Dan, right? You're sure about that?" Cody questioned.

Because if she wasn't, if she had somehow managed to slip away, no matter what anyone else said, Cody would feel that it was somehow his fault, that he had overlooked something and hadn't kept the woman safe.

"You know she's been through a lot," Dan tactfully reminded him. "Her being asleep is a good thing. The body does its best recuperative work when it's asleep. That way, it's only focused on that one thing."

Cody could buy that. But what if she remained that way? What if she never woke up? he worried. "How long do you think she'll, you know, be asleep?"

"She'll wake up when she's ready. Meanwhile, I'm going to have her stay here." Guessing Cody's next question, Dan added, "Don't worry. She won't be alone. I'll have someone stay with her."

Which was his euphemistic way of saying that *he* would be that "someone." He knew his wife, Tina, wouldn't exactly be overjoyed about having him stay the night, but she had long ago made her peace with the fact that that sort of thing went with the territory and she was nothing if not supportive.

Cody never hesitated. He had made up his mind the moment the doctor said Devon was going to remain at the clinic overnight. "Can I be that someone?"

Dan looked at the deputy, surprised and a little skeptical. "You?"

Cody nodded. "I found her and I'd kind of like to see this through if you don't mind. It's something that Connor taught us was important—to finish something that you've started."

Dan nodded. "Well, I certainly can't argue with that." He made a quick assessment before giving Cody an answer. "Everything should be fine. But if she wakes up suddenly, or if you feel uneasy about how she's doing for *any reason at all, call me,*" Dan ordered. "I'm only five minutes away." That was the advantage of living in town instead of on one of the outlying ranches, as both of his nurses did.

Cody was already pulling up a chair, positioning it beside the bed. "Thanks." And then he suddenly remembered—appalled that he could have forgotten, even for a moment. "The baby—" he began, looking around as if he expected the infant to be close by.

"—will be coming home with me," Dan informed

him. "Nothing Tina likes better than to have a baby to fuss over." He could see that Cody was about to offer a protest. Like the rest of his family, the deputy obviously didn't know when to stop shouldering responsibility. "You'll have enough to do just watching over the baby's mother. By the way, Holly's going to need some information from you about the patient," he told Cody, nodding at the woman in the hospital bed.

"Can't help you there," Cody confessed. "I don't know much, just her first name. Devon."

Dan nodded. "It's a start. Listen, have you had anything to eat since this whole thing started?" he asked.

Cody shook his head. Food was the very last thing on his mind. He hadn't taken his eyes off Devon since he'd walked in and he really wished that the woman didn't look so pale.

"No."

Dan's eyes met the deputy's. "I can stay here and wait until you swing by the diner and get something to go," the doctor offered.

"That's okay, Doc. I'm good" he said, turning the doctor's offer down. "You've already done more than enough," Cody added gratefully.

Dan smiled, brushing off the thanks. "It's what I signed up for," he reminded the younger man.

It wasn't every doctor who felt morally bound to care this much. Despite the fact that they'd had to wait thirty years, everyone in town felt that they had really lucked out when Dr. Davenport reopened the clinic.

"Even so, she'd be dead by now if it weren't for you and Dr. Alisha," Cody said with all sincerity.

Dan smiled. Cody had forgotten one key point. It was so like the McCulloughs. "And don't forget you. If you hadn't found her and come to her aid, none of this would have been possible."

Dan paused for a moment to study the younger man's profile. Cody already appeared to have settled in for the night. He wasn't going anywhere.

"Okay, then," he said, resigned, "if you don't have any more questions, then I'm off. Remember, just five minutes away." He got a nod from Cody in response. The deputy's eyes were once again trained on the sleeping patient.

Dan took his cue and quietly slipped out of the room, leaving the door open.

"Who are you?" Cody asked the unconscious woman after a few minutes had passed and the clinic had slipped into stony silence, letting him know that everyone was gone. "And what kind of a man would have let you go, especially in your condition, carrying his baby?

"Unless he had a damn good reason for it, he should be horse-whipped if he shows up here, looking for you." Cody quickly amended, "Not that we whip our horses around here. But for someone like that guy, an exception could definitely be made.

"Come to think of it, I can't come up with *any* kind of a reason for him to have let you go off like that by yourself. The guy has to be dumber than a box of rocks—" he concluded "—and I'm probably insulting the rocks. I can see why you wouldn't want to be around him. More important—why you wouldn't want your baby to be around him. Babies need someone to look up to, to stimulate them. That sure doesn't sound like the man who let you go off by yourself."

Cody sighed, dragging his hand through his hair. He was at a loose end, not to mention somewhat confused.

He felt like a man who had been on a roller coaster for too long, having taken both the uphill climb and the harrowing, steep plunge once too often.

In short, he knew he wasn't making any sense, but all these emotions were suddenly popping up, rising to the surface like bubbles in a shaken soda can—dangerously ready to explode.

Cody struggled to get his emotions back in line. "You just take your time waking up," he told Devon. "Doc said you needed your rest and he should know. Until Doc Alisha came along, Dr. Dan had been taking care of the town on his own for a while now. Word has it that his brother was supposed to be the one coming to take care of us—first doctor in thirty years since the clinic closed—but the night before he was supposed to fly out, he was killed in a car accident, so Dr. Dan came in his place.

"I never knew the other Dr. Davenport, but speaking for the town, I'd say we got ourselves a really good deal, getting Dr. Dan."

Cody made himself as comfortable as he could as he continued talking to the woman he'd saved:

"And speaking *of* the town, you'll find that, if you decide to stay here a while, this is a really nice place, both for you and for your daughter. People here like to watch out for each other. It's the kind of thing that makes you feel safe and protected without feeling like you're confined or imprisoned. I should know. I'm a deputy sheriff—" he quickly clarified "—not that we imprison anyone."

His words and Devon's even breathing filled the silence. He went on talking, hoping that he could somehow comfort the woman. He'd read somewhere that people in comas responded to the sound of someone talking to them.

"Having a sheriff's department is just putting window dressing on the notion of a town," he said honestly. "Not that I don't like being a deputy," he went on, "but I would have done what I did this morning even if I was still just one of the ranchers around here." He confided, "As a deputy, I'm supposed to keep the peace, but mostly the peace keeps itself." Still, he liked the idea of being part of a law enforcement department in Forever.

"Did you get to the part about me yet?"

The raspy, honey-whiskey voice startled him. Cody twisted around in his seat to see Miss Joan standing behind him in the room. The thin redhead was holding a tray full of food.

"Miss Joan, I didn't see you there," Cody confessed, immediately jumping to his feet out of an ingrained sense of respect.

"Obviously. You probably also didn't hear what I just said," she assumed and then repeated it. "I asked if you'd gotten to me yet, seeing as how you're giving this poor, unconscious girl a verbal tour of the good citizens of Forever. Not fair," she judged, "since she can't get away."

"I just wanted her to know that she was safe," Cody explained philosophically.

Miss Joan set down the tray on the counter beside the sink that the medical staff used for washing up before procedures.

"Nothing wrong with that," she agreed. "I was going to have one of the girls bring this to you, but I decided to come myself."

He assumed that someone from the clinic, possibly

Mrs. Moretti, had stopped by the diner to share what was going on with Miss Joan. Everyone knew that nothing ever seemed to take place in Forever without Miss Joan somehow being aware of it. Aware and ultimately involved in her own way, she was thought by many to be the veritable heart of the town.

"You really didn't have to go to the trouble," Cody told her, even as the tempting aroma of fried chicken, mashed potatoes and green beans with bread crumbs filled the room.

"I did if I didn't want to have you on my conscience, sitting here, keeping vigil and slowly starving." Besides, she added silently, she wanted to see the young woman for herself.

Coming around closer to the bed, Miss Joan took her first good look at the young woman at the center of the little drama that had everyone in Forever talking.

"Pretty little thing," she pronounced. "Kind of young, too, to be out on her own this way."

Long-ago memories whispered across the frontier of her mind before Miss Joan shut them away.

Turning away from the young woman, Miss Joan looked at Cody. "You need anything?" she asked him in her take-charge tone that everyone was familiar with.

Cody looked at the tray. Miss Joan had even brought dessert. His favorite. Boston cream pie. Even though he knew the meal had been prepared by Angel, another one of the people Miss Joan had taken under her wing, the woman herself never ceased to amaze him. She somehow always instinctively managed to be there, filling needs no one had voiced.

"No, ma'am, I think you've taken care of everything as usual. Thanks," he told her. Sliding back on his chair so he could dig into the pocket of his jeans, he asked, "What do I owe you, Miss Joan?"

The withering glance the older woman gave him had Cody stop reaching for his money.

"We'll come to terms" was all she said. Everyone knew that she believed favors were to be paid forward. It was a given. "You know where she was heading?" Miss Joan asked.

Cody shook his head. "Haven't a clue, ma'am."

"Well, if she decides that she doesn't want to keep on going there for some reason, let her know that I could always use another girl at my place once she gets up on her feet," Miss Joan told him. "And she'll need somewhere to stay," she added, stating the obvious.

The town had a new hotel—their only one—but hotels were expensive.

Cody suppressed a sigh as he turned back to look at the sleeping young woman. "First, she needs to wake up," he said more to himself than to Miss Joan.

Miss Joan nodded. "First things first," she agreed. It was time to leave. Miss Joan made a point of never staying longer than she felt necessary. "Don't let that get cold," she told him, nodding at the food on the tray she'd brought.

Cody was already drawing his chair over to the tray. When he glanced up to thank her again, he realized that Miss Joan had gone.

Smiling to himself, he began to eat, discovering only then just how hungry he actually was.

Cody saved some of the food that Miss Joan had brought, just in case Devon woke up hungry. But the hours passed and the young woman continued sleeping.

Reminding himself that the doctor had told him this was a good thing—and checking on Devon a couple more times to assure himself that she was breathing—Cody finally settled back in the chair he'd relocated by her bed. Within minutes, he fell into a light, uneasy sleep.

Fragments of dreams kept collecting, then colliding and ultimately breaking apart in her head. They were all different from one another, but they still had one thing in common.

They were all dreams that revolved around being lost. Hopelessly lost. Lost in the desert, lost in an amusement park, lost in a large city, lost in a school she remembered from her childhood. In each instance, for however long or short that particular dream fragment lasted, she was trying to find her way home, trying to find something she had lost besides herself. Though, in the scope of the dream, she had no idea what it was that she was looking for or even exactly where this "home" was.

Or even *if* it was home.

All she was aware of was this urgent need within her to find it.

It felt as if it went on for hours, this odyssey-without-end that she was on, going from dream to unsettling dream. A few times, as the kaleidoscope of locations kept changing, she somehow felt that she was close to journey's end only to have home suddenly disappear, leaving her stranded. And then the so-called adventure began again, taking on a new scenario, but accompanied by the same feeling.

Eternally lost, Devon felt exhausted, frightened and incredibly sweaty as she continued trudging to nowhere.

A despondency began to eat away at her, making her feel as if she was in some kind of a loop, a loop that kept sending her through the motions of this search-without-a-solution over and over again.

Somewhere in her dream, Devon came to realize that the baby that had literally been a part of her for so long was missing, abruptly taken away from her very body. The sense of urgency to find the infant, to find *home* increased exponentially. She strained to wake herself up, somehow sensing that if she could just do that one thing, if she could succeed in waking herself up, then this futile search would be over and her baby would be returned to her.

She tried to cry out, to somehow rise above the downward pull that was attempting to submerge her once and for all.

Opening her mouth, she felt water rushing into it, threatening to drown her. She had no idea where it had come from, but if she wanted to remain alive, she knew she was supposed to close her mouth. But if she did that, then she couldn't wake herself up and, eventually, that would completely suffocate her.

Feeling she had no choice, afraid that retreating would ultimately lead to her baby's demise somehow, Devon opened her mouth and screamed, even as water once again came rushing in to silence her.

She screamed again, louder—and finally, just before drowning, succeeded in waking herself up.

She woke up looking at the sky.

No, not the sky. She was looking into the bluest eyes she'd ever seen.

And she wasn't drowning anymore.

Chapter 6

Cody had just managed to doze off, despite his best efforts not to. In this case, although he was generally a light sleeper, he had somehow fallen into a deep sleep. So much so that the screams he heard initially incorporated themselves into his dream and, suddenly, he was back in Devon's truck, doing his level best to help her bring her daughter into the world.

But because he was always so logical, even when asleep, something nudged at Cody's consciousness, making him realize that the scenario he believed himself in was all wrong.

They had both been through this already. Devon had already given birth to the baby and, since she'd only been pregnant with one child, this couldn't possibly be real no matter what it felt like.

She couldn't be giving birth again.

But the scream was very real, so there had to be another reason for it.

Devon was in trouble.

Sheer will and almost military discipline forced Cody to wake up. He did so with a start.

The second he did, he was up on his feet and beside Devon's bed. A railing was all that separated them and Cody hardly noticed it. He hovered over Devon, wanting to wake her up. The only thing that stopped him was that he'd once read that it was bad to wake up someone who was sleepwalking.

The moment's hesitation evaporated as he reminded himself that she was *not* sleepwalking, she was obviously in the throes of some kind of nightmare.

Before Cody could put his hand on her shoulder to rouse her, Devon's eyes flew open. He saw fear mingling with confusion within the deep blue orbs.

But what he also saw—and what seemed to grow at nearly lightning speed—was relief.

"It's you," she breathed. Devon felt as if she was still gasping for air. She struggled to tamp down the sense of panic.

"It is," he replied, only hoping that she wasn't mistaking him for the low-life scum who had allowed this woman to be out on the open road by herself.

The look of relief on her face gave way to concern as Devon attempted to prop herself up on her elbows while looking around the room at the same time.

"Hey, you're supposed to be lying back and resting," Cody insisted, gently putting a restraining hand on her shoulder. "Don't exert yourself."

"My baby," Devon cried. Still scanning the area as if she'd somehow missed seeing the baby in the small room the first around. "Where's my baby?" There was panic in her eyes as she clutched Cody's arm. "She's not—"

It didn't take much to guess at what Devon wasn't saying.

"Oh no, no, she's fine," Cody reassured her. "She's better than fine. Layla's with Dr. Dan."

"Layla?" Devon repeated, bewildered, her brain still somewhat foggy. She was having trouble processing information. Nothing seemed to be making sense to her. "Dr. Dan?"

To Cody's relief, he began to see color returning to the young woman's cheeks. If she seemed addled, that was just because the last few hours of exertion had caused her to forget some things.

He backtracked. "Layla's what you decided to name the baby," he told her patiently. "And Dr. Dan's one of the two doctors at the clinic who saved your life. He lives in town. Dr. Dan thought it might be easier for you, as well as the baby, to have someone else take care of Layla while you just concentrate on getting better yourself." He saw that she was about to protest so he quickly pointed out, "By the time I got you to the clinic, you'd lost a lot of blood. You gave us all quite a scare."

Devon blinked, trying to absorb everything this man had just told her and make some kind of sense of it. It wasn't easy. Her brain felt like a giant piece of Swiss cheese with information falling through the holes. Devon looked at him more closely.

And then she remembered. "You're the guy who stopped."

Cody supposed that was as apt a description for him as any. Except that there was one important thing missing. "And the guy who delivered your baby," he added matter-of-factly.

It began coming back to her in large, all-encompassing chunks. Her eyes widened as she suddenly recalled his name. "You're Cody."

Sharing the moment with her, Cody felt almost triumphant.

"That's right." He leaned in a little closer to her. "How are you feeling?"

That was an easy one. She didn't even have to pause before answering his question.

"Like one of those Saturday-morning cartoon characters who was run over and flattened by a truck."

Cody laughed quietly. "There's a reason for that," he told her.

Devon eyed him warily, trying to understand. "You ran me over with a truck?"

Cody suppressed a grin. He didn't want her to think he was laughing at her. "No, but you did lose a lot of blood. That would explain why you feel the way you do now."

The room was well lit and Devon was able to focus on the man sitting beside her bed. There were streaks of blood evident along both halves of his tan uniform.

"Is that some of mine?" she asked, nodding at the blood.

Connor had brought him a change of clothes, but Cody hadn't wanted to leave her side long enough to change—and it didn't seem right to do it in her room, even though she *was* unconscious. After a bit, to be honest, he'd been too concerned about Devon to even think about his own appearance.

Looking down at himself now, he saw what Devon was seeing. There were streaks of blood, dried now, along the front of his shirt, as well as additional amounts, not nearly as pronounced, along his pants legs.

"Yes, it is. Sorry," he apologized. Getting up, he walked over to where he'd left his other clothes. Removing the bloodstained shirt, he switched into the clean one.

Devon's head was still spinning a little and there was no question that she felt pretty woozy, not to mention shaken. But, even factoring that in, Devon could still appreciate the fact that the person she was looking at was more than just a passably attractive man. He was the closest specimen to bone-melting gorgeousness she had ever seen. His solid muscles testified that he was a man who didn't allow others do his work for him but tackled head-on whatever came his way.

She caught herself wondering if those muscles felt as hard as they looked.

Get a grip, Devon.

"I can wash that for you," she told Cody, feeling somewhat guilty that he had gotten his clothes dirty on her account.

He flashed a quick smile of thanks even as he shook his head. "You're in no shape to do anything right now," he told her.

"I didn't mean right now," Devon protested. Right now, she doubted that she could even stand up. But she was determined to be better by tomorrow. "But when I get back on my feet… Where am I, anyway?" she asked suddenly, trying to look around again.

This time, she didn't try to sit up. Exhaustion prevented her from doing very much of anything but lying there. Still, she was able to take in her surrounding area, such as it was.

"This is the clinic I told you about earlier," he reminded her, doing his best to give her a sense of continuity. "The doctors have this room set aside for any emergency surgeries that might come in."

"Why not just have people go to the hospital?" she asked.

Cody shook his head. He had lived here all his life, so to him what the doctors did at the clinic wasn't unusual, but he knew that an outsider wouldn't see it that way.

"The closest hospital is fifty miles away," he told her. "A person can't always get there in time. It would be too dangerous to wait that long."

Devon took in a deep breath as the fact that she might have actually died today began to dawn on her. "Like me."

"Like you," Cody confirmed. He thought of the meal that Miss Joan had brought him. There was still a little of that left. Devon needed to eat something so she could build up her strength. "Are you hungry?" he asked.

The mere mention of food caused her stomach to bunch up and threaten to rise up in her throat.

"Oh Lord, no," Devon cried with feeling. Cody had already seen her close to naked, but she found the thought of throwing up in front of him extremely embarrassing. It took her a moment to catch her breath.

When she did, Devon asked him, "Did I say thank you yet?"

Without specifically answering her question, Cody grinned and replied, "As I recall, you were kind of busy screaming and pushing."

That part was still rather a blur, with the events all running together into one murky whole.

Her eyes held this. "Then I'll say it now." Her voice softened. "Thank you."

Cody wasn't a man who felt comfortable in the face of gratitude, even though he appreciated the fact that she felt that way.

He shrugged off her words, murmuring, "Well, I couldn't very well have left you like that."

"Someone else did," Devon said under her breath before she could stop herself.

She was referring to the SOB who'd gotten her pregnant and then abandoned her, Cody thought. Ordinarily an easygoing, mild-mannered man, he could feel his temper spiking. Who did that kind of thing?

"About that—" Cody began.

"I don't want to talk about it," Devon responded, her tone shutting down any conversation that might have gone in that direction.

"Then we won't," he told Devon.

But mentally, Cody made a note to look into the matter for his own edification as soon as the dust settled. Someone needed to be taught a lesson about basic responsibility.

Looking back at the entire incident now, Cody was well aware that had he not happened along when he did, Devon could have very well died, either in childbirth or right after that from blood loss. It wasn't something he wanted to think about, but, on the other hand, the man who had gotten Devon pregnant and then pulled a vanishing act had to be held accountable for this.

Unless she had felt compelled to run away from him, Cody thought suddenly. But for some reason, as he reconsidered the matter, he didn't think that was the case.

Telling himself to revisit the subject later, when he could do something about it, Cody turned his attention back to the woman in the hospital bed for now.

"Are you thirsty?" he asked her. He could see not wanting to eat right now—although that had never been his problem. But she needed to stay hydrated. "Do you want something to drink?"

The second he asked, Devon became aware of being thirsty. Very thirsty. She couldn't remember the inside of her mouth ever feeling as dry as it did right at this moment.

She nodded. "Some water would be nice," she told him.

But as he rose to his feet, a sense of panic suddenly swooped out of nowhere, seizing her. Looking back, her reaction made Devon feel ashamed of herself, but at the moment she felt completely overwhelmed by the feeling. She reached out and grabbed his hand, trying to hold on to it.

"Don't leave me." It was almost a plea. The nervousness undulating through her took Devon's breath away.

If her request surprised him, Cody gave no indication. "I'm not going anywhere," he assured Devon. "There's water right over here." He pointed to the faucet over the sink. "Just a couple of steps away."

Devon flushed, feeling like a complete idiot. What the hell was wrong with her? This wasn't like her at all. She wasn't normally needy or clingy. If anything, she prided herself on being the total opposite.

"Sorry," she murmured as she accepted the water-filled paper cup he brought back to her. "Must be all these hormones acting up," she told him. "You can leave if you want to. I'll be fine."

He didn't buy it for a minute. And even if she really wanted him to, he wasn't about to leave her alone. Cody planted himself on the chair that he'd pulled up next to her bed earlier and got as comfortable as he could.

"Don't have anywhere I need to be but here," he replied simply.

"No wife and family waiting for you at home?" she asked. She'd taken up enough of his time. If he had people waiting for him, if wasn't fair of her to make him stay.

"No wife," Cody told her.

"No family?" she pressed, unable to imagine someone like Cody being utterly unattached.

"Oh, I've got family," Cody assured her. "But it's not like we tuck each other into bed."

Half the time Connor did act like their father, but it was Connor who had always said to never leave a job unfinished and, as far as Cody was concerned, seeing to this new mother's needs through the night qualified as a job that he had undertaken.

"Do you have brothers and sisters?" she asked, curious.

It was a question, but he also caught a rather wistful tone in her voice, which in turn had him asking a question of his own.

"Are you an only child?"

Cody could see that Devon was struggling to erect a protective wall around herself or, at the very least, a protective shield. But she wasn't fast enough. He'd glimpsed the vulnerable woman who was just beneath the bravado and the careless act.

Devon frowned, ignoring his question.

"How many brothers and sisters?" she asked, stubbornly pressing on.

Cody felt he had gotten his answer about her family dynamics. "Two of the first, one of the second," he told her.

Devon tried to envision them all around the dining table, talking over one another, arguing, laughing. "Parents?"

Cody shook his head. "Not for a while now," he told her quietly.

So his life wasn't as perfect as she thought. Devon felt sympathy stirring within her. "Me neither."

"Guess that gives us something in common," Cody replied.

Devon nodded. For just a single moment, she felt close to the man who had rescued her. "Guess so," she murmured.

He wanted to keep her talking and thinking of something else. "Were you headed somewhere?" When she didn't answer him, he gently pressed, "When I found you, where were you going?"

A single tear spilled out of the corner of her eye, leaving a trail along her cheek until it stained the sheet beneath her ear.

"Doesn't matter now," she told him quietly.

Jack was gone and he had left intentionally, deserting her as well as the baby she now realized he'd never really wanted. She was not going to lower herself any further by continuing to search for him. Jack wasn't going to take her back and even if he did, she didn't want him to. But it would have been nice to recover her mother's jewelry.

The next moment, she banished the thought. Time to get on with her life. Hers and her daughter's. She just needed to find somewhere to stay until she could figure out what her next move was going to be.

"Is there anyone you want me to call for you?" Cody offered. "Anyone you want to come for you?"

Devon shook her head in response to each question. She had a few girlfriends, but they were more like acquaintances than people she could turn to in a time of need or share anything of importance with. Besides, they were all in another state. She couldn't think of a single person who would go out of their way for her.

"Nobody," she told him stoically.

"No family at all? No friends?" he pressed, doing his best not to sound incredulous. In his experience, everyone had *someone* to turn to. He couldn't begin to imagine how alone she had to feel.

His protective instincts went up several degrees.

"Nobody you need to waste your time or your breath calling," she told him flatly.

He'd taken in enough strays in his time to know one when he saw one. It didn't matter that the former were all animals and she was definitely a flesh-and-blood human being.

The woman was obviously without any binding ties and most definitely on her own.

"And no," she said, her eyes meeting his—hers daring him to display even an ounce of pity, "I have nowhere to go."

"Don't worry about that," he said dismissively. "We've got plenty of room at the ranch. You and Layla can stay there until you can get back on your feet and decide what you want to do."

"You mean stay with you?"

And here she'd thought that he was different. How gullible could she be?

Cody could hear the wariness in her voice. He did what he could to set her mind at ease immediately.

"With my family," he corrected. "Those siblings you

asked me about, we all live together on the ranch my father left us. And, if you don't want to stay with us, there's always Miss Joan's." He saw a quizzical look enter Devon's eyes. "She's taken in her share of people who were passing through Forever, on their way to nowhere."

"You mean charity cases," she said indignantly. "I'm not—"

"Nope," he said, cutting in. "She's already been by. Told me to tell you she's got a job waiting for you once you're up to it. She runs the local diner and could always use another waitress." Devon was looking very tired, Cody thought. "Okay, enough talking. Right now," he told her, "your only job is to get stronger."

She started to protest that he had no business telling her what to do or acting as if he was in charge of her life.

She wanted to, but the words didn't come because she had fallen asleep again.

"Attagirl," Cody murmured, drawing the blanket back up over her, tucking Devon in. He ran the back of his hand along her cheek.

She looked so vulnerable and innocent. Something stirred a little harder within him.

"Get some sleep," he whispered as he planted himself back into the chair.

Chapter 7

Open six days a week, Forever's medical clinic's doors were not officially open this morning until nine o'clock. That didn't mean that neither Alisha or Dan came in at that time. Both doctors, especially Dan, made a point of arriving at least forty-five minutes to an hour earlier.

This morning, because he had a patient who had remained at the clinic overnight, Dan came in a few minutes after seven to see how both she and her impromptu "nurse" were doing.

Dan considered *everyone* in and around Forever as patients he had either previously ministered to or would be ministering to in the near future. The health and welfare of the good citizens of Forever were a perpetual concern for him.

Since arriving in Forever several years ago, Dan hadn't even remotely been tempted to do things in half measures.

Entering the clinic through the back entrance, Dan eased into the single-story building and made his way into the room where he had left Devon recovering from her emergency surgery. The operation, plus the ordeal of childbirth, had taken a heavy toll on the woman. She was going to need some time to recover even though she struck him as otherwise being a rather healthy, strong woman.

The doctor found Cody in a chair right beside the young mother's bed—just as he had expected he would. Dan made a quick assessment of his patient's condition. His first overall impression was that Devon looked a great deal better than she had last night. There was color—not just a flush but actual, well-distributed color—back in her cheeks and that was always a good sign.

At first glance, both his patient and her rough-around-the-edges guardian angel appeared to be sound asleep.

But within a few seconds, Dan saw Devon stirring. And then she opened her eyes.

It never got old, Dan thought, pleased. Although he had been practicing medicine for a number of years now, the exhilarating feeling he experienced whenever he witnessed someone getting better because of his efforts still flashed through him like a bright, gleaming thunderbolt.

Best adrenaline rush ever, Dan thought as he smiled at Devon.

"You gave us all quite a scare, young lady," he told her. His smile widened. "How are you feeling, Devon? You don't mind if I call you Devon, do you?"

"You're the doctor?" she asked. He was still dressed

in jeans and a bulky sweater, so she wasn't sure. She'd been unconscious when Cody had brought her into the clinic.

"One of them," Dan confirmed.

Devon's eyes crinkled as she smiled at him. "Seeing as how I'm told that you saved my life, you can call me anything you want."

"Just part of a team," Dan told her, neatly deflecting the compliment. "If anyone deserves credit for saving your life, it would be Cody over there," he said quietly, nodding in the sleeping deputy's direction. "If he hadn't found you and brought you in when he did, the only thing I would have been able to do for you is call the official time of death. You might want to think about buying a lottery ticket because you really *are* the definition of *lucky.*"

The emptiness suddenly and unexpectedly got to her. Cody had said that Layla was spending the night at the doctor's house. Had Cody lied for some reason? Or was her baby not well and had to be rushed to a hospital?

"My baby—" she began.

"—is perfect," Dan told her with a smile. "She spent the night at my home with my wife. She'll be bringing your daughter in shortly. So," he continued in the manner of a doctor who had done this countless times already, "to get back to my question, how are you feeling?"

She didn't even have to stop and think before answering. "Relieved. Tired. Very, very sore," Devon told him, rattling off her answers.

Dan nodded as he calmly took down a blood pressure cuff from a hook on the wall. Wrapping the cuff around Devon's arm that was closest to him, he proceeded to pump it up, then slowly released the air through a valve. He took note of the numbers.

"Sounds wonderfully normal to me," he confirmed. "You took excellent care of yourself during this pregnancy and this is obviously the payoff for all your conscientiousness," Dan acknowledged. Removing the cuff, he folded it and set the machine aside.

"So I'm free to go?" Devon asked. Her tone sounded far more eager than she actually felt.

"I think an extra day in bed would be advised," Dan counseled, writing down the reading that had registered on the blood pressure's monitor.

"Here?" she asked uncertainly.

Dan nodded. "It's a bed and there are four of us here to look in on you. Can't beat that," he told her cheerfully.

Despite the various situations she had found herself in over the course of her young life, the one constant that had never changed was Devon's sense of pride. Poor or not, she had always found a way to pay her way, even though, as a substitute elementary school teacher, she had never been even remotely flush.

"I can't pay you right now," she qualified, letting him know that she did consider it a debt she intended to make good on.

"I'm not really concerned about that right now," Dan informed her. "This isn't exactly a cash-and-carry business, you know."

"But—" she began to protest.

"Devon," he went on firmly, "if I were in this for the money, I would have never left New York."

Surprised, Devon looked at him more closely. "You're from New York?"

He liked the surprise in her voice. It meant that he was finally on his way to shedding the accent that had been such a major factor in his speech pattern.

"Yes."

"Why did you leave?" she asked incredulously. It had to be a complete shock to his system, going from New York City to a town like this.

In his place, she knew she wouldn't have come out. To her, New York represented the very best of the civilized world and being part of that was everything she would have ever aspired to.

"I made a promise," Dan answered vaguely. Never mind that the promise he'd made was to his younger brother, who, at the time he made it, was no longer among the living—something he would feel eternally responsible for.

Before she could ask another question, their conversation—even though they had kept their voices at a low level—succeeded in rousing Cody.

Cody was awake and automatically on his feet in the same instant.

"What's wrong?" he asked, even as his brain struggled to get itself back into gear.

He really didn't remember falling asleep. The last thing Cody could recall was tucking the blanket around Devon again. Turned out that the woman was a fitful sleeper.

"Nothing," Dan answered him, his tone laid-back and easy. "Everything seems right on track with our new mother here. You, however, look like hell," Dan commented, taking a longer, closer look at the younger man.

"Yeah, Connor already mentioned that." Looking

past the doctor, he glanced at Devon. He was far more concerned about her condition than he was about his own appearance. "So she's okay?" he pressed, wanting to be reassured. Wanting to leave no margin for doubt.

"Appears that way. Her blood pressure is remarkably low, all things considered. I'm going to have Dr. Cordell-Murphy give her a thorough physical exam later to confirm that." Dan said, "Why don't you go home now and get some sleep?"

"I slept here," Cody answered, dismissing the well-intended suggestion.

"And you look it. These chairs weren't exactly built to give anyone a comfortable night's sleep," Dan pointed out.

Cody shrugged the words away. He was about to say something else in his own defense when they heard the back door being opened.

The next moment, Dan's wife, Tina, walked into the room, a pink bundle in her arms.

The second she saw her baby, Devon immediately began to pull herself up into a sitting position.

"Hold it," Dan cautioned. The doctor pressed a button on an attached keypad and raised the mattress that was beneath her shoulders until he'd achieved an upright position for her.

"That's better," he pronounced.

"Your mama's been waiting for you, precious," Tina Davenport cooed to the baby she was holding. "There you go, say hi to your mama," the doctor's wife instructed, shifting the baby from her own arms into Devon's. "Your daughter has to qualify as one of the sweetest-dispositioned babies I've ever had the fortune of interacting with." As she took a step back from the bed, she added, "I'd say that's a pretty good omen." She told her husband, "See you tonight," and then paused to assure Devon, "You're in very capable hands."

And with that, Tina left the clinic the same way she had entered.

"Okay, she's been fed and changed as of forty minutes ago. Hopefully, the latter will last for a little bit. If she needs changing, use that buzzer," Dan told his patient, indicating the keypad he had previously used to raise the mattress. "Holly or Debi will be in to do the honors for you." His grin was infectious as he went on to tell the brand-new mother, "I'd take advantage of that if I were you."

Turning from Devon, the doctor took another long look at Cody. Except for yesterday, he had never seen the young deputy in anything but top, alert condition. That wasn't the case at the moment.

"Go home, Cody. You really do look like hell."

"That seems to be the popular assessment of the day," Cody murmured. But he had a job to get to and if he was leaving the clinic, he was going to the sheriff's office. He'd already missed too much work. "Okay, since everyone seems to think I'm bringing down the atmosphere, I'll get out of your hair." He asked Dan, "Do you know when you'll be letting her leave?"

"All things being equal, I'll release Devon and her baby tomorrow morning around when we open the clinic." Turning toward his patient, he told Devon in the next breath, "You're quite welcome to stay with my family and me once you're discharged."

"My place is closer," Alisha interjected, coming in and presenting herself to Devon and her baby. "So you might want to come and stay with Brett and me. I have a ground-floor spare bedroom that—"

"Devon already has a place to stay," Cody informed the two doctors, then nodded back toward Devon and the tiny pink bundle in her arms. "She'll be staying at the ranch." Shifting to look at Devon, he promised, "I'll be back."

And with that, Cody left the room.

Nodding at Holly and Debi, who were both already in the reception area, pulling files and bracing themselves for the onslaught of patients, Cody walked out of the building.

Flint was no longer tied to the hitching post. In place of the stallion, his truck was now standing there, apparently ready for travel.

Connor, Cody thought gratefully. *Always there to fill in the gaps.*

True to his word, Cody went straight to the sheriff's office.

He half expected the office to be empty. Unlike the clinic staff, who were in almost constant demand, Rick and his deputies were considered necessary in terms of generating goodwill within the town and its surrounding area. Their job was not so much focused on keeping the peace—what he'd told Devon was true: the peace more or less kept itself. Their jobs were focused on pitching in to help its residents with whatever they needed.

Occasionally, it was to locate a child who had wandered off. And every so often it was to mediate a dispute between two citizens, both of whom believed they were in the right over, like as not, some trivial matter.

The department got its share of phone calls asking them to find pets that had gone astray or to tackle an aggressive coyote or two that had gotten too brazen for the town's own good.

And, of course, there was Nathan McLane, the de facto town drunk. Nathan was harmless. Long ago he had chosen resting on a stool in Murphy's Saloon over sitting in his living room, listening to his less-than-sympathetic wife recite a list of all his shortcomings and outright failures.

On a few occasions, Nathan had actually attempted—never successfully—to walk home from the saloon. Those were times that either Cody, Rick or one of the deputies would bring the man in and lock him up for the night to sleep it off.

Gabe Rodriguez was already at his desk when Cody came in, searching through something on the computer.

"'Morning," Cody murmured as he passed Gabe on his way to the rather ancient-looking coffee maker.

There was a full pot of freshly brewed coffee in the decanter, the enticing aroma filling the air.

"'Morning, stranger," Gabe murmured before looking up.

And then he did.

Gabe had been filled in on yesterday's excitement. News traveled like the proverbial wildfire in a town where sighting the first robin of spring was considered newsworthy.

"Hey, have you been to bed yet?" Gabe asked the department's newest deputy. "'Cause you really look like he—"

Cody held his hand up to stop the rest of the sentence.

"If you say what I think you're going to say, you need to know that I can't be held accountable for my reaction."

Gabe laughed. "I take it that someone else already told you?"

"I don't think there's anyone left in town who *hasn't* told me," Cody commented wearily.

He had to admit that he felt pretty worn-out right about now. Yesterday was finally beginning to catch up to him.

"So, then, why don't you go home and get some rest?" Gabe asked. It struck him as the only logical conclusion.

"Because I was already out yesterday and I don't want to lose my job for taking too much personal time," Cody explained, adding, "I really like this job."

Gabe clearly wasn't following Cody's reasoning. "Why would you lose your job? You were busy saving a tourist's life. That's supposed to be one of the things we get paid for, remember? Saving people. It's not like you took time away from capturing the culprits responsible for some kind of crime spree."

Cody's head was definitely foggy and he wasn't absorbing things as quickly as he normally did.

"Too many words," he muttered, tipping back his coffee mug.

Gabe tried again. "In a nutshell, Rick clocked you in. You were on the job yesterday, protecting and serving, not playing hooky." Getting up, Gabe came over to Cody's desk, where the tired deputy had more or less collapsed into his chair rather than simply sitting down. "That means you're free to go home, Cody."

But Cody shook his head. "I'm waiting to get my

second wind. If I lie down now, I probably won't get up until tomorrow morning."

Gabe sighed and turned back to go to his desk. "Suit yourself," he said with a shrug.

I generally do, Cody thought with a smile. The tricky part, though, he couldn't help thinking, was getting through today without falling asleep on the job.

The fact that he intended to look in on Devon and the baby at lunchtime and then at the end of the day helped him to rev up his engine.

Chapter 8

"How is she?" Sheriff Rick Santiago asked Cody less than half an hour later as he walked into the office.

Cody looked up to find that the sheriff had paused by his desk on his way to the crowded cubbyhole in the rear of the office that served as his work space.

Cody couldn't help thinking of the sick feeling he'd had in the pit of his stomach when he'd first become aware of all the blood that Devon had lost.

"Better than I actually thought she'd be at this point," he confessed. "Turns out that she's pretty resilient and has a great constitution. Doc thinks she'll be strong enough to leave the clinic by tomorrow morning."

Rick nodded, taking in his deputy's words. "Dan thinks a lot of the credit belongs to you," Rick said matter-of-factly. Through the whimsy of fate, Dan Davenport was his brother-in-law, married to Olivia's younger sister,

Tina. They'd all had dinner late last night. "Word around Murphy's Saloon has it that you'll be able to amass a lot of free drinks on that particular story," Rick commented.

"I don't really drink," Cody reminded his boss.

"I'm sure the details can be worked out when the time comes," Rick surmised. He was fairly certain that if he didn't want alcohol, then Cody was going to be in for his share of hot meals at Miss Joan's. "I really didn't expect to see you in today."

"Planning on giving away my job already?" Cody asked dryly.

"Nobody I know would be a good candidate for it. Takes a certain talent to be able to mix boredom with getting things done. Right now, there're no takers."

"I tried to tell him to go home, Sheriff," Gabe told Rick, speaking up.

"The McCulloughs have always been a stubborn bunch," Rick reminded his other deputy. He turned toward Cody. "You find out what her story is yet?" he asked.

"Story?" Cody repeated. His brain felt as if it was wrapped in a thin layer of cotton. Maybe he should have gone home to grab a quick nap, he thought, beginning to reconsider his position.

The sheriff nodded. "What was she doing out there by herself in her condition?"

He had a feeling that Devon felt that she'd had no choice in the matter.

"She didn't give me any details and when I asked her, she really didn't want to talk about it," Cody told the sheriff. "I thought I'd give her a few days to get better before I start to ask her any questions, if it's all right with you."

"No problem," Rick agreed. "It can wait. Got a place for her to stay yet?"

There was probably no shortage of doors that would be opened to the young mother. If nothing else, the good people of Forever were generous to a fault.

"Several places," Cody said, not wanting to get into the fact that it didn't matter who else volunteered to take Devon and her baby in. At the end of the day, he was still taking the two of them to the ranch. The way he saw it, she was his responsibility until such time that she was able to leave on her own power.

"Do we know who she is?" Rick asked.

"Her name is Devon Bennett," Joe Lone Wolf said as he walked in. The sheriff's brother-in-law was carrying a box of pastries that he proceeded to deposit on the center table.

Rick gave the box and its contents a quick once-over. "What's the occasion?" Rick asked.

"I stopped at the diner to get some coffee—no offense but ours hasn't been good since Alma retired," he complained, referring to Gabe's sister, who had brought him into the department before she married Miss Joan's step-grandson, "and Miss Joan said to bring these to 'the hero.' I figured that meant you," Joe said, looking at Cody.

Cody shook his head, disavowing any connection to the title. "I'm not a hero," he protested.

"I figure the young woman might have a different opinion about that," Rick commented, selecting a cream-filled pastry from the top. He took a bite before heading to his office. "Damn but that's good. That's got to be Angel's handiwork," he said to Gabe. "You are one lucky son of a gun, Deputy. It's a mystery to me why you haven't blown up to at least twice your normal size since you married that woman."

Picking out a pastry for himself, Gabe sat down at his desk. "It's not like that. Angel cooks and bakes all day long at the diner. The last thing she wants to do when she comes home is cook."

There was genuine pity in Rick's eyes as he looked at his deputy. "You mean you're not going home every night to fantastic meals?"

"I wouldn't say that," Gabe corrected and told the sheriff, "I make most of our meals."

Cody laughed for the first time that morning. "So then I take it you're living on sandwiches? No wonder you're not fat—don't forget, I've had some of your cooking," he reminded his friend.

Gabe drew himself up to his full height. "I'll have you know that I'm a damn good cook," he informed the man he'd known since childhood.

"You just keep on telling yourself that, Gabe," Cody said as he got back to the search he'd started to conduct on his computer.

It was, Rick thought with a hint of a smile as he finally walked back to his small office, business as usual.

Couldn't ask for better than that.

The following morning, Cody popped into the sheriff's office to let him know that he was going to be picking up Devon and the baby at the clinic.

"Take all the time you need," Rick told him. "Nothing of consequence is going on here."

Cody lost no time in getting over to the clinic.

Over the course of the day before, he'd been out on patrol twice, walking the streets of Forever, and maybe it was just his imagination, but he could have sworn that people were smiling at him more broadly than usual.

Cody knew he should just enjoy it and ride the wave of warm approval, but he was a man who felt more comfortable fading into the shadows than being thrust out onto center stage.

Still, as he made his way to the clinic this morning, there were people out who were more than willing to call out their approval.

"Way to go, Deputy."

"Nice job, Cody."

"You did your daddy proud."

The last one, coming from one of his father's oldest friends, tugged at his heart, even though he did his best not to show how affected he was by it.

Cody nodded in response to each and every acknowledgment, trying to be polite while still remaining as self-effacing as usual.

Making his way to the back of the clinic, he saw that the door to the room where Devon was was partially closed.

He would have knocked on the door if he hadn't heard the buzz of mingling voices. He paused for a moment, thinking that perhaps one of the two doctors was in the room with Devon. He definitely didn't want to intrude, especially if she happened to be getting an exam.

"You don't have to stand on ceremony."

The deep male voice was coming from behind him.

Cody turned around just in time to see Dan.

"Go on in," Dan urged, waving him into the room ahead of him. "I'm giving her a clean bill of health," he told Cody.

Opening the door, Cody saw that not only wasn't

Devon alone, several women were in the room with her. In addition to Devon, Holly, Miss Joan and his sister, Cassidy, were all gathered around the hospital bed, leaving precious little space in the room.

They all seemed to be talking at once.

Cody wasn't surprised to see Miss Joan—the people in town had long since given up attempting to pigeonhole the older woman. She was the source of never-ending surprises. Miss Joan showed up wherever she damn well pleased, whenever she felt she was needed. It was obvious by the tray on the side counter that Miss Joan had brought in breakfast for Devon.

And Holly was the nurse, so of course she had every reason to be at a patient's bedside.

It was Cassidy's presence here in Devon's room that threw him.

Beating around the bush had always struck him as a waste of time. He got right to the heart of the matter.

"What are you doing here?" he asked his sister.

Rather than answer him immediately, Cassidy tossed her long blond hair over her shoulder, narrowed her blue eyes and gave him a long, thoughtful once-over.

"Since when have you been put in charge of where I go and what I do?" she asked. Before Cody could comment on his sister's unofficial challenge, Cassidy told him, "If you must know, I'm convincing Devon here that you're harmless." Taking him aside for a second, she added in a lower voice, "I also brought her some clothes I thought she might find handy."

It was Cassidy's tactful way of not mentioning the fact that he'd told her that Devon only had the clothes on her back—and those had been cut off her when he'd brought her in to stop the hemorrhaging.

The *harmless* remark Cassidy had made had caught his attention. Cody looked quizzically from his sister to the woman he had come to take back to the family ranch.

"Come again?"

"I'm vouching for you, Cody," Cassidy said cheerfully. "For all of us at the ranch, really. You do have a shifty face," she patted his cheek by way of underscoring her statement. "Can't blame the poor woman for holding your invitation to come stay at the ranch suspect." Cassidy shrugged carelessly. "I thought that if she knew that you weren't offering to take her to some den of iniquity, she'd relax and agree to stay there while she recuperated."

Flashing a smile at the woman in the bed, Cassidy went on to tell her brother. "It's all settled. She's going to be coming with us."

Despite the fact that she liked the idea of being with Cody and his siblings, Devon felt compelled to offer at least some sort of token protest.

"Layla and I could always stay at the hotel," she told Cody. "Holly said that the one in town is only about three years old."

"And just what would you be using for money, my dear?" Miss Joan asked bluntly. "You said that no-good SOB took your joint savings when he skipped out on you."

Cody shook his head. Leave it to Miss Joan to find out more about Devon in the space of a few minutes than he had in all the hours he'd sat by her bedside the other night, keeping vigil.

Devon attempted to brazen her way through it. "I was thinking of offering to work my debt off once I was on my feet."

"Very noble of you," Miss Joan commented. "Also pointless since you have all these people here offering to take you in, including me. Hospitality beats servitude seven days a week and twice on Sunday," the older woman pointed out.

Feeling outnumbered and outtalked, Cody glanced at the only other male in the room.

As if reading his mind, Dan said, "Dr. Cordell-Murphy gave her a physical yesterday." He smiled at Devon. "Mama and her baby are free to leave the clinic whenever she's ready." Looking at his patient, he added. "You're also free to spend another night here if you'd feel better doing that. You know, one more night to build up your strength."

Devon flashed the doctor a grateful smile. "No disrespect intended, Doctor, but if it's all the same to you, I'd rather get out of your way and settle in somewhere else."

"No disrespect taken," Dan assured her. "So, where'll it be? Miss Joan's home, the McCullough ranch or Holly's house?"

She appreciated the overwhelming generosity of the people in the room. Even so, she wished she had the option of politely turning down all three offers and getting on with her life on her own.

But it wasn't just her life that she was accountable for. She didn't have the luxury of pride where her daughter's comfort was at stake.

"The ranch," Devon finally said quietly. "But I want you to understand that I intend to pay you back," she insisted.

"There's nothing to pay back," Cody replied.

"It's not like Connor has a rental rate posted for the extra bedrooms," Cassidy told the other woman. "Just having that little darling around—" she nodded at the infant lying in the cradle that had been donated to the clinic "—will be payment enough for Connor, trust me." Cassidy gave Devon an encouraging smile. "For all of us, really. The two of you will brighten up the house," Cassidy assured her.

"I guess it's settled, then," Devon said, praying she was making the right decision and that she wouldn't regret it.

But if she was being honest with herself, she really had no other options open to her at this point.

"Good," Cassidy pronounced. "By the way, I brought you a change of clothes, just in case you don't have anything serviceable to wear."

Devon exchanged looks with Cody's sister. "You heard," she guessed. Word apparently got around very fast. She'd been in town only a little more than forty-eight hours.

"That that bastard made off with your clothes when he left?" Cassidy wasn't really asking a question. "Yes, I heard."

"You're better off without that lowlife," Miss Joan declared firmly. "You ask me, losing a few articles of clothing is well worth the price," she told Devon, patting the younger woman's hand. Miss Joan was the heart of the town, but she came with a crusty shell— except when it came to children. The transformation was enough to render a person speechless. "And when you're feeling up to it, I plan to hold a baby shower for you at the diner."

Devon looked at the woman, clearly confused again. "Baby showers are held before the baby's born," she pointed out, skipping over the part that was glaringly obvious to her. Baby showers were thrown by family and friends. These people were neither to her. In her opinion, they had already gone over and above the call of duty helping her.

Since her mother had died, Devon had come to expect nothing from people. That way she found that she was never disappointed.

"At my age, I've learned not to let a few silly rules get in my way or stop me," Miss Joan was saying to her. "And in my opinion, this little lady is definitely in need of a shower."

She had already assessed that the young mother had absolutely nothing when it came to the various items that a newborn required.

"Why don't we clear out and let Devon get dressed?" Holly suggested tactfully. Turning toward the young mother, she made her an offer. "I can stick around if you need any help putting on your new clothes."

"And that'll give me a few more minutes to hold this little darling in my arms," Miss Joan said, cooing to the baby she held close as she walked out of the room.

Miss Joan was followed out by Cody and Cassidy, as well as the doctor.

"Well, I've got a backlog of patients still waiting for me," Dan said by way of parting. He looked over his shoulder back into the room. "Call me if you need me," he told Devon.

Miss Joan waited until the doctor had disappeared into an exam room. "Did you happen to catch sight of the scum who robbed her blind and then cut out on that poor girl?"

"He probably took off in another direction," Cody guessed. He didn't add that he intended to check any reports of recently stolen vehicles within a thirty-mile radius. Layla's father would have needed some mode of transportation since there was no other way to get around.

After he found the man—and he had little doubt that he would—he wasn't sure exactly what he would do. But that wasn't something he had to work out yet. First, he had to catch the bastard. The rest would follow.

Chapter 9

"*That's* your house?" Devon asked Cody in unabashed wonder.

She was sitting in the rear of the truck just behind the passenger seat. Layla's car seat—Tina Davenport had insisted on lending it—was next to her, strapped in right behind the driver's seat.

Devon's question referred to the building she was looking at, a warm, rambling, three-storied structure that seemed to grow larger and more overwhelming the closer the truck came to it.

Cody nodded. "Well, mine and my family's," he told her.

A sliver of wistful envy stirred through her. For Devon, home had been a series of one-bedroom apartments, studio apartments and, on the occasions when her mother couldn't find any work, the backseat of a second-hand SUV or a truck.

"How do you keep from getting lost in it?" Devon asked.

"You get used to it," Cody assured her. "Besides, it's not as big on the inside as it looks."

"It couldn't be," she murmured under her breath, awestruck. And then a practical question occurred to her, one that she hadn't even considered earlier when Cody had convinced her to stay at his place. "Are your brothers okay with my staying here? I know that it's all right with your sister, but a lot of men don't like having their space invaded," she pointed out.

She certainly didn't want to repay Cody for coming to her rescue by causing his brothers to give him grief.

"Well, as you already noticed, this is a large house," Cody told her. "You're not exactly going to be in anyone's way unless they come looking for you."

Cody pulled up the truck in front of the main house. Devon still felt rather uncertain about staying here, but it was too late to change her mind. By the time she had unbuckled her seat belt, Cody had already rounded the truck's hood and was on the passenger side, ready to assist her in any way that she needed him to.

The front door opened even as Cody was pulling open the passenger door on the truck.

Devon saw what appeared to be a slightly older version of Cody run down the three steps that led from the porch.

"Hi," he said, flashing what looked like an identical smile at her. "Welcome to the house. I'm Cole."

"Hi, Cole," she said, returning his greeting. "I'm... dizzy. Wow."

Devon blew out a breath, suddenly feeling a wave of weakness washing over her. It took her completely by surprise because, over the course of the day, she'd felt she was getting stronger. In her opinion, this was a definite setback.

It occurred just as she was stepping out of the vehicle on the passenger side. The second her foot touched the ground, her leg buckled right from under her, sending her straight into Cody's arms. Luckily he'd had the presence of mind to position himself right in front of her, just in case.

Devon flushed, embarrassed. She wasn't supposed to feel like a limp rag doll. "I'm sorry," she said.

"For what? Being human? Not necessary," Cody told her. He was holding her to him and did his best to search her face from that angle. "Do you want to go back to the clinic?"

"Oh Lord, no," Devon cried emphatically. "Not that everyone wasn't nice to me there—they were." Especially when she considered the fact that she had no ties to the town or anyone there. "But I've got to keep moving forward."

"Well, for now, we're putting that 'moving forward' exercise on hold." The next second, rather than putting her back into the truck, he easily lifted her in his arms. "If you don't want to go back to the clinic, okay, but you're going straight to bed,"

She couldn't put him out like this, nor could she allow herself to depend on him. The man was no one to her and owed her nothing. In contrast, she and Jack had planned forever together and that hadn't stopped him from leaving.

"Put me down. I can take care of myself," she protested with feeling.

"That's debatable," Cody answered, making no effort to set her down.

Devon tried again. "My baby," she protested, reaching out to the infant still in the backseat.

"Got her covered. Cole," he called out to his brother, "bring the baby."

For his part, Cole looked a little perplexed. "How do I get her out of this contraption?" he asked, referring to the car seat.

"Bring the whole thing," Cody said. "Just open up the straps tethering the car seat to the truck," he told his older brother.

"If you say so," Cole murmured, trying to get the seat loose.

Cody debated taking Devon inside and putting her in the guest bedroom before coming back out to lend Cole a hand. That would have been the simplest way to go, but he sensed that it would also cause Devon more than a little stress and concern.

"I'm going to set you down for a minute," he told Devon, returning her to her seat. "Okay?"

The world insisted on spinning, even though she was doing her very best to focus on keeping it still.

"Do what you have to do to get her untangled," Devon urged, trying not to let Cody see just how weak she suddenly felt. The last thing she wanted was to divert his attention away from Layla.

Despite Cole's consternation, it took very little effort to untangle the straps that had constrained Layla's car seat.

"*Now* you can take her into the guest bedroom," Cody told his brother, turning his attention back to Devon.

This time, she allowed Cody to pick her up without complaint. She had to admit that having his strong arms around her made her feel safe.

The next moment, she was silently upbraiding herself for feeling that way.

Safe?

What's wrong with you? When are you going to learn? No one is going to be your crutch. You're the only one you can depend on, not some good-looking, sexy deputy sheriff.

She was doing her very best to rein in her feelings while also holding them at arm's length, but she was failing at both. There was this hunger within her to allow someone in, someone who would help her banish the incredible loneliness that had hollowed out her insides.

Cody was aware of her tightening her arms around his neck. Despite the warm feeling being generated within him, he told himself that she was doing it just because she was afraid of being dropped.

Don't make anything of this that it isn't, he warned himself.

"Not too much longer," he promised out loud.

Devon didn't loosen her hold.

Cody carried her into the house and then made a sharp turn to his left. There was a bedroom just off the main living area, its window looking out on what amounted to the front yard.

"This is your room for now," Cody told her, then quickly corrected himself. "I mean it's your room for however long you need it." He didn't want her to feel as if her presence here created any sort of an inconvenience for him or his family.

"Why?" she asked him unexpectedly as he deposited her on the bed.

He wasn't sure what Devon was asking him. "Why what?"

Just then, Cole came in with the baby. He set the car seat on the floor right next to the bed, then backed off, getting the impression that his older brother wanted to have a few words in private with the woman he had brought to the ranch.

"Why are you doing all this? Why are you taking me in, giving me a place to stay without any strings or deadlines attached?"

He didn't see what the big deal was. In his world, you helped people out, no questions asked. "Because you look like you need it," he told her simply.

"And that's it?"

He looked at her, seeing the suspicious expression in her eyes. Again he caught himself wishing he could get his hands on the man who had run out on her, who had stolen her sense of well-being, not to mention her possessions.

"What more should there be?" he asked her.

"Well, for starters," she said, pointing out the obvious, "I'm nobody to you."

"I wouldn't go that far," he told her. "I mean, I did deliver your baby."

She still couldn't really make any sense out of his behavior. She and Jack had made plans, shared dreams— or so she had thought—and none of that had stopped him from ultimately running out on her.

Not just running out, but taking all her money with him, leaving her stranded and on her own without so much as a backward glance or a note of apology. He hadn't even wasted crocodile tears on her and here was this stranger, someone she hadn't even known three days ago, taking her in and behaving as if he was her newly appointed guardian angel.

"I know," she said to Cody. "But that doesn't obligate you to stick by me."

In a way, she reminded him of Flint. When he'd first come across the stallion, the colt had been extremely skittish and it had taken him a great deal of patience to get Flint to trust him.

He viewed Devon the same way.

"I'd say that we've got a difference of opinion there," he told her mildly. "Now, why don't you get some rest?" he suggested. "Cassidy and Cole will look in on you periodically, make sure that everything's okay."

"Where will you be?" That didn't come out right, Devon realized. She didn't want Cody thinking that she was being clingy because she wasn't. She was just trying to get her bearings and the lay of the land. "I mean—"

"I know what you mean," he told her gently. "I've got to get back to work before they figure out how dispensable I actually am."

Before he could say anything, Cassidy walked in, carrying what appeared to be a drawer. "Where do you want this?" she asked.

"Put it over there." He pointed to the side of the bed. "That way," he added, addressing Devon, "it'll be within reach, but still give you plenty of space to get up."

"What are you doing?" Devon asked, watching him as he arranged the drawer. From her vantage point, she could see that the drawer wasn't empty as she had assumed. It was lined with what appeared to be two blankets, one on top of another.

"Well, it's been a long time since there were any babies in this house, so there are no cribs stored in the attic. But Layla has to sleep somewhere, so until we can get a crib for her, this is going to have to do."

"A bureau drawer?" she questioned incredulously.

"Sure. As long as no one decides to close it, it should be just what she needs." Taking the remaining safety belts off the infant, he lifted her out of the car seat and placed her inside the drawer. "Perfect," he declared.

Even as he made the pronouncement, he saw the infant's eyes flutter shut. "I guess she thinks so, too, because she's falling asleep. I suggest that you do the same," he told Devon.

He started to leave the room when she called him back. "Cody?"

Cody retraced the few steps back to her bed. Devon raised herself up as far as she could and then beckoned him in a little closer. When he bent down, expecting her to share some whispered secret with him, he was surprised to feel the fleeting pass of her lips against his cheek.

He could have sworn he felt a glow spreading out through him in its wake.

Moving back a little, Cody looked at the woman in confusion.

"Thank you," she whispered, her voice brimming with emotion.

And then, the next moment, before he could tell her that she had nothing to thank him for, he saw that Devon had fallen asleep, just like her daughter.

Cody lingered there for a moment, just watching her sleep.

"Don't worry," he whispered to the sleeping pair, "I'll take care of you."

He felt the lighter-than-air imprint of Devon's lips on his skin throughout the drive back to the sheriff's office.

* * *

"Feeling better?" Cody asked. His shift over, he'd lost no time in hurrying back to the ranch.

Once there, his first order of business was to look in on Devon. There'd been no phone call from either Cassidy or Cole, so he could only assume that everything was going along peacefully.

Devon was up, out of bed and sitting in the rocking chair where Cody's mother had once sat, rocking each one of them to sleep when they were infants. Layla was in her arms. It struck Cody that, somehow, things seemed to have come full circle.

"Yes, much," she answered with a welcoming smile. "Looks like a little angel, doesn't she?" she whispered, still very much in awe that she had given birth to this miracle.

He came around to her side and peered at the tiny, sleeping face.

"She looks like her mother," he told Devon.

The comparison surprised her. "You really think so?"

There was no question about it in Cody's mind. "I do."

Devon looked down at the baby in her arms and then shook her head. "I don't see it," she confessed.

If anything, she thought she could see traces of Jack in the baby and that bothered her a little. She didn't want to be reminded of all the heartache and humiliation that were involved with Jack's memory.

"Well, she does," Cody said simply. "Have you had anything to eat?" he asked.

"Cassidy brought me something earlier, but I don't have much of an appetite," Devon confessed.

"You need to force yourself," he told her. "You're

still eating for two, you know. You've got to build up your strength. You don't want to be bedridden forever."

"I'm not going to be bedridden forever," she protested.

"Good." Opening the bag he'd brought with him, he set out a covered dish on the makeshift tray Cassidy had dug up for her. "This is for you."

Devon raised an eyebrow at the sight of the foil-covered offering.

"Miss Joan had Angel prepare this for you," Cody told her. "She told me that if I didn't make you eat this, she was going to hunt me down and find a way to make me pay for it."

"No, she didn't." Devon dismissed the threat with a laugh.

"Oh yes, she did," he told her in no uncertain terms. "Miss Joan doesn't accept any excuses. She expects results. In your case, that result is in the form of fattening you up."

Cody sat down beside the tray. She allowed him to remove the foil. She had to admit that the scent of the tri-tip sirloin had her mouth watering, which surprised her. She was at the point where she'd assumed no meal would be appealing to her.

Devon had to ask. "Why would she or you care if I eat or not?"

"Why's the sky blue?"

Devon wasn't sure she had heard him correctly. "What?"

"The point is," he clarified, "some things just are— we don't waste time questioning them. Now, start eating so I don't have to try to lie to Miss Joan tomorrow."

"Try to lie?" she repeated. "I'd imagine you're probably very good at it."

He didn't rise to the bait. "Well, I don't lie," he told her simply. "And even if I did, I'd never attempt to lie to Miss Joan. The woman is a human lie detector machine."

"Okay, now I know you're kidding."

"Nope," Cody deadpanned. "That woman has a way of looking at you that makes even a hardened criminal start to confess to things."

Devon was fairly certain he was putting her on, but the sandwich Miss Joan had sent her was far too delicious for her to reject—so she didn't even try.

Chapter 10

The scent of fresh brewing coffee had the allure of a siren's song for Cody as he came down the stairs the following morning.

As a rule, Cody, his brothers and sister took turns making breakfast for the others, although between over-sleeping and running late, that breakfast more often than not consisted of something simple and basic, like orange juice and dry cereal.

This morning, if he recalled correctly, it was Connor's turn to prepare breakfast. Connor, he knew, favored oatmeal, something the rest of them preferred to pass on.

"Guess you decided to go all out this morning, Connor," Cody commented as he walked into the kitchen.

He stopped dead when he saw that Conner was sitting at the table instead of standing at the stove, preparing four breakfasts. Layla was in her car seat on the table right in front of him, occupying all of his attention.

"Not me," Connor replied, nodding his head at their houseguest.

Devon was standing in front of the stove, her hair clipped back, and it was her, not Connor, who was busy preparing breakfast for the family. She looked like a vision, Cody couldn't help thinking.

"What's going on?" Cody asked his older brother.

"Hey, don't look at me," Connor protested. He was gently rocking the baby's car seat. "When I came in, Devon was already busy getting breakfast ready. Wait until you try her coffee," he told his brother. It was obvious that the brew had gotten his vote.

"And you let her?" Cody questioned. That wasn't like Connor. His brother normally liked being in control of every situation.

Connor exchanged glances with Devon before answering his brother, "Hey, I learned a long time ago not to get in between a woman and her spatula."

Trying not to look annoyed, Cody crossed over to Devon. "You are supposed to be in bed," he told her sternly.

Devon gave him a wide smile as she kept an eye on two frying pans at the same time. "I'm feeling much better now."

Frustrated, Cody looked at the woman. He couldn't order her around, but he really wished she'd listen to reason. He doubted if she understood how close she had come to dying.

"Just what do you think you're doing?" Cody demanded helplessly.

She spared him another quick glance. "Paying you

back in some small way," she told him. "Really, I'm much better," she said, and then, because he didn't look convinced, she added another emphatic "really."

Cody blew out a breath. Talk about being stubborn. "You know, there's no need for you to do this," he insisted.

"Yes, there is," she countered. "I told you yesterday, I am not a charity case."

"Nobody here thinks of you as a charity case," Cody assured her. "Tell her, Connor," he said, enlisting his older brother's help.

"Nobody here thinks of you as a charity case," Connor parroted.

"Then don't make me feel like one." Devon's words were directed at Cody.

After sliding what amounted to a giant omelet onto a plate, Devon cut it into four sections and a sliver. She distributed them onto five plates and added several strips of bacon from the other frying pan to each one.

"Let me do this," she requested as she placed a plate before him and then one in front of Connor. "I promise I won't poison you."

Cody had to admit that the omelet not only looked tempting, but smelled it, as well. He gave up trying to resist.

"I'm not worried about that. If we can survive Connor's cooking, we can survive anything you come up with," he told her. "And if this tastes even half as good as it smells, you will have turned us all into true believers."

"Hey, what is that great smell?" Cole asked, coming into the kitchen. "Did Connor suddenly get some cooking lessons?"

Connor looked up from his plate. "What's wrong with my cooking?" he asked.

Devon had met Connor only fleetingly yesterday when Cody had brought her to the house. She didn't want the man to think she was trying to upstage him. After all, Connor was head of the household, even though, according to Cody, the house actually belonged to all four of them and they shared equally in all the duties that were involved in running it.

"There's nothing wrong with it. Dinner was wonderful," Devon told the oldest McCullough. "I just thought you and the others might want a reprieve from kitchen duty."

"Amen to that," Connor agreed. "And for the record, Cassidy made dinner last night, not me." In between healthy forkfuls of his serving of Spanish omelet, he told her, "Well, I have to admit, this tastes even better than it smells."

Devon smiled broadly, relieved. She knew that the breakfast she'd prepared was good, but some people might still have taken offense. She was relieved that Connor was not small-minded.

"Hey, what's going on?" Cassidy asked, straggling into the kitchen and joining her brothers. "You guys are making enough noise to wake the dead."

"The hungry dead," Cole interjected, taking in another forkful of his omelet.

Smiling at Devon, Cassidy took a seat. "Well, this is different," she commented as she took her usual seat at the table and pulled over one of the last two plates that Devon had prepared. "Are you getting creative in your old age, Con?"

"Connor can't take the credit for this," Cody told her. "Devon made breakfast today."

"Devon?" Cassidy echoed, looking around the table at her brothers. "Why are you putting the poor woman to work?"

"Hey, I had nothing to do with it," Cody protested, raising his hands to ward off Cassidy's words of accusation. "When I came into the kitchen, she was already cooking."

"Did she make the coffee, too?" Cole asked. He was nursing a mug that was twice as large as a regular cup.

"Yes, *she* did," Devon answered, wondering if hers didn't measure up to what they were accustomed to.

Cole grinned at her. "Well, I don't know about the others, but as far as I'm concerned, you can stay here forever. Hate to tell you, Connor, but this is a *lot* better than what you come up with. What did you do to this?" he asked after taking another long swallow. "This tastes great." He got up and helped himself to another mugful.

"I used chicory to cut the bitterness," she confessed. It was something her grandmother had taught her, years ago.

"We have that?" Cassidy questioned.

"I found some in the back of your pantry," Devon told her. She'd come across it while rummaging around to see what she could add to the omelet.

"Pure heaven," Cassidy pronounced after draining her cup. "Well, you've got my vote," she told their houseguest cheerfully. "Connor's coffee tastes more like semisoft mud."

Connor leveled a seemingly reproving look at his sister. "You never complained before."

"That's because if I did, you would have stuck me

with permanent KP duty." Her eyes shifted to Devon, who had taken a seat beside Cody. She smiled at the other woman. "But now we've got an alternative."

"Hey, Devon's not here to cook for us," Cody said defensively.

Devon put her hand on his to stop him from making any further protests. "It's okay. I need to feel useful," she told him and the others.

"Like Cole said, you've got a place here for as long as you like," Connor told her.

Devon smiled her thanks. She knew that Connor and the others were most likely just being polite, but it was nice to hear and she did like to feel as if she was pulling her own weight. Their approval, well-deserved or not, felt good. It made her realize how much she'd missed hearing that.

Jack never had any actually kind words for her. He'd once told her that if he didn't like something, *then* she'd know about it. To him, the absence of criticism was supposed to be taken as an unspoken compliment. She could never make him understand that she needed more than that, that she needed to actually *hear* praise once in a while. Heaven knew she'd been more than generous and loving when it came to flattering him. But the lesson never seemed to take root with him.

As if feeling left out of the adult conversation, Layla began to stir and within a few seconds, she was mewling.

"Sorry," Cole apologized to her. "I guess we got a little too loud."

Devon was quick to absolve him of any guilt. "No, I think she just got jealous, watching everyone eating breakfast except her," Devon said. Putting everything else on temporary hold, she extracted the infant from her car seat. "She wants some of her own. Let's go, little one," she murmured lovingly to her daughter. "Time to get you fed."

As she began to make her way out of the room, Devon paused to look over her shoulder. "Leave everything the way it is. I'll clean up after Layla's been fed."

"Did you find out anything about her yet?" Connor asked Cody once Devon had retreated to the guest room with Layla.

"No, not yet." He didn't add that he felt it best not to prod Devon for any information. Instead, he wanted to present himself as a willing listener if she decided that she wanted someone to confide in. "Some people take longer to open up than Cassidy," Cody added.

"Hey, I resent that," Cassidy pretended to pout. "Just because I'm friendly—"

"That's one word for it, little sister," Cody countered.

Cassidy raised an eyebrow. "Oh? And what's another word for it?"

"Okay, you two, time-out," Connor told them as he stood up. "Well, I've got a ranch to run so I'd better get to it." His eyes swept over his siblings before he left the table and walked out. "I suggest you do the same. Good meal," he murmured before he disappeared.

"Love to linger over this coffee," Cole told Cody, "but I promised Jackson White Eagle I'd be back to lend a hand at The Healing Ranch," he said, referring to the ranch that had recently had an influx of twice the applicants they normally received. Ever since an article in a national magazine had appeared, citing the ranch's success rate in turning troubled youths around, there had been no shortage of requests for a spot in the innovative program.

"Gotta run, too," Cassidy announced, making a hasty retreat before Cody could ask her any questions.

"Looks like it's just you and me," Cody murmured to the collection of dirty dishes around him at the table. He'd already told the sheriff that he would be coming in later than usual and had gotten the man's blessing.

Despite what Devon had said about leaving everything just as it was, Cody made short work of cleaning up. The dishes were washed, dried and put away. It went faster than he'd thought it would.

He knew he should get going, but he didn't want to just leave without letting Devon know that she would be alone in the house. He wanted to give her a phone number so she could reach him just in case.

Making his way to her room, Cody knocked on Devon's door.

She responded immediately. "Yes?"

Taking that to be an invitation, Cody opened the door. The next second, he stopped dead, stunned and freezing in place.

Devon was sitting on her bed, Layla gathered against her breast. She was still nursing her daughter.

It was—he later thought, looking back—probably the most beautiful sight he had ever seen. But he certainly wasn't free to give voice to that feeling. At the very least, he didn't want to embarrass her.

So he swung his head in the opposite direction, looking away.

"I'm sorry," he told her with feeling. "I didn't mean to just walk in like that. I thought you'd put her down for a nap. I mean—" He fumbled, not knowing what to say to convey just *how* sorry he was for intruding on her in such a private moment.

"It's okay," Devon assured him, her tone understanding as she absolved him of any perceived wrongdoing. "Seems that this little lady is an extremely slow eater."

Deftly pulling her blouse back into place, she put the baby up against her shoulder and began to pat Layla gently on the back.

"Did you want to tell me something?" Devon asked, taking the focus off herself and what Cody had just seen. Theirs, after all, was a rather unique relationship. Cody had already seen far more of her than any other man except for Jack.

Cody was exceedingly grateful to Devon for not making a big deal out of what happened, but by the same token, *because* she was being so nice about it, he felt guilty that it had happened in the first place.

Clearing his throat, he grasped at the excuse she had handed him. "I wanted to know if you needed anything before I went to work."

"You're leaving?" she asked, mildly surprised.

Cody sensed what wasn't being said. "I can stay if you'd rather have someone here."

Devon shook her head. She didn't mean to make him feel that he had to stay with her. Thinking about it, she could use a little alone time herself.

"You've already done a lot for me. I'm not going to make you stay and hold my hand," she told him. "Layla and I will be fine, won't we, little one?" she said, addressing her question to the infant who was curled up against her shoulder.

Cody took out one of the business cards Cassidy had made up for him as a gift when he'd joined the sheriff's department. It was meant to show Cody how proud they all were of him.

He handed the card to Devon. "That's the phone number at the sheriff's office. Call me if you need anything—or," he added as an afterthought, "if you just want to talk."

She looked at the card before she tucked it into her pocket. "To be honest, what I need right now is some time alone to just pull myself together."

"You look pretty put together to me already." The comment came out before he could censor it. What was wrong with him? He usually exercised more control over himself than this. "Okay, then," he told her as if he hadn't made the other comment, "Connor should be back sometime around noon or so."

"Okay, anything else I should know?" she asked.

He felt she needed to know how much they appreciated what she'd gone out of her way to do, despite what she'd been through herself. "Only that everyone walked out of here smiling because that had to be the best breakfast we've had in a really long time."

Devon couldn't help beaming, even as she dismissed his compliment. "Then I'd say that you and your family are very easily pleased."

"Not really," he interjected, and then told her, "The phone's in the kitchen if you need to call."

Devon nodded, suppressing an amused smile. "I noticed this morning," she replied.

"Right, of course you did." She had to think he was some kind of country bumpkin, Cody upbraided himself.

"You want me to bring you back anything?" he asked just as he was about to leave her bedroom.

"No, I'm good," she assured him. "But be sure to thank Miss Joan for me for the sandwich."

He'd forgotten about that. That Devon had remembered gave him a good feeling about the young woman. She obviously didn't take anything for granted.

"She'll appreciate that," he told her.

He was lingering again, Devon noted. And, as much as she found that she liked having him around, she couldn't allow herself to get used to it or feeling that way.

"You should go," she prompted. "You don't want to be late, especially not on my account."

"Okay, then—you're sure you'll be all right?" he asked one last time.

She rose from the bed and crossed to where he was standing. "I've been on my own for a long time now, Cody. I'll be fine," she assured him.

Then, as if to end the discussion and put an end to any lingering concern he might be harboring, she placed one hand on his shoulder to anchor herself and then rose on her toes. The next moment, she brushed her lips against his cheek.

"Now go," she instructed.

Cody backed out of the room until he felt the heel of his boot hit the threshold. Only then did he turn around and leave.

He caught himself wanting to remain, just in case, but he knew she was right. He needed to get to work and she probably needed her space right now, just like she had said. He didn't doubt that she needed to sort out her feelings and emotions, not to mention find a way to adjust to being a first-time young mother, something that was bound to throw her world into a tailspin.

As for him, he needed to get to the sheriff's office not just because it was his job, but because he wanted to use the search engines available to him there to see if he could somehow track down the man who had run out on Devon. He wanted the man to own up to his responsibilities. He'd stolen her money and at the very least he needed to make some sort of restitution for that.

If Cody could possibly help it, he wasn't about to let that rotten SOB get away with it.

Chapter 11

There were those in and around Forever, Cody among them, who felt that Miss Joan really did have eyes in the back of her head. How else would she be aware of every little thing that was happening, often simultaneously, in her crowded diner? It was a given that nothing got past the titian-haired woman with the deep, penetrating hazel eyes.

Today was no different. Cody had barely made it in through the diner door at lunchtime—always an incredibly busy time of day for Miss Joan—before she was suddenly next to him. He'd come in to get food to go and to express Devon's thanks for the sirloin sandwich the woman had sent over last night.

"Missed you this morning," Miss Joan informed him, startling Cody. "When you didn't come in for your morning coffee, I thought you'd decided to stay home and lend that little girl a hand with her baby."

Cody congratulated himself for giving no indication that the woman had caught him off guard. "No, actually, Devon made coffee for all of us this morning." He added tactfully, "It was almost as good as yours, Miss Joan."

Far from acting slighted, the owner of the diner was very displeased by what he was telling her. "You've got that girl making coffee?" Miss Joan asked him in an accusatory tone. "What else are you having her do?"

Cody deflected the blame easily. "No, she insisted, Miss Joan. By the time I got down to the kitchen, Devon had already made coffee and she had breakfast going, as well. She said she needed to do that not to feel like a charity case."

Cody held his breath, waiting for the older woman's reaction. Miss Joan was nothing if not unpredictable. Finally, the woman slowly nodded her head in approval. "Spunky. I like that."

He breathed a silent sigh of relief. "She wanted me to thank you for sending over that dinner last night. She really enjoyed it."

He could see the older woman was pleased, even though she waved the words away. Miss Joan drew him over to the counter, and then made her way behind it. In a second, she was filling customers' coffees.

"How's she doing today?" she asked.

Cody smiled. "She looks a lot better than she did when I brought her into the clinic." Anything would have been an improvement over that.

"Well, I should hope so," Miss Joan said sharply. "And the baby?"

"Sounds happy, looks healthy." He knew that Miss Joan appreciated brevity. She didn't like wading through miles of words to reach the answers she wanted.

"You got everything you need?" she questioned. "Because I had Henry pick up a couple of packs of disposable diapers to tide her over." To prove it, she took out the packs from behind the counter and placed them in front of Cody.

The woman was a godsend. "She could definitely use those," he agreed.

Miss Joan's next question came right out of the blue and caught him off guard, although it did reinforce his belief that the woman was all-seeing. "What's the baby sleeping in?"

"Right now, a drawer," he told her, watching for her reaction.

The pencil-thin eyebrows narrowed above her piercing hazel eyes. "A what?" she demanded.

Cody tried to make it sound more accommodating. "We put blankets and a sheet into a drawer. It was the best I could come up with on the spur of the moment. It's been years since there was a crib set up in the house," he told her by way of an excuse.

Miss Joan pressed her thin lips together and he knew that what he'd just told her was not making her happy, but there wasn't anything he could do about it. His father had gotten rid of the crib years ago, when Cassidy turned five.

Just as he decided that she wasn't going to say anything else to him, Miss Joan instructed, "All right, stop by here on your way home tonight."

"Why?" He'd planned on not wasting any time and just going directly to the ranch the minute he clocked out at the sheriff's office.

"Because I just told you to," Miss Joan retorted. "Didn't your father ever teach you not to question your elders?"

"I guess he must've skipped that lesson," Cody told her with a grin.

Miss Joan pinned him with a look. "Don't give me any snappy answers, young man. Just be here." She waved him over to one of the waitresses. "Now, tell Margarita your order and go get back to work," she told him, and then specified, "Pronto."

"Yes, ma'am," Cody replied, turning toward the waitress she had pointed out.

Like a woman on a mission, Miss Joan went back to her small office at the rear of the diner. She had phone calls to make.

Cody pulled his packed truck up right in front of the house. This would definitely *not* have been a good day for riding Flint to work.

He eased his way out from behind the steering wheel, barely being able to wiggle passed the various items that had been stuffed into his truck. As it was, there wasn't enough space leftover in the cab for an oversize cough drop.

Miss Joan had been exceptionally busy playing the sharp-tongued fairy godmother.

Closing the driver's side door, Cody decided to leave everything Miss Joan's husband and step-grandson had loaded onto his truck. He would need help getting the things out and, since he didn't see any other vehicle in front of the house except for Devon's beaten-up truck, he assumed that the others hadn't come home yet.

So, for the time being, he left everything where it was, except for the diapers. Those he took in with him.

After tucking one bag under his arm, he unlocked the front door. Ordinarily, the door was rarely locked.

Safety around here was not an issue. But because he'd left Devon on her own with the baby, he felt justified in taking the extra precaution.

"Hi, I'm home," he called out, closing the door behind him.

He thought it best to announce himself—just in case. After accidentally walking in on Devon when she was breastfeeding the baby, he didn't want to take a chance on that happening again. She had enough to deal with without thinking that she had temporarily thrown her lot in with a voyeur.

"Devon?" Cody called out, although not too much louder. He didn't want to risk waking up the baby if she'd fallen asleep somewhere close by, such as the living room.

But Layla wasn't in the living room. Neither was Devon.

Because he was focused on finding her and her baby, Cody didn't realize until he'd taken several steps into the living room that there was something else missing, as well.

The chaos that had been in the room as he'd left this morning was no longer there. Haphazardly thrown shirts and jackets, books and notepads, actually *all* the things that had been strewn around were no longer evident. In their place, order had been restored.

Out of all of them, Connor was the orderly one, but in the last few weeks, he'd been too busy with calving season on the ranch to pay attention to the growing piles in the living room that had all but taken on a life of their own.

Everything was neatly stacked, folded or just plain put away.

Cody made his way through the room, looking around uncertainly.

"Connor?" he called out, even though he hadn't seen Connor's truck parked anywhere outside. "Are you home?"

This time, he got a response, although it wasn't from Connor or anyone else in his family. Instead, Devon walked into the room looking fairly pleased with herself.

"You're home early," she observed. "I didn't think you'd be back for another hour.

He noticed that she had on a pair of jeans and a blouse that looked vaguely familiar. Her midnight black hair was loose and seemed to swing about her face as she walked. He had to force himself not to stare.

Another man might have said something about wanting to rush back home to see how she was doing, but Cody was nothing if not honest. His father had once observed that he didn't think Cody *knew* how to lie.

"Everybody was fixated on having me go home early, so I finally took the hint."

"Everybody?" Devon questioned, not exactly sure who he was referring to.

"Miss Joan mostly," he clarified. "But the sheriff, too. He told me I'd do more good at home than at the office." He looked around. "Did Connor come home during the day?" He thought that would be odd because, at breakfast, Connor had mentioned having to stay out all day.

"No, why?" she asked uneasily.

Was this about the living room? She'd wanted to do something nice and she'd wanted to keep busy, but maybe she'd overstepped her boundaries. She certainly didn't want to annoy Cody and the others or offend them for some reason.

Cody gestured around the room. "It's neat," he said, clearly confused.

She watched his expression as she explained. "Oh, that—well, I thought since the baby was asleep and I had time on my hands…"

To her relief, he didn't look angry, just mystified. "If you had time on your hands, you should have taken a nap, too," he told her.

Devon shook her head. "Not my style," she said, and then hastily assured Cody, "Don't worry, I didn't get rid of anything. I just organized it. The books are on shelves in the bookcase and the clothes are hung up in the hall closet."

He looked around the room again, clearly impressed. It hadn't been this uncluttered in a long time. "You did a nice job," he said belatedly.

She beamed but made no comment. Instead, she pointed to the two large bags he was still holding in his hands. "What's that?" she asked.

He'd almost forgotten. "Oh right. Miss Joan sent over some disposable diapers."

The expression on her face couldn't have been brighter than if he had just presented her with a five-carat diamond. Still, she was a little wary. "Why would she do that?"

"Because she's Miss Joan," he told her, adding, "It doesn't get any more complicated than that, trust me. When she thinks something needs to be done or taken care of, she just does it."

For now, Devon set aside her suspicions. "Really? That's wonderful," she cried.

Now that her guard was down, at least temporarily, Devon looked like a kid on Christmas morning, he thought. "She sent other things," he told her.

This was beginning to feel like a dream, Devon thought. Who *were* these people anyway? She looked at him a little uncertainly.

"What other things?" she asked.

"They're in the truck." He decided not to wait for help. After all, he wasn't exactly a weakling. He just had to exercise caution in lifting some things out. "I'll bring them in," he told her.

Within a few minutes, the newly uncluttered living room was filled with a different sort of clutter. There was a large box of baby clothes, ranging from newborn to twelve months old, a bassinet that looked as if it had come straight out of a fairy tale and a box of toys of various sizes, most of them stuffed.

It was too good to be true.

She could feel her eyes welling up as she ran her hand ever so lightly over the bassinet. Since it was mounted on wheels, it would be easy for her to move to any part of the guest room as well as into the living room and the kitchen if she needed to.

"This is wonderful," she said in a small, halting voice, afraid to speak up because she thought her voice would crack. "Where did you get all this?"

"Miss Joan is very resourceful," he told her matter-of-factly. "And," he added, "there have been a number of babies born in Forever in the last few years. Miss Joan just knew who to call.

"Technically," he specified, "these are all on loan—except for the diapers, of course."

"I don't care if they're on loan," Devon told him.

"The fact that I can use them even for a little while is just wonderful," she said, tearing up completely.

Cody noticed immediately. He'd heard her voice crack. Nothing made him feel more helpless than tears. "Oh, hey, you're not going to cry, are you?"

"No," she said and then promptly had several fat tears go cascading down both of her cheeks.

Unable to talk for a moment, she waved away any words that he was going to say. She knew she couldn't answer him.

It took her a moment to catch her breath.

At a loss, not knowing what else to do, Cody took her in his arms and just held her, saying nothing. He didn't want her to feel he was trying to intrude on her feelings or take advantage of her. He just wanted her to know that he was there for her, no matter what she needed.

Regaining control over herself, Devon took a deep breath and stepped back after a second. Cody handed her his handkerchief and waited until she'd fully composed herself.

"It's okay," he told her. "Just take your time. There's no hurry."

She pressed her lips together, still trying to regain control and to sound coherent. It took her another couple of minutes.

When Devon could finally talk, she told Cody, "It's just that no one's ever done anything like this for me. Ever."

"Well, they should have." It was all that he would allow himself to say. He knew that if he gave voice to what he was feeling, if he said the negative things he was thinking about the man who had skipped out on her, it would do her no good to hear them.

Because he needed something to divert her attention for a moment, Cody directed it toward the bassinet.

"Let's get this into your room and see how the princess likes her new sleeping accommodations," he suggested. "Anything has to be an improvement over that drawer."

Devon wiped away her tears, grateful to Cody for what he was attempting to do. "Oh, I don't know," she said, playing along. "The drawer wasn't such a bad idea. Actually, I think it was kind of sweet, seeing her in it. And," she added, "it was definitely original."

"Well, maybe not that original," Cody admitted. "Before they found out about me, my parents really weren't expecting another baby. Cole was in the only crib they had and they didn't think putting both of us in that one crib was a good idea, so for about the first month, until they could find a second-hand crib for me, my dad had me sleeping in what used to be the sock drawer."

She laughed, charmed. "Thank you for this."

"Hey, don't thank me," he told her. "Thank Miss Joan. This was all her doing. She knew who to call and nobody says no to Miss Joan." He winked. "It just isn't done."

"Well, tell her I think she's wonderful," Devon said and then added, "And I think you're wonderful, as well."

Overwhelmed with gratitude and just plain happiness, Devon meant to underscore her thanks with a kiss to his cheek. But this time, just as she was about to brush her lips against it, Cody turned his head to say something to her.

Which was how her lips wound up on his.

To say that Cody was surprised to find himself in that position would have been a huge understatement. He more than half expected Devon to pull back.

But she didn't.

Once what had happened registered with her, instead of quickly pulling away and mumbling some sort of embarrassed, half-coherent apology, Devon surprised them both by continuing the contact.

And just like that, the kiss transformed to one that was meant to be a person-to-person kiss rather than just a quick, fleeting peck on the cheek.

The moment the kiss deepened, it became a genuine kiss.

For just a moment, she let herself go—all the pent-up feelings, anxieties, emotions, *everything* that was inside her rose within her chest and found release in the timeless contact.

Stunned, Cody was afraid that if he reacted accordingly, he'd scare her off.

But then he decided to risk it by folding his arms around her and drawing her just a hint closer. Her mouth tasted sweet, sweeter than anything he could recall ever having sampled.

If he continued on this route, emotions might just spike, rising to a level where they were not easily kept in check.

So it was with the greatest reluctance that he forced himself to break contact and end the kiss.

"Sorry," he murmured, "I didn't mean to take advantage of you."

"You didn't," she whispered.

Then, afraid of what he might think of her for needing him like this, Devon stepped back. "I made dinner," she told him. "I hope Connor won't mind."

"Mind?" he repeated. "He'll be relieved and thrilled. Connor hates cooking. He just does it out of necessity."

He confided, "We all do. But I didn't bring you here to clean and cook,"

"I know that," she replied. "But I didn't know what else to do with myself."

He smiled at Devon. "The word *rest* comes to mind."

"I did," she told him. "But I couldn't do that all day," she protested.

Cody laughed. "I know several people who could argue that point with you." He was about to say something else, but Layla began to cry. "Is she hungry?" he asked.

Devon checked the baby's bottom first. "No. You brought those diapers home just in time," she told him.

"Need help?" he asked.

She was about to tell him that she could do it herself and then had second thoughts. "An extra set of hands might be nice," she told him.

"Funny you should say that. I just happen to have a set," he said with a grin, holding his hands up in the air the way a surgeon might when entering an operating room. "Let's get your daughter dry."

Devon could only smile at that. Smile and fervently pray that she wouldn't wake up too soon.

Chapter 12

"Well, it's official," Connor declared, pushing back his empty plate on the dining room table. For a moment, he sat there, feeling too full to even move. For once he'd eaten too much, something he rarely did. But it had definitely been worth it. "You have a place here for as long as you want, Devon." A sigh of contentment escaped his lips. "That has to be one of the best meals I can remember ever having eaten. Where did you learn how to cook that way?" he asked her.

Color crept up into Devon's cheeks. The oldest McCullough's compliment had embarrassed her even as it pleased her.

"Necessity," Devon replied simply. "My mother taught me how to make do with whatever I found in the refrigerator and the pantry. Adding a few spices and flavored breadcrumbs to the mix can really work miracles if you do it right," she said modestly.

"Well, whatever it is that you're doing, keep right on doing it," Cole told her, joining the chorus of approval.

Cody had enjoyed the meal as much as everyone else had, maybe even more, but he really didn't want Devon to feel obligated or put upon. "C'mon, people, you don't want to make her feel like she's got to keep cooking for us," he protested.

"I'm with Cody. You're going to make her feel like an indentured servant who can't say no," Cassidy said.

"No, really, I don't mind," Devon said. "It makes me feel that I'm at least paying you back in some small way for all your kindness," she told the others as she started to gather up the dinner plates and silverware. "Besides, I like cooking."

"Well, you can go on cooking for us if you don't mind doing it, but no way are you going to wash the dishes after the meal's over," Cody informed her sternly, moving the stacked dishes away from her.

"Cody's right," Cassidy told her. "Cooking is a talent—washing dishes is just grunt work."

"Glad you feel that way," Cody told his sister. "As I remember, it's your turn in the kitchen." He pushed the dishes in front of Cassidy.

Cassidy pursed her lips, frowned and then, with a sigh, got to her feet as she picked up the stack of dirty dishes.

"No, really," Devon insisted, "I don't mind cleaning up after a meal."

"You might not," Connor allowed, "but we do. Cassidy's right. Cooking is more than enough. Cleaning up would turn you into a maid and you're our guest," Connor informed her.

The discussion was abruptly cut short by the Mc-Culloughs' tiniest guest. Devon had wheeled Layla's bassinet into the dining room, placing it in the far corner so that she'd be able to hear her daughter when she woke up.

Which she did.

"I believe that settles the argument," Cody quipped with a laugh. Not waiting for Devon to cross to the bassinet, he got there ahead of her. "And what's your complaint?" he asked the infant, looking down at the little puckered face.

"Well, I fed her and changed her just before dinner so my guess is that she probably just wants attention," Devon speculated.

"Then attention is what this little princess is going to get," Cody declared.

Leaning over the bassinet, he deftly picked up the baby. Layla settled down the moment he had her against his shoulder.

"If I didn't know any better, I'd say that it looks like she's taken a shine to you," Cole told his brother.

"Why not?" Cassidy spoke up. "They're about the same age."

"Don't pay any attention to them, Princess," Cody told the infant in his arms. "They're just jealous because you like me better than them."

Infants weren't supposed to be able to recognize anyone and most likely it was gas that was responsible for that funny little twist of her lips, but Devon chose to believe otherwise.

"She does seem to light up around you," Devon agreed, smiling.

And Layla isn't the only one, she added silently. She shut out the thought since she was in a vulnerable place right now and Cody was being nice to her. There was no reason to make anything of that. She knew what could happen if she wasn't vigilant about her feelings.

Out loud she told Cody, "I guess she senses how kind you are."

"Or maybe she just thinks you need a friend your own age," Cole cracked.

Cody turned his back on Cole, ignoring his brother. The baby had all his attention. "Don't pay any attention to him, Princess. He just likes to hear himself talk."

"C'mon, sweetie, it's time to give you your first bath," Devon told her daughter as she took the infant from Cody.

"A bath?" Cole echoed, concerned. "Isn't she a little small for that?"

"Not really." Devon laughed. "I'm bathing her in the bathroom sink, not the bathtub," she assured Cody's brother. Seeing the somewhat-concerned looks on all their faces, she assured the others, "She'll be fine. I'm going to be in complete control."

"Want some help?" Cody volunteered.

She wanted to tell him that she didn't need help, that she had this covered, but that was just her independent streak talking. The truth of it was that every new thing she attempted with her daughter had her trembling inside.

So rather than turn Cody down, Devon flashed a relieved smile at him and accepted his offer. "That would be very nice of you."

"Nice is my middle name," he told her in a low voice, hoping not to be overheard by any of his siblings.

He hoped in vain. Cole and Cassidy rolled their eyes in response to his comment. Connor merely shook his head. But since none of them said anything in response, Cody counted himself ahead in the game.

"Good to know," Devon replied before pushing the bassinet back into the guest room as Cody followed her with the baby.

After moving the bassinet into a corner, she turned around to face Cody. There was something so very heartwarming about seeing him cradling her daughter in his arms.

Snap out of it, Devon. No more entanglements, remember?

Squaring her shoulders, she told Cody, "Why don't you continue to hold her while I get everything ready?"

"Don't have to ask me twice," he answered. Layla looked perfectly fine with this arrangement, Devon couldn't help thinking.

She swiftly laid out the baby's new diaper and a change of clothing, thanks to the box of clothes Miss Joan had collected for Layla.

With that ready, she went to the bathroom sink and ran the water, making sure it was just the right temperature for the infant. Aside from a large, fluffy towel, she also got a cup ready, placing it nearby.

"Okay," Devon said, taking the baby from Cody, "Time to make a water baby out of you," she told Layla as she laid the infant on her bed.

She removed the baby's clothing, secretly relieved that Layla had seen fit not to leave any unexpected deposits in her fresh diaper.

Cody watched her as she got the baby ready for her bath. "You sure you didn't have any younger brothers or sisters?" he asked her.

"Nope," she verified, "it was always just me."

She seemed to be too confident about what she was doing to be a novice, he thought. "But you babysat a lot of infants, right?"

"No. Why would you say that?"

Slowly immersing Layla's lower half into the water, she gently splashed a little water along the baby's tummy. Layla made a noise that sounded as if she liked what was happening.

"You just seem very comfortable with all this. I thought maybe you'd done it before." And then he shrugged. "I guess you're just a natural."

She laughed. For a second, she considered letting his impression stand, but then she thought better of it. She didn't want him thinking she was something she wasn't. There'd been enough of that in her life with Jack. She couldn't play any games, even if they were the kind that was totally inconsequential.

Tilting the baby back a little against one arm, she cupped her other hand and allowed a little warm water to wet the fringe of dark hair on Layla's head.

"Look in my purse," she prompted. When he glanced at her curiously, she added, "It's on the desk."

He wasn't sure why she wanted him to look in her purse, but he retrieved it and then opened it the way she instructed. Inside was an extremely worn, dog-eared copy of a paperback book written by a popular pediatrician.

"That was a new book when I got it," she told him when he held up the book to make sure it was what she'd wanted him to find. "I was determined to be the very best mother I could be—and to be as prepared as possible for all the bumps and hiccups that were bound to come up in the first few months of this little partnership," she told him. Devon leaned over and lightly kissed the top of her baby's wet head.

Devon made a face, wrinkling her nose.

"What?" he questioned.

"Shampoo," she explained. "I guess I didn't get all of it out. Here, I'll tilt her back again. Fill that cup up and pour it along the back of her head," she instructed.

The directions sounded awkward, but he got the general gist of it. Very carefully, he allowed a stream of warm water to cascade along the back of her hair.

A tiny squeal pierced the air.

Devon raised her eyes, meeting Cody's. "I think she likes it."

A wide, wide smile curved Cody's mouth. He seemed to all but radiate pleasure. "You know, I think that you're right."

She had the infant cradled against one arm while she gently used a washcloth to pass along the baby's body with the other. She could see he appeared surprised at how well she was doing.

"I practiced with a doll," she confessed. She didn't add that Jack had ridiculed her for it. She should have known then that it wasn't going to work out for them.

"Well, it looks like it paid off," Cody told her. "You've got it covered."

The compliment pleased her more than she thought it would.

"I do, don't I?" she responded. "But I'd still like to know I've got backup, just in case," she told him.

"I'm not going anywhere," he assured her.

Between the two of them, Layla received her first bath—and got through it with flying colors.

Lifting the infant out of the water, Devon wrapped the large white towel around her, gently patting the baby's body.

Her eyes met Cody's. "We did it," she declared happily. She placed Layla on the bed and then patted her completely dry.

"*You* did it," Cody corrected. He let out the water. "I was just a bystander."

"You were more than that," she told him. There was gratitude in her eyes as she looked at him. "You were moral support."

Having dried off the baby, Devon diapered Layla and then slipped on a onesie that Miss Joan also had sent over with Cody.

"Okay, you're clean, changed and fed," she pronounced. "Time for bed, little girl."

She placed the infant back into the bassinet, and then went into the bathroom to make sure everything had been cleaned up. To her surprise, Cody had missed nothing. Everything was back in its place. The man was incredible, she caught herself thinking.

When she came back into the bedroom, she found that Cody was sitting on the edge of the bed, gently pushing the bassinet to and fro. The motion created a soothing sensation.

Devon paused over the bassinet and peered in. Layla's eyes were closed and she looked very peaceful. The infant was asleep.

She glanced back up at Cody. "You're an absolute wizard," she told him.

"The bassinet has wheels," Cody responded. "They did the hard part."

Devon sat down on her bed, suddenly feeling as if the very air had been drained out of her. She hadn't realized that she was this tired. Just remaining upright took effort.

"I really had no idea I was so exhausted," she confessed.

"You put in a full day, making breakfast for all of us as well as dinner," Cody enumerated. "And being a mom, especially a new one, is a full-time job. If you *weren't* exhausted, I would have said there was something seriously wrong with you."

"Then I guess there's nothing wrong with me," Devon told him, "because I can hardly sit up."

"Then go to sleep," he suggested simply.

Cody began to get up so she could do just that. But he found that he couldn't leave. Devon had caught hold of his arm. When he looked at her quizzically, she said, "Don't go yet. Talk to me."

Sitting back down, he acted as if she'd just made the most normal request in the world. "What about?"

A long sigh escaped her lips. "Anything you want." And then, because that was so vague, she got him started. "Tell me about your day."

"It wasn't very exciting," he told her.

She was starting to feel very sleepy—but she still didn't want him to leave. She felt as if he was her good-luck charm.

"Did you get to talk to anybody?" she asked.

"Sure." The sheriff's office could be a very noisy place.

"Then it was exciting," she assured him with a yawn.

Devon settled in against him, surprising Cody when she leaned her head against his shoulder. "Talk," she requested again, and then tempered her plea because she didn't want him feeling like a prisoner in his own house. "Just for a little while longer."

"I'll talk for as long as you want me to," he promised, slipping his arm around her shoulders.

Cody doubted that she even consciously noticed that, although she did seem to curl into him a little bit more, not unlike a kitten seeking shelter.

"Okay, then," he murmured.

Cody started to talk, giving Devon a full report of his earlier interaction with Miss Joan as well as with the sheriff and the other deputies, Joe and Gabe.

He talked slowly, purposefully, stretching out his narrative as much as he could. As he spoke, he tried not to get distracted by the feeling of her hair brushing against his cheek or the scent of what he took to be her perfume, which seemed to be everywhere.

Or maybe that was just her shampoo, he amended. Whatever it was, it was something light and herbal, but he still found it extremely stirring and distracting.

It also made him realize that it had been more than a while since he had socialized with any of the young women in the area who were around his own age.

That had not been a conscious decision. It had evolved on its own because he'd been so busy learning all the ins and outs of his relatively new position as deputy. This while still lending a hand on the ranch whenever Connor got in over his head and needed him and the others.

His life might not have been exciting by anyone's standards, but it definitely could be taxing at times. The salary he earned as a deputy went into a communal account, along with the money that Cole brought in and whatever Cassidy managed to earn working part-time both at the diner and at Olivia Santiago's law firm as her assistant.

It wasn't an easy life for any of them, but Connor had been there for them when they needed it and they were returning the favor. If not for Connor, they would have been farmed out to foster homes, most likely *separate* foster homes. And though Connor never talked about it, he had given up his dreams in order to keep them all together while running the ranch. The three of them had agreed long ago that they would never be able to actually pay Connor back for what he'd done, but they could damn well try at least.

In a way, this helped Cody understand why Devon insisted on finding a way to pay them back.

Cody realized after a few minutes that he was telling Devon all this, sharing more of his life with her than he had ever done with anyone else outside of the family, besides Miss Joan. But then the older woman had just intuitively known the details without his having to say them.

She always knew everything.

Sharing this with someone else, namely Devon, was a new experience. As soon as he realized what he was doing, he abruptly stopped.

Cody began to rise, trying to gently shift Devon's weight so that she would be lying down in the bed.

But as he started to do so, he heard a little noise of complaint escape her lips. Glancing down at her face, he saw that Devon was still asleep.

Still, he was sure he'd just heard her whisper, "Stay."

Debating, Cody decided to remain just a little longer, at least until she had fallen into a somewhat deeper sleep. After all, he had nowhere to go and nothing pressing to do.

And there were worse things than sitting beside a beautiful, sleeping woman, he thought with a smile.

So Cody remained where he was, sitting on Devon's bed, keeping his arm supportively around her so that she wouldn't just slump forward or fall over.

It occurred to Cody that a lot of people would have considered this to be the perfect ending to a rather hectic day.

A kernel of contentment opened up within him and spread even as darkness tiptoed into the bedroom, wrapping all three of them in a blanket of peace.

Inexplicably, a fresh wave of her shampoo filled his senses. Cody smiled again.

Perfect.

Chapter 13

Without any actual planning or real forethought, Cody found that, over the course of the next few weeks, a routine had fallen into place.

His mornings didn't officially begin until he'd looked in on Layla and her mother. Usually, they were in the kitchen, with Devon effortlessly preparing breakfast for all of them. He always pitched in despite her initial protest. Being around Devon and her baby, even if it was just until he drove off to work, gave Cody something to look forward to the minute he opened his eyes.

He knew that, eventually, this would come to an end, that Devon would one day, most likely soon, announce that she was ready to start forging a life for herself and her daughter somewhere apart from the McCullough household. But that day didn't have to be today—and, as long as it wasn't, he put it out of his mind and just enjoyed each minute as it happened.

Living in the moment took on a whole new, vivid meaning for him.

And all too quickly, it began to feel as if it was always this way, as if Devon and the baby had always been a part of their lives.

A part of *his* life.

And it didn't go unnoticed.

"You're getting too attached," Connor warned him one morning, following him out of the house just as he was about to leave for work.

Cody kept walking, heading for his truck. "No, I'm not," he protested, trying not to sound defensive.

Connor kept pace with him. As Cody opened the door on the driver's side, Connor put his hand on it, temporarily keeping it in place.

"Yeah, you are," Connor contradicted, concerned. "Things change all the time, Cody. You have to be prepared for that."

Cody planted his feet firmly, stubbornly turning to face his older brother. "I'm not twelve, Connor."

"No, you're not," Connor agreed. "Which is why it'll really hurt when she leaves. And she is going to leave, you know that," Connor emphasized. "She's not the type to let things slide and have other people take care of her." He nodded back toward the house. "That's a lady who pays her own way."

Devon was already doing that. There was no reason for her to leave yet, Cody thought, resisting the idea that Connor was expounding upon.

"According to her, she is paying her own way. She's saving us from your cooking," Cody said pointedly.

"Very funny." But Connor wasn't going to let him put up a smoke screen.

Cody tried not to get annoyed. He knew that Connor meant well. But he was getting a little too old to have his older brother meddling in his affairs.

"I know what you're saying—that this is just temporary. But that doesn't mean I can't enjoy it while it lasts," Cody told him.

"Nobody said that," Connor agreed. "Get to work before you're late," he said, waving Cody off and stepping back.

Once at work, since the atmosphere was so relaxed, Cody went on with his search to find the man who had abandoned Devon. He'd managed—working with the little that he had been able to get out of her—to discover the man's name. Jack Tryon. That led him, after a great deal of effort and searching through various databases, to a New Mexico driver's license that had Tryon's picture on it. He circulated the photo, sending it to the various motels in a hundred-mile radius.

He got no hits, but he refused to give up. The man had to turn up somewhere.

"What's that?" Devon asked one afternoon several days later.

Cody had come home early and, as was his habit, his first stop was the kitchen. He liked to hang around, talking to Devon while she prepared dinner.

Devon's question pertained to the bouquet of wild roses that Cody was holding out to her.

Cody flashed an engaging grin. "Most people call them flowers," he quipped.

"I *know* what they are," she said, and then tried again, "but why are you giving them to me?"

"To celebrate," he told her simply, deliberately doling out his answer slowly in small pieces.

"Okay," she allowed. "Are you celebrating anything in particular?"

His grin was irresistible—she found that she didn't stand a chance. "Today marks four weeks since you came here and made mealtime bearable instead of just something to get through."

Rather than laugh at his quip, Devon looked surprised. Since she'd arrived at the ranch, her days had begun to run into one another and she'd lost track of time more than once.

But even so, she had to admit, if only to herself, that she hadn't been this happy in a long, long time. She'd admonished herself, telling herself not to get used to it, but the truth was she just couldn't help it.

His words now were a jarring reminder. "My lord, has it been that long?" she cried.

It felt as if she'd only arrived the day before yesterday. She hadn't meant to take such advantage of them, she thought, the wheels in her head beginning to turn madly.

"Actually," Cody told her, "it feels like time's just glided by."

But Devon didn't see it that way. Still holding the flowers Cody had given her, Devon sank down at the table with a look on her face that Cody could only describe as dazed.

There was almost shock and wonder in her voice as she realized, "I've taken advantage of your hospitality for an entire month."

"No," Cody corrected firmly, "you've made our lives *better* for an entire month." Devon still looked unconvinced. She couldn't possibly be thinking of leaving, he thought nervously. "These are flowers," Cody pointed out, "not an eviction notice. If anyone's taken advantage of anyone, we've taken advantage of you."

The look in her eyes told him that she didn't see it that way. "I should have found a place for Layla and me by now."

"You didn't have the time," he said. "You've been too busy taking care of her and cooking for us," Cody reminded her, adding, "There's no hurry. The invitation to stay on is open-ended," he insisted.

That made her feel worse. "You're just being nice."

"I'm only being practical," Cody insisted. He needed to make her understand. "Having you and Layla here brightens up the place." And then he smiled at her. "I can't even explain exactly why, but there's a lot less bickering going on in this house with you here." He looked at the bouquet in her hands. It had all started with the bouquet. "If the flowers upset you, I'll get rid of them," he offered, about to take them out of her hand.

"No!" Reflexes had her pulling the bouquet out of his reach. "The flowers are beautiful." Devon could count the number of times she'd received flowers from someone on one finger of one hand. This was a first for her. "It just reminds me that I should get busy finding a niche for myself and Layla."

No matter what he said, she couldn't expect Cody and his family to put her up forever.

"And by 'niche' you mean a job," Cody guessed, reading between the lines.

"Exactly."

He could understand how she felt. The inevitable became a little more so to him as he asked, "What did you do before you came here?"

"You mean what did I do for a living back in New Mexico?" she asked.

"Yes. What sort of job did you have?" Maybe if he knew what she'd done for a living he could help her find something in Forever.

"I was a substitute teacher." She'd wanted to teach full-time, but Jack had been selfish with her time, wanting her to be around whenever he felt he needed her. A part-time position allowed her to be available.

Cody noticed a rather wistful expression slip over her face when she said the word *teacher*.

"What?" he coaxed. "You were thinking of something. What was it?"

She debated just waving his question away. Jack had ridiculed her for giving voice to her dreams. But Cody looked genuinely interested, so she took a chance and told him. "I was going to enroll in an online college, get some credits toward my degree. I want to eventually teach at a junior college." And then she shrugged away the notion. "Or I did before something more important lay claim to my time," she added, glancing toward the baby, who was in the bassinet, having a wonderful time entertaining herself by playing with her toes.

Cody nodded. "Sounds like a noble idea," he told Devon. His reaction totally surprised her. "You can still do that here. Connor has a computer he doesn't use unless he absolutely has to. It's set up in the den. I'm sure he'll let you use it. And, on the plus side, you have a lot of babysitters to watch Layla for you while you take your classes."

Excitement warred with common sense. "I can't ask you or your brothers and sister to do that," she told him.

"You're not," Cody pointed out to her. "We're volunteering."

She really wanted to take him up on that, but it wouldn't be right. "You mean you're volunteering for them."

"Only because they don't know about this plan of yours," he replied simply. "Once they know, they'll be only too happy to get on board."

He was painting a very rosy picture, but she couldn't allow herself to get swept away. She'd survived only by having both feet planted in the real world. "I still need to get a place of my own."

"Nobody's arguing with that. It just doesn't have to be today—or tomorrow," he pointed out.

She felt herself waffling. "But I've already imposed more than enough."

"Nobody's complaining," he told her, "and no, you haven't. Look, I know that you've pretty much been on your own a lot and maybe the concept is hard for you to grasp, but *this* is what family and friends do—they're there for each other, they make life easier for each other." Trying his best to get through to her, he underscored, "Let us help."

Didn't he understand? "You already have."

The corners of his mouth curved in an appealing smile. "Let us help more."

Devon sighed. It would be so easy just to let him take care of things for her. But she knew better than that. She couldn't allow herself to depend on anyone too much—that was how she'd wind up getting hurt.

"There is no arguing with you, is there?" she asked Cody.

"Oh, there's arguing," he contradicted. "But if you mean winning, then no, there's not. You can argue all you want, but in the end the house wins. In this case," he told her with a smile, "the 'house' means me—and the others."

She shook her head, knowing it was futile to keep trying to persuade him, at least for now. But she was still also afraid to allow herself to believe things could be this simple, this easy. For now, she turned her attention to dinner. "How do you feel about chicken parmesan?"

"Passionate," Cody answered, tongue in cheek.

Her eyes smiled as she said, "Then lucky for you, that's what I'm making."

In his opinion, that wasn't why he was lucky.

"But where are we going?" Devon asked as Cody ushered her toward his truck.

It was Saturday and while he wasn't working today, he still seemed determined to go on an unannounced outing with her.

"I thought you might want a break from everything," Cody said matter-of-factly. "You've been cooped up in the house much too long so I'm taking you into town. Think of this as a field trip," he advised.

She'd come outside with Cody because she'd thought he wanted to show her something, She wasn't prepared to just take off like this.

"But what about the baby?"

"Cassidy and Cole have watched you enough to know what to do with Layla for a few hours." Opening the passenger door, he helped her up into the seat as he spoke. "She'll be fine."

Devon twisted around in her seat as Cody slipped the metal tongue into the seat belt slot. "I'm not worried about her. I'm worried about them."

"Don't be." Quickly, he rounded the hood and got in on the driver's side. "Don't even think about the house or the things you need to do." He buckled up quickly. "Just think recreation."

She looked at him suspiciously. Something was off. "What are you up to?" she asked.

He thought of a number of excuses to give her, things to mislead her for the time being. But he'd never been one for lies, even little white ones. So he told her the truth—or at least the partial truth—as he drove into town. "I thought I'd take you to see Miss Joan, seeing as how you two didn't get to visit much when she came to the clinic after the docs fixed you up."

Devon took in a deep breath, trying to steady the onslaught of nerves that had suddenly materialized out of nowhere. Miss Joan had already done a great deal for her. How could she ever thank the woman for everything she'd done for a stranger?

"She's helped me so much. What do I say to her?" she asked Cody when they arrived at the diner half an hour later.

"'Hi' comes to mind. Don't worry, she'll take it from there," he assured her. After getting out, he opened the door for Devon and helped her out.

Devon took a tighter hold of Cody's arm than he'd

expected. It was probably the closest thing to a tourni-quet he'd ever experienced, he thought.

"If you say so," Devon murmured, her eyes all but fixed on the entrance to the diner.

Cody leaned his head in so she was able to hear him. "You've met her. You know she doesn't bite."

Devon tossed her head, her hair brushing along her shoulders. "I know that," she murmured, still holding on to his arm as hard as she could.

The moment she walked into the diner, Devon realized that he wasn't bringing her there to say hello to Miss Joan or even to undergo the woman's scrutiny. He'd brought her there because Miss Joan had instructed him to. One look at the crammed diner and it became apparent that the woman had finally gotten the word out to the people she wanted to reach. They had all turned out and came bearing gifts. This wasn't a command performance, Devon realized belatedly. As improbable as it seemed, this was a baby shower.

As soon as he'd opened the door for Devon, she saw the balloons and the various other decorations. A look of delight passed over her face even as the next moment she seemed to freeze in place.

"You didn't," she breathed.

Taking hold of her arm, he steered her across the threshold and into the diner. "Nope, *I* didn't. Miss Joan did," he said, setting her straight.

Why would the woman do this? Devon couldn't help wondering. Why would Miss Joan put herself out for someone she didn't even know?

That question, along with half a dozen others, throbbed in Devon's head as she allowed herself to be led into the heart of the diner.

"Cody?" she said uncertainly.

"Just keep walking," he coaxed. "One foot in front of the other. It gets easier."

She felt as if her head was spinning. There were boisterous voices all swimming into one continuous noise. "What *is* all this?" Devon cried, not knowing where to look first.

"It's your baby shower," Olivia Santiago said as she came around to Devon's other side, ushering her in and acting as her unofficial guide.

"But—but I'm a stranger," Devon protested, not knowing what to make of these people who were so different from anyone she was accustomed to. Baby showers were thrown by friends, by family, none of which these people were to her.

It still felt enchanted, she couldn't help thinking.

"A stranger's just a friend you haven't met yet," Ramona, the sheriff's sister, told her, joining the growing circle around the new mother.

Devon was still having trouble wrapping her head around what was going on.

She looked toward the woman standing at the counter. Miss Joan. Their eyes met and then Miss Joan came forward, smiling a greeting at her.

"Welcome to your baby shower," Miss Joan told her, a regal smile of welcome on her lips.

Unable to contain herself, Devon just started talking. "But you already sent me all those baby clothes and things." Her point was that there was no need for a shower, but something kept her from saying the words.

"Those were hand-me-downs," Miss Joan informed her, beckoning her over to a table that was piled high with gifts. "Every baby deserves to have some brand-new things of her own," she maintained. "Sit," she instructed, pointing to the chair before she waved over one of her waitresses to bring Devon something to drink.

"And don't worry about a thing," Miss Joan told her, continuing. "This is about that sweet little baby—and her mama," she added pointedly, looking at Devon. She had picked out a few items that every new mother needed in order to preserve her own identity, but there was time enough for Devon to unwrap those things later, Miss Joan thought. Right now, the young woman needed to just sit back, relax and enjoy herself.

Miss Joan's eyes narrowed into thin hazel beams as she focused on Cody. "You can make yourself scarce now, Deputy. Someone will come to get you when it's time to load all the gifts onto the truck and take them back to the ranch for the new mama."

Devon turned to look at him, a sliver of panic slicing through her. "You're not staying?"

Cody glanced at Miss Joan. The latter's expression remained firm. "Apparently not."

"Sorry, dear. I'm old-fashioned," Miss Joan informed her, even as she shooed Cody out. "Baby showers are strictly for the softer sex."

On his way out, Cody laughed. Softer sex. As if that described Miss Joan in any manner. But he knew better than to say that out loud, even as she gave him a piercing look.

"Something funny, Deputy?" Miss Joan asked.

"Not a thing, Miss Joan," he told her.

Cassidy was part of the gathering, having managed to get here just a hair's breadth ahead of them. He waved her over to sit beside Devon. When she took her seat, he looked at Devon.

"See you later," he promised just before he left.

Devon watched him exit the diner and desperately wanted to go with him.

Chapter 14

In an effort to kill time until the baby shower was over and he could take Devon and her gifts back to the ranch, Cody decided to swing by the general store. He figured it was his turn to stock up on basic groceries and supplies anyway.

Since that hardly took any time at all, once he had deposited the groceries into his truck, Cody stopped by the sheriff's office next, but it was even slower there than it normally was during the week. After talking to Gabe, the lone deputy who was on duty this weekend—and being unable to return to the diner, which was technically closed because of the shower—Cody went to the only other place left in Forever where he felt he could kill a little time. Murphy's Saloon.

There was a tacit agreement of long standing between Miss Joan and the three Murphy brothers who owned and ran the saloon that the diner wouldn't serve any alcohol and Murphy's wouldn't serve any food beyond the accepted staples of all bars: pretzels and peanuts.

But that was all right with Cody. He wasn't hungry. He was just at a loose end.

The oldest Murphy brother, Brett, was tending bar and he looked up in surprise when he saw Cody walk in.

"Been a long time," Brett commented as he made his way over to the far end where Cody had parked himself. "What'll it be, Cody?" he asked.

"Got any coffee?" Cody asked. He half expected to have Brett tell him "no."

Brett looked at him thoughtfully for a moment, as if debating his answer. And then he said, "Well, that all depends."

"On what?" Cody asked. Had there been a change in policy?

Brett continued massaging the counter with his cloth, buffing it to a high gloss. "On whether you're asking for yourself or acting as a spy on behalf of Miss Joan."

"For myself," Cody answered. "But I know for a fact that she wouldn't begrudge you serving coffee to your customers if they were trying to sober up." The woman always put safety first.

Brett looked amused. "You do realize that in order to sober up, you'd have to have been drinking first, right?" he pointed out.

Cody shrugged. Had he been interested in drinking, he would have ordered a drink. But it was far too early to cut the edge off the day that way. "Yeah, well, let's just skip that part."

Brett nodded agreeably. Going behind the counter, he

picked up the pot of coffee he kept for himself, poured some into a mug and then brought over the pitch-black brew. He placed it in front of Cody.

"You waiting on the baby shower to be over?" he asked as he set a small container of milk and a sugar bowl beside the mug.

"Yeah." Cody just availed himself of a light dusting of sugar. "How'd you know?" The baby shower at Miss Joan's was possibly the last thing he would have thought Brett knew about.

"Because that's where Alicia is," Brett answered, referring to his wife. "As a matter of fact, that's where all of Forever's women are as far as I can tell." He frowned ever so slightly as he looked off in the general direction of the diner. "Seems almost too eerily quiet without them, doesn't it?"

Cody merely shrugged in response, not really wanting to agree with Brett, not because it wasn't true, but because saying so would have been admitting something to the bartender that he hadn't admitted to himself yet. That he missed the sound of a particular woman's voice.

Brett smiled knowingly. He didn't need any verbal confirmation. "Kind of funny how quick we get used to having them around, isn't it?"

Cody raised his eyes to Brett's. "Are you trying to tell me something?"

Brett's smile just widened a little more. "Nothing you don't already know," he replied.

This was a small town and people talked. Sometimes way too much in Cody's opinion. He didn't want rumors going around about Devon. He had a feeling that it could be way too easy for some of the good people of

Forever—well-meaning though they might be—to read between the lines and create scenarios that weren't true.

"Devon's talking about getting her own place as soon as the baby's a little older." That really had nothing to do with it, but he thought it sounded good.

Brett focused on what he felt was the important part. "So she's staying on in Forever."

Lord, he hoped so. But out loud Cody merely said, "For now."

A look he couldn't quite read passed over Brett's face. "If I were you, I'd make it worth her while."

Cody raised an eyebrow. "What's that supposed to mean?"

"Just about anything you want it to," Brett replied guilelessly.

Cody decided it was best not to take the conversation any further. Finishing off his coffee, he put the mug back on the counter and asked Brett, "What do I owe you for the coffee?"

The expression on Brett's face was the soul of innocence. "Nothing." He shrugged, taking back the mug and passing his cloth along the counter again. "I don't sell coffee here."

Cody laughed shortly. The man's secret was safe with him. "Thanks."

Leaving, he got back into his truck and drove it back to the diner. Cody parked the vehicle across the street and decided to set up camp and wait it out. He felt the shower couldn't go on much longer.

He was right.

Forty-five minutes later, the doors of the diner opened and several of the women who had attended the baby shower came down the steps.

That was his cue, Cody thought, getting out of the truck. Politely nodding at the women and exchanging a few words with Ramona, the town vet and the sheriff's sister, as she came out of the diner next, he made his way inside the restaurant.

He found Devon sitting at a table positioned smack-dab in the center of the diner. There was another table behind her and it was piled high with all sorts of baby furnishings and things designed to make a new mother's life a little easier. The gifts ranged from the very basic to one-of-a-kind items.

"Looks like you cleaned up," Cody remarked, looking over the table.

Devon swung around to face him and it occurred to him that she'd never looked happier to see him.

Or maybe she was just plain happy, he amended.

"I don't know what to say," she confessed, gesturing at the gifts the women had brought to the party. Even Christmas had never looked like this. This was definitely something out of the ordinary.

"You'll think of something," Cody assured her. The other guests who'd attended the party were filing past them and leaving the diner, saying their goodbyes. "You ready to go home?" Cody asked her.

Home. It had such a nice ring to it. She knew she shouldn't allow herself to get carried away, to feel like this, but she just couldn't help it.

Out loud she said, "Just as soon as we get this into your truck."

At first glance, it looked like a lot, but he'd always been good at organizing things. "No problem. You just sit tight," he told her.

She shook her head. "But I want to help," Devon protested.

Miss Joan came up behind her. "Man wants to do it all, let him do it all," she told Devon. "From what I hear," she continued, crossing over to the guest of honor, "you've been returning the favor by keeping him and his family well fed."

"Seems like a small thing to do," Devon protested.

"Don't underestimate yourself," Miss Joan warned. Turning to face Cody, the woman waved a thin hand all around the immediate area. "Those are all her things, Cody," the older woman informed him, adding in a no-nonsense voice, "Get busy."

"Yes, ma'am," he replied, doing his best to look solemn. Secretly, he was extremely grateful to her.

Miss Joan had outdone herself. He felt confident that all of this—the shower, the gifts—would go a long way in helping Devon feel more secure about her new life here in Forever.

Cody moved quickly as he brought the gifts to his truck. On his last trip, he noticed that Devon had gotten up. He assumed she was getting ready to leave. Instead, he saw her crossing over to Miss Joan. To his surprise, she threw her arms around the older woman.

"Thank you for everything, Miss Joan," Devon murmured.

Knowing Miss Joan's nature, Cody half expected the diner owner to extract herself and say something vague and distant about being physically touched. Instead, as he watched in surprise, Miss Joan not only allowed Devon to hug her, but the woman actually returned the embrace for several seconds before she stepped back and said, "Go home to your baby, Devon. She'll be full grown before you know it."

Brushing aside a tear, Devon nodded in response, afraid that if she said something, her voice would wind up cracking.

Cody sped up his pace. He took the last of the shower gifts from the table and loaded them onto his truck. Out of the corner of his eye he saw several of the regular customers walking into the diner.

Business as usual had resumed.

Devon was already sitting in the passenger seat when he got in behind the steering wheel. Cody had buckled his seat belt and was just putting the key into the ignition when he heard Devon finally break her silence and speak up.

Glancing at him, she said the obvious. "Miss Joan is an amazing woman."

Cody tactfully suppressed a laugh before responding. "She sure is," he verified.

Devon nodded her head, more to herself than for Cody's benefit. "I wasn't sure what to expect," she confessed.

He turned on the ignition. "So what's your final verdict?" he asked, curious about her impression of the woman.

To his surprise, Devon summed it up rather neatly. "She's scary and sweet at the same time. An angel."

He laughed. "Yeah, I guess that's one description of the lady."

Devon shifted in her seat with her seat belt digging into her shoulder. "Why would Miss Joan do something like that for me?" she asked suddenly. "I mean, I'm nobody to her."

"Because she's Miss Joan," he answered simply. That unadorned statement was the explanation for a good many things the woman had done that remained a mystery to the rest of the town. "And because I think long ago she might have found herself in the same position as you," Cody added.

He paused, and then decided that it might be helpful to Devon if he told her his own story about Miss Joan.

"When my dad died, leaving us orphaned, Connor stepped up to take care of us. If he had gone his own way, Cole, Cassidy and I would have been put into foster care. Lucky for us, he didn't. But Connor didn't manage to take care of us alone. There was always Miss Joan in the wings. She came through with odd jobs for us to do in order to make ends meet. She also fed us on more than one occasion, insisting that if we didn't take the food, she'd only wind up throwing it out because she'd ordered too much."

He smiled to himself. "Nobody can remember Miss Joan miscalculating her inventory. She always knows down to the last serving how much to order, how much to have on hand. Yet for the first couple of years after my dad died, she always seemed to have this 'surplus' lying around." A philosophical smile curved his lips. "Most people in town just think of Miss Joan as this rough-talking guardian angel."

She could add herself to that number. "Well, I think she's wonderful."

She wasn't going to get an argument out of him, Cody thought. "Most of us do, too.'

Twisting farther around in her seat, Devon looked at all the things that she'd gotten as a result of the baby shower. It seemed a little overwhelming now that she looked at it.

"I don't know where you can put all those things," she confessed.

He'd already thought about that. "Don't worry about it, we'll find space."

That seemed to be the go-to catchphrase, she thought. *Don't worry about it.*

The problem was she did.

Her concerns were somewhat abated when they reached the house and, rather than make any remarks about her "taking over" the way she feared, Cody's brothers pitched in and helped Cody unload the gifts, which included a brand-new crib that Mrs. Hennessey from the general store had given her, saying that it was a model that someone had ordered and then failed to pick up.

Cole helped to ease the crib out of the truck, bringing the parts into the living room.

"Why don't we set this up upstairs?" Cody suggested. And then he looked at Devon and said, "It's about time the baby had a room of her own so that you can get a good night's sleep."

"But I won't hear her crying if I'm down here," Devon protested.

"Which is why we moved your things upstairs into the bedroom next to the nursery," Connor told her.

She looked from one brother to the other. "You're saying that I can take over two bedrooms?" she asked incredulously.

"Why not?" Connor asked with a shrug. "They're just standing around, empty, going to waste."

Devon's astonished gaze swept over all three brothers. She kept thinking that she was going to wake up at any minute and find out this was all a dream. "You don't mind?" she questioned.

"Why should we mind?" Connor asked. "We're the ones who came up with the suggestion." And then he seemed to read between the lines, guessing why she seemed so wary. "Don't worry, we don't plan to hold you here against your will. Whenever you decide you want to leave, you can leave. But until then, this just seems like the more logical arrangement for everyone."

She didn't know what to say. No one had ever treated her so well or been so thoughtful about her needs and situation.

Not since her mother had passed away.

Tears shimmered in her eyes as she said, "I have to tell you, you all make it very difficult to leave."

Cole and Connor exchanged looks. Connor grinned. "That did cross our minds," he admitted.

She didn't want to break down and cry in front of them. She didn't want them to think she was crazy.

Turning away, she murmured, "I'd better feed and change the baby."

"Already done," Cole informed her proudly.

"Then I'd better get dinner started," Devon said. More tears welled up in her eyes and she hurried into the kitchen quickly.

Connor poked Cody in the ribs and nodded his head in Devon's direction. His message was clear. Devon was definitely a woman in need of comforting.

"Go to her," he told his brother when Cody continued to stand there.

Cody eyed him uncertainly. "Maybe she wants to be alone."

Connor sighed, shaking his head. "Every crying

woman needs a shoulder. You don't have to talk. You just have to be there," Connor maintained.

Cody was still undecided about what to do. Which was when Cole pushed him toward the doorway.

He had no choice but to enter the kitchen,

"Are you all right?" he asked Devon quietly.

Rather than answer him, Devon nodded her head.

"Are you sure?" he pressed. He watched the way her shoulders were moving. Connor was right. She was crying. She stopped and turned around to face him. Since there were tears sliding down both cheeks, she couldn't very well protest that she wasn't crying.

Instead, she drew in a ragged breath and said, "These are happy tears."

He could never wrap his mind around that. "How can you tell?"

She tried to smile and didn't quite succeed. "Because I'm happy."

"Okay, you could have fooled me," Cody admitted.

The next thing he knew, Devon had thrown her arms around his neck. "I'm so sorry about this," she sobbed.

"Hey, nothing to be sorry about. You're dealing with a lot here. From where I stand," he told her soothingly, "you're doing a damn fine job of it."

"No, I'm not. If it wasn't for you…" Devon couldn't bring herself to finish her sentence.

"Shh," he said softly, and then told her, "we'll argue about it later." In an effort to soothe her, he held her closer and, ever so slightly, kissed the top of her head.

Devon looked up at him.

The next thing he knew, like a man in a dream, he brought his mouth down to hers.

Chapter 15

In the next moment, Cody forced himself to step back, murmuring an apology. He wasn't about to say he didn't know what had come over him because he *did* know. He wanted to comfort Devon, just as Connor had said. He wanted her to know she wasn't alone in this. He wanted her not to feel lost.

He wanted her.

Which was why, Cody sternly upbraided himself, he absolutely needed to keep his distance. And that, he realized, would be a challenge—because her room was now next to his.

Devon quickly wiped away her tears with the back of her hand. "I'd better finish getting dinner ready," she said brusquely, turning away from Cody and trying very hard to regain control over herself. She'd slipped, but she wasn't going to allow that to happen again.

For her own survival, she couldn't.

* * *

He hoped his feelings would change, but after two more weeks, they still didn't. If anything, as far as he was concerned, it became more prominent for him. He was never more aware of Devon's proximity after everything had settled down for the night.

With no effort at all, he came up with a dozen different reasons to look in on Devon, to offer his help with the baby or just to talk. It was a struggle each evening to talk himself out of every one of those excuses. At times he wound up all but barricading himself in his room.

The last thing he wanted was for Devon to feel that he was crowding her—or worse, that because of everything that had transpired, she *owed* him something. It was hard on him, but he forced himself to pull back. That came in the form of his putting in longer hours. He knew that his brothers and sister would handily fill up the space that he left behind. It was in their nature to step up and pitch in whenever Devon needed help.

Eventually, Cody talked himself into believing that Devon didn't even notice what he was doing—except perhaps, that she might feel less hemmed in.

Each day was supposed to grow easier for him. It didn't. After two weeks he still found himself actually missing her despite the fact that he saw Devon every morning before he left the house and every evening after he came home.

It couldn't be helped, Cody thought, but at least his plan was proceeding the way he intended it to. Devon wouldn't feel obliged to him for anything.

There was only one sad side effect of this program of self-denial. Since he'd started keeping his distance from Devon, he found that sleep had become a rather elusive commodity. The main reason for that was because he caught himself straining to hear sounds that would let him know whether or not Devon had gone to sleep or if she was up with the baby.

Moreover, each time he heard any indication of the latter, he had to struggle to keep from getting up and volunteering to take over for her so that at least *she* could get some rest.

It was beginning to take a toll on him. Rather than getting used to this, he found that things were just getting more difficult for him. People were noticing the dark circles under his eyes. Shrugging it off didn't help the basic situation.

Cody had just resigned himself to spending another sleepless night when he thought he heard a light knock on his door.

Sitting up, he stared at the closed door, wondering if he was imagining things. Up until this point, the house had been as quiet as a tomb. Apparently everyone else, including the baby, was asleep.

Curious, Cody got up and opened the door a crack. It allowed him to see that Devon was just turning away from his room. She was wearing an old, oversize T-shirt.

His old T-shirt, he realized. Cassidy must have found it somewhere and given it to her. She was obviously using it as her nightgown. The hem only came down halfway on her thighs.

Something tightened in the pit of his stomach.

"Devon?" When she stopped in her tracks and turned around to face him, Cody felt his mouth go dry. "Is something wrong?"

For a moment, she appeared to be waffling, as if she

was undecided whether to say something or not. Or maybe the sight of him bare-chested, wearing a pair of old, torn jeans that hung precariously off his hips had rendered her mind blank.

Her internal conflict was short-lived. She squared her shoulders.

Blowing out a deep breath, Devon asked. "Can I come in?"

Because he wanted her to so much, Cody almost asked her if whatever she wanted to talk about couldn't keep until morning.

But something in her expression kept him from asking that. Instead, he stepped back and opened the door farther for her.

"Sure."

Devon took another deep breath, as if to fortify herself, and then crossed his threshold. Before she said a single word, she closed the door behind her.

"Is something wrong with the baby?" Cody asked when she didn't say anything.

Devon shook her head. "No, not the baby," she told him.

"Then what?" He was getting a very uneasy feeling that something was definitely wrong. He might have been avoiding her for her own good, but he didn't want that to keep her from coming to him if something was troubling her. "You can tell me anything," he coaxed.

Rather than pouring out her heart, she looked at him for a long moment.

"Can I?" she questioned.

That threw him. "Sure."

Cody watched her press her lips together as if she was wrestling with a problem. It suddenly occurred to him that she wasn't saying anything because what was bothering her was a woman thing. He told her the only thing he could. "Maybe you'd feel better if I got Cassidy—"

"No," Devon said sharply. She didn't want to talk to Cassidy. She wanted and *needed* to talk to *him*, to have it out with *him*.

Gathering her courage, she asked, "Have I done something to offend you? Because if I have, you have to know that I didn't mean it. I don't know what I did, but I am very sorry." Her eyes met his and she told him with all sincerity, "I would rather die than have that happen."

Cody stared at her, stunned. Where had she gotten that idea?

He stepped forward to put his hands on her shoulders and then caught himself at the last moment. If he touched her, that would lead to something else.

Frustrated, he kept his hands at his sides. "You haven't done anything to offend me," he assured her.

Devon was far from convinced. His answer and his tone of voice only served to confuse her further. This didn't make any sense.

"Then why?" she asked.

"Why what?"

She spelled it out for him. "Why have you been avoiding me?"

Denial was becoming second nature to him. "I haven't been—"

Devon cut him short. She was in no mood to play games.

"Yes, you have. You've been skipping breakfast, staying longer at work and when you actually do come home, if you *do* sit at the table, you don't say anything," she concluded, underscoring her grievances. "And don't," she warned, "tell me that I'm imagining things, because I'm not." She tried to make amends again. "If I somehow hurt your feelings or did something to make you angry, you know I didn't mean to."

"Devon—" he began, searching for some way to reassure her while still maintaining the distance he felt was necessary for his own good "—you haven't done anything."

Frustration clawed at her. Devon felt as if she was going around in circles. "Then why won't you talk to me anymore?" she asked.

This was hard for her because she was all but baring her soul to him and it wasn't getting her anywhere. But Devon knew that she wasn't going to have any peace until she found some way to resolve this.

Her eyes met his. She played her ace card. "I miss you, Cody," she told him.

That look on her face was going to be his undoing, he thought.

"Oh damn, you're making this really hard, Devon."

She raised her eyes to his. "Making *what* hard?" she asked.

He debated saying it, but she left him no choice. So he did.

"Staying away from you," he told her simply.

"Then don't," she entreated.

With his last fiber of resolve, Cody struggled to hold himself in check.

"I don't want you to feel that you're obligated to me in any way." He could see by the look on her face that she didn't understand what he was trying to tell her.

He let out a ragged sigh, trying again. "I don't want you thinking that I helped you in order to help myself to you."

And then she understood.

Idiot, she thought.

"Did it ever occur to you that maybe, just maybe, I'd *want* you to?" she asked him in a low voice that seemed to undulate throughout his entire being.

He didn't believe that for a second. He couldn't shake the feeling that he'd be taking advantage of her. "Your emotions are all in an uproar and you're confused, Devon," he told her.

"Don't tell me how I feel," she said, raising her voice. "I *know* how I feel and I'm only confused because you did such a U-turn on me. Now, if I did nothing to offend you, why won't you talk to me?" she asked. "Why don't you hang out with Layla and me the way you did before?"

Once he said this, he didn't know how to unsay it. But she left him no choice. There was nothing else that he could do.

"Because I want you," he said simply.

Cody expected her to look upset or at the very least, retreat from him. Quickly. He did not expect her to say, "Thank God."

Cody blinked, certain he hadn't heard her correctly. "What?"

"I said, 'Thank God,'" Devon repeated, her eyes on his.

He'd heard her the first time. That wasn't what he was asking her. "I heard you," he told her. "But—"

The rest of his words died in his throat as Devon put her arms around his neck, bringing her body up against his.

"Enough talking," she said.

And then, before Cody could say anything further, she pressed her lips against his, initiating a kiss that seemed to go on forever, growing deeper and more passionate with each second that went by.

A moment later, all his good intentions seemed to dissolve. Cody wrapped his arms around her, the feeling of her body against his warming his very soul. Desire suddenly spiked up so high within him that it all but swallowed him whole.

At the very last second, before he felt himself going down for the third and final time, Cody managed to draw his face back from hers, terminating contact even as his body pleaded for him to continue.

"You don't want to do this," he told her.

Devon's soul-melting smile began in her eyes, which crinkled as she informed him, "See, you don't know everything."

"But we can't," he protested. "You just had a baby." He knew nothing about the way a woman's body worked at a time like this, but he was attempting to be cautious for her sake.

"Everything's back in working order. Trust me," she whispered seductively. "I know my own body."

It had been more than six weeks since she'd given birth and prior to that, there had been several months of complete abstinence, not because she hadn't wanted the intimacy, but because Jack didn't. He had come up with one excuse after another to keep her at arm's length. He hadn't so much as kissed her in the last two.

The longing she felt right now was overwhelming.

Cody wanted to resist, to be noble for her sake. But good intentions only went so far and all of his disintegrated in the face of the passion that had come to the surface.

His lips locked with hers, Cody carried Devon over to his bed, gently laying her down as if she was the most precious of packages. A fire had been lit within him, a fire that wasn't going to be easily sated, not until they'd made love.

Maybe not even then.

But again, guilt raised its head and he struggled to put an inch of space between them, giving Devon one last chance to change her mind and come to her senses. He couldn't do any more than that.

"You're sure?" he asked breathlessly.

His question only made her want Cody more. No one had ever cared about her feelings, about how she *felt*, certainly not to this extent.

"I'm sure," she murmured. "If it'll make you feel better, I'll sign an affidavit later," she breathed against his lips. "Now make love to me before I go up in smoke entirely."

She felt his lips curve against hers as he smiled. "Can't have that happening," he told her.

Finally!

She kissed him back with a fresh wave of passion that all but submerged them both, a giant tsunami of unleashed desire that only kept building, heightening, making her feel almost frantic as she twisted and turned beneath his large, capable hands.

Cody stroked her—over and over again he stroked her—bringing her up higher with every pass of his hand, every wild beat of her heart.

It took a huge effort to hold herself in check, to keep from reaching the final climax on her own.

But she wanted more than that, more than just gratification.

She wanted Cody to feel what *she* was feeling. Wanted him to experience what *she* was experiencing. Whatever was going to happen, she wanted it to happen to both of them together because she had no idea what tomorrow might usher in.

She needed this memory to cling to if everything that was transpiring tonight suddenly went away.

Shifting, moving her body along his, Devon reached for him, her fingers deftly caressing his muscular back, slipping along his hard biceps and then, with swift, eager strokes, she brought her hands gliding along his hard thighs. Hearing him moan excited her, bringing her up to an even higher plateau.

She moved ever lower until she managed to come to the very essence of him.

As her hands worked their magic, she could feel Cody responding, could feel his body hardening. Pulsating.

He wanted her and it was time.

Devon parted her legs and arched her back, the invitation unspoken but clear.

Just before his next move, she opened her eyes. She saw that Cody was looking back at her. Their eyes locked even as their bodies forged a union.

His hips moved, thrusting and she mimicked the movement, eager to ride out the wave with him. Eager to feel that final, wild, ecstatic thrill that would have her gasping as it stole her breath away.

She held on to him as hard as she could, absorbing the thrill. Something stirred within her that, until this very second, she hadn't realized had been missing all those other times before, when she'd made love with Jack.

The emotion burst open within her chest like a hungry spring flower searching for the light. It took everything she had not to say the words aloud.

Because she instantly knew what she was feeling, even if she had never felt it before.

Because nothing but love could feel this way.

It took great effort not to shout "I love you" even as the sensation filled her. She knew that she would continue to feel that way long after tonight was just a mere memory.

Happiness mingled with sadness. Because she was in love and because she had no idea what he felt.

Chapter 16

Euphoria's hold on him tiptoed away slowly, slipping back into the shadows where it had come from.

Cody held fast for as long as he could. He didn't want to let the moment go, didn't want to allow the outside world and reality to come barging in, taking its place.

All he wanted to do was hold on to this feeling.

Hold on to her.

He lost track of time. Maybe he dozed off, maybe he didn't. But he kept his arm tucked around Devon, comforted by the sound of her even breathing.

Had she fallen asleep, or…?

And then he heard it, heard the tiny cry that swiftly heralded in the outside world like nothing else could.

Devon raised her head from his chest, cocking her ear and listening. He felt her breath rippling along his chest as she sighed.

Devon glanced in his direction. "I'd better get her before she wakes up everyone else."

"Stay," he told her, gently moving her aside so that he could slip out of his bed and look in on Layla. "I'll go see what she wants."

She felt extremely confused by everything that had transpired tonight, even as her heart quickened just to look at him. But she didn't want him feeling that he needed to help her. The baby was her responsibility.

"But—"

Cody was already shrugging into his jeans. Standing up, he leaned over and kissed the top of her head.

"Just this once, Devon, don't argue," he requested. "I've got this. You get your sleep."

With that, he padded out of the room barefoot and into the baby's new room.

His path was illuminated by the light from the new lamp Devon had gotten at the baby shower. A shy pink lamb was gamboling across the lamp shade. Cody crossed to the crib.

"So what'll it be, Princess?" he asked as he lifted the fussing baby into his arms. Taking a deep whiff of her diaper, he ruled out one reason for the middle-of-the-night summons. "Well, you don't need changing," he concluded. "That leaves hungry or bored."

One look at her small, intent face answered his question for him. "Hungry, it is. What say you and I go downstairs and raid the refrigerator? How does that sound?"

Layla's face was pressed against his chest and he could feel her little lips rooting around.

Tickled, Cody laughed softly. "I guess that answers that."

Holding Layla close to him, Cody made his way down the stairs and into the kitchen. Although for the most part, Devon was still breastfeeding Layla, she had prepared several small bottles of formula to be used just in case.

"What do you say we let Mommy get her beauty rest—not that she needs it," he went on. "You grow up to be half as pretty as your mama, I'm going to have to make sure that all those young bucks out there know that they'll have me to reckon with if they so much as step one inch over the line."

The bottle warmer Devon had received as another gift at the shower was set up on the counter. Cody took out a bottle from the refrigerator and placed it in the warmer. It did its job quickly. He smiled to himself as the timer went off.

"That's a hell—I mean heck—of a lot more efficient than just putting it into a pot of boiling water." Even so, he tested the bottle's contents to make sure it hadn't gotten *too* warm. "Perfect," he murmured. "Okay, let's get you back upstairs."

Cradling Layla against him with one arm, Cody held the bottle with the other and slowly made his way up the stairs back to Layla's room. Cody wasn't accustomed to moving so slowly, but he wasn't about to take a chance on jostling the infant.

When he got to her room, he crossed over to the rocking chair by the window. He sat down.

After positioning the infant, he began to feed her and gently rock at the same time. He hoped the combination of warm milk and rhythmic motion would help Layla fall asleep again.

And after a while, it did.

Despite the hour, Cody sat for a few minutes just looking at her. No doubt about it. Layla held his heart captive in that tiny fist of hers just as much as her mother did.

Ever so slowly, he removed the bottle's nipple from the rosebud lips that had been so intently clamped around it.

He set the bottle aside but continued sitting there for a moment longer, just watching Layla sleep.

Feeling guilty, Devon had gotten out of bed to look in on her daughter and to see if Cody needed help.

What she saw warmed her heart to such an extent she could feel tears gathering in her eyes. If she hadn't already admitted to herself that she was in love with Cody, she would have fallen in love with the man right at this moment.

For however long this lasted, Devon promised herself, she was going to enjoy it and be grateful that their paths, hers and Cody's, had crossed just when she'd needed him. But being with Jack had taught her that nothing lasted forever, so she intended to savor this while she could.

Suppressing a sigh, Devon tiptoed back away from the room.

When he finally put Layla down and then went back to his own room, Cody found that his bed was empty. Devon had obviously returned to her room.

For a second, he thought of going to her. Not to make love again but just to slip into her bed. He liked the comforting sensation of having her next to him, of holding her. But he had no idea how Devon might react to his presence there. She might think that he wanted to make love again—he did, but that wasn't the main reason he wanted her beside him.

She needed her sleep, he told himself, surrendering the notion. He resigned himself to sleeping alone.

His bed felt cold and empty as he slipped into it.

"Are you up to meeting someone?" Cody asked Devon suddenly as he walked into the kitchen. He made no effort to hide his excitement. Less than a week had gone by since the parameters of their relationship had shifted.

He'd initially thought about pretending that nothing had happened, but that was a lie. Something *had* happened. And over the course of the next few days, it kept on happening by very mutual consent.

"Who?" she asked as she turned from the stove for a moment.

Whatever she was making smelled really good, he thought absently. As did she, he added as a silent afterthought. Just looking at her stirred him and made him think of things that had nothing to do with cooking.

He paused for a moment to choose his words, but then gave up and just let them come tumbling out. She'd get the gist of this soon enough.

"Her name's Julia Shaw and she's the principal of Forever's only elementary school. She's an old friend," he qualified. "And she'd like to meet you whenever it's convenient."

Devon stopped stirring the beef stew she was making and looked at Cody. She wasn't following him. "Why would she want to meet me, Cody?" she asked. "Just what's this all about?"

"Well, you mentioned that you'd been a substitute teacher in New Mexico and that you were thinking of getting back to teaching someday. I happen to know that one of the teachers at the elementary school is leaving Forever, so I checked it out. I found out that there'll be an opening for a fifth-grade teacher in the fall. Now, I know you said that your goal is to teach at a junior college, but I figure maybe some baby steps might be in order."

Devon was stunned to say the least and very close to speechless as she looked at him. When she finally found her tongue, she had to ask. "How did you manage this?"

The corners of his mouth curved into a grin that could be called nothing short of sexy.

"There are some advantages to living in a small town," he told her. "For one thing, everybody knows everybody—or knows someone who knows the someone you want to meet." Cody realized that he was getting lost in his explanation and so he simplified it. "Bottom line is that Julia would like to meet you and talk to you about your experience."

"Well, I have teaching credentials," she said. "But I actually didn't teach for that long."

"Then that shouldn't be a problem," Cody concluded. He knew for a fact that Julia was actively searching for a teacher to plug up the unexpected hole in her staff. And then it occurred to him that Devon looked less than excited about this prospect. Had he misunderstood something? "I mean, if you still want to be a teacher."

"Oh, I do," she assured him quickly. And then she sighed. Nothing was black-and-white anymore. "But things have gotten a little complicated the last few weeks. I mean, I'd need to find someone to watch Layla for me while I was teaching every day, so—"

"We'll come up with something," he promised her. "That's not a problem." He handed her a folded piece of paper. On it was Julia's private number. "Why don't you talk to Julia and make an appointment to meet with her?" he suggested.

Devon opened the paper and stared at it for a moment. "Really?" she asked, unable to believe that it was going to be this easy. Almost *too* easy, she couldn't help thinking.

He smiled as he went to pick up Layla out of her portable playpen.

"Really," he assured her before he looked at the infant and cooed, "Hi, Princess. Miss me?"

Devon pressed her lips together as she watched Cody with her daughter. *Temporary, it's just temporary*, she reminded herself. *Don't get used to it.*

But it was hard not to.

All twelve grades of Forever's school system could essentially be found within the confines of one building. The first eight grades were located in the larger wing of the building while the last four were in the other, far smaller wing.

In the center, connecting the two wings, was not just the lone kindergarten class but a preschool class, as well. There were only three children enrolled for the fall term in the preschool class. The teacher who oversaw the kindergarten class did double duty with preschoolers as well since each class was held at a different time of the day.

Accustomed to larger schools, not to mention larger

classes, Devon thought the whole thing seemed charming and quaint. Julia Shaw had arranged to meet with her on the school grounds and had taken her on a tour of the entire building before conducting the interview.

Cody had insisted on taking the day off to bring her to the school and to introduce her to Julia.

"You don't have to do this, you know," Devon had protested when he'd told her. "I can drive over myself," she reminded him, since she had her own vehicle.

He'd let her talk until she was finished and then said, "Humor me."

"Thank you," she murmured as an afterthought.

He'd merely smiled at her and replied, "Don't mention it."

He made her feel special and beautiful for no reason at all, but she kept waiting for the other shoe to drop—because it always did.

The interview, conducted in the principal's office, lasted all of thirty minutes and that included the tour. Julia Shaw was an attractive blonde who looked more like a model than a newly appointed school principal.

When the interview ended, Julia sat back in her chair and smiled at her as she nodded. "Well, I'm satisfied," she told Devon. And then she extended her hand. "Welcome aboard, Devon. The fifth-grade position is all yours."

Devon looked at her in disbelief. "Don't you want to send for my records first to verify everything?" she asked uncertainly.

"Yes, I will definitely check your credentials and references, but I'm confident in my decision."

"Are you sure?"

"Why?" Julia asked her, amused. "Did you lie about them?"

That caught Devon completely off guard. It took her a second to find her tongue. "No, of course not."

Julia spread her hands. "Well, then I know all I need to know. Besides, I went to school with Cody. If he's vouching for you, that's certainly good enough for me," she informed the younger woman. "Moreover, you sound as if you really like children."

"Oh, I do," Devon assured the principal with feeling. She loved not just their innocence but their honesty, as well. As far as she was concerned, children were far more trustworthy than adults.

"I thought so," Julia said with approval. "Well, here's the employment packet the board makes me hand out. Just fill out the forms and bring all that back with you on the first day of school. I'm planning on holding a meeting before then, but I'll let you know the date once it's set." Rising to her feet, she coaxed, "C'mon, I'll walk you out."

Julia led the way through the hall. Stopping at the front door, Julia pushed it opened and held it for Forever's newest teacher.

Cody was waiting just outside the entrance. As soon as the door opened, he crossed to it.

"How'd she do, Jules?" Cody asked the woman beside Devon.

"Thanks to you, a crisis has been avoided. We have our teacher," Julia told him. Looking at Devon, the woman smiled. "See you in the fall."

Once the principal had retreated back into the building, Cody beamed at Devon. "Congratulations! Why don't we go to Miss Joan's and I'll buy you lunch so we can celebrate?"

Her smile was somewhat forced. "No, that's all right."

"You're not hungry?" he asked. For someone who had just gotten the job he thought she was hoping for, Devon didn't exactly strike him as being overjoyed—or even very happy.

"I'm too excited to eat," she told him. "Everything's happening so fast."

Cody abruptly stopped walking and just looked at her. "What?" she asked.

"Nothing," he replied. "I'm just waiting to see your nose grow."

She blinked. "Excuse me?"

"Like Pinocchio when he told a lie," he explained.

Indignant, she squared her shoulders. "I'm not lying," she protested. And then she sighed. Cody was going to keep looking at her until she came clean. "You didn't tell me you knew her that well."

"Knew who that well?" he asked. Devon had managed to lose him without taking a single step.

"The principal. Ms. Shaw. Julia," she finally said.

He shrugged. "I went to school with her," he admitted, and then asked, "So?"

She shrugged, embarrassed by how she was feeling, but unable to shake it off. "Nothing. She just seemed rather taken with you, that's all. Did you two date or anything?"

"No to both questions,' he told her. And then it hit him. "You're not jealous of Julia, are you?"

"Of course not," she said much too quickly.

"Because there's nothing to be jealous of," he assured her. "She had a crush on Connor for a while, but I doubt if she even noticed me until I asked her about a teaching position for you."

"How could she not notice you?" Devon challenged. The woman had to be blind not to react to Cody's looks, Devon thought.

"Very, very easily," he assured her. "And I think it's very cute that you're jealous."

"I am *not* jealous," she retorted, and then thought better of it. There was really no point in protesting the obvious. "Well, maybe a little."

He laughed and then he kissed her, right there in the street. Her heart shot up to her throat and then fell down again, pounding hard. "You're messing with my head," she told him.

"Seems only fair because you're messing with mine," he told her as he held the passenger door open for her.

"I need a clear head to think about my next move," she said as she got in.

He rounded the hood and got in on the driver's side. "Which is?" he asked.

"Finding a place for Layla and me," she told him. The words tasted almost bitter in her mouth. "I mean, that's the next logical step, isn't it? I can't expect to impose on you and your family indefinitely."

He studied her face before answering. "I wasn't aware that you were imposing," he told her. "But if you feel awkward about staying now that we've—" How could he put this delicately, he wondered, searching for the words. He finally settled on a euphemism. "—now that we've *been* together, I understand. Although," he went on as he put his key into the ignition, "if it'll make you feel better, what happened the other night—and the nights after that—doesn't have to happen again."

Devon felt her stomach sinking. "Then you *do* think it was a mistake," she concluded.

"If it makes you leave, then yes," he told her simply. Then he felt honor bound to add, "But honestly, no, I don't think it was a mistake." He challenged, "How could I?"

Devon shook her head. She didn't know what to think. "You're confusing me."

He put the question to her point-blank. "Do you want to move?"

Devon bit her bottom lip, and then said, "I should."

"That's not what I asked you," he pointed out. "I said do you *want* to move."

This time Devon pressed her lips together, knowing what she thought she should say and what she actually *wanted* to say.

"I've never been part of a household where people care about each other, where they watch out for each other. I have no right to be here, but I do know that I am very grateful for the time I got to spend at your ranch with your family."

"It doesn't have to end," he told her. "At the very least, there's no rush for you to leave anytime soon. Listen, we're all crazy about Layla and, this way, there's always someone there for her, freeing you up to do what you need to."

"But that's imposing," Devon insisted.

There was that word again. Cody was not about to back off. "We don't see it that way."

"You can't speak for the others," she told him. For all he knew, his siblings were counting the minutes until she left.

"Sure I can. After you've been through as much as we have together, you get to know what the others are thinking and feeling. And I can tell you with certainty that if I let you move out without at least *trying* to talk you out of it, the others will have my head, no doubt about it. I might not be the best-looking guy around, but I promise I'll look even worse without a head."

She had no idea why, but that struck her as funny. So funny that she couldn't stop laughing for a couple of minutes.

Finally, when she did, she told him, "You're crazy, you know that?"

Yeah, crazy about you, Cody thought.

"Whatever you say," he said out loud. "Now, about that lunch at Miss Joan's," he reminded Devon. "This way, you can tell her the good news. Miss Joan loves being the first one to hear good news."

Devon inclined her head. He'd won her over with that argument. "Okay, sounds good."

"Knew I'd convince you," he said.

Now all he had to do was convince her about the rest, Cody added silently. And that, he had a feeling, was not going to be easy.

Chapter 17

Despite her background, Devon had never been one who allowed herself to be consumed by worry. For the most part, she'd always managed to face life with a healthy resilience, determined not just to take whatever fate threw her way but to triumph over it. No matter how bad the situation might be, she had always found a way to stay true to herself and forge on. She felt that, as long as she kept moving, she would survive.

But all that was when she only had herself to think about. She didn't have just herself to think about anymore. Now she had to view things through the eyes of a mother, always mindful that there was a little person who was totally dependent on her. A little person whom she needed to watch over and take care of.

Not exactly an easy feat when she didn't even have a dollar to her name.

That was what Jack had left her when he took off—nothing. He'd stolen not just her love but everything he could put his hands on. That included her credit cards and the money in her wallet. All the money she had managed to save up.

All the money she had in the whole world.

Devon had been quick to cancel all of her credit cards—there'd been only two—but the money, perforce, was a lost cause. As was ever getting back the necklace and earrings her mother had left her.

Being completely penniless made her extremely aware of the fact that she couldn't provide even the most basic of things for her baby.

Thanks to Cody, she had a job that would begin in the fall, but that still didn't pay any of the bills right now. The fact that she couldn't pay for anything had her frustrated beyond words, not to mention exceedingly hemmed in.

Stress and tension all but radiated from her.

Certainly this tension was not lost on Cody. He felt it the moment he got home and walked into the kitchen to see her.

"Something wrong?" he asked.

It was far better to meet any problem head-on than to pretend that it wasn't there. In Cody's opinion, the latter approach only made things fester and grow worse. Besides, he preferred things out in the open.

Devon hardly spared him a look. With Layla dozing in her bassinet in the corner, Devon was busy preparing dinner.

"No," she bit off.

Cody didn't believe her. "You're pacing," he pointed out.

She shrugged off his observation. "I'm getting dinner ready."

Cody frowned slightly. It was time to correct that, he thought. "About that—" he began.

Devon stopped dead, but she still didn't turn toward him. "Getting sick of my cooking?" she guessed, her voice on edge.

He'd always been good at picking up both blatant signals and subtle nuances. There was a definite shift in her voice as well as her personality. Devon was being defensive for no reason that he could see.

"No, nobody's even remotely tired of your cooking, but we talked it over and decided that it wasn't fair to keep having you make the meals, no matter how good they are." Cassidy had even voiced the feeling that it was taking advantage of Devon.

Devon raised her chin as if she was preparing for a fight.

"You talked it over?" she repeated. "When?"

Definitely defensive, Cody thought. He was going to have to tread lightly here until he discovered exactly what this was all about.

"Last night," he answered mildly. "There's no doubt about the fact that you really have a gift when it comes to cooking," he assured her. "But we feel that we've been taking unfair advantage of you by *letting* you do all of it these last two months."

That was how she was paying them back for allowing her to live there. She thought they'd already had this discussion. "What else am I supposed to do?" she asked, some of her annoyance coming through.

Cody shrugged. He hadn't thought of anything specific. "Something else," he told her. "You have a life."

"Not really," she countered almost defiantly.

"Okay," he said, taking her by the hand and leading her off to the side. They were alone in the kitchen, but bringing her into the alcove created more privacy in case someone else walked in on them. "What is this *really* all about?" he asked.

She lifted her chin again. "I don't know what you're talking about." She sniffed.

Cody continued watching her, determined to wait her out. When she said nothing, he resorted to coaxing. "Level with me, Devon. What's bothering you?"

She wanted to snap and tell him to stop badgering her, that there was nothing wrong, nothing bothering her. But even as the words rose to her lips, she owed him the truth. There *was* something bothering her.

"Layla needs to go in for her two-month checkup," she told him.

"Okay," Cody allowed, waiting for Devon to get to what was bothering her.

Devon threw up her hands impatiently. "I can't take her."

Cody asked the first thing that came to his mind. "Something wrong with your truck?"

Devon closed her eyes, searching for a vein of inner strength. "No—"

"Because if there is," Cody continued, "I can take the two of you in. No problem."

"It's not the truck," she firmly emphasized. Devon found she had to struggle not to raise her voice.

"Then what is it?" Cody asked patiently.

So far, Devon seemed to be talking in riddles and he really hoped that they were coming closer to the problem so he could know what was bothering her and what omissions he was dealing with.

Devon threw up her hands again. "I can't afford it,"

she cried. "I don't have any money to pay the doctor."
Just admitting it embarrassed her.

"Is that all?" he asked, relieved that it wasn't anything that was actually serious.

"That's not an 'all,'" Devon declared, frustrated.
"That's *everything*."

Didn't he see that? Didn't he see how awful it felt
not to be able to provide for her daughter's basic needs
at all?

Cody had a solution, but he tested the waters slowly,
not know how it might affect Devon. "I can pay for it,"
he volunteered.

Her eyes almost blazed as she cried "No!"

The woman just had too much pride as far as he was
concerned. It made things difficult.

"All right," he qualified. "I can *lend* you the money
to pay for it."

Devon shook her head. "I already owe you too
much."

"There's no running tally on any of this," he told her.

Her pride was wounded and hemorrhaging. "I told
you before, I am *not* a charity case."

That again, Cody thought. It took effort to curb his
impatience. "And no one said you were," he insisted.
"Look, did it ever occur to you that it might make me
feel good to help you?"

"Why would it?" she asked. "You've got better things
to do with your money than throw it away like that,"
she insisted.

"My money, my decision. Besides," Cody continued,
raising his voice to stop her from saying anything further, "we do things differently here. A lot of the peo-

ple the docs treat at the clinic either pay the visits off slowly or make a trade."

"Trade?" Devon repeated. She wasn't sure what he meant by that.

Cody smiled. "One hand washes the other. Like you cooking for us in exchange for your room and board," he pointed out, hoping that would put a lid on the subject once and for all.

But Devon shook her head. "It just doesn't feel right."

They could go around and around about this all night. "It's right if we say it's right," he told her once and for all.

Rather than concede, Devon took the so-called argument they were having in a completely different direction.

"I'm getting much too dependent on you," Devon complained quietly.

He kind of liked having her depend on him. It made him feel useful in an entirely different light. "And that's a bad thing because…?"

Devon stared at him. "Because someday, when I least expect it, you'll grow tired of carrying me and suddenly, the rug'll be pulled out from under my feet and I'll go plummeting down into this deep, dark abyss."

Okay, now it was making sense to him. "That's a very colorful scenario, but it's not going to happen."

"There are no guarantees in life," she insisted.

Cody's eyes met hers. He felt the same ache within him that he always did lately. An ache that had its roots in fear. Fear that she was going to just disappear on him. That one day, he'd reach out for her and she wouldn't be there.

Wouldn't be anywhere.

"Sometimes, there are," he told her quietly.

"Like what?" she challenged.

He spelled it out for her. "Like I can guarantee that I'm going to feel the same way about you tomorrow that I do now and that I will the day after that and the day after that—to the nth degree," he said.

"What way?" she asked, feeling shaky inside. She was cornering him and she knew it. But she already knew that Cody wasn't the kind of man who lied and, if she pressed him for an answer, he would give her an honest one. She was counting on it and hoping against hope that it would be enough to break through her wall of fear and convince her.

"I love you," he told her quietly. "I'm not Jack," he insisted. "Get that through your head. I'm not going anywhere. Ever."

I love you.

She stared at him. She'd heard the words before. Heard them and clung to them and they had turned out to be as binding as soap bubbles. Jack had told her he loved her and then took off soon after that without a backward glance.

"You don't mean that," she said flatly.

Cody measured his words carefully. "No disrespect, Devon, but you don't have any right to tell me what I mean or don't mean. If I say I love you, then that's what I mean." A little more fiercely, he repeated, "I love you."

"Why?" she asked. "*Why* do you love me?"

Rather than get annoyed with her for pressing him, he did his best to make her understand. "For more reasons than you can possibly imagine. Looking back, I probably fell in love with you the first moment I laid eyes on you."

As she recalled it, she had her legs spread out and she was screaming, not to mention that she'd looked like a mess. "Not my finest moment."

"Oh, but it was," he said. And then he grinned. "And I want to love you through every moment for the rest of my life."

She shook her head, unable to accept that. "You just feel sorry for me."

"No," he corrected, "I feel sorry for *me* because you're giving me such a hard time over this." He took hold of her shoulders to keep her in place and to force her to look at him as he spoke. "Now, you may not like hearing it and I really can't help that, but I love you." He took a breath and went for broke. "And I'd like to marry you."

Stunned, her mouth dropped open. "No," she whispered in disbelief.

Cody took it as a rejection, but he tried not to let it slice him up inside.

"Not the answer I wanted to hear, but there's no hurry. You can take your time, think it over, work it out." He emphasized, "Like I said, there's no hurry. Because I'll still be here when you finally realize that maybe marrying me isn't such a bad thing. Bottom line is *I am not going anywhere*."

She realized that she'd stopped breathing and took in a deep one now before asking, "You're serious?"

Out of the corner of his eye, he saw Cole about to enter the kitchen and he waved his brother back. Cole took the hint and disappeared.

Facing Devon, Cody's expression was the soul of solemnity. "I've never been more serious in my entire life."

Devon never took her eyes off him. "You're not just saying this to make me feel better?" Devon asked.

"No," Cody corrected. "I'm saying this to make *me* feel better."

As if she believed that. "Why would you want to marry me?" she challenged, silently demanding that he somehow convince her.

Maybe he needed to enumerate the reasons for her, at least to some extent. He began with the most obvious. "Because you're beautiful. I look at you and my heart all but stops. Because you're a good person. You could have taken advantage of all of us—we would have gladly let you—but you didn't. And maybe most of all because I need you to need me."

The reasons were all valid, but somehow, she just couldn't see how they applied to her. She didn't feel worthy of that sort of sentiment or capable of generating it in someone else.

"Is that all?" she asked quietly.

"No, that's just the beginning," Cody answered. "But I promise that if and when you do decide to marry me, I'll make sure that you never live to regret it, not even for a single moment."

"That's a tall order," Devon told him, struggling really hard not to smile.

"In case you haven't noticed, I live up to all my promises," he told her with a touch of pride. "Just ask around."

She didn't have to. She knew the kind of man he was. He was offering her the world on a platter. It didn't seem fair to him. "I don't have anything to give you," she told him.

"Now, there you're wrong," Cody contradicted. "You

have yourself to give and I couldn't ask for a more precious gift," he told her honestly. "And don't worry," he quickly told her, "I'm not going to ask you for an answer yet. I told you you could take your time and you can. Take as long as you want—as long as, eventually, you come up with the right answer, the one I need to hear." He added, "No pressure."

"Yes," Devon said.

"Yes, we have an understanding?" he asked, not quite sure what she was telling him.

"Yes," Devon repeated. Her eyes had locked with his and remained that way.

"Yes to the understanding?" he asked again uncertainly. She still wasn't making herself clear and he refused to jump the gun in case he was wrong. Because being wrong would hurt too much.

"Yes to the question," she told him.

"Which question?" he asked.

The corners of her mouth began to curve. "The only question that counts."

He looked at her apprehensively, still afraid that he was grasping at the one thing he wanted to hear. But he knew that he couldn't just walk away from this without knowing, without being *positive*.

"This question—Devon, will you marry me?" he asked.

Her eyes crinkled as she threw her arms around his neck and brought her mouth up to his.

"Yes," she repeated with feeling and then, in case they were still bogged down in rhetoric, she made herself perfectly clear by saying, "Yes, Cody, I will marry you."

His heart all but leaped out of his chest as he asked for one final confirmation. "You're sure?"

Her eyes were laughing as she said, "I'm sure."

"I'm not pressuring you?" he asked her.

"No, you're not pressuring me." Her eyes were smiling now. "You are, however, driving me crazy."

"Well, that's only fair," he told her as his arms around her tightened. "Because you're doing the same to me."

She didn't want to talk. More than anything, she needed him to kiss her, to finally seal this bargain they had struck up. "Shut up and kiss me."

He pulled her even closer as he brought his mouth within a hair's breadth of hers. "Oh, with more pleasure than you can possibly imagine."

"Does this mean someone else is making dinner?" she asked teasingly.

There was mischief in his eyes as he asked, "What do you think?"

"I don't want to think," she told him. "I just want to feel."

"That can be arranged," he promised her.

"Show me," she whispered.

He did.

And Layla slept through it all.

Both her mother and her father-to-be took that as a good omen.

Epilogue

Devon looked at her reflection in the full-length mirror in the church's antechamber. She hardly recognized the person in the wedding gown looking back at her. That person was positively glowing.

She put her hand over her stomach, willing the butterflies away.

They stayed put.

"Maybe we should have eloped," she said, addressing the other reflection she saw in the mirror.

Cassidy, resplendent in a blue maid-of-honor dress, was fussing with the bottom of Devon's wedding dress, making certain that the veil's train wasn't trapped beneath it.

"Don't you even dare think about it," Cassidy warned. "This is the first McCullough wedding and there's a church full of people out there, not to mention your little fifth-graders, who would be heartbroken if you suddenly turned tail and became Forever's version of the runaway bride," she admonished.

"Runaway brides leave grooms at the altar," Devon pointed out. "I don't want to leave Cody at the altar. I just don't want everyone watching me show up to marry him."

"Too late," Cassidy said. She dropped the train and stood back for a moment to admire her handiwork. "You're good to go," she pronounced happily.

Cassidy glanced over to the corner where Layla was sitting up in a colorfully decorated car seat. She was wearing an infant's version of Cassidy's dress. "Too bad she's too little to be your flower girl, but I guess you can't have everything."

"You're wrong, there," Devon corrected her. "I *do* have everything." She smiled at Cassidy. "I'm even getting the sister I always wanted."

Cassidy laughed. "Just try getting rid of me." There was a knock on the door and Cassidy exchanged glances with the bride. "I didn't think that Connor was coming for you for another ten minutes." Because her father had long since passed away, Devon had asked Connor to give her away. "He's probably early to make sure you're not changing your mind."

Devon shook her head. "Not a chance."

Cassidy opened the door. Then she tried to close it again.

"You're not supposed to see the bride before the wedding, Cody," she admonished. "Don't you know anything? It's supposed to be bad luck."

Cody stuck his foot in to block his sister from shutting the door. "I just want to give her something," he told Cassidy. "I thought she would want to wear it during the ceremony."

"Let him in, Cassidy," Devon said.

"It's against tradition," Cassidy insisted.

"So's everything that's happened in my life so far," Devon told her.

She felt that if Cody wanted to see her right before the ceremony, it had to be about something important. Telling him he couldn't because of some ancient superstition wouldn't be starting out their marriage on the right foot.

Cassidy frowned. "Okay, but this is against my better judgment," she said just before she opened the door farther. "Okay, buster, what's so important it can't wait?" she demanded of her brother.

"I'd like a minute alone with my fiancée if you don't mind," Cody said, amused that his sister had turned into a guard dog in a bridesmaid dress.

Cassidy picked up Layla. "Let's get you situated out there, Princess." Since Cassidy and her brothers were all in the wedding party, Miss Joan had volunteered to hold the baby for the duration of the ceremony. "Make it quick," she told Cody. "Connor's due in less than ten minutes."

"This won't take long," Cody said. As Cassidy left, he turned to face Devon and really looked at her. She took his breath away. "I didn't think you could be any more beautiful than you already were, but I was wrong."

"Is that what you came to say?" Devon asked. She was no longer afraid that he was going to call the wedding off at the last minute, but, for the life of her, she couldn't come up with a reason for Cody showing up like this just before the ceremony.

"No," he replied. "I came to give you this. I thought you might want it."

"This" was what he was holding in his hand. He held it up in front of her before he drew back his fingers. There in the palm of his hand was a necklace and a pair of earrings.

Her necklace and earrings. She would have known them anywhere.

Her eyes widened as she stared first at the items and then at him. "Where did you get these?"

"Then they are yours?" He was fairly certain that they were, but he wanted her to confirm it.

"Yes!" she cried, taking both from him and looking at them in wonder. She never thought she'd see the necklace and earrings again. "Where—? How—?"

"They were in a pawnshop thirty miles outside of Houston." It had taken him all this time to locate the items, circulating Jack's photo to all the pawnshops between Forever and Houston. Jack was nowhere to be found, but at least the jewelry was. He felt extremely triumphant about locating it, especially when he saw the look in Devon's eyes. It was priceless. "I thought you might want to wear them."

There were tears in her eyes as she put the earrings on. Then, turning her back to Cody, she gave him the necklace so that he could fasten the gold clasp for her. She held very still, almost afraid to breathe. She was that happy.

"I don't know how to thank you!"

Finished, Cody turned her slowly around to face him. "Don't worry, we have the rest of our lives together to work on that."

The wedding march was starting. In the next moment, Connor was in the doorway. He rapped once.

"Time," he declared, giving his younger brother a piercing look.

Cody grinned, withdrawing. "It sure is," he agreed. "See you at the altar," he told Devon just before he hurried away.

Connor shook his head as he offered Devon his arm. "Well, at least you know what you're getting into," he said to her.

Devon could only beam as she replied, love in every word, "I certainly do."

* * * * *

"The Joshua trees and saguaros sure are pretty," Jack said reflectively. "This sort of looks like the land west of the Three Rivers Ranch house. Where you showed me the North Star, remember?"

Remember? Those moments had been burned into Vanessa's memory. Even if she never saw him again for the rest of her life, she'd always have those special moments to relive in her mind.

The thought unexpectedly caused her throat to tighten, and she wished the waitress would get back with their drinks. She didn't want Jack to think she was getting emotional. Especially because she could feel their time together winding to a close.

"I do. And I just happen to know a place not too far west of here where there's another special view of the evening star."

His eyelids lowered ever so slightly as he looked across the table at her. "After we eat, you should show me."

Did he expect her to look at him in the moonlight and not feel the urge to kiss him? Or maybe she'd get lucky, Vanessa thought, and the moon would be in a new phase and the light would be too weak to illuminate his face.

Damn it, Vanessa. Who are you fooling? You could find Jack's lips in the darkest of nights.

Thankfully, a waitress suddenly approached their table, and the distraction pushed the mocking voice from her head…but not the idea of being in Jack's arms again. She was beginning to fear she'd never rid herself of that longing.

Don't miss
The Other Hollister Man *by Stella Bagwell,*
available August 2022 wherever
Harlequin books and ebooks are sold.

Harlequin.com

Love Harlequin romance?

DISCOVER.

Be the first to find out about promotions, news and exclusive content!

Facebook.com/HarlequinBooks

Twitter.com/HarlequinBooks

Instagram.com/HarlequinBooks

Pinterest.com/HarlequinBooks

YouTube.com/HarlequinBooks

ReaderService.com

EXPLORE.

Sign up for the Harlequin e-newsletter and download a free book from any series at
TryHarlequin.com

CONNECT.

Join our Harlequin community to share your thoughts and connect with other romance readers!
Facebook.com/groups/HarlequinConnection

HSOCIAL2021

HARLEQUIN

Heartfelt or thrilling, passionate or uplifting—Harlequin is more than just happily-ever-after.

With twelve different series to choose from and new books available every month, you are sure to find stories that will move you, uplift you, inspire and delight you.